Shadowmakers

Shadowmakers

RALPH WETTERHAHN

CARROLL & GRAF PUBLISHERS
NEW YORK

SHADOWMAKERS

Carroll & Graf Publishers
An Imprint of Avalon Publishing Group Inc.
161 William St., 16th Floor
New York, NY 10038

First Carroll & Graf edition 2002

Interior design by Simon M. Sullivan

Library of Congress Cataloging-in-Publication Data is available.

ISBN: 0-7867-1080-2

Printed in the United States of America
Distributed by Publishers Group West

For

Carol

Tireless, supportive, my inspiration throughout

Acknowledgments and Disclaimer

Heartfelt gratitude goes to my ever-persistent agent, Nancy Ellis-Bell, and to Publisher Herman Graf, Executive Editor Philip Turner, Assistant Editor Keith Wallman, and Managing Editor Claiborne Hancock at Carroll & Graf. Thanks is also due to the late Paul Gillette, the members of his workshop, and especially to Col. Jimmie Butler whose counsel and advice started it all.

To the hundreds of hardworking members of the Joint Task Force for Full Accounting and the Central Identification Laboratory in Hawaii, I offer a hand salute for opening my eyes to the world of forensics and anthropology. A note of appreciation goes to Candace Hoffmann for help with symptoms and diseases, and to the staff at the University of Southern California School of Dentistry for insight into dental anthropology.

Thanks also goes to all the members of my family, but most of all to my wife Carol, who edited every draft, and without whom this undertaking would never have proceeded.

While this book could not have been written without the generous aid of all the above, they are not responsible for what is, in fact, fiction. Any similarity to actual persons living or dead is purely coincidental. The use of actual historical names and locations is employed merely for verisimilitude.

Prologue

HANK DALTON NEVER KNEW what hit him that December morning in 1968. And later, when pain no longer seemed to matter, they told him of the irony during the last of the beatings. That nearly ended his screams forever.

Dalton had been at Hollomon Air Force Base in New Mexico back in 1962, where from test-bed fighters he fired improved U.S. AIM-9 Sidewinder missiles at target drones. But the heat-seeking missile that would change his life forever was built by the engineers at Vympel Machine-Building Design Office in Moscow. The Russians had stolen one of those enhanced Sidewinders after it was deployed to an American air base in West Germany. They duplicated the missile piece by piece, calling it the K-13A. An exact copy.

In 1968, K-13A serial number 0012BF was delivered to Haiphong Harbor in North Vietnam by a Russian cargo vessel. Then the Soviet missile went by barge up the Red River to Hanoi and from there by truck to Noi Bai Airfield where it was slung under the right wing of a Chinese-built MiG-21. On December 5 of that year, a Vietnamese pilot took off carrying missile 0012BF, then headed northwest until he spotted two U.S. Air Force F-105 fighters twelve miles from Hanoi.

In the front cockpit of the lead F-105F was the pilot, Major Hank Dalton, his fingers flipping switches as he muscled the bomb-laden fighter into a steep turn. His G-suit bladders inflated, squeezing his legs and torso like a stack of steel bands. Sweat poured down his face while the cooling system spit a steady stream of cold fog from around both sides of the front canopy. Behind him sat his electronic warfare officer, his Ee-Woh (EWO), Captain Jack Cadence. Both men were busy lining up to attack a North Vietnamese radar that was tracking the F-105. Dalton rolled to begin the dive-bomb run. The nose of the plane dropped through the horizon. Dalton's thumb eased on top of the pickle button as he steadied out in a forty-five-degree dive. Almost ready . . . ready. Now!

The plane shuddered as the bombs kicked clear of the racks. Dalton pulled the stick back, the G force squeezing them hard against the seat cushions as the plane came roaring out of the dive. Neither man saw the MiG approach. Neither man saw missile number 0012BF leap from the MiG-21's wing pylon. The missile streaked toward them making jerky corrections, its ashen smoke trail closing the distance like a skeletal finger whose touch augured death. The KA-13 flew up the tailpipe of the F-105's engine, passing through an inferno of flaming jet fuel inside the afterburner. It continued forward until it smashed into the spinning turbine wheel. The explosion shattered the turbine. One hundred fourteen titanium blades tore loose and, along with steel shrapnel from the warhead, hurled outward like an expanding buzz saw to sever the tail from the rest of the plane.

Dalton was shoved backward by the impact.

"Sweet Jees! . . ." An instant sense of dread froze Dalton in mid-breath. The plane yawed left. His foot, now pressing against the right rudder pedal, shot all the way forward. The control stick went slack. The nose of the plane plunged down. His knee board, with all the numbers and code words needed to find the target or to keep him alive, was no longer of use. Ripped from his thigh, the pages sailed past his face to the canopy above.

Simultaneously, Dalton's legs whipped up. The extended right one caught the sharp underside of the instrument panel. The tibia snapped like a matchstick. Intense pain shot up his spinal cord. Blood gushed into Dalton's skull at six times the force of gravity. His left hand was jerked from the throttle while his right clung to the useless stick with a vise grip. He tried to pull his left hand down to grab one of the ejection handles that sat alongside each leg but could not move his arm. Panic rose as the retina of each eye flooded, and he went into red-out, unable to see.

"Eject!" Dalton yelled.

"I can't . . . move," Cadence managed.

The main wing spar was never designed for the stress being applied. It bent, and hairline cracks sprouted along its length. The skin on the bottom of the wings rippled. Then the nose came up. The G load reversed to eight positive—eight times the force of gravity—pressing Dalton deep into his ejection seat. His arm flailed down, slamming his hand into the side console. The blood supply in his torso did an about-face and surged into his buttocks and legs, bursting capillaries by the thousands all along the extremities of his lower body. Dalton gritted his teeth, and the tendons in his neck stretched taut while he tried to hold up the G-induced, 110-pound weight of his head.

The wing spar flexed in the opposite direction. Now, the excesses of years of use and thousands of pullouts came to bear. The spar snapped on the right side, the sound crackling through the plane like a thunderbolt. A blurry image of his surroundings emerged in front of Dalton. The outer half of the wing had collapsed upward, but had not separated from the fuselage. Then a molten orange flash lit up the instrument panel as the fuel tank behind the cockpit exploded. He felt a flash of heat and sensed the end as blood drained from his eyes and his vision tunneled into gray-out.

What remained of the forward half of the plane began a rapidly increasing spiral into a fiery spin.

Dalton felt a numbness descend. Images of his dead wife, his mother—stern, accusing—a child and the woman he now loved merged together in front of his sightless eyes. He felt a warmth, a release, an acceptance. Then the G load relaxed. Like a slow-motion opening of a camera shutter, he began to see again. Dalton sensed no danger, as though the inevitability of death was not in doubt—a mouse in the cat's jaw. His gaze fell on the cockpit mirror where he saw Jack Cadence, head back, body slack, arms wobbling like a rag doll's. He heard a sound, as though from far away, a quavering voice on the radio. His wingman.

"Bail out, Hank, you're on fire!"

A spark, an instinct of survival deep in the cortex of Dalton's brain, rose in his senses. *Alive, I'm still alive!*

The next second would determine everything. His right hand

opened, releasing its grip on the stick. Then, as if commanded by something beyond his control, his hand inched to the side of his seat. His fingers wrapped around a yellow-and-black metal grip. He rotated the mechanism. A small lever was now exposed. He squeezed the lever, triggering ejection.

Both canopies flew off. The EWO's seat was automatically ejected first. Dalton blacked out three-tenths of a second later as the rocket under his seat fired.

PART I

1

On this otherwise normal July evening, in an otherwise normal America, New Mexico senator Hank Dalton was hosting a thousand-dollar-a-plate fund-raiser. For the occasion, he wore a charcoal gray tuxedo adorned with a silver bow tie. His hair, thick and gray at the temples, was styled longer than during his military days. He looked out on life through narrow slits, his eyes highlighted by crow's-feet that gave him a rugged look, one hardened not in the West, but in the crucible of pain in the Far East as a prisoner of war for five years.

Senator Dalton, whose banner read Dalton for President, the Man Who Can, had been on the campaign trail for nine months with his running mate Tyler Anderson. Tonight Anderson was out west in Los Angeles at a similar function.

The Grand Ballroom at the Mayflower Hotel in Washington had been centerpiece to a number of historical events. Every president since Calvin Coolidge had spoken there, and FDR, Eisenhower, and Kennedy had pressed the flesh in that very arena. Dalton showed a visibly upbeat mood in these renowned surroundings. His Independent Party campaign was closing fast on the Democrat and incumbent Republican's slim lead over him.

A sign draped along a side wall read POW/MIA League of Families Salutes Hank Dalton, One of Our Own.

Senator Dalton shook hands with members of the glitterati near the head table. Next to him loomed another former POW, Major General Bradley Stoner, his broad chest implying a natural, almost unconscious power. Pale from spending too much time in the office, Stoner's dour expression seemed framed by dark, imposing eyebrows. This evening, he wore a civilian tuxedo instead of the mess dress uniform normally worn by the military at formal functions. Behind Dalton stood staff aide Gary Bennett. With cell phone at the ready, Bennett was poised to address the senator's slightest whim. Flanking the group were security men, one from the office of the Secret Service and two from Dalton's private detail, identifiable by the ever-present communication line appearing at the collar and disappearing into the left ear.

Nearby, surveying the group, stood a scarlet-haired woman clad in a basic-black cocktail dress. She shifted her stance from one high heel to the other, looking a little out of place, staring with sad, childlike eyes that rolled over Senator Dalton, steadily probing, then singularly focusing on, General Stoner. She took a photograph from her purse, glancing at it as she eased forward.

The senator, his arm around General Stoner's shoulder, spoke to a middle-aged socialite who wore her wealth, a diamond necklace that curved above a strapless gown that swept beneath deep cleavage. "Brad's here unofficially, of course," Dalton told her. "My old roommate—"

"Cell mate!" General Stoner said with a guffaw. He was on his second scotch and soda.

The socialite laughed, then touched the senator's arm. A CNN crew moved close to video the action around Dalton, while flashbulbs from print reporters rippled in explosions of light.

This presidential candidate was a very eligible widower.

The woman with the photo approached and caught the scrutiny of the nearby Secret Service agent. The agent held his position as she thrust her empty hand in front of General Stoner. "Pam Robbins. My father is Major Randall Robbins, shot down September nineteenth, 1971."

Stoner shook her hand, then eased her away from the senator. "I'm familiar with his case. My condolences."

Robbins offered him the photo. Stoner opened his hand to receive it, all the while holding his gaze steady on her face. Only when the photo touched his hand did his eyes dip to study it. A black-and-white image, it showed two middle-aged men standing together. One had a curious sort of grin, as though a joke was over and he didn't get the punch line. He held a placard with the numbers 2N-4W-L79 written on it. Finally, Stoner looked up, a questioning expression on his face.

"I show you this," Robbins said, "because your task force erroneously declared my father deceased—"

Stoner blanched. "That was before my reign."

"I'm not blaming any errors on you, but that photo was taken in Laos where my father is still being held."

Stoner's head twitched, almost imperceptibly, in response to the tone in her voice. He straightened, inhaling deeply, in an attempt to cover the reflex. "I'll have my staff in Hawaii take another look. May I keep this?"

"Please do." She pointed to one of the men in the photo. "A computer analysis has matched my father and *that* man."

"As I said, I'll look into it." The general slipped the photo into his breast pocket, then abruptly turned his back.

Robbins stood in place for a moment, churning inside as she watched Stoner withdraw. Senator Dalton raised an eyebrow at Stoner who shook his head as though nothing of consequence had transpired. Stoner then moved behind the group to speak with security. The bodyguard nodded as he brought a cell phone to his lips. When Stoner returned to Dalton's side, they had a brief conversation. Then both men laughed.

Robbins had seen enough. They might brush her off like an autograph seeker, but find a laugh in it? No. She surged toward the senator, waving her hand to get his attention. "Senator . . . Senator . . . could I have a moment—"

The two men from Dalton's private detail moved to block her path. "This way, please, ma'am," the taller one said as he motioned with his chin toward the rear of the room.

"No, I want to speak with the senator—"

The shorter one spread his arms as though any attempt to move around him would result in an open-field tackle. "Security, madam. Would you please come with us?"

"Bullshit! I paid to get in here!" Robbins whipped her purse against the man's arm. Then, with a move she perfected on the soccer field years before, she ducked around him the other way before he could react.

"Senator Dalton, I must speak with you," Robbins shouted.

At the sound of the outburst, everyone within earshot turned to watch. Dalton's eyes skimmed the room, clearly checking first to make sure he was safe and this was not a diversion.

The Secret Service agent sprang in front of Robbins, but the private guards were already on her. The tall one's hand seized Robbins's shoulder, spinning her away from the senator.

The short agent, obviously miffed at having been faked out by a 115-pound female, swung behind her and wrapped his hands around her elbows with viselike force. "Okay, lady, we'll do this the hard way."

The two men took her in tow, heading for the exit as cameramen and reporters moved in like vultures spotting carrion.

Senator Dalton looked behind him and signaled his staff aide. Bennett practically jumped to the senator's side.

Dalton pointed at the door. "Gary, go out there, find out what that constituent's needs are, and take care of them."

"You bet, sir," Bennett said as he took off.

2

THE CHAPEL AT THE U.S. Air Force Academy was an aluminum and glass edifice jammed hard against the backdrop of the Rocky Mountain Rampart Range. Major Will Cadence stepped inside, took off his cap, and ran his fingers through dark hair that had begun to gray at the temples. Shafts of light beamed down through stained-glass windows that stretched vertically between accordion-like spires rising on both sides. As he moved forward through refracted rays, his gait a little unsteady, he recalled so many Octobers ago when he had been led down this very aisle.

Now, dressed in his blue uniform, Will stepped to the second row of pews and sat. Through his left trouser, he adjusted a knee brace. The smell of candle wax and the images that surrounded him made him think he should pray, but that's not how he felt. He suppressed a twinge of guilt over the thought that he seldom went to church. Weddings provided the occasional exception, including his own. He used to go to funerals but not anymore. The last, of his wife, Elena, he considered his fault. The ones before that, his mother and father's, had wrenched his childhood away, thrusting him into the world before he was even remotely ready. No, he had not come to pray. His life was in transition. Flying had been his life, a jet plane his mistress, all rolled up in an air force career. But he had failed at it and, like everything else, all of it was swept away in a rush of memory. What he needed now was a place to think things out, where quiet contemplation might provide answers, might stop the nightmares and headaches that had returned after the accident.

He glanced up, remembering the initial sight of the chapel spires at the first two funerals. Then came the wedding, years later. June Week. He marched in wearing his brand-new mess dress, white jacket, silk bow tie, and second lieutenant shoulder boards. Prince Charming. Then Elena entered the church in her wedding gown, all nervous, stepping tentatively as she dragged an eighteen-foot train up the aisle. Princess Elena. Everyone smiled, cried, and smelled the flowers.

"Let no man put asunder."

They had kissed. Then under crossed swords held by eight lieutenants, they walked out to face reality.

Reality was Enid, Oklahoma: hot, dusty, flat.

Pilot training. They'd only be here a year, he had told Elena. He had her student loan to pay off and a car payment to make. They rented an apartment two miles from the field and checked out furniture from the base warehouse, any color sofa you might want as long as it was brown. Built in the '50s, the flat had a window air conditioner that shook the whole unit when the compressor kicked in. It didn't always kick in, but it always made noise. The clatter drowned out the sounds of children laughing, or, in many cases, crying. The complex was bursting with servicemen, wives, kids with dirty faces. A fenced pool was fifty feet from their front door. Waterfront property. There was a lot of drinking, a lot of complaining from the wives, never enough money, and always the blazing hot sun.

The mess dress gave way to a green bag, his flight suit. Instead of shoulder boards, he came home with salt stains across his back. Life's focus was on perfecting dizzying aerial maneuvers from inside a cramped and stifling-hot cockpit. The wedding flowers gave way to the smell of his sweat and vomit.

Then winter set its teeth. The apartment shook from icy winds that swept the plains day and night. Elena became bored and restless. He discovered a dark side to her that replaced those splendid illusions of a fairy-tale life. Moodiness became her nature. She talked about getting a job, but there was nothing decent for someone who would only be around a few more months.

They hung on—it'd only be a year—but he sensed Elena was getting another message. *Happily ever after* was not supposed to be like this. She spent her days crammed together with young military wives, some of whom had three kids before they were twenty-five. Elena began drinking. A few beers with the neighborhood girls, then empty six-packs began showing up in the trash.

Elena heard the stories about what the men did on temporary duty, TDY away from home, and about how three of last year's graduates were already dead, killed in crashes of fighter planes. Friday nights she would ride to the base for happy hour with one of the wives. She'd be plastered before Will showed up, other pilots hovering over her like carnivores. Will and his bride would drive home in his car, she with her head tilted on the headrest staring into space, he thinking of nothing but sleep.

As the training program wound down, flying assignments loomed. Elena pointedly mentioned that a cargo plane was the thing he should ask for. Put in his time and he could get out, go to the airlines, get a *real* job with a *real* paycheck and have a *real* house in a nice neighborhood where their kids could graduate with friends they grew up with. Happily ever after.

She was right, of course, but he felt drawn by an inexorable force, and it wasn't to a *real job* in the airlines where he would wake up mornings with a groan in some strange hotel room, live for the days off, bitch about seniority, own two cars, a dog, and a charge card at Sears. He wanted more. He needed answers to things neither Elena nor the airlines could satisfy. The only way he felt he would find them was to enter that same life his father had chosen. Only then might he find forgiveness in his heart. That was his own dark side, unfathomable to all but himself.

The last Friday in August the assignments came down. He told Elena at the Officer's Club that night. They were going to Luke Air Force Base for six months so he could train in the F-15 fighter. She just sat at the bar and stared. *Phoenix, Arizona: hotter, dustier, but less flat.* She finally reeled off the bar stool, said she needed to powder her nose. When she did not come back, he checked the parking lot. The car was gone. One of his friends gave him a lift. They came upon flashing lights and a wreck a mile from the base. As the medics rolled Elena's lifeless body into the ambulance, the policeman said, "Tried to take the curve too fast."

He knew it wasn't speed that killed her. They let him in the ambulance, and he pulled the sheet back. Blood covered her chest, her accusing eyes were open. It was midnight. The ball was over. The princess was dead. The blame placed.

All that happened years ago. Now, with a newer calamity on his mind, Will spent the minutes sitting alone in the chapel until a tour group interrupted his thoughts that October morning. He got up, using the pew in front of him to steady himself, then headed back to the nearby parking lot.

Winter comes early above seven thousand feet in Colorado, and Will, dressed only in his thin uniform jacket, jammed his hands into his trouser pockets, ignoring the disapproving eyes of by-the-book cadets who pressed past him and saluted. "Good morning, sir!" they barked. Their breaths puffed out, then were stripped away by the sharp drafts that rolled down the mountains.

Thin cirrus clouds washed over the sun, turning it pallid yellow, then obliterating it completely. Snow flurries dotted Will's windshield as he opened the door to his polished blue '56 Thunderbird.

His father's car. It had aged well, was still full of life—cylinders that moved, oil and water pumps that pressed fluids through hoses and tubes, wheels that spun. The car was Will's one physical connection to that earlier world, one that could have been normal but never was. His knee had begun to stiffen in the cold, and Will used one hand to lift the limb inside the open door. He slid onto the seat and turned on the ignition. The engine coughed, kicked over, then fell into a ragged faltering idle, its timing set for denser air.

He drove to the Academy Cemetery and parked along the little road that ran through the graveyard. Will swung his right leg out, then reached behind the seat to retrieve a cane. He hated the sight of his "crutch." It stripped away his independence, and whatever manhood was left to him. In public he seldom used it, but here, alone among the ice, snow, and stone markers, he might need it. He had already caused enough pain to his body. Will moved off, his gait awkward, the use of the cane a still-unfamiliar skill.

On both sides of his narrow path lay acres of grass, crew-cut yet matted, yielding to the constant wind that lashed the soil this time of year. Will's shoes crunched across those frozen remnants of a summer past. Patches of ice-hardened snow struggled for a hold in small depressions. He shivered involuntarily as leafless skeletons of aspen, ash, and cottonwood rattled in the wind.

The graveyard had no headstones, just flush slabs of gray granite with brass plates listing the vital details. Will had been back a few times over the years, and he wandered along the familiar path glancing from plaque to plaque: Robert Michael Gilchrist, Born: July 7, 1941—Missing-in-Action, Declared Deceased: October 7, 1966. He moved on, his mind a jumble of faded memories—the shock, a lost childhood, trying to reconnect by living someone else's dream, and finally his personal failure and the returning nightmare and accompanying headaches that had brought him back to this place. James Donald Goodman, Born: March 15, 1940—Killed-in-Action, January 9, 1967.

He held his cap tight to his head as the wind took a savage swipe at him. Will steadied himself, then stepped carefully around the marker to the next row, moved a few more halting steps, and leaned heavily on the cane.

A grief more potent now than ever flooded back as he gazed upon the two slabs before his feet. JACK INGRAM CADENCE, BORN: FEBRUARY 14, 1942—DIED: PRISONER-OF-WAR, DECEMBER 12, 1972. Next to it: NANCY IRENE CADENCE, BORN: JUNE 4, 1943—DIED: OCTOBER 27, 1973, BELOVED WIFE OF JACK. At the time of his father's funeral, his mother lay in the hospital, run down by a hit-and-run driver while crossing a street. Will remembered standing here stiff and silent, his neighbor's hand guiding him, helping him toss a rose on his father's casket. Then his eight-year-old body jerking in terror as the honor guard fired their volleys, the sound striking him like a blow, the concussion sucking the wind from his lungs. Will stayed on at McConnell Air Force Base in Kansas, moving from one officer's home to another every few months, calling each couple "uncle and aunt" while his mother struggled to recuperate. She didn't. Ten months later he was led back to Colorado for his mother's burial.

Will bent low, half kneeling, his lame leg remaining rigid as he placed his bare hand on his father's stone. "Well, *now* what do I do?" he heard himself say, his voice sounding tired, distant, even to him. There was no answer, of course. There never was.

After his mother's death, he had bounced among relatives from California to Paducah, Kentucky, trying to fit in but never quite succeeding. An aunt and her certified public accountant of a husband took him in. They changed his last name to Peasley in the process. Those six years became a game, with *them* trying to mold him into shape, while he fought every correction. All he wanted was what he had lost. He felt drawn to the past and the memory of an aviator father he knew not enough about, so he applied and was accepted into the Air Force Academy when he was seventeen. Two months before graduation, he turned twenty-one. His first legal act was to have his name changed back to Cadence. With that symbolic deed of defiance complete, he found himself walking to the podium for his diploma without a single relative in attendance.

Will shifted his weight to the cane and rose.

A woman's voice sounded behind him. "Major Cadence?"

Will flinched, embarrassed, then annoyed that someone might have eavesdropped on his one-way conversation with the dead. He turned on his good leg.

A woman stood twenty feet behind him, hands clasped in front. She wore a navy blue overcoat, black leather gloves that matched her calf-high boots. Her collar was pulled straight up underneath thick red hair that whipped in the breeze like a tattered ensign.

She had that *look,* one he had come to despise. Women would learn of his past, the young widower, the orphan, and would descend on him as though he were a wounded bird. They would quickly discover that his broken wing did not mend easily, especially when the wound seemed self-inflicted. He resented the sympathy these women offered. The guilt he felt over Elena's death could not be washed away by sentiment. Soon these women would drift off, or was it he that pushed them away?

"I'm Pam Robbins," this one said, offering her gloved hand as she stepped forward. In a shivering voice, she announced, "My dad's marker is in the next row." She shook Will's hand, then stepped over the matted grass toward her father's marker. "I called the Nellis base hospital. They were kind enough to tell me you were visiting the academy. I live in Denver, so I drove down."

Will moved to follow her. "On the chance of bumping into me?"

"The doctor mentioned you had a classic T-Bird. I cruised the parking lots, finally spotted it leaving the chapel area."

Will glanced toward his car. A white Toyota was parked behind it. "I'm impressed." He returned his gaze to her. "But why me?"

She took another step and pointed at the closest marker. RANDALL B. ROBBINS, BORN: AUGUST 12, 1946—MISSING-IN-ACTION, DECLARED DECEASED: DECEMBER 28, 1972.

"Because of him." She spoke without looking up. "My mother and I came here last August, as always, on his birthday. She to mourn, and me . . . well, I just rage inside." She turned, and with eyes now full of bitterness, looked directly at Will.

He stared, reading the anger in those wild, childlike eyes. Her wrath intrigued him, but still he wanted his question answered. "What does it have to do with me?"

"It's a little complicated." She started off, the crunch of her boots adding rhythm to the rush of the wind. A flurry of snowflakes lifted from a nearby drift and swirled around her. Pam lifted her shoulders to block the wind as she raised her voice. "I'd like to tell you over a cup of coffee, if that's all right."

Will glanced back at the row of markers, then nodded.

They had coffee in the cadet snack bar. The Saturday lunch crowd was filing in, cadets and dates chattered away in groups of two and four as they seated themselves at nearby tables.

Maybe it was the coffee, but Will noticed an edginess come over Pam as she made idle chatter. He sensed a feigned casualness, an amateurish, let's-not-get-into-this-too-fast-or-we'll-scare-off-the-mark kind of show. Then her expression hardened.

"She's lucky," Pam said as she glanced at a female cadet. "So were you. I would have liked to have been a combat pilot, too, just on the off chance I might somehow get even, but women pilots weren't allowed in combat during my college days."

Will had no interest in pursuing vengeance. "Actually, my father wasn't a pilot. He didn't pass the physical because of his hand. Dupuytren's syndrome. It's genetic, develops slowly, causing your fingers to curl as you age. They let him in navigator school though. He was nuts about fighters, so he wangled a job flying as an EWO in the backseat of F-105s. My mother told me he could have skipped the war. By then he couldn't straighten all the fingers on one hand, but every year he'd go in and browbeat the flight surgeon into signing him off."

"Chose war over family life." Pam stirred her coffee. "The hurt never goes away, does it?"

No it doesn't, Will thought, but chose not to respond.

"I still cry whenever I hear 'Taps,'" Pam continued, "even in movies." She looked away, composing herself, then began fidgeting in her bag as though she were going over a sales pitch one more time.

When she pulled out a manila envelope, Will glimpsed the shiny black grip of a handgun nestled inside her bag. Pam placed the envelope on the table and looked away again, out the window.

"I was Daddy's little girl, always hoping the next minute he'd come running in the front door, scoop me up, and shout, 'I'm home, pumpkin!'" The corners of her lips curled upward as she seemed to relish the thought. Suddenly, the hint of a smile vanished. "Then they declared him dead. It broke my mother's spirit."

"But not yours?"

"Not mine. I kept hoping." She let out a sigh. "But I went on living, too. I even got engaged. You know, my mother wanted me to have her wedding ring. Said she would feel better if it was on a hand that a living, loving man could grasp." She straightened, taking in a deep breath. "Well, the wedding's off, but I wouldn't have accepted the ring anyway, not until I resolve this."

She opened the folder, then placed a photo in front of him.

Will looked at the picture, two men standing together, both aware that their picture was being taken, but only one had a forced smile, betraying any hint of pleasure in the event.

She pointed to the figure on the right. "That once was my dad."

"Once was?"

"I sent a copy to the CIA. After months hearing nothing, I gave a copy to the two-star head of the Joint Task Force in Hawaii. A colonel at JTF got back to me a few weeks later and said that the face in the photo had been tampered with, a forgery. I was suspicious, so I had what I thought was my original analyzed again, and this time the result was different—it corroborated the JTF finding that the image had been altered. I'm convinced someone stole the original and replaced it in my file with the same modified version JTF sent back."

"What about the CIA copy?"

"When I asked for that one to be returned, they claimed they had sent it to JTF for action."

Will studied the photo, looking for a resemblance to Pam in the man's face or a sign that the image had been changed. He saw neither.

"He's still alive. That's why I won't take my mother's ring."

Now he was really puzzled. "Didn't we just come from your father's grave?"

"His marker, beneath which is a handful of bones sent by the Vietnamese. For all I know, it could be Ho Chi Minh out there."

"Ho Chi Minh's body is on display in Hanoi." The words flew from Will's mouth. He caught the look of surprise on Pam's face but felt no remorse. He did not want to encourage her in the direction he felt she was headed: a plea for support from him to finance some ill-conceived MIA search effort.

"Bad homework, I guess," Pam said, her tone measured, cool, in control. "I was just trying to make a point. The original photo was analyzed by a private firm that finds missing persons. They sent it back claiming a ninety-nine percent correlation using pictures of my father taken before his capture."

Will studied the picture, noting the man holding a placard with 2N-4W-L79 written on it. "Any significance to these numbers?"

"I learned that the air force had a navigation beacon on top of a peak in Laos during the war. Our pilots used it to find their way into North Vietnam. It was called Lima Seventy-Nine. A Laotian brought the photo to our embassy this past summer. I can't tell you yet how I obtained it. Dad looked twenty years older in the original photo than during his Vietnam days, but it could have been taken after only ten or so years of imprisonment, given the way he had probably been fed and treated. I think my father was trying to tell us he's imprisoned two miles north and four west of the Lima site.

"I don't get it. Have you approached anyone high in the government?"

"Yes, my congressman suggested I contact the Joint Task Force. Everyone passes the buck, right to JTF. I've been stonewalled," Pam said. "The colonel in Hawaii sent back the altered photo and a form letter stating my claim would be considered along with thousands of others. It could take years before they find anything. Meanwhile my father rots in some jungle prison."

Will rubbed his chin. "Obviously, you think I can help."

"Yes. I'm convinced there's a cover-up here, and I'd like you to work with me to expose it."

Will leaned back in his chair.

"I know," she said. "It sounds like the ravings of some crackpot, but believe me, there *is* a cover-up at the highest level." Her voice resumed that sharp tone that Will had earlier sensed was held in check with great effort. "There are over two thousand MIAs. If just ten percent are still alive, hundreds of millions of dollars in back pay is at stake. Can you imagine the embarrassment, my God, the *lawsuits,* if it became known that the government knowingly abandoned POWs all this time and did nothing about it?"

Will spread his hands, palms up. "You're looking at a grounded fighter pilot, who'll be a civilian in six months."

"I know your record."

Will sat in silence. *Was she getting ready to give her two-cents'-worth about his plane crash?*

"History major at the academy with a minor in Russian studies, three years Russian language, pistol team captain, graduated eighty-first out of nine hundred ten. Four combat missions over Baghdad. Instructor pilot. Currently on medical leave from the F-15 Fighter Weapons School, Nellis Air Force Base." She ended with, "Good homework?"

Will remained motionless, his attention locked on the smug look she now had, but she was not finished. "I also sense you'd like to fly again."

Will looked away. The truth was, she had him dead to rights. Flying was the one thing that filled the emptiness left by parents too-soon gone, his wife's death, and the solitary world he knew.

She took back the photo. "I'd like you to get assigned to the Joint Task Force. Working together, we can blow the lid off this travesty. When it's over, they'll give you anything you want."

Will was intrigued by her spunk but had no intention of becoming a zealot on her behalf in the lets-not-forget-our-MIAs business. "Thanks for the offer, but you don't understand. The air force wouldn't let me in the MIA program even if I asked."

"Please, hear me out. Senator Dalton on the Armed Services Committee can get you in, and I know you're close to him."

"Bad homework again. No one's close to that man anymore . . .

except the Secret Service." Will glanced at his watch. When he looked up, she was glaring at him.

"I have something else." Pam opened the manila envelope again. As she reached inside, she looked up, her eyes flashing. "If you can't help me search for *my* father, would you do it for yours?" She slid a Polaroid toward him that had been taped together. A figure standing near the camera appeared to be waving. "I've had *it* privately analyzed, too."

A little underexposed, it showed a man from the chest up, hair askew. In the background was a chain-link fence with a few bushes growing along its base. The man's hands were raised in surrender. The face looked familiar. Then Will focused on the man's left hand. The pinky and ring finger were curled, but the middle and index finger were straight as though giving a Boy Scout salute—a hand Will remembered only too well.

Will's gaze slowly shifted up to Pam. Words failed him, his mind a blur.

3

October 3—Capitol Hill, Washington, D.C.

A Capitol Hill regular could spot Senator Dalton a mile away by his determined forward-leaning stance and the slight hitch in his gait, his chin jutting ahead like the bow of a cruiser plowing through heavy seas. The odd step was a permanent souvenir from a broken leg set by a less-than-enthusiastic Vietnamese medic.

The senator's leather oxfords pounded down the underground corridor that linked his office with the Capitol Building. He was accompanied today by his campaign manager, Janet Mills, a professional image maker who jogged and dieted to appear ten years younger than the forty she had lived. Two steps aft strode Special Agent Anthony Ganetta from the Secret Service. With a neck like an oil drum, Ganetta strode with the swagger of a longshoreman, his fatigue-ringed eyes sweeping the scene in front and behind.

Ganetta had spent his early years working in internal security at the Defense Intelligence Agency, the military spy operation. After officials analyzed the 1981 attempt on President Reagan's life, the Secret Service revised its work rules and began recruiting additional agents. Ganetta took an interdepartmental transfer to the more glamorous, though more demanding, job on the Hill.

Mills flipped through a stack of papers as she walked. She had to work hard to keep up with Dalton and was accustomed to rushing after him as he strode along, a purpose to his conspicuous step. She and Ganetta kept a pace or two behind, in the wake of this imposing human ship.

Ganetta held his distance, a communications wire running to his ear, while Mills caught up alongside Dalton to brief him. The senator inclined an ear as she spoke, his eyes never wavering from the path ahead. She enjoyed her role as campaign manager, a take-charge position that involved handling the detail part of the show while keeping her boss fully informed. She had joined his prior run for the Senate late in the campaign as a speech research assistant, but Dalton pulled her aside and told her how impressed he was with her grasp of the issues and details. When the previous campaign manager stepped down for health reasons, Dalton promoted her. Between campaigns she was his chief of staff. Now she felt he owed a large measure of his success to her contributions. She knew she tended to be abrupt, even blunt to the point of rudeness, never hesitating to speak her mind about even the most sacred cows like Social Security and national defense. That ability to take a stand apparently pushed the right button with Dalton, who did not want his most important staffer to be a sycophant. She could be irascible with him one minute and concerned to the point of tenderness the next, depending on what she sought. On the other hand, she knew the rest of his staff resented her. She cracked the whip over them, but in so doing took the pressure off the senator. Dalton reined her in at times, but together they clicked and she had an affection for him, beyond her professional veneer, that grew over the years. When she dropped a thinly veiled invitation to expand their relationship, he had taken a step back, becoming distant. She interpreted his reaction as a message that he had no intention of letting a woman get her hooks into him in this political age. Though shaken by his rebuff, she had learned a valuable lesson, promising herself to use that experience to advantage in the future. The future had rushed center stage with a cryptic heads-up she had gotten over the phone that morning.

Unlike the Senate run, the current campaign was a much tighter race since he had become an independent. The opposition candidates, the incumbent president, and the Democratic Party nominee were running neck and neck. Pressure was building as Dalton closed to within two points in the polls. Mills had learned that the president was about to raise the ante. Up to now, the senator had been on the defensive, having to counter the weight of recent policy gains made by the administration. With Mills's help, Dalton had neutralized those obstacles and was ready to go on offense. The president needed something decisive to swing support from undecided voters. A debate had been proposed by the League of Women Voters. The contest was to be held in less than two weeks, and Dalton felt confident in spite of the president's experience in debates. Times were tense for all three candidates and a tiny miscalculation could have disastrous effects.

When Mills had finished going over the rest of his schedule, she paused. The insider phone call that morning had alerted her to a new twist in the campaign. The one subject she had hinted at before but never readdressed had reared itself. She would have preferred to work the problem in private, but events were moving too rapidly. Mills moved closer. "Senator, being unattached when running for the Senate was one thing, but the prospect of a White House without a first lady is presenting a formidable challenge for this campaign."

Senator Dalton continued walking, his expression frozen except for the knot that slowly appeared on the side of his face as his jaw muscles tightened. He tapped his neck scar. "Surviving throat cancer was what I call a formidable challenge. Being *unattached* didn't seem to hold back President Buchanan, or Jefferson for that matter."

"Women didn't have the vote then."

"Thank you for refreshing my memory, Janet, but I didn't get this far by satisfying conservative perceptions all the time. If it costs a few votes—"

"We're not talking a few votes here. You hired me for my campaign savvy, and I'm just saying that right now it would make a hell of a difference."

"Humph."

She checked to make sure Agent Ganetta was still out of earshot. "You should consider doing something to take the edge off that touchy issue."

"Exactly what are you suggesting?"

"Ellen?"

Ellen Vincent was a Washington socialite who often accompanied the senator to events where having a lady on his arm was the right thing to do. There had been just the slightest tabloid hint—unfounded—of something more than friendship in the relationship, Ellen having come to enjoy her role in the business and political world after inheriting a fortune from her late husband's shipping business. She was older than Dalton, yet still attractive, and enjoyed taking part in the Washington scene. Together they made a handsome couple.

"Think engagement. After you're in office, what happens, happens. Meanwhile Generation X will switch from watching *West Wing* to C-SPAN. The gray conservatives will be satisfied. Ellen would be a good choice," Mills continued, "if you are so inclined."

Dalton glanced sideways at her. "Janet. *If* I was so inclined, would I be the first to marry in the White House?"

She was certain he didn't care about the answer since he held his gaze toward her as if only interested in her reaction.

She brushed back the single thick wave that covered her profile on that side of her face and felt her tough, driven veneer begin to waver. She was sure even her makeup couldn't hide the flush of color she felt rising in her cheeks. "Second," she said, back in control, "Cleveland did it in 1886."

The senator smiled. "Second, hmmm?"

Though she knew the senator was highly conscious of his public image, that image apparently had its limit, and a drastic change of lifestyle, like marriage, seemed to exceed the limit—a limitation she for some time had an uneasy sense about, a vague perception that forces beyond the campaign weighed heavily upon him. There were phone calls to his secure line, the installation of which came with his appointment to the Armed Services Committee, and abrupt cancellations of important meetings after which the senator would be driven to the Defense Intelligence Agency for a few hours without so much as an "oh-by-the-way." She knew where he had gone though. She checked the vehicle log.

"I may be seeing too much of Ellen if thoughts like marriage are crossing your mind," Dalton said, "but I'll take your suggestion under advisement." Then he picked up speed.

Mills followed, satisfied that so far she had worked the issue perfectly.

Will sat across from Senator Dalton's secretary, Arline Haske, who kept an anxious eye on him while she worked. Haske had been with the senator even longer than Janet Mills. As his secretary, she was used to pop-up requests to meet with the senator. Because he was in uniform and also on the official access roster, her sixth sense was at work telling her not to treat this visitor offhandedly, but instead to let the senator deal with the intrusion.

Will stood as Senator Dalton entered, followed by Janet Mills and Agent Ganetta.

Dalton saw Will at once and laid on a campaign smile. "Will, what a surprise!"

Will shook the senator's hand. "I know how busy—"

"Look at that uniform, will you?" Dalton stepped away. "Trim as ever. Couldn't squeeze into mine if my life depended on it."

"Janet," the senator said, catching her eye, "this is Will Cadence."

"Pleased." Mills didn't part her lips a fraction when she smiled. Then she turned to the senator. "Sir, we have twenty minutes before your session with the League of Women Voters."

"Okay, fine. Things are in a tailspin around here, Will, but give me a minute. Then we'll chat." Dalton signaled for Haske and Mills to follow him into his private office.

Once inside, Haske spoke first. "He's been out there since eight this morning. Won't say what he wants to talk about." She paused. "I thought it better not to brush him off."

"You did right," Senator Dalton said.

Mills was wide-eyed. "Is there something I should know?"

Dalton hesitated, then said, "Will's father, Jack Cadence, and I were shot down together. Jack didn't make it back, and at times I've tried to treat Will like a son." Dalton hesitated.

"Even if he's your *prodigal* son," Mills cut in, well aware of Dalton's past, "couldn't he get an appointment—"

Senator Dalton raised his hand like a stop sign. "He has recently been involved in an aircraft accident. I'll see him, and that's all there is to it," he declared. "Five minutes."

Mills rolled her eyes. "Whoa-kay, but I hope he's not after something that could be . . . distracting, that would upset today's schedule."

"All *right,*" Senator Dalton said raising his voice. "Five minutes."

Mills pursed her lips, closed her eyes, then nodded. She was aware that Dalton had placed several calls to an air force accident board after a personal call came in from Cadence a few months ago. She had been in Dalton's office at the time, and he had asked her to leave when Haske buzzed him regarding the call. Now she knew the subject of the phone conversations. She wondered what else Cadence was after. She spun around and stalked up to Haske who was about to open the door. "When he comes out," Mills hissed at Haske, "I want him gone before any media snoops grab him."

After Mills and Haske departed, Dalton looked himself over in the full-length mirror mounted by the exit so that he could always see himself before the public did.

Then the doorknob turned. A moment later, Will limped in, his gaze quickly taking in the surroundings.

The office reeked of history—fireplace, antique cherry desk, a nineteenth-century oil of Pennsylvania Avenue, sofa, a few color photos of D.C. monuments, and a straight-back chair with armrests that made it easy for the senator to get into and out of. A twenty-four-inch TV was on, the sound muted, C-SPAN broadcasting live congressional testimony, which was being recorded on the VCR below the set.

Dalton put his smile back on. "Having a gimp leg is becoming a fighter pilot trademark."

Will feigned a grin. "Except that my midair collision has taken me out of the fighter pilot business, which is one of the reasons I'm here. The other is to thank you for intervening with the accident board."

Dalton sat gingerly in his chair and invited Will to sit on the sofa. "After your call during the board proceedings, I got the releasable copy of their report and was disturbed by the recommendations. I supposed that's what you'd hoped. Well, it worked. I hoped you'd eventually give me the rest of the story, your version. 'Closure,' I think they call it."

"For me, yes." After a deep breath, Will began. "As the report showed, I was flying Boyd's wing during a midair refueling mission with a KC-10 tanker over the Gulf of Mexico. No moon. Stars merged in the blackness with lights from fishing boats below, giving no sense of up from down. Flying wing was like floating in space—total vertigo. One moment I'd feel right side up, the next instant upside down.

"I was delighted when my tanks showed full, and I finally disconnected from the KC-10's refueling boom. Boyd radioed me to rejoin onto his wing. I remember glancing inside the cockpit to peek at the attitude indicator and finish turning on my exterior lights after refueling. Checklist stuff. A second later I felt the bump. I thought it was just a bit of turbulence, but I'd rammed Boyd's plane. The night sky filled with an orange glow . . ."

Dalton seemed to pick up on Will's uneasy delay. "Take your time."

Will was lost in the moment, reliving those fateful seconds after his midair collision, hearing again the screech of the wing as it sheared from the fuselage.

The plane then snap rolled. In an instant Will became disoriented, being hurled against his harness restraints, legs slamming against the side of the cockpit. Flames! *Oh, God, I'm burning up!* His fingers found the ejection handle. He pulled and felt the brute kick from the rocket that propelled him out of the jet. A rush of air, blackness, tumbling, pain in his leg, total loss of control, then his head whipping down as his parachute opened. He peered into an inky void below. Somewhere down there the ocean was waiting for him, but as his vision cleared, he noticed a glow from above reflecting off his gloved hand. He looked up. His parachute was on fire!

Seconds later with flaming risers starting to rain down on him and terror gripping his heart, he slammed into the sea and went under. Stunned, Will reached out, trying to grab something solid. The next second he was on the surface, but what remained of the parachute canopy and risers had collapsed on top of him. The flames had been doused by the sea, so he was in total darkness again. He could hear a hissing sound. Smoke and salt water filled his mouth and lungs as he tried to breathe. Panic rose as he flailed, trying to find some clean air. He could feel his legs, already tangling in the risers. *Training, training, got to remember my training!* He stopped struggling, pulled a glove off, found a chute panel seam, and pulled his way along until his hand bumped against the canopy edge. He shoved it aside, poked his head above a roiling sea, and sucked in a lung full of cool air. A swell washed over him and under he went again. He felt for his life preservers. Both had failed to inflate automatically. He found the toggle cord for the left side and pulled. Once more on the surface, he heard the sound of an engine and discovered himself looking into a floodlight from a fishing trawler, the captain of which had seen the flames and come for a look.

"Will," Dalton continued, "my exit from an airplane was pretty traumatic, too."

"They all are," Will said, his palms sweaty and his mind returning to the present. "I punched out really low and got picked up by a crew on a fishing boat. That's all there was to it." He was unwilling to discuss the ordeal any further. "Boyd's wing tip was damaged, but he managed to land safely. The accident board found Boyd at fault, saying he didn't allow enough time for me to finish my cockpit tasks and stabilize. I thought that to be in error and wanted you to review the findings, with an open, experienced eye."

Dalton nodded.

Will continued. "I was hoping you'd have problems with the board's recommendation regarding Boyd. They didn't take my wings. I guess it's because they didn't have to. I can't fly 'em any longer, anyway." Will tapped his leg brace. "Tom Boyd lost his chance to command a fighter squadron but thanks to you still flies—hauling embassy cargo around the planet."

"I'm glad my intercession helped."

"It did, and I thank you for that. As for me, I have one more request. I want to do my last tour with the JTF program."

"The MIA Task Force in Hawaii?" Dalton asked. His fingertips, tented in front of his lips, began pressing together, firmly.

"Yes, sir. Trouble is, they have an assignment policy against next of kin—"

"And for good reason: no personal agendas."

Will swallowed hard, then spoke softly. "The only agenda I have is to do something about MIAs, for the father I never knew."

The senator paused, then pointed behind his desk to a picture of the Vietnam Veterans Memorial. "Have you been to the Wall?"

"I've made it a point to avoid it."

"Why is that?"

"It's hard to put into words . . . my feelings."

"Go. You'll cry. Everyone does. Get it out of your system. Put it behind you, and I'll help you get a fresh start."

Will looked at the image of the black granite memorial. "Cry? Then turn away from it?" The suggestion seemed odd. He glanced back at Dalton. "Have you?"

Dalton looked eye to eye at Will for a long moment, as though analyzing something perhaps threatening in what Will had just said. "I'll see what I can do," Dalton said.

After Will had left, Dalton pressed the intercom. "Arline, get Colonel Bustamente at the Joint Task Force on the line. As soon as we're finished, I'll need to talk to General Stoner there as well."

4

THE DEBATE COMMITTEE FROM the League of Women Voters was waiting in the second-floor conference room when Senator Dalton and Janet Mills arrived. Elizabeth Stanton Herman, renowned for her flamboyant feminism, led the four-member committee. Her smile belied the *I can use the f-word and go from zero-to-bitch in 2.0 seconds flat* potential that lurked behind her pleasant facade. She stood to greet the senator, gave Mills a passing nod, then sat. "We have arranged a tentative schedule for you and your running mate, the rules for each debate, and the makeup of the panel that will present questions. I hope you will find these satisfactory."

Mills eyed Herman as Senator Dalton reviewed one of two folders that Herman slid toward him after he sat. Finally, Dalton looked up. "It looks to be in order." Dalton smiled, then Mills caught his sideways glance for concurrence as he gave her the paperwork. Having already reviewed the program, she nodded assent while wondering how Herman planned to broach the subject of the insider phone call she had received that morning.

Herman picked up the other folder. "There has come a suggestion for a third session, one where the candidate's wives offer their views in a seminar, to be aired after the presidential and before the V-P debate."

"What?" Dalton blurted.

As Mills had been warned, the opposition was trying to score points by highlighting the fact that their opponent was not married, something they were hesitant to bring up openly due to the political sensitivity involved.

Dalton took on the look of a cornered bobcat.

Mills and Dalton both knew that as a possible stand-in, Barbara Anderson, wife of the senator's running mate would get devoured in a two-on-one seminar, a term Mills considered a blatant way to soften the term *debate.* Up to now, Barbara's backstage role in the election campaign was considered an asset since it served to lessen the impact that Dalton's not having a spouse had on the electorate. But now, if the offer was declined, word would get out, and Dalton could lose a chunk of conservative women's votes. If he allowed the seminar to go forward, the empty chair would speak volumes.

"That's a ridiculous proposal," Mills spat out.

"The other candidates understand your position," Herman continued speaking to Dalton without looking at Mills. "The president suggested that you, Senator, could be present in order to express your views on women's issues."

"That's very generous of him," Dalton said, chuckling. Mills caught another glance from Dalton, which she read as an interrogative. *Had she known about this?*

Mills shrugged. It was not quite a lie. The phone call that morning gave her an idea about what was coming but was not detailed enough to pin it down.

Dalton winced, his hand going to his jaw, kneading the clean-shaven flesh there. Finally, he leaned toward Herman. "Tell you what. I accept my opponent's offer."

"Then you'll attend the seminar?"

"No," Dalton said. "My campaign manager will."

"I will?" Mills saw Herman's mouth form an enormous puckered O, which then transformed to a cynical smile. Mills returned the grin while inwardly musing over the media frenzy that she was sure Herman had instantly begun conjuring at the prospect of breaking the news about the seminar. Mills turned to Dalton. "Are you sure that's a good idea? You know how I tend to spout off." She chuckled as a knot in her stomach tightened like a noose.

Dalton placed his hand on her forearm. "You'll do fine."

"I see," Herman said as her eyebrows inched up. "I'm sure there will be no objections."

Mills covered a huge sigh. From her earlier lessons with Dalton's emotions, she had learned that he was open to proposals when it came to routine problems, office staffing, or the campaign schedule, but when it came to certain personal and political issues, the senator could be counted on as a control freak. This tendency was the only vulnerability she had uncovered in the man. Otherwise he was as solid as they come. He had developed into the most popular politician New Mexico had elected in decades, ably working tough issues like welfare, crime, immigration, and pressing matters that could be considered in the light of statistical analysis and fiscal alternatives. He had even coaxed a meeting of the minds between industry leaders and environmental advocates to bring his state to the forefront in that effort, a model other states were rapidly adopting.

Janet's biggest coup was convincing him he had to become an independent to win the White House. The problem for Mills came when an issue touched deep personal nerves, an issue that could not be broken down into a numbers drill. Then she had the delicate task of finessing the senator's train of thought in the proper direction. Suggest he elevate Ellen Vincent's status, and he lowers it. Advise that there should not be a distaff debate plus you, Mills, may not be a good choice to be in it, and there *is* one and you *are* in it. The more personal aspects of Henry Dalton's candidacy were his alone to decide. She was aware that he seemed to lean toward contrariness when decisions were of that nature, so she manipulated this idiosyncrasy. Pressing Henry Dalton's buttons was becoming more and more productive. What bothered Mills was how Dalton seemed to push the limit, bending rules whenever an issue connected to Will Cadence popped up. Dalton routinely eschewed doing favors for acquaintances. "One has to earn one's way," Dalton had insisted on many occasions, yet he had made those calls to the air force accident investigation board while its outcome was still undecided. Now he had made another move that she knew was risky: greasing the skids on a military assignment for a personal friend. That kind of action could open him up to criticism. Was the close personal interest in Cadence simply a favor to the memory of Cadence's dead father? Could be, but Dalton seems to behave differently whenever

Cadence enters the scene, particularly this time. *A little too edgy,* she thought. He had raised his voice to her regarding meeting him, and that seemed out of character. She would try to find out if there was more to this, in case the major held something over Dalton. Mills wouldn't use the background investigative channels normally open to her, though. That might get back to Dalton. Instead, she would press another button she controlled on the elevator wall of her ride to the top, this one attached to Thornton Bishop, the powerful and discreet director of the CIA.

5

MONDAY, NOVEMBER 1, HAWAII

WILL CHECKED OVER HIS Thunderbird at the Pearl Harbor port of entry, marking NO DAMAGE on the inspection sheet. When he finished, he lowered the convertible top, then deposited a suitcase and duffel bag in the trunk where he retrieved his cane. On his way back to the shipping office, he tested his injured leg, putting extra weight on it as he stepped. Satisfied, Will dropped the cane in a Dumpster outside the office where he went to sign release documents for the car. While there, he got directions to Camp Smith.

The morning traffic coming in the main gate was heavy, but he was headed opposite the flow. Will turned on the radio and waited patiently as its cathode tubes warmed. He rotated the dial until he hit upon KUMU, featuring '50s and '60s hits. The sky was bright and clear, but the sun had not crested the Koolau Mountains yet, so the air felt chilly as it surged up his sleeves. He regretted having put the top down.

Three minutes later he crossed the H-1 Freeway and turned his T-Bird right on Ulune Street, then took the first left onto Aliipoe and up a steep, hilly incline. He drove through a residential section, single-family homes jammed chockablock on tiny parcels, most with a manicured lawn in front and a papaya or banana tree sticking up out back.

He gazed at the ridge, the colors of tropical flowers crisp to his mainlander eyes. The distinct texture of this verdant reality contrasted with the blur, the disbelief he felt regarding Pam Robbins's contention that his own father might still be alive. When he had questioned Pam about the origins of the Polaroid, she claimed to have received it from a friend. In due time she would reveal who, but her contact was "living in a place of extreme danger." Intriguing as her story had been, he could not truly believe in the possibility that both their fathers were still alive. How could prisoners still be held captive decades after the end of the war and, more disturbing, how could a government that sent these men to war refuse to investigate what might be their continuing plight? In spite of doubts, her assertion had interrupted his personal dilemma over his aircraft accident, plummeting him into an emotional dive with a force so powerful that control was out of his hands for the moment.

Will dropped into second gear and accelerated up the hill. Foliage partially covered a stop sign where Paihi Street intersected, and Will was late in spotting the sign. He squealed to a stop in the middle of the intersection just as a motorcycle zipped around a curve.

The rider saw Will's T-Bird blocking the intersection and hit the brakes. The motorcycle skidded on a patch of sand, the bike's rear wheel swinging forward. Both rider and bike slid to the ground and came grinding down the incline. The motorcycle came to a stop inches from Will's door as a shower of gravel pinged off his car.

Will could not open his door without bumping the machine. "Sorry," he blurted, as he looked down on the spectacle. The rider stood, then spread feet wide apart. Tucked into brown leather ankle boots were skintight jeans that rose up long legs to a right hip, where a furious hand was planted. Elbow out. The left arm hung at the rider's side, veins visible on the back of a slender hand and wrist. She wore a leather bomber jacket. Every curve, every sinew of her being screamed, "You idiot!" but all she said was:

"Shit!"

Will noticed that from the look of it, the machine had seen a lot of miles. The model name HUGGER was emblazoned on the rear fender, but she was definitely not in that kind of mood.

"You okay?" He attempted to rise, intending to leap over the door, but could not maneuver his bad leg clear. Frustrated, he gripped the door handle, waiting for her to hopefully make enough room for the door to be opened.

The sun had risen above the Koolaus and it reflected off her helmet visor into Will's eyes like a laser scoring steel.

She righted the machine in a deliberate, exasperated heave as Will tried conversation again. "Drivers like me are a prime reason you won't get me on one of those things."

She checked the machine over. "You're damn lucky there's no damage to this *thing.*"

Will was about to offer another apology when the woman kick-started the cycle, then zoomed past him down the grade. He watched her disappear in his mirror, then headed up the hill, making the turn at Halawa Heights Road, which led to Camp Smith, home of the Joint Task Force and his new assignment.

The entrance was guarded by a marine, who leaned from the sentry post, checked Will's ID, then gave directions to an ominous blockhouse of a building.

Will studied the place through the windshield as he pulled up. The JTF Headquarters had no windows. *Perfect,* he thought. *Wouldn't want to enjoy the Hawaiian daylight when one could grind out paperwork with eyes shielded to the real world outside.*

A car beside the building pulled out of a parking slot near a modest wooden sign that announced: MIA JOINT TASK FORCE, MAJ. GEN. BRADLEY M. STONER, COMMANDER.

Will parked and got out. He bent low, a few tiny scratches of the kind small pebbles might make were near the T-Bird's doorsill. "Damn," he mumbled. When he rose, he saw another building across the street with a sign indicating the local office of the Defense Intelligence Agency, DIA.

After straightening his uniform, Will headed for the JTF entrance. He saluted two officers who were just leaving. One was a two-star general who appeared agitated, the other a marine major, wearing the yellow fourragère of an aide. The major popped a crisp return salute, but the general returned Will's with a forearm flick that looked like a karate chop snapping a brick in half.

As Will entered the building, he glanced back and saw the two officers approach the entrance to DIA. Will passed through building security and ambled down the hall looking at a sign above a office that read INVESTIGATING OFFICER (IO) SECTION. Then he saw one marked COL. ROBERT L. BUSTAMANTE, DIVISION CHIEF. As Will opened that door, he saw a banner on the far wall, this one made from continuous-feed computer paper that read GOOD LUCK, BETTY. WE'LL MISS YOU! The room was filled with military and civilian workers all chattering as they ate cake. After a moment, a colonel on the other side of the room noticed Will. He had a tanned Mediterranean look, with permanent five o'clock shadow and a head of black hair that gave him a youthful, virile look. He stabbed his remaining cake with his fork and put the plate down. "Cadence, Will Cadence, the new IO from Nellis! Am I right?" The conversation around them ground to a halt.

Will extended his hand. "That'd be me, sir." He noticed the lack of wings above the colonel's shirt pocket, signifying that the officer was not a flier.

"I'm Colonel Bustamante, your new boss." They shook hands. Then the colonel indicated a sprightly woman who stood next to him cutting slices of cake. "This here's Cath, my secretary, and you might say this is a hi-good-bye for Betty." He wrapped his arm around a chubby, rumpled woman who was all smiles and tears. "New job at DIA in D.C. Her husband got reassigned to the Pentagon."

"Don't get me started on that," Betty roared.

"She's taking it kinda hard," Bustamante said with a frown. The others laughed dutifully at the remark. Bustamante made the rest of the introductions, after which he opined, "Your father would be proud you're here."

"You knew my dad?"

"I pulled your file and his when I saw the assignment come through, so in that way I guess I know you both." Bustamante picked up a napkin to clean his hands. "I need to run an errand, and these folks need to get back to work. Follow me. I'll give you the cook's tour."

"Party pooper," Betty countered. The others booed lightly.

"Have that case folder ready for me when we get back, Cath," Bustamante said as he bustled out the door. He led Will down the hall. "Didn't expect you until tomorrow." The words rattled out, sounding like a rebuke.

"With tomorrow being Election Day, I wasn't sure who might be in and anyway, after months of therapy, I'm eager to get back to work."

Bustamante nodded. "An attitude that will fit in nicely here, as will your history background, seeing as how we deal with the past. By the way, how's the leg coming?"

"It's coming, thanks. Shouldn't be needing this too much longer." He tapped the metal support of his knee brace.

A navy chief petty officer stood as Bustamante and Will entered an office marked RECORDS SECTION. Behind him were two computer operators entering data into their machines. The chief's desk had its own monitor and a small baseball-sized object for a paperweight that Will recognized as a cluster bomb unit, a type of antipersonnel weapon used extensively during the Vietnam War. Holes drilled in the side of this one indicated deactivation.

Bustamante introduced the NCO, then swept his arm toward the files and equipment. "Chief Jackson has a pretty spiffy operation—all the bells and whistles tax money can buy."

Jackson smiled. "Southeast Asia MIA info is catalogued here—over thirty thousand items. We link across the street to the Defense Intelligence Agency and their main office in Washington."

"We used to be under DIA," the colonel added. "Now we operate directly for the Pentagon, but still share data with DIA.

Will hefted the paperweight bomblet.

"That CBU came out of Laos on our last visit," Jackson said. "Mean little things. Kids still find them and *boom.*"

Will replaced the device on the desk.

Bustamante moved near one of the operators. The man was scanning a document onto his monitor. Will noted that the item was in a foreign language. When the man used his mouse to click an icon, the document was immediately translated into English.

"Impressive," Will said.

The operator looked up. "Yes, sir. A handy system, but it does have its problems. Some idiomatic expressions don't do a neat translation. We still have to make a complete line check."

"What language was that?" Will asked.

"A dialect from a Laotian hill-tribe."

They moved to another computer station. A sergeant maneuvered an image of a man's face on his monitor. Then he clicked an icon and the man's hairline changed.

"This is Sergeant Larson," Bustamante said. "Our image-enhancement guru. Come back later, and he can show how you'll look in twenty years. I don't recommend it, though. Damn depressing."

Will chuckled. "I imagine so."

Bustamante led Will from the room. Back along the hall they passed the investigating officer section that Will had seen earlier. The colonel stopped in front of an unmarked office.

"Because your assignment came through as an overage, we're one man top-heavy, so you'll be working in here for a while." Bustamante opened the door to another windowless room. Inside, a phone, computer and monitor sat on a gray steel desk near empty in/out baskets. Across from it was another desk, stark, including its own empty in\out basket. A bank of file cabinets separated the desks serving to give the room an artificial feel, as though it had been hastily altered from other uses.

"General Stoner asked his aide, Major Byron Chase, to help you get your feet on the ground—be your sponsor." Bustamante indicated the other desk. "That's his desk, part-time. He's a hard-charging leatherneck."

Will walked over and toyed with Chase's in/out basket. There was neither a note nor pen, not even a paper clip in sight. He scanned the room wondering where he might take a hammer, as he had seen done in a prison-escape movie, and begin banging out a porthole to the outside world. He'd cover the hole with a picture of John Wayne. No marine would mess with the Duke.

"Enough of this," Bustamante said. "I've got an errand to run at the Central Identification Lab, so come along."

Colonel Bustamante picked up the case file from Cath, then led Will outside to a staff car. The colonel drove. As they sped down the incline, Bustamante pointed out the *Arizona* Memorial and the sprawling runways of Honolulu International Airport. The colonel explained that the runway area was once part of Hickam Field, an army post back in the forties. What remained of the base belonged to the air force now and was squeezed between the civilian terminal and the navy facility at Pearl Harbor.

After they passed through Hickam's main gate, Will sensed that little had changed in this part of the base since the Second World War. The streets were lined with tall shade trees. Along Hangar Avenue the old army air corps insignia was mounted with retro-pride on the facade of each renovated hangar.

They drove onto Vickers Avenue near the headquarters, the road now cordoned off to dissuade terrorists. The colonel pointed to the outer walls of the structure. "See those pockmarks . . . bullet scars from strafing done during the Pearl Harbor attack. They've been left, a permanent reminder of what results from failed vigilance." Farther to the west, he nodded in the direction of a two-hundred-foot-tall concrete structure that looked like a monument. "That's a water tower. The Japanese gave it a wide swath. Their pilots were briefed that it was a religious symbol; attacking it might rile us far more than from the destruction of purely military installations." The colonel laughed.

Will glanced at the tower. How ironic, he thought, that a nation's leaders and its military could be so misguided into thinking that America's reaction to their act of treachery would be anything but a consuming desire for vengeance.

"Sixty-seven ships of the Imperial Japanese Navy took part in the attack," Bustamante said. "When the war ended, sixty-five had been sunk. Striking this country is not conducive to the attacker's longevity."

They came to the end of Vickers Avenue, then found their way onto Fort Kam Road, a blacktop that wound around the aircraft parking ramp. The colonel followed signs that led to the lab, a long beige-colored building. He pulled into a visitor's slot.

With folder in hand, Bustamante led the way into the building. He waved at the receptionist and immediately turned down the hall and entered a large open room. To the right, Will noticed two offices, one of which had a nameplate above it announcing it belonged to Dr. Gabrielle DeJean. To the left, behind a glass partition, he saw row after row of examining tables, each one had a set of remains spread on it. Twenty tables in all, containing skulls, rib cages, femurs, arm bones, feet, hands, teeth. The human remains were assembled alongside personal articles, flying suits, dog tags, ID cards. Some of the remains still had flesh attached, some were bleached white, others were dark brown, some coal black. A male technician wearing a mask and medical smock was seated at one table, taking skull measurements with a pair of calipers.

Bustamante glanced inside Dr. DeJean's office. It was vacant. He crossed the hall and tapped on the glass. The technician looked up. The colonel raised his voice, while pointing at the doctor's office. "Excuse me, is Dr. DeJean around?"

The technician got the message and pointed to a lab door.

Surgical masks poked from a box near the door that had a sign on a frosted-glass panel indicating WET ROOM.

Bustamante grabbed two masks and tossed one to Will. "Put this on. You'll need it. The doctor is *in*."

Will donned the mask.

The colonel opened the door and Will looked past his shoulder as they entered. Someone was working over a dark object that was stretched out on a gurney inside the chamber. Will heard the high-pitched whine of what sounded like a dentist drill. The noise gave him shivers.

A tall woman, gloved and masked, her hair covered in a plastic surgical cap, looked up from her work. Something glinted near her hand. A circular blade spun at the end of the instrument she held.

The dank odor of decay hit Will full force as it penetrated his mask. Her hand was poised above the crotch of a corpse whose skin, blue-black and leathery, was peeled back. *Sweet Jesus.* Will felt a twinge in his gut and blood drain from his face. He had been on a fatal-accident board two years before and had worked with detailed photos of the victims. Will had been glad that only the investigating flight surgeon had to do the hands-on work.

The cadaver's mouth was open, teeth bared as if grimacing. A dead hand was raised, fingers reaching out as though caught in stop action yet trying desperately to defend itself from the violence being done to what was left of its masculinity.

"Hope we're not too much of an interruption," Bustamante said. "Dr. DeJean, meet our new IO, Major Will Cadence."

"Give me a minute," she said through her mask. Then she turned and positioned the blade above the hip bone on the cadaver and began to cut. The pitch of the sound increased as bone fragments flew into the air. A moment later, the woman lifted a two-inch segment of bone matter from the corpse. She placed it in a plastic bag, then put down the sample.

Her dark eyes met Will's and seemed to scan his face. They had a seductive, fluid quality, eyes that somehow he could never imagine would willingly gaze upon the horror within that room.

She slowly lowered her mask. The crease on her lips looked finely sculpted and her full lower lip glowed, reflecting the overhead lighting. She stared, eyes narrowing, not quite sure of herself until Will dropped his mask.

"Oh, it's you," she said with disdain. Her words jumped from those extraordinary lips and hit Will like a slap.

Bustamante's brow furrowed. "You've met?"

Will, puzzled, took in a shortened breath. The mask, now damp, clung to the side of his neck.

"We sort of," she said, "ran into each other this morning," Then she faced Will. "I was on the Harley."

Will winced with recollection, the imaginary slap now reinforced with his very real blush of embarrassment.

"Uh-oh," Bustamante said. "A story I probably don't want to hear."

"You really don't." She pointed at the corpse. "Hope you're not too skittish, Major. You'll be seeing a lot of this."

Will swallowed. "Oh?" His mind a blur.

"And who do we have here?" Bustamante stared at the remains.

"According to the dog tags, a Major Waxman, Caucasian, but this guy's Mongoloid, an Asian," she said, moving in a quick, surefooted way as she pulled off a glove and led them into the outer office. "I still have to send a bone sample to the lab in Maryland for the mitochondrial DNA analysis, but this is another con job." She closed the door.

Inside the office, the scent from an air freshener and normal office surroundings changed the ambiance. Will felt better until he spotted a clothes tree where a leather jacket hung, its scuffed elbow unmistakable. Inside on the crossbar hung her jeans. *Wonder Woman's phone booth,* he thought as he looked around.

The doctor offered a handshake. "Call me Gabbie."

Will felt her grasp, firm and certain. "Gabbie it is," he said, then continued. "So . . . who's conning who?"

"The Vietnamese are conning us. Desperate for cash, villagers bring in remains, complete with phony dog tags, claiming they're our guys and demand reward money—a booming cottage industry."

"With what little was left of him in there, how did you determine he's Asian?"

"That's a two-beer story, Major." She pulled at the other glove, and it came off with a *thwack*. Even the colonel flinched.

Will rose to the sardonic challenge. "And you don't drink on the job."

Gabbie flashed a momentary grin.

Bustamante coughed. "Dr. DeJean has a Ph.D. in forensic anthropology, Major. The good doctor knows whereof she speaks."

Will's eyes remained on the good doctor. "I never doubted it." To Will, she was an incredible beauty, tucked away in a morgue like an orchid in a trash heap. Was the acid tongue her norm, or just the result of their inauspicious meeting on the street?

Bustamante fingered the file he held. "Well, Gabbie, we won't keep you from your duties." He laid the file on her desk. "I'd like you to look this over and give me an opinion."

"Yes, sir."

As Will went to follow Bustamante out the door, he hesitated, feeling a compulsion to get in a last word. Maybe it was the whole macabre scene he had just witnessed, or maybe it was simply a need not to be so passive. There was something about her feminine imperiousness he found captivating. When the colonel was a few steps down the hall, Will leaned back inside. "About this morning, I really am sorry."

He saw her glance toward the clothes tree where her leather jacket hung. "Apology accepted," she said. Then she raised her hand, palm down, and shooed him away with her fingers, the expression on her face inscrutable, suggesting either that she was tired of his presence or felt his traffic lapse was not such a big deal after all.

6

NOT THAT GABBIE THOUGHT Will's driving gaffe *was* a big deal. A *big* deal was watching your father die when you were thirteen. A *big* deal was what happened in California and later at Fort Huachuca in Arizona.

She grew up adoring a chain-smoking, power-company lineman of a father who the adults in the cul-de-sac called Vince. They lived with her mother, Évelyne, in a high-desert subdivision aptly named Mercury Heights in Victorville, California, where each look-alike house came complete with an evaporative cooler on the roof. When she was old enough to hold a .22 pistol steady, Vince took her on the back of his motorcycle into the desert where they hunted. He always had a cigarette dangling from the corner of his mouth, and she gave him grief over the habit.

"Stay behind me, girl," he said as they stalked game. "You don't smell that smoke, means we're not moving upwind. That happens, you tell me straightaway, girl!" And he'd cuff her lightly on the ear and move off into the bush.

When they came home he would hone his taxidermy skills. "Gotta preserve these . . . and our legacy," he told her. His Cajun ancestors had moved west after the Louisiana Purchase in 1803. Back then the DeJean clan worked trap lines on the upper Missouri River in Montana. Her great-grandfather wound up marrying a Blackfoot. Vince told her that's where her dark eyes and complexion came from. He said his "Injun blood" is what made him fearless up high on the power lines.

Together in the garage, they shoulder-mounted whitetail deer. From her father, she learned the craft of taxidermy and how to use borax to preserve everything from rainbow trout caught at Big Bear Lake to desert pit vipers that the locals paid to have tanned and mounted. But one evening in the garage, her father couldn't control his hand while trying to insert a glass eye into the empty socket of a largemouth bass. His smoking had cost him a lung the year before, and when he went to the doctor this time, the diagnosis was a metastatic brain tumor—inoperable. She watched her father waste away, succumbing three months later. His death put Gabbie into a depression. Her school grades plummeted. She began cutting classes and was caught at an underage drinking party, which got her mother on her back, and, after a second offense six months later, a probation officer on her case. But not everyone had heard of her father's death. One afternoon she came home to find a cooler on the doorstep. Inside, a dead black-tailed rattler lay atop a bag of ice, along with a note that the owner would pick up the mounted reptile that weekend. Gabbie stepped into the garage, stared at her father's workshop gear for a long moment, then went to work. When the owner of the snake returned, he paid Gabbie and left. More hunters came by. Word got around about the teenage girl who did top-notch taxidermy. A lot of business came her way and she began to hang out with rednecks and country boys who roared around in pickup trucks and on Harley hogs.

At sixteen, when the other high school girls carried exotic makeup cases, her prized possessions were scissors, scalpel, forceps, teasing needles, dropper, and ruler, all stuffed inside an elementary dissection kit. Classwork bored her, but she was a quick learner. She spent little time on study, in spite of her mother's complaints. Biology was the exception, especially the lab work, which she aced, doing extra assignments on species she would bring in from the desert after lonely forays. Then at seventeen, with more spending money in her pocket than her mother had any idea about, sullen and still deeply missing her father, she began keeping late hours, getting more attention from the authorities, until along came a *really* big deal.

On a particularly hot evening in July, Florence Mather, her probation officer, leaned forward inside the holding room. "Gabrielle, do you know what your biker pal is wanted for?" Florence waited for the reply.

"No," Gabbie finally answered.

"Rape and attempted murder!"

Gabbie felt a chill as the words registered. She could hear her mother suck in her breath as Évelyne lurched backward in the chair beside Gabbie.

Florence poured it on. "Do you really think he was taking you to Las Vegas?"

"I guess not," Gabbie managed.

"You *guess* not," her mother moaned.

Florence looked to the ceiling. "You'd probably be dead now if that police officer hadn't been so observant!"

Évelyne had learned from a neighbor about Gabbie's leaving on the back of a motorcycle after dark and had called the cops. An APB with her description had gone out, and near midnight a police cruiser had spotted the pair just outside Baker, headed east. Joe-Bob Weldon—that was the name her biker pal was using—then stuffed a sleeve of cellophane envelopes into her jean pocket as they were being pulled over. "Be cool," he had told her. Well, things weren't so "cool" after they found the "hot" stuff.

"Here's the deal," Florence continued, but Gabrielle wasn't looking at her. "Are you listening?"

"I am." She straightened up. As a prior delinquent who had violated restrictions, she knew she had become a status offender. Probation was not an option.

"Your hearing is set for one week from now, unless you come back sooner to show the judge your enlistment papers for the army, navy, air force, or, heaven help you, even the marines, if they'll accept you. If you take off again, you'll be apprehended and sent to Ventura, the youth correctional facility." Florence then picked up her briefcase and went in to deal with the arresting officer.

Évelyne used the house as collateral to make bail, and the next morning Gabbie was out. One week later she was in. The army, that is. She had crammed, then passed the high school equivalency exam, and reported to basic training the next month. Boot camp was a snap. She was strong and quick and used to the outdoors, was comfortable with pistols and rifles, and knew how to hit what she aimed at. She graduated with honors, then selected her specialty: mortuary affairs. *Why not,* she thought? She had always been fascinated with things that were dead.

She got a stripe on her sleeve and wound up at Fort Huachuca in Arizona, home of the Buffalo Soldiers. Assigned to Graves Registration, Search and Recovery Team, she was part of the Quartermaster Corps at the fort. Duty was pleasant, and she began taking night classes for college credit. Her mother came to visit the second year.

"Mortuary Affairs?" Évelyne asked, exasperation evident in her tone. "When, Gabbie, are you going to get over this fixation on dead things?"

"The dead don't complain," she answered.

But those *responsible* for the dead were about to complain.

The word had come in on a Thursday afternoon in August. Gabbie went in the ambulance, then hiked to the scene. She waited as the authorities were finishing with their sweep for evidence, photography, and footprint search—of which there were many since a group of hikers had come upon the body. She heard from a military policeman that they had found and bagged a dead rattlesnake, an empty canteen, and a backpack near the corpse. The John Doe had a bloodstained rock in one hand. Gabbie then helped load the decedent's remains into a body bag for the trip back to the fort morgue. The next afternoon she assisted Dr. Steens, an army medical examiner, in conducting the autopsy. The deceased, Lamar Combs, was a "light-skinned African-American," a corporal. He had been reported missing since August 14, three days prior, and had been carried on the roster as an unauthorized absence.

X rays, photographs, measurements, and weight had already been recorded. Dr. Steens began the autopsy procedure, describing each step and observation into a microphone attached to his green surgical scrubs. He examined, then removed every item of clothing—all of it civilian garb—which Gabbie then placed in separate plastic bags. She wondered about that, why a man would put on casual civvies and go off into the desert in August with only one canteen.

Dr. Steens did a preliminary visual examination. The bowels had been ripped open and the swollen body showed evidence of numerous animal bites and insect invasion. Then Gabbie handed him a scalpel. He made a Y incision across the chest and down through the open viscera to the pubis. He removed the heart, lungs, esophagus, and trachea and she weighed each one before he sliced them into sections for analysis. An hour later, he was examining a black-widow-spider tattoo on the gluteus maximus above the right leg's vastus lateralis muscle and missed something.

But Gabbie didn't. She knew a snake bite when she saw one, so she pointed to tiny puncture wounds on the edge of the tattoo.

Dr. Steens adjusted his overhead light. The skin around the wounds was discolored from decay but reflected a greasy sheen. He described what he saw, then switched off the mic. "You thinking snake bite?"

Gabbie nodded. "Looks like venom leaked onto the skin surface. Might explain why there aren't any animal bites around the holes."

"Or . . . maybe those critters are like me, afraid of spiders." Dr. Steens smiled as he poked the tattoo, then measured the distance between the wounds. He shifted around, getting into better position to fillet a skin sample from near one of the holes.

"He was on the ground when he got hit," Gabbie offered.

"Really?" The doctor sliced a sample.

"A rattler won't strike that high unless it's coiled above ground level on a rock or ledge, plus the orientation of the holes is wrong for a hit on an upright person." Gabbie waited until the doctor finished placing the cutting on a slide, then added, "The ground was frying-pan flat where the body was found."

Dr. Steens mused, "Why would a man go out alone onto a mesa in August, lie down and surprise, surprise, get bitten on the ass by a snake?"

Gabbie shrugged.

Dr. Steens turned the mic back on and discontinued the conjecture.

It wasn't until they got around to checking the remains of the rattler that Gabbie got *her* surprise. The snake had already been bagged when she had gotten on-site, but when she saw it in the autopsy room, she felt a shiver. She was quite certain she had seen that snake before. When Dr. Steens checked the mouth of the viper, he found fibers imbedded in the reptile's jaw. When he projected the fibers onto a viewing screen, the color was army brown. Gabbie checked the clothing samples. Combs wore nothing colored brown that day. Then she knew where it must have to come from, given her opinion that the victim had been bitten while prone. An examination of the blanket on Combs's bed produced a perfect fiber match. Though the blanket had been washed, the investigators even found the puncture marks.

How she knew all this eventually drew her into another *big* deal, but that was in the long-ago past. Now grad school was behind her, and she had a job she loved, a home in "paradise," and her own motorcycle. It would be nice, though, as her mother had once said, to find a living thing that caught her interest as much as her fascination with the dead.

7

THE PARKING LOT WAS crowded, but Will finally found a spot near Camp Smith's Sunset Club. His first day on the job finished, he walked to the entrance. The sun was already down but still managed to dab each fold in the base of a cirrus cloud with crimson.

Inside, after-work drinkers elbowed stout wooden tables,

crammed around a horseshoe-shaped bar. The air was thick with the scent of fresh popcorn. Backlighting was soft. Animated voices rose and fell to the clatter of dice as players, in quest of free drinks, rolled them from leather cups.

Will waited until his eyes adjusted to the dimness. He spotted Gabbie sitting at a table across from Colonel Bustamante. Between them sat the marine officer whom Will had seen leaving JTF with the general. At the bar, Will ordered a Coors, then observed the proceedings. The marine jabbered away while continually tossing peanuts from a basket into his mouth. Gabbie sat in profile to Will's angle. Her hair, unleashed now from its surgical-cap confinement, glowed ebony in the muted light. Pulled back on one side, ringlets fell across her shoulder above a sleeveless black shift. He wondered where the blue jeans were as he watched the marine edge close and touch her forearm while uttering something for her alone to hear. She laughed, bringing her hand to her chin and in the process, discreetly withdrawing her arm from his touch. She possessed a mysterious quality, those sensuous lips and languid eyes that had seemed so out of place in a death room. Maybe that was part of the allure that touched Will again as he looked beyond the bar at her. Then she turned and saw him. A shadow, curious yet anxious, seemed to fall across her face as she caught his stare. She held her gaze a moment, then turned to the marine.

Will felt a strong tug. Maybe it was the fact that Gabbie seemed unattainable, so secure in her own world. No broken-wing seeker, she. He dropped some change on the bar, then ambled over and put his hand on the empty chairback next to Gabbie. "Taken?"

Gabbie shook her head in the negative as Bustamante took note.

"Have a seat," the colonel offered. "Byron, this is our new IO, Will Cadence. Will, meet Major Byron Chase."

"Ah, my sponsor," Will said. "The colonel mentioned you'd help get me get squared away."

The marine stood. "That's my charter, but I wasn't ready for your early arrival." He was a tall, handsome man, with a regulation half-inch crew cut. In an automatic gesture, he tucked his shirt front in with his thumbs. "Welcome aboard." He thrust his hand out and firmly shook Will's hand.

Will sat, then noticed Gabbie's nearly empty glass. "Buy you one? I've got time for that two-beer story."

"I prefer Coke, but no, thanks. We're about to have dinner. Plus, talking my kind of shop in here usually sends folks stampeding for the exits."

"Some other time, then."

Chase leaned across the table. "Jet jockey, huh?"

Will faced the major. *Was the question meant to inflict the mental pain that came with it?* "Used to be. How about you?"

"Choppers. To keep my sanity around here, I fancy my desk as a flyin' machine in a hover." He grabbed a peanut, tossed it into his mouth, then chewed for a moment while studying Will. "Can't imagine how you fighter guys keep from losing it doing staffwork."

A waiter approached. "Your table is ready, sir, ma'am."

Gabbie slid her chair back, and everyone stood.

"Well," she said, "if you'll excuse us."

Will looked at Gabbie, then at Chase, but Colonel Bustamante took Gabbie's arm. They moved off toward the dining room. Will noticed heads turning throughout the room as she left.

Chase smirked. "Rank doth have its privileges, Major." The marine tossed down another peanut. "Woman's like a wild horse. Did a stint in the army. They couldn't tame her. Probably untamable, but it sure would be fun to saddle up, huh, ace?"

"If you say so."

"I say so. When she showed up, every stud was drooling over her. Body to kill for and brains to go with it. By eleven she'll be home, though, the only thing in bed with her a good book, I'm betting. She lumps us fly boys in the hot-dog category." He reached for a dice cup. "How about a game of liar's dice." He smirked again. "Maybe you'll get lucky!"

8

WILL DROVE THAT NIGHT to a bungalow in Nanakuli. A Russian-studies classmate from the academy, on temporary duty in Kazakhstan, had offered to let Will house-sit until he found his own place. The termite banquet of an abode had a kitchen–dining room combination, single bedroom at the rear, an office-den, and a bathroom whose tiled floor was straight out of the 1940s.

Will made a tour of the place, hung his things in a closet, put his toilet articles in the bathroom, and made up the bed. He washed and undressed, stowing his knee brace on the nightstand. Then he flipped off the light and slipped beneath a sheet, pulling it to his waist. The moon cast a pale glow through the bedroom window. A breeze lifted the curtains, held them away from the window, then gently released them. Warm ripples of air eddied across Will's bare chest. He thought about the "good doctor," as Colonel Bustamante had called her. He tried to push her out of his thoughts, yet the woman lingered, a shadow in the moonlight.

Will diverted his mental focus onto the purpose of his coming to Hawaii. Was Pam Robbins's certainty about her father's existence and government cover-ups anything more than the invention of a vulnerable soul grasping at whatever might bring the grieved dead to life? His own father had shared a cell with Hank Dalton a month before the POW release but had gotten sick, deathly ill according to Dalton—diphtheria, cholera, Dalton wasn't sure. The guards finally came with a stretcher and hauled away his emaciated body. Earlier that same month, Will's mother had been critically injured in that hit-and-run accident.

The first group of POWs came home in January of '73, and the last man, prisoner number 451, came out in April. Jack Cadence was not among them. Eight-year-old Will watched with a heavy heart as scenes of POW family reunions splashed across TV screens. A grateful country opened its bosom in welcome. The few voices who argued for a full accounting were washed aside by the cheers of a relieved nation in no mood to start drums beating again in Asia.

The Vietnamese released what they claimed were Jack Cadence's remains—ashes. They came with a note from the Vietnamese stating that the prisoner had contracted cholera and died "despite courageous attempts by the Revolutionary People's Medical Staff to save him." They claimed that the body had to be cremated. That generated a letter to Will's mother from the U.S. government offering its condolences and requesting disposition instructions for the ashes and other belongings, which were being kept in storage. For nearly five years his father had endured a squalid existence, only to succumb a month before the prisoner release.

Now Pam Robbins had reopened all those tender scars with the intriguing mystery of the photographs and her conviction that both of their fathers still lived. Will felt as if he were riding a rubber raft, hurling down white waters, totally out of control, yet certain that jumping was not an option. At JTF, a subtle sense had been conveyed that he was an intruder, the little puzzle of the isolated office—away from the other IOs—and the veiled attempt to keep an eye on him by moving the general's aide there. Maybe it was as the colonel had said, Will being an overage, they had to make do with an office in a file room.

He would get to the bottom of things eventually, he thought. Meanwhile, better to bide his time before pressing-to-test the establishment. The *establishment.* There would be a new one by the end of the next day. And if it was headed by Henry Dalton, then what could he expect? Dalton . . . why were thoughts of him so unnerving?

Will finally drifted off to sleep, then began twisting, knotting himself in the sheets until he could no longer move his legs. He struggled to free himself, then awoke, the sound of a scream—his scream—ringing in his ears as he got his bearings in the darkened bungalow. Digging an elbow into the mattress, he pushed himself up and blinked, trying to shake fleeting images, trying hard to suppress what he knew was coming. He rolled off the bed. Wood creaked as he delicately shifted upright, his bad leg wobbly, but there was no time to deal with the brace. He groped in the dark for the doorway, found it, then shuffled into the hallway, running his hand along the wall to steady himself.

Water was dripping in the shower. He crept down the passageway toward the sound, feeling the rough grain of the floorboards under his toes. Flickers of red and amber light danced in his head, signaling the birth of another of his horrendous migraines. His quivering hand reached into the darkness, searching until he found the doorknob. It felt cold against his clammy palm. Heartbeats began pounding in his chest, throat, and on up to his temple. A violent struggle was being waged inside his head, as though his subconscious kept suppressing the end of the dream while a dark, angry part of his brain kept hammering away in search of access to the conscious mind. He pushed the door open and staggered toward the medicine cabinet, smelling the tropical mildew that filled the air from rotting panels behind the shower. No light. That would bring the assault on with a vengeance. His hand found the mirrored door. Rusty hinges squealed, the sound magnified in the still night until the safety chain went taut, abruptly stopping the screech that jolted his nerves like an electric shock. He reached in, fingers fumbling for the vial of Fiorinal, on the left side, bottom shelf, where he had carefully placed it earlier, just in case.

Glimmers pulsed, colors exploded across his brain with each heartbeat. Grotesque images formed themselves into incoherent patterns. Vision in his right eye telescoped and his face went numb on that side. Now, half blinded, he stuffed two pills between cheek and teeth, bent over the sink, then twisted his head so that his mouth slid under the faucet. Portraits of distorted faces, black on green, then red on black, flashed in his mind's eye. He turned on the water. The flow washed across his numb cheek and sloshed cool into his mouth, mixing with the bitter taste of the pills. He swallowed just as the pain from the migraine hit him with fistlike sharpness. In front of the sink he collapsed on both knees—oblivious to that new pain—pivoted toward the commode, and waited for his breath to catch up with his heart and the nausea to begin.

9

On the drive to work, Will felt drained from the misery of his long night, the dream that never seemed to end, and the headache that eventually did. Was there some meaning to the dream? It always stopped abruptly at the same point. Why? He had thought about seeking psychiatric help, but in the military that was a sure way to stay grounded. So he put it off. Last night's episode was the fourth since the accident—months earlier. The previous time had been on the night following the Pam Robbins encounter.

In the dream, his childhood home appeared. Then Will found himself floating above a street, watching his father come out the front door onto the steps. He saw his house with its brass address number, 5117, mounted on the wall. Fastened beneath it was a nameplate reading Capt. J. Cadence. To the left was another house, its nameplate reading Maj. H. Dalton.

The dream shifted to the rear of the property where the '56 T-Bird, his father's car, was parked in their garage. Will saw his mother, Nancy, standing outside the garage.

Jack Cadence always appeared wearing fatigues and carrying an olive-green B-4 bag, a bulging canvas suitcase.

Will tried to call out but could make no sound as he watched from hiding, above in the garage rafters. He began crying and his mouth formed words that were never voiced.

Will's father stood motionless for a time, his hands on his hips, looking, listening. Then he picked up the bag, carried it to the car, and tossed it in the trunk, which he slammed shut.

Will's mother's eyes welled with tears as Jack Cadence went to her, lifted her head, and gazed into her eyes. He bent over to kiss her. Nancy pushed away slowly after the embrace and moved to lean against the garage as Jack got into the car.

The car vanished.

Then Will sensed a deep foreboding and would wake up screaming.

Will had actually fallen from the garage rafters and knocked himself cold when he was almost four, so he knew there was some basis for the nightmare, but in the dream he never falls. It always stops at the same place. He again considered consulting a psychiatrist now that the recurrences were becoming more frequent. *I'm no longer flying anyway,* he thought ruefully. The worst that could happen was that he would learn the latest speculation on dream analysis. He made up his mind to do it as soon as this business about missing POWs was settled.

Will turned on the radio for news of the election. The polls had been open for hours on the mainland and Will guessed they were already making predictions. He had mailed in an absentee ballot while still stationed in Nevada, so finding a voting place was not his worry. He had felt an obligation to vote for Dalton, but something deeper, troubling yet elusive, made him unable to mark that name on the ballot. He had left the presidential selection blank. Who might become the next president was a concern, not a choice, for him. The newscaster on the local station made no prediction, the campaign being so close: the polls carried all three candidates neck and neck at the finish.

At the office, Major Chase swiveled his chair, then tossed a manila folder on Will's desk.

"Your first chance to excel," Chase announced. "You get to do the final take on this package. Concur, and we put one more action to bed."

Will opened the file. In the left pocket was an interview form that had been filled out by a caseworker at a displaced-persons' camp in northeast Thailand. It related a claim of a POW encounter by a Lao refugee. Paper-clipped to the report was a hand-scrawled note, all penciled in block letters. The creases where it had been folded showed that this document had enjoyed a much-circulated existence. Will read rambling prose purportedly written by a POW, whose main thrust was to plead for military intervention to secure his release. Behind the note was a grainy blowup, apparently cropped from another photo. This one showed a white male, a thousand-yard stare in his eyes.

Will pulled forms from the right side pocket. On top was the investigating officer's report. A Captain Steve Andres had concluded that the note, ostensibly written by a U.S. pilot, was not authentic. "The grammar is full of bad English, sentence construction consistent with Lao language." After flipping the page, Will noted Sergeant Larson's comment: "No conclusive facial match. Two images, cases 1322 and 1648, indicate ten percent probability." Attached to Larson's evaluation were two photographs of American servicemen, their haunting likeness to each other staring out from mat-finished prints. Both men's pictures had been forwarded for anthropological analysis.

Will flipped to the next section. He felt a sudden tremor as he encountered the carefully scripted words from Dr. Gabrielle DeJean. He noticed her precisely crafted words as his scan drifted across the script. The writing seemed unusually neat for a medical practitioner.

Anatomical Photo Comparison—

Case 1322: Negative correlation. Subjects have .07mm difference in the optical lobe diameter. Cranial displacement of the right ear is .15mm lower on case subject. Similar jaw-to-nose axis anomaly, yet offset is 1.2° for case subject, 1.4° for potential match.

Case 1648: Negative correlation. Subjects have .33mm difference in jaw hinge placement versus lip line. Cranial arc shows .02 milliradian difference.

Will turned to the last form. He noticed that Major Chase's name had been curiously typed in below his own, the letters offset slightly, as though Chase's review had been required later as someone's afterthought.

On the form's recommendation section there were three blocks: OPEN, CLOSE, and CONTINUE. All of the other action officers except Major Chase had marked the CLOSE block, signifying they disputed the authenticity of the Lao refugee's claim. Chase's blocks were still vacant.

Will checked the CLOSE block and dropped the file in his out basket. He then took out his wallet. Inside was a snapshot of his father. He opened his briefcase and removed the photo Pam Robbins had given him. He compared the two for at least the hundredth time, only now he paid more attention to the ears, the placement of the eyes, the position of the nose.

Chase's phone rang. He listened for a moment, uttered an "Okay," hung up, then spun toward Will. "That was the general's secretary. He's ready to meet you."

Will saw Chase's eyes drop to the photos he held, so he flipped Pam's upside down into his open briefcase, then folded his wallet and put it back in his pocket.

The major's eyebrows lifted slightly. "Something I can help you with?"

"No, I just find this photo analysis business fascinating." Will felt a chill, as though a shadowy cloud had just floated through this weatherless room.

General Bradley Stoner rose from behind his desk when Will and Major Chase entered the office. He puffed out his chest as he came around to shake Will's hand.

"Welcome to the command," he said. "I trust Byron is being of some help easing your in-processing."

"He's been great at getting me squared away in the office," Will said. "Beyond that, the move is turning out pretty routine." Will moved a little to the side, keeping them both in sight and feeling like a lamb run to ground by two coyotes. He suspected that Chase's function was to filter Will's staff work, and that the general may already suspect Will's arrival at JTF brought with it a personal agenda. He recalled how Pam Robbins had called him after he got the assignment and had suggested he play things slow and deliberate, not raising the issue of the Polaroid until the time was right, and Will knew where people stood regarding the issue.

Stoner beckoned Will to a seat on a sofa, then sat in an easy chair.

Will took in the room; its dark oak paneling set a subdued mood. There were oil paintings of nineteenth-century battles, but none of the trappings such as personal photos with VIPs, unit plaques, or service awards found in so many commanders' offices. On a credenza by the window stood a bronze sculpture of what looked like a World War II–era aviator.

When Will's eyes returned to Stoner, he noticed Stoner staring at him.

"Ah," the general blustered. "You don't recognize Francis Gabreski, I'll bet? Besides being an ace, he was a POW."

"I know of him, but you make it sound as if getting captured was a feat equal to becoming an ace."

"Surviving capture *is* a feat," Stoner said. He gave Will a hard look before switching to pleasantries about the base and the many opportunities for sports and entertainment in Hawaii. Finally, he came to the point. "This is a touchy business we're in. We have a tremendous amount of congressional oversight and get beat over the head by the VFW, the American Legion, the Alliance of Families, the press, not to mention the Vietnamese on every issue we address. You can understand our sensitivity."

"I can."

"Good. That's why it is imperative that what you see and learn here, stays here. Loose talk at the bar tonight will find its way into the tabloids tomorrow. We have all learned some very time-consuming lessons over the years. That's why I've asked Major Chase to show you the ropes. He's been privy to most of what I call the horrible examples. Gain from his experience." General Stoner's brow lifted on one side, flecks of warning shimmering in those eyes like sparks.

"I'm sure I will, sir," Will said, not breaking eye contact.

The general commanded a presence that Will felt must be useful in the intimidating halls of Congress or in front of reporters, but Will was beyond the point of being browbeaten with menacing looks. His life and recent experience with the aircraft accident board had hardened any tendency toward that frailty.

The general smiled. "Fine, then. Unless you have any questions, let's get back to work."

Honolulu Advertiser, *dateline: Wednesday, November 3rd, 2004*

INDEPENDENT DALTON WINS BY NARROW MARGIN

Can politics get more electrifying? Not since the Bush/Gore election, not since history's closest three-way race in 1912 when the Progressive Party nominated former president Theodore Roosevelt, has America seen anything like this. Although Roosevelt polled the highest percentage of the vote ever attained by a third-party candidate, he lost. So did the winner of the popular vote last election. This time things turned out differently.

Victorious President-elect Dalton emerged from his home in New Mexico after private telephone conversations with the president and Democratic candidate. He spoke briefly with reporters and thanked his supporters before retiring inside to meet with key members of his staff. Campaign manager Janet Mills was beside the president-elect as he made his statement. She looked resplendent in a beige Classique Entier suit. Many insiders consider Mills an odds-on favorite for future first lady and credit her active participation on the campaign trail, particularly her appearance with the candidate wives during the campaign's expanded debate format, as the key element that won the female voters over to Dalton.

10

As far as Phil Garcia was aware, he was the only naturalized Cuban employed as a CIA agent. There had to be others, he thought, but he had never met one. He took great pride in having passed muster through one of the tightest screening programs ever devised. His facility in Russian, Spanish, and accentless English probably made a big impression on the Agency recruiters.

Phil's university professor father, Ernesto Garcia, and Phil's mother, Marlina, raised him in a strict household where he spoke Spanish to his mother and English to his father. He learned Russian in school. Everybody did. Ernesto fled Cuba with his family in 1970 after becoming disillusioned with the way Castro's politics had turned. In 1975, Phil was taken to Miami's Dade County Courthouse where his parents took the oath of citizenship.

Phil Garcia joined the air force at seventeen. He was sent to the Defense Language Institute in Monterey, California, for more intensive Russian. Four years later he had tired of translating Soviet radio transmissions that came out of Havana. Aspiring to loftier employment, he left the air force and used the GI Bill to enter Fordham University and study law. In his third year, he wandered by a recruiting booth on Career Day. He met a CIA veteran and was captivated by his pitch.

Now, two decades later, CIA officer Garcia peeked through ten-power binoculars from a bedroom window on Aiea Heights, a ridge to the west of Camp Smith. A tripod-mounted video camera hummed away near his ear, its grapefruit-sized lens observing the comings and goings at JTF and DIA. At another window, a feed-horn antenna, shaped like a baseball bat, was aimed at the microwave tower on top of the DIA Building. A clock radio on the floor was on at low volume, tuned to the local Honolulu National Public Radio station.

CIA Officer Dan Markle, a Chicago native, spun around on a swivel chair to face Garcia. Markle operated the audio and visual recording equipment that was set up on two card tables where the bed normally would have been. He had a blank face, with droopy eyelids and a double chin. Markle took off his headphones. "He just hung up."

"Where'd he call?"

"D.C., on the secure net." Markle slid his chair over to his computer, then dialed a number via modem to a CIA e-mail location. Once the connection was made, he typed a coded message using his keyboard, then transmitted a data stream. "It'll take the boys at Langley a couple hours to unscramble it."

"It'd be nice if they told us what DIA is talking about." Garcia rubbed his eyes. "I've been doing this a bunch of years, but this is a first. You ever worked this close-hold before?"

"Hey, I never even worked stateside before. This shit ought to be FBI business."

Garcia looked up over the top of the binoculars at the huge American flag that fluttered above the Pacific Command Headquarters Building. "What do you think, Dan? Are we the good guys in this or are they?"

"Fuck'd if I know. Why don't we call the FBI and ask? They've probably got a team on the next block watching us watch the goddamn DIA."

Garcia resumed his scrutiny through the binoculars. "No, really. Sometimes you have to break the rules, but there's got to be a damn good reason. I have yet to hear it on this caper."

Markle put his hands behind his head, twisted his chin back and forth, and cracked the vertebrae in his neck. "Look Phil, you got a *bad* company attitude. What else we got to do on such a lovely day in Hawaii?"

"Wonder if the Russians still spend as much dough watching each other as we do."

Markle noticed a change in voice on the radio, so he reached over and turned up the sound. A recording of President-elect Dalton's acceptance of the Republican and Democratic candidates concessions of the election was being aired. After the statement, Dalton opened the floor to reporters. After two easily answered questions, a journalist asked, tongue in cheek, who the president planned to elect as first lady. After the laughter died down, Dalton addressed the issue. "Where did you folks ever get the idea that being unattached was a detriment to running the White House or the country? Thomas Jefferson had a rather respectable term. So did Andrew Jackson, Martin Van Buren, James Buchanan, and Chester Arthur. All of them served unmarried. Next."

Dalton answered one more question, then ended the session. Markle turned the radio off. "You vote, Phil?"

"Yeah, mailed it in."

"Me, too. You wanna know who I voted for?"

"Putin."

"Hey, I shoulda!" Markle cracked a huge grin. "But I voted for Dalton. The way I figure, with his background, he hadn't had time to become a brainless political amoeba like the rest of them."

Garcia stayed riveted on the scene at Camp Smith. "You know what political organism is the most dangerous?"

Markle looked up at the video repeater but did not answer.

"A secret organization *within* a secret organization."

Garcia watched as General Stoner and his aide exited the DIA Building and got in a staff car. "The players find themselves answerable," Garcia looked over at Markle, "to no one but each other."

"Yeah," Markle said, "and who's around to enforce the rules in a setup like that?"

11

WILL FELT THE ELECTION of Dalton might help him in his effort. Who would choose to interfere with someone whose assignment had been worked by the next president? Of course, no supervisor liked it when an officer used influence to gain that assignment within his or her domain. Displeasure or jealousy could cause a reaction from above or from the most seemingly innocent of places below.

Will processed paperwork through Major Chase for the remainder of the year without an incident. During the Christmas holidays Will spent an afternoon at the Bellows Air Force Station recreation area on the windward side of Oahu. General Stoner hosted a luau on the beach for JTF, complete with native dancers and roasted pig. Stoner seemed pleased that Will showed up and remarked how well Will seemed to be fitting into the program. He invited Will onto the tennis court for a set of doubles against Colonel Bustamante and Major Chase. Though they lost, Will was happy his knee seemed to take the pounding well. Meanwhile, Will noted that Gabbie had not accompanied Bustamante. Though he had considered calling her and asking her out, he had decided that she would likely turn him down. Then what? No, he wanted to find a way to ease within her circle, get to know her better, but not a single opportunity had presented itself in the months that had seemed to fly by.

By the first of the new year, the general's aide was spending less and less time looking over Will's shoulder while the other IOs joined Captain Steve Andres, the officer whose POW report Will had reviewed his first day on the job. The three men were affable and seemed glad to have an extra hand to work the flood of reported MIA sightings pouring in from Asia. The majority were obvious fakes, most attached to requests for humanitarian asylum in the United States. One case involved a photo of the cropped head of a missing pilot, reproduced from his college graduation album, then crudely superimposed on another man's body.

Will was stunned by the quantity of flimsy evidence that crossed his desk and how the media gave hype to it, having alleged over the years that more than a hundred MIAs might still be held captive somewhere in Laos. During the past months he began to think that his continuing curiosity about his father's alleged death might be merely a symptom of paranoia contracted from Pam Robbins. But his mind kept going back to the Polaroid she had given him, that hand in a distorted clench so like his father's. Because his father avoided having the disfigurement photographed and official photos only show him from the shoulder up, a forger would probably not be aware of the impairment. He had no real idea about how to broach the subject through normal channels without being accused of a personal agenda, so he decided on another route to tap JTF's kneecap on the matter. If he triggered a reflex, the repercussions might be revealing.

Chief Petty Officer Jackson looked up as Will entered the Records Office. "What can we do for you, Major?"

"Thought I'd take up the colonel's invitation the day I arrived to see how I'd look in a couple decades." Will noticed the blank expression on the chief's face. "That is, if you're not too busy."

"No problem," CPO Jackson said, his answer accompanied by an agreeable smile. "Sergeant Larson can accommodate that."

At Larson's workstation, Will handed over a wallet photo of himself. "Sarge, can you make me, say, a dozen years older?"

Larson looked at the photo. "Can do. One future general coming up." He placed the photo on the scanner and moments later transformed the picture. Will's hairline receded; crow's-feet appeared beside his eyes.

Will studied the image, then said, "Add another dozen."

Larson entered the data. Will's likeness looked thinner, more gaunt, with the outline of his cheekbones more pronounced.

Larson sat back in his chair and peeked at Will's reaction. "Mine gave me kind of a creepy feeling."

"Yeah, no kidding." Will stared at his future, the impact more personal than he had expected.

Larson picked up the computer mouse. "You want a copy?"

"No, thanks, but you know . . ." Will pointed at the image. "That's the age my father would be right now, if he were still alive." Will reached for his wallet and removed a snapshot, which he dropped on Larson's desk. "Let's compare. You'll have to add about thirty years to this one."

Larson glanced at the photo showing a man standing over the open hood of a T-bird, his left hand out of sight as his right hand waved at the camera. Larson shot CPO Jackson a look, but Jackson merely shrugged.

"Can do," Larson repeated. He scanned the picture, then entered the data. An older version of Jack Cadence emerged on the monitor. Larson went split-screen. Both Will's and Jack's images appeared side by side. They differed noticeably.

"You must resemble your mother," Larson said.

Will tapped his finger on his father's image. "Can you bring the face around to the right a little?"

Larson shifted Jack Cadence's face around until the image had rotated about ten degrees.

"There," Will said. "Print it."

Larson clicked on an icon and a moment later a sheet of photo-grade paper slid into the output tray of his printer.

Will took the printout, said thanks, and left.

As soon as the door closed, Larson made copies of both Will's and his father's aged images.

12

WITH THE NEWLY AGED likeness of his father, Will headed back to his desk to compare that version to the one in the Polaroid Pam Robbins had given him. He found similarities in both, but the two images needed professional evaluation. Gabbie had been in and out of his thoughts ever since the first night at the club, and though he had not run into her too many times since, he did remain curious about the marine's remark that the army wasn't able to "tame" her. Will made copies of the two photos, grabbed a file, jumped in his car, and headed for harm's way. Twenty minutes later, Will tapped on Dr. DeJean's office door at Fort Kam on Hickam Air Force Base, intent on initiating part two of his scheme.

"Come on in." Gabbie was doing paperwork at her desk, her medical smock unbuttoned at the neck, her hair tied back. One ringlet had escaped control and hung by itself near her temple. She gazed up at him with an inquisitive look as though she had expected someone else, her lips and dark eyes made darker with suspicion as she recognized him. Gabbie eased the folder closed, its outside marked in bold lettering, CLASSIFIED, LIM-DIS, a clearance above Will's level.

Will laid his file on the edge of her desk. "Sorry to bother you, but can you check and initial this brief?"

Gabbie indicated her in basket. "We do have a distribution system for passing casework, you know."

"I was just following the colonel's lead."

Gabbie stared at him for a moment, perplexed.

"The first time I was here, remember? Colonel Bustamante hand-delivered a file. Only trying to expedite the paperwork like my boss."

"Really?" Gabbie pointed at her in basket. "Leave it there. I may get to it, but I've got a ton of things to finish."

Will then produced a copy of the Polaroid Robbins had given him, the snapshot of Jack Cadence working on the T-bird, and the aged enhanced photo from JTF. He set them on Gabbie's desk. "Could you do me a little favor?"

"Then this visit isn't just to expedite paperwork." Gabbie picked up the photos. "You know," she continued, her voice softer, accommodating, "I prize directness. If you need something, ask."

"I'm wondering if you might compare these," Will said.

She picked up the images. "Do we know who I am looking at?"

"My father."

"I'm sorry about whatever happened to your father, but I can't work cases without approval, particularly closed cases, and especially now." She started to hand the photos back, then glanced at the photo of Jack Cadence with his hands up. She hesitated, giving it a long look.

"Was the original a Polaroid?"

"Yes," Will answered.

She dropped the photo on her desk as though the answer was of no real consequence. "Maybe I can take a look . . . after work. No promises."

Suddenly she had gone from "no time" to "overtime" to accommodate him. Will popped her a friendly little half-salute. "I owe you one." Will remembered the incident with her motorcycle. "Maybe two."

"Two," Gabbie said, accompanied by a long look at Will as he closed the door on his way out.

"See me, ASAP," read the colonel's note stuck to the door of Will's office when he arrived at work the next morning. He grabbed his briefcase and headed down the hall.

As soon as Will entered Colonel Bustamante's outer office, he got the distinct feeling that the personal price of doing his rendition of MIA business in JTF was about to rise.

"He's expecting you," Cath said. "I'll buzz you in."

Will tapped lightly on the door, entered, reported, and stood at attention. Bustamante did not look up from his seated position behind a polished mahogany desk, spotless except for an ink pad and a copy of the computer printouts of Jack and Will Cadence that Sergeant Larson had made. Bustamante was studying the images. After an awkward silence, his eyes came up slowly, his expression remote and hostile.

"So, Major, would you mind telling me what this is all about?" Bustamante shoved the photos toward Will, who stepped forward and glanced at them.

"I took your suggestion. Wanted to see how I'd look a few years down the road."

"That's not all there is to this?" Bustamante inhaled deeply. "Could we kindly get to the bottom of things?"

Will sensed the colonel was holding something back, as though setting a trap. *Did he have the Pam Robbins photo, too?* He decided that to be caught in another evasion would end his tour abruptly. He wanted to know if both Dr. DeJean and Sergeant Larson had betrayed him. The only way he might find out would be from Bustamamnte's reaction to the Polaroid that he assumed Larson had not seen.

Will opened his briefcase, then handed over the photocopy of the Polaroid. "I wanted to compare the result with this."

Bustamante glanced at it, his expression frozen, too well checked, in Will's mind.

The colonel looked up. "Who gave you this?"

He had seen it before, Will felt certain. His mind flashed angrily at the thought that Dr. DeJean had turned him in. "I've been asked not to say, sir."

"Oh? Fine. Let me guess. One of those crusaders from the Alliance of Families. Am I right?"

Bustamante's eyes focused so hard that Will felt as if a laser beam were boring through his head. Finally, in a flat tone, he said, "Yes, sir."

The colonel grunted. He compared the Polaroid with the computer-aged print of Jack Cadence. "What *I* see is an imagination working overtime." He indicated Larson's print. "Photo aging is not an exact science."

"But—"

"Major, we get photos like this in here all the time. Last year it was a picture of three bakers from Romania that were supposed to be MIAs. We found its origin in an old Soviet travel magazine at a library in Phnom Penh." The colonel's brows came up in warning. "I got a hundred eighty people in this organization. If they all started diddling around like you have, the tabloids would have a field day. I'd have fifty congressionals a week to answer."

"We are talking about my *father!* I had to check it out."

The colonel's voice dropped to a growl, his words coming slowly, deliberate. "Major, *I* will check it out. If it's a phony, as I think it is, that'll be the end of it. Understood?"

"Yes, sir."

"Good. Now get your nose buried in only what comes through your in basket."

"Yes, sir." Will turned to leave, but the colonel was not quite through. "One more thing, Cadence."

Will looked over his shoulder.

"Now you know why we have a no-next-of-kin rule."

13

SECRET SERVICE AGENT ANTHONY Ganetta kept his bedroom intentionally dark. The unpredictability of the Dalton assignment and his additional duties made for irregular hours. He used heavy window drapes with Velcro strips to completely cut off outside light.

The air conditioner fan ran continuously, even in winter, to block out street noise.

He had just finished a four-day duty cycle and had barely fallen asleep when the phone rang. He picked up the receiver while noticing the time on his clock radio: 4:05 P.M.

"This is Uncle Harry," the voice at the other end said. "I need you to stop over. Bring the blueprint."

Ganetta shook the sleep from his eyes as the coded phrase registered. "Can do. It'll take me about half an hour."

"Fine," the voice said.

Ganetta made a quick pass over his face with an electric razor, then dressed. Five minutes later, he entered Foggy Bottom Metro Station, boarded a blue-line train, and got off four stops later at the underground station that served the Pentagon.

The platform was crowded with homeward-bound commuters who jostled Ganetta as he made his way against the flow of pedestrian traffic to the escalator. On the concourse level, he showed a photo ID to the guard, passed through the metal-and-bomb-detector devices, and entered a subterranean shopping mall complete with gift shops, florist, barbershop, post office, drugstore, even a medical clinic. It was here, during his brief marriage to a fiery Latin beauty years ago, that he could have stopped at the flower shop on his way home to make up for missing dinner, but did not. It was here that he could have bought her a cake for her birthday, but did not. He hardly thought about those things then, and he was just barely conscious of them now.

Agent Ganetta made his way across the mall to the ramp that led to the Pentagon offices located above. He passed through another metal detector, on up the incline, then took a stairway to DIA Headquarters on the third floor. Ganetta was in a bit of a sweat. He was a big man, trained to handle himself in just about any kind of physical scrap, but he had reason to be unnerved. The few times he had been called in before were due to a serious miscalculation by a member of the inner circle, the triumvirate, as the director liked to call their little group. Ganetta adjusted his tie, not quite getting it centered beneath his seventeen-and-a-half-inch collar, then entered the agency reception office. From there he was led to the Blue Room, code word *blueprint,* a carefully constructed conference chamber built like a vault, which was regularly swept for recording devices, and where the director awaited his arrival.

The director of DIA, air force lieutenant general Jarret Kraus, ran the second-largest intelligence gathering operation in the Western Hemisphere. Director Kraus used to claim his network was second only to the CIA in the "free world," a term that had become passé with the demise of the Soviet Union, an event for which Kraus liked to assign himself much of the credit. Unfortunately, getting that credit was not possible, because Kraus had engaged in a number of actions outside his area of responsibility over the years. These actions would have raised congressional eyebrows had they come to light. The resulting outcry would have put limitations on DIA's power, and power was one thing the director guarded zealously. So he kept the power and did without the credit.

The position as head of DIA was unlike most other military assignments. It was considered a critical appointment requiring an extensive intelligence background. When a director proved himself effective, his boss, the secretary of defense, tended to stick with him. In Kraus's case, he had held the job for twelve years. Even his mandatory retirement at thirty-five years' service had been extended by congressional action in order for him to continue in the three-star position. After a dozen years at the helm, Kraus was not bothered by the fact that his rank was frozen. He liked the job, and his devotion to the cause surpassed any need for higher military rank.

The director was slight of build, as though unsuited to military service. Although pale and frail looking, all who knew him feared his authority. He remained seated as Agent Ganetta entered the Blue Room. The walls were barren of paneling or pictures, and the overhead fluorescent lighting gave the gray paint its blue hue, hence the name. Director Kraus was dressed in a custom-tailored suit. His razor-cut hair was parted neatly on the right side and his fine brown mane tapered evenly to the neck. He preferred civilian attire, an option he had approved for DIA's military employees during his second year as director. The wearing of the uniform was reserved for special functions or when testifying before Congress. He also preferred to be addressed as director rather than by his military title.

Kraus sat at the head of a polished conference table. To his right sat army general Richard Ellis, the four-star head of the Joint Chiefs of Staff. Ellis was in uniform, with seven rows of ribbons dominating the left side of his chest. Though General Ellis outranked Kraus, that distinction was not in evidence here. General Ellis's seat was where the DIA deputy director normally sat. Fourteen years ago, then Lieutenant Colonel Ellis had worked for Brigadier General Kraus when Kraus spent a year as the deputy assistant at the Defense Nuclear Agency, another Department of Defense directorate. The changes in rank had never eroded their subordinate-to-supervisor relationship. Director Kraus had been able to leak certain bits of embarrassing information about a number of Ellis's rivals over the years, thereby clearing the way for his protégé's rise to the top. In the process, Kraus had cached negative information on Ellis, a fact that the general suspected and was enough to keep him in line.

"Good of you to come so quickly, Anthony," Kraus said, then forced a smile as Ganetta nodded and took his seat. The door was closed by a sentry. When Kraus heard the lock engage, he glanced at both men and continued. "There has been a security breach."

Ganetta, his forehead looking as suave as the back of a greasy spoon, said nothing. His eyes flitted from Ellis to Kraus.

"Jack Cadence's son managed to get himself assigned to JTF," Kraus announced. "He approached our candidate before the election, asking for help with the assignment."

Ganetta shifted uncomfortably in his chair. "I saw him at the senator's office months ago but they spoke in private. You think he holds something over Dalton for him to make a move like that?"

"Supposition is not my concern at the moment. Why was I not informed when you know how sensitive the Cadence issue is?"

"Dalton told me he'd personally handle the situation," Ganetta said. "He told me about the assignment request and claimed he'd already worked out a solution. They planned to let the major work at

JTF long enough to satisfy any curiosity he might have about his father's disappearance, then move him to another staff position. From the way he talked, I assumed he had spoken to you."

"Sodid our man at JTF, but you're both wrong." Kraus shook his head. "Dalton took it upon himself to get the one man who might jeopardize *Shadowmaker* assigned right where we don't want him. There's a curious disparity in that."

An awkward silence settled over the room.

"Next," Director Kraus continued, the word sliding out like an acid hiss, "would anyone like to hazard a guess at what else has been breached?"

Kraus's question went unanswered.

"A Kharkov-operation photo has turned up."

General Ellis straightened. "From where?"

"From Cadence," Krause said. "He got it from that Robbins woman. We should have taken her persistence more seriously. I should never have let myself be talked into that scheme with the modified photo of her father. She was bound to see through it and become even more zealous."

General Ellis was not about to let the slur regarding what had been his idea go unanswered. "You didn't go far enough."

"I'm all ears," Kraus said.

"Our JTF people found some singed bone fragments at her father's wreckage site. Those are buried at the academy. Her father graduated in the academy class of '65. It would have been hard to refute a class of '65 graduation ring turning up. We could have gotten one there with all the right engravings."

Kraus stared at the wall, considering the claim. "No, that woman would rationalize even the truth if it doesn't fit her fantasies." Kraus took several breaths as his eyes remained fixed on the blank wall. "But your idea may be useful in convincing others that she is misguided." Then he shrugged. "Before we do anything, we'll need to find out what is going on inside the young major's head at JTF." Kraus shot a look of reproach at Ganetta. "Can you handle that, Anthony?"

"Definitely." Ganetta coughed to clear his throat.

General Ellis was not through with the subject. "Are we certain the CIA isn't involved in placing Cadence at JTF?"

"CIA?" Kraus closed his eyes. "I doubt even those fools would use an amateur in that manner." Kraus seemed to deflate. "C . . . I . . . A . . ." he repeated in a voice filled with languor. Then Kraus's lips curled into a patient smile. "On the other hand, we've done their work for them, so who knows? Maybe they've decided to snoop on us to learn how we get it accomplished."

Ganetta forced a laugh, but General Ellis remained glum.

"Bumblers with fat wallets. If only we had half the budget that is wasted at CIA." Kraus reconsidered. "Then again, if we had all their money, we'd have ten times the congressional oversight."

Once more, there was no comment until Ellis finally piped in. "Maybe we should simply have briefed Dalton fully on *Shadowmaker.*"

"No. That might have brought on too many questions. Our successful candidate has to remain totally in concert with our goals. The less he knows about necessary decisions, the better."

Ellis looked down at the polished table. "Necessary decisions?"

Kraus homed in on Ellis. "You've never understood, Richard. Oh, you answered the call all right, put on the uniform, then went into Kuwait and Afghanistan and killed the enemy. When you did, some of your people died. In fact, you knowingly sent them to almost certain death. A few were even killed by friendly fire, yet they call you a hero. Well, I still wear the uniform on occasion, too, but I'm in the spy business. If I kill the enemy I am reviled. If I send our men to their deaths, there are those who point accusing fingers. For me there are no parades, but more victories are won by espionage than by bullets. Do you think those megalomaniacs Montgomery, De Gaulle, and MacArthur would have succeeded without our clandestine service breaking both the German and Japanese codes? Our spies killed, and some of them died, to get and break those codes! Look how poorly we did in Vietnam when we no longer had access to the enemy's every move. Look at how terrorist cells ply their wares of destruction relatively unimpeded today."

Ellis's face turned red. "Thank you for the history lesson."

"Yes, history. A brutal master that does not abide lessons unlearned. Keep in mind one other thing. During World War II, we as a nation considered everyone in Germany, Italy, and Japan as our enemy, even though many of the people were duped by their leaders. In those countries, women, children, and the elderly all contributed to the war effort, and we attacked them. Not a single American newspaper came out against the fire raids or the atom bomb. We plastered them, fixed what was wrong with their thinking, and now they are staunch allies. These days, we try to hunt down our enemies one by one, creating martyrs in the process, rather than going directly after the source nations and all the people behind the scenes who support them, and trust me, the current misguided populace in many places overseas wholeheartedly supports our destruction. So, the administration blusters and threatens, but does little because of fear the media in this new world of ours will print, 'Shame, shame.' Another flaw in our thinking." Kraus leaned back in his chair, as though trying to lower the temperature a notch. He looked directly at Ganetta and his tone softened. "I know your association with the president-elect has created problems for you, but I ask you to keep the big picture in mind at all times. In order for progress to remain on track, I need to know about these little hiccups before they become disruptive, no matter what Dalton tells you otherwise." Kraus raised his eyebrows, then smiled. "No more surprises, eh?"

"None, sir," Ganetta replied, greatly relieved, sensing his oversight had been excused. In his mind, he had made the right decision. Kraus had learned about the action regarding Will Cadence without Ganetta having violated the future president's trust.

"That's settled, then," said Kraus, a brief tone of clemency in his voice. "Let's keep close tabs on Cadence. I need to know at once if he becomes a further problem. As for this Robbins woman, I really want her meddling terminated. We need to have a little talk with her." Kraus glanced over at Ellis.

Ellis diverted his eyes away.

Kraus returned his attention to Ganetta. "Anthony, go tell her why we are doing this."

Ganetta looked from Kraus to Ellis and back. "Tell her the truth?"

"Yes," Kraus said. "It's the only way she'll ever understand what we've had to do and the need for silence."

"But—" Ganetta still wasn't sure he understood.

"Ensure silence." Kraus reached for Ganetta's tie and gently centered it on his collar as he scolded, "And remember, neatness counts!"

Kraus dropped his hand, then smiled at General Ellis. "All right then, next subject. You've raised the Ukrainian issue with the president?"

"Yes, but he's still unconvinced. The Ukrainians acknowledge the parts of the SALT agreement that are still in force, but they're stalling the destruction of the launch vehicles."

Kraus pursed his lips, then nodded. "That republic still has more than eighty ICBMs inside its borders. A great number of those launch vehicles can be rolling around the countryside on goddamn flatbed trucks driven by vodka-soaked corporals, and the president is happy because they acknowledge a piece of paper *we* have essentially discarded ourselves?" Kraus shook his head slowly. "Politicians have a knack for underestimating military threats. That is precisely why *we* . . . must never underestimate them."

"Agreed," Ellis said.

Kraus nodded. "There are elements in the Ukraine that are unhappy about our continued coziness with Russia. Should these reactionaries assume power, legitimately or otherwise, I have grave misgivings about what might become of those ICBM assets. Even though the Russians have removed the nuclear warheads, it is a simple matter to insert into the reentry vehicles chemical or biological weapons."

Ellis nodded. "Lord knows they have tons of that stuff."

Kraus began drumming his fingers. "Gentlemen, providence has thrown us together in this undertaking. Some might call it serendipity, but I believe it is our destiny calling, one that requires loyalty to our cause above all else. Our little triumvirate controls this country's ace in the hole . . . or should I say wild card. Let's make sure we don't turn it over until all the bets are down."

The session was over.

After Ganetta and Ellis were gone from the room, Kraus remained seated, his mind reviewing his decisons regarding Pam Robbins, Will Cadence, and Henry Dalton, but his thoughts eventually focused on the issue that concerned him most: the rise of one of the key military leaders in the Ukraine and how the man's past was intimately connected to Kraus's.

Kraus's father was the son of an ethnic German from Kiev in the Ukraine. He met and married his mother, a stunningly attractive blonde, while studying medicine in Heidelberg, Germany, in the thirties. In school, he was recruited by the Nazis for their fifth-column efforts, and the couple returned to the Ukraine. When the Wehrmacht rolled through the country in June 1941, the locals welcomed the German army with flowers and the traditional Ukrainian bread and salt of hospitality. German soldiers were regarded as liberators from the Communist yoke of Moscow. Kraus's father surfaced, and since Stalin had evacuated the government, Dr. Kraus was for a time appointed as administrator of the Radenberg region of the Ukraine.

When the Germans pulled out in 1944, his father stayed behind, where he had resumed practicing medicine at the hospital until a Ukrainian partisan unit allied with the Soviet army overran it. Every horse and swine had been long butchered and devoured. The populace was on the verge of starvation, most of them having fled ahead of the Russian juggernaut. Jarret Kraus retained the vivid memory of the sight of his father being beaten and dragged from the hospital. His young mother left him beside a woman she knew as she went to plead for her husband's life. "He is only a doctor," she argued.

A young partisan arrived in a jeep. He wore a Ukrainian army field jacket and German jackboots and was obviously someone in authority. When told what was going on, he checked Dr. Kraus's identification against a list he possessed.

"The man is a collaborator," the partisan said.

"No," she pleaded. "He quit the Party when they started the deportations. He refused to help them! We have papers to show this."

The partisan hesitated, for a moment seemingly struck by her attractiveness, then ordered the couple into a truck packed with wounded German soldiers and civilians from the hospital.

None but Kraus's mother was ever seen again.

She and Jarret wound up in West Berlin and eventually immigrated to the United States where his mother obtained citizenship. The day after his eighteenth birthday, she committed suicide. Kraus would learn the details of what happened near Radenberg from a letter his mother left behind.

My Dear Sweet Jarret,

You are now eighteen and old enough to care for yourself, so I write to you in hopes that you will understand what brings me to this passing. Do not wonder about my love for you. It is eternal.

When your father and I left the hospital that terrible morning in the truck, the young partisan leader you saw followed in his jeep. The truck stopped well east of town and the strongest of the men were made to carry the seriously wounded to an open pit. Two of the captives tried to slip away and were immediately gunned down. Meanwhile, the partisan leader separated your father and me.

"We are not monsters, like the Germans, but we will take our vengeance," the partisan shouted. Then he pointed at me, "And if you shed one tear for him, I will have you shot." Then he made me watch as your father was executed.

I did not cry. Who would be left to care for you?

When they were through, he shoved me into the jeep and drove back toward Radenberg. On the way he produced a half-empty bottle of vodka and began drinking. He told me how he had been a good defender of the Third Reich. In the jeep he mentioned a big battle, after which the German leadership ordered his division to "stand still." Later, a regular German SS brigade came upon his unit well behind the front lines. Most of the Ukrainians were without weapons by that time. Many had rags wrapped around their feet for warmth in place of ruined boots, he claimed. The Germans were well armed. They singled out the Ukrainian officers.

Then to prove their loyalty, the SS made the Ukrainian troops fire on their own superiors. One of those officers was the older brother of the partisan.

"I watched my own brother die," he roared in my face, "like you did your husband."

Nearing Radenberg, the man began ranting. He asked me how it felt to watch tearless as a loved one died. I gave him no answer, my shame too great. Then I felt my eyes welling up. I turned away, but he guessed the movement for what it was, because he pulled over. I am yet sickened by what I allowed in order to take another breath, to live a few more seconds. What he did to me was unspeakable, but at one point he released his grip. I struck him with a rock, stunning him. Then I hit him again and again, until I thought he was dead. I took the jeep and left it at the edge of town, but there were some papers, the collaborator list, and the partisan's name was on a military order. Slava Podvalny, a name seared into my memory. I destroyed the list, found you at my dear friend Johanna's home, and fled west.

But your father and I had played a role in all the misery that befell the world. Forgive your father as I have. He was a fervent Nazi until he had a change of heart, convinced that Hitler's vision was wrong. Now I have learned that this monster Slava Podvalny has survived. Him, I cannot forgive. The weight of all this has become too heavy for me. I am joining your beloved father this night. Forgive me.

All my love,
Mother

Kraus's mother also left behind an undated news article, written in Cyrillic that included a photo. The article announced the promotion of Slava Podvalny as a tank regiment commander in the then Soviet-controlled Ukraine.

So with both parents dead, Jarret Kraus picked up the pieces of his young life and began taking care of himself. After his mother's funeral, Kraus joined the U.S. Army and, because of his language ability, chose the intelligence route and was later commissioned as an officer. His career path was heavily influenced by his need to locate and destroy the man he held responsible for the death of both his parents. Kraus used his archival research access to discover that Podvalny had been conscripted into the 14th Waffen-Grenadier Division der SS in May 1943. He fought in the disastrous Brody-Tarnow pocket, which decimated his unit in July 1944. A postwar debriefing indicated that Podvalny survived the SS massacre of his unit because the Germans needed manpower to haul provisions, so Ukrainian drafteees and enlisted men were put to work. They were eventually sent to Sadgorsk concentration camp, where during a wood-chopping detail in a heavy snowstorm Podvalny slipped away and eventually joined the partisans in fighting against his former masters. After the war, he survived Stalin's purges, primarily by joining the Party and carrying out many of the killings himself.

Over the years, as Kraus achieved promotions, he kept track of Podvalny's career, watching but unable to stifle his moves toward the top. Four decades later, though, his vigilant drive for a means to extract vengeance had led him to become an expert in Soviet- and post-Soviet-era intelligence-gathering; he now found himself in charge of keeping tabs on the Russian bear and its Ukrainian cub.

14

THE GYMNASIUM AT CAMP Smith was located inside a renovated warehouse. It contained a basketball court, six racquetball courts, men's and women's saunas, and a fitness center complete with free weights, Stair Masters, treadmills, stationary bicycles, and the latest aerobic and anaerobic training equipment.

The gym was a popular place, especially after work. Will had been using it most evenings since his arrival in Hawaii. He came to do therapy on his leg and to sort out how he would handle the tornado that was sure to descend should he continue with his agenda.

As Will placed a towel on the bench of a leg-extension machine, he noticed a man doing sit-ups nearby. He was sixtyish, on the chubby side, with sagging jowls. A shock of slicked-down hair gave him the look of a bulldog. Will turned away, shinnied his right leg, then his left, into position on the exercise machine, all the while searching his memory, trying to place where he had seen that face before.

When Will's feet were comfortably under the cushioned ankle pad, he began his routine. First he raised and lowered the healthy limb; then, with a grimace, the right leg. His brow furrowed. Sweat beaded up by the time he finished the first set. He twisted his torso and reached behind to add weight. As he did so, he paused ostensibly to watch three enlisted men taking turns spotting each other and doing bench presses with a barbell that, when lifted, bent in an awe-inspiring arc.

Will still could not identify the familiar older fellow. The man sweated heavily as he rested on a mat. Then the man looked over and caught Will's eye.

Will smiled with recognition, blurting out, "Uncle Russ?"

"I'm Russ Whitten," the man said, then came ambling over with more grace than his bulk would have indicated.

"Will Cadence," Will said, and stuck out his hand.

"No lie?" Whitten shook his hand, then tugged, nearly launching Will from the exercise machine, and gave him a bear hug. "Yeah, I was one of your 'uncles' back in the old days."

"Jeez, how are you?"

"Hanging tough. Hey, been a group of years." He stepped back, sizing Will up. "You were just a tyke, and I was a head-down, ass-up, hard-chargin' Yankee air pirate."

Will let go with a hearty laugh. "Unk, it's good to see a friendly face. So what have you been doing with yourself?" Will got back on the leg-extension machine.

"Oh, I keep busy with a little company I started after I got out." Whitten glanced at the leg brace and scar on Will's knee. He pointed to skin graft–like scars on his own arm. "Got mine courtesy of a Vietnamese prison camp guard we named Warthog."

Will tapped his knee brace. "This is my reward for punching out of an F-15 at three hundred knots."

"No shit? You . . . an air force pogue?"

Will nodded. "Newly stationed right here at Camp Smith."

"Shows how much I keep in touch. Don't get much time to hang out with blue-suiters anymore. They still let me in the gate, though, to do my rehab. I'm classified sixty percent disabled. I ain't complainin', mind you. Livin' in paradise and working government contracts is about as fine a way to goof off as ever invented. My ex-wives keep me working overtime though."

"Sounds like things are pretty much going your way. Say, things turned out pretty well for Uncle Hank, too, didn't they?"

"No lie. Hey, you going to his shindig in D.C.?"

"The inauguration?"

"Aw heck, Henry T. calls it a promotion party. The night before they stamp 'Commander-in-Chief' on his ass, all the POWs are invited to the Mayflower for the real pinning on, but damn it, you ought to be there, represent your dad. If you want, I'll call and square it with the committee. I got a suite reserved at the Mayflower. You can hang your hat there, 'cause there ain't no vacancies left in the whole damn town that weekend."

Will pondered, then made his decision. "Why not?" Then he casually swung his right leg from under the lift cushion and let it dangle back and forth. "Say, Uncle Russ, what do you think about POWs maybe still being held in Asia?"

"All that old MIA stuff in the papers?" Whitten scoffed. "No way are a couple hundred jocks still sitting over there." He looked away, as if reconsidering, then spoke more softly. "Not this long, there ain't."

Two mornings later, Will got a call at the office from Russ Whitten's secretary, wondering if he would be available at eleven o'clock for a tennis session with Whitten at nearby Hickam Air Force Base. Will was keen to ask Whitten more about the past and also wanted to continue putting his leg to the test. He accepted the invite, then stopped by the cafeteria to grab a sandwich and bag of ice which he wrapped in his towel for insulation before driving out the gate.

Pulling to a stop at the tennis center, Will saw four cement courts laid out adjacent to an Olympic-size swimming pool. The entire exercise area was framed by sprawling trees aflame with orange blossoms.

Whitten, sitting in the shade by the pro shop, saw Will exit his car. He waved, then shouted, "Court two!" He hefted his racket and bag and made for the playing area.

They shook hands at midcourt.

"Now, Will, you go easy on me. I'm spotting you twenty-five years and thirty pounds."

Will flexed his injured leg, still wearing the metal and leather brace. "Come on," he chided. "You're playing a diagnosed cripple."

Whitten banged his racket against his knee. "I'll trade you this knobby old joint for yours, no questions asked." He opened a fresh can of balls, then faked a limp and moan as he headed for the other side of the net.

Will was surprised that Whitten could move so well for a man with a gut like his. He was pleased with how well his own leg took the pounding. It took two of Whitten's service games before Will could win a break. Finally Will sent an overhead smash into the open court to end the set.

"Whew!" Whitten said, as sweat dripped from his face onto a soaked shirt. "Ask a guy to go easy and he tries to give a man a coronary. You got to remember, kid, when I was your age it was haul ass with a G suit, a bottle of whiskey, and a hard-on. Now it's drag ass to liposuction, O'Douls, and Viagra." He dropped his racket by his gym bag and stretched his spine. "Damn. Getting old is a pisser."

"It beats the alternative," Will said, smiling as he set down his own racket and followed Whitten to the water fountain.

"That it do. That it do." Whitten got to the fountain first. "Tell you what. Just to show you what a good sport I am, let me buy you a drink." He pressed the valve button and water squirted into the air.

"On you," Will said, and bent to drink. When he was through, he watched as Whitten took a long swallow. He noticed how the man savored the water, letting it splash about his face, into his hair, filling his mouth as though the whole event were a special occasion. Will guessed that after the treatment he had received at the hands of the Vietnamese, even the smallest of pleasures took on significance that others might deem trivial. Whitten stood, and they began to walk back to the court. As they sauntered along, Will bounced a ball up and down on his racket. "Say, Unk?"

"The answer is no, I don't have another set in me."

"Me neither." Will stopped bouncing the ball as they reached a bench where Will unwrapped the ice bag from the towel and put it on his knee. "Russ, did you run into my father during your days in prison?"

Whitten sat heavily next to Will. "Once," he said, the words flowing as if his mind were suddenly far away, "near the end, when they brought Jack to the Hanoi Hilton. He looked fine then. A couple weeks later, they hauled him from the cell he shared with Hank Dalton. I heard he looked real bad, all yellow and jaundiced, but I didn't see him." Whitten stared at the ground. "Damn shame. Lived through all the shit they threw at us, then with a month to go, he catches a bug and buys the farm."

"Is it possible he recovered?"

"Hell, anything's possible. You thinking he did?"

"I'm not sure, but all the Vietnamese sent back was a note about cholera and some ashes."

Whitten's interest suddenly piqued. "You got something that says the ashes ain't his?"

"Yup. A photo taken years after the war ended."

"Of Jack?"

Will nodded. "I ran into pretty strong headwinds when I showed it around."

"At Camp Smith?"

"Right," Will said.

"You got the photo with you?"

Will reached into his bag and produced the Polaroid. "I've been accused of having a personal agenda. They want us to work without emotional bias."

Whitten studied the photo, then shrugged. "Seems to me a little emotion might be just what that outfit needs." He looked at the picture again. "Does kinda look like him, and I remember those gangly hands. Had some weird malady with his fingers."

"They call it Dupuytren's," Will said, "a genetic disorder."

Whitten nodded. "Hey, why don't I run some interference for you. Let me give Brad Stoner a call." When Whitten saw the look on Will's face, he was quick to add, "I know him. I'll just rattle his chain a little. Won't use your name."

"No thanks, Unk." Will took back the Polaroid copy. "If anyone gets the idea I'm bringing pressure from the outside, I'll be JTF history. All I've got is a picture that might be phony. I need time to come up with something concrete. Can you think of any reason why the Vietnamese might want to hang on to Dad?"

"Well, he was a Wild Weasel," Whitten said, referring to the nickname given to elite two-man crews of the F-105 squadrons that attacked surface-to-air missile sites in North Vietnam.

"Why would those guys be special to the Viets?"

"We Weasels knew all the classified info about detecting and defeating their Soviet SAMs."

"By 1972, that information was probably old hat."

"To you and me, maybe."

"Sorry if it sounds like I'm groping around in the dark, but that's exactly what I'm doing." Will sat on the bench. "How many Wild Weasels were captured?"

"What is this, a quiz . . . to see if I've still got the names memorized?" When Will said nothing, Whitten added, "That was my prison job, rememberin' all our names so we'd know who came out and who didn't." Whitten scratched his head. "Let's see, five front-seaters and six backseat Weasels, including your old man."

"How many came back?"

"That's easy. Henry T. and me."

"Did you know Captain Randall Robbins?"

"Yeah, sure, Robbie was a Weasel, front-seater."

"Is there some new info on him?"

"Just met his daughter recently, but you say only two of eleven came back?"

Whitten glanced at Will as though trying to figure out how to soften the impact of his words. "The others died, Will. Most of them, except your dad, went pretty quick. You see, the Commies were pretty desperate to find out everything we had on those missile systems." Whitten swiped angrily at a fly buzzing around his head. "We knew that by giving them the info it would mean more of our guys would get shot down. When we refused to cooperate, they beat the living shit out of us." He rubbed his arm and swallowed hard, his eyes tearing as his head came back up. He flicked sweat off his brow. "I had to listen while they worked on my buddies for six straight days. I've heard kids yell and women cry, but there ain't nothin' like the sound of a grown man screaming." He looked away. "A few guys died holding out. Finally they got around to me. I guess I wasn't as tough as some of the others."

Will glanced at the scars on Whitten's arms. "Maybe tougher."

15

THE CONVERSATION WITH WHITTEN fueled Will's curiosity. Did the number of Wild Weasel crew members who were assumed dead have any significance beyond the fact that they were tortured more than the other prisoners? How many Wild Weasel POWs had come back in a stone urn like his father? Will planned to find out.

When he returned to JTF, Will went straight to the Records Office. Chief Jackson stood as Will entered. "Sir?"

"I want to see all the data we have on Wild Weasel crews."

Chief Jackson made no move. "I'll need a statement of need-to-know from the head-shed. Sorry, sir. New rules from the colonel came in yesterday."

Will went back to his office, angry and confused. The system had closed ranks trying to keep him in the dark about something the hierarchy seemed anxious to suppress. He now fully understood Pam Robbins's frustration. He also was alert to the fact that most but not all of those who were trying to stop his efforts were doing what they thought was right. He had seen the number of bogus reports that flooded in from all over Asia. He remembered the wild look on Pam's face as she detailed the coverup she alleged. Was his own persona changing, becoming more intense, more paranoid in other people's eyes?

Will considered backing off, biding his time. Maybe they, whoever *they* were, would make a misstep. On the other hand, he might spend the rest of his military career, brief though it might be, shuffling paperwork that had been sanitized by the higher-ups. No, he had to find out who wanted to curb his efforts and why. His access to data now restricted, he needed an ally inside the system, someone who believed in his suspicions and supported him. He considered calling Pam Robbins to give her an update but decided she might overreact. Also, his phone at JTF might be monitored. Who could he confide in?

He thought about Gabbie again. Had she gone to Bustamante with his Polaroid? She continued to fascinate him—a complex woman who combined a daredevil streak with a scientific mind. A phone call to her might raise a warning flag, but Will punched up her number anyway. When she answered, he asked her if she'd had a chance to look over the photos he had left. She had a dinner engagement at Camp Smith but agreed to meet him briefly at the Sunset Club to discuss the matter.

After work, Will found a parking space at the rear of the lot, then headed for the club entrance. On the way, he spotted Gabbie's motorcycle.

Inside, the place was crowded, so he glanced around, thinking the one-on-one conversation he had in mind might prove difficult. To Will's relief, Gabbie sat alone at a table near the jukebox. She had on a white cotton blouse, buttoned at the collar. He wondered about her conservative dress, with her motorcycle waiting outside. There was no drink in front of her, and she had not yet noticed his arrival. He intercepted the waitress at the bar and, with a healthy tip, convinced her to let him deliver the Coke she had ordered. He had the bartender add a draft beer, then carried the tray from the bar.

Gabbie looked up as he approached. If not entertained, she seemed intrigued by his unwieldy maneuvers as he weaved around the crowded tables toward her.

He placed a napkin on the table in front of her, then set her drink on it. "Your cola, ma'am."

She smiled, a bit taken aback, then reached for her purse. "And how much—"

"On the house."

From her hesitation, Will guessed she was searching for a reason to decline his generosity. "Actually," he admitted, "I'd like a chance to make up for that first encounter."

She glanced at the tray. "Officers aren't supposed to work in bars, especially majors. I may report you, you know."

Again? Will thought about the session with Bustamante, but came back instead with, "You don't always play by the book do you?" He stood still, waiting for her response, the beer glass looking as though it might tip over in the next instant.

She reached out and plucked it from the tray, placing it on the table across from her. "Have a seat."

Outside the Sunset Club, a Nissan Maxima pulled up beside Will's car. Victorio Anagni sat in the driver's seat. He had obtained a visitor's pass at the Camp Smith front gate by using a fake defense-contractor's card. From there he had picked up Will's trail at JTF.

Victorio had a colorful past. He had escaped the stinking, narrow alleys of Naples, Italy, by walking step by lawless step out of the squalor that was the lot of most Neapolitans. After two attempts on his life by criminal adversaries, however, he saw the light and hired on as an ordinary seaman aboard a tramp steamer. Four months later, when it ported in Baltimore, he jumped ship to renew his life of crime. A year later he noticed the dizziness and weakness. Diabetes mellitus, the doctor had told him. He had no medical insurance, but he adjusted, as he always had. A controlled diet and insulin injections became a regular part of his life, a life of work that required precision and concentration. Then came the numbness. He was slowly dying. When he became aware of the partial night blindness, he flew into a rage, punching holes with his fist in the drywall of his bedroom, breaking four bones in his hand.

Darkness was important to Victorio. To see better in dim light, he took medication to dilate restless pale irises hidden behind yellow-tinted glasses. As the years progressed, his skin drew tight against his skull, with tiny veins becoming visible at his cheeks. He was a lot younger than he looked.

Working at night made it possible for Victorio to enjoy what daylight he had left in life. Ironically, ending people's daylight was what Victorio was all about now, and he was very good at it.

Victorio had never seen Will's car until this day, but after being briefed on his target's background, Victorio had purchased a similar Thunderbird from an antique car dealer. He determined the best way to disable the vehicle. A week later, he sold the car at considerable loss.

Victorio walked along the path above the parking lot and frequently glanced at Will's car, sitting in the lane directly behind his own vehicle. He felt fortunate that Will had beat the crowd, arriving before the lot was half full, allowing Victorio to park so close. He monitored the nearby activity, waiting for twilight and for cars to fill in around the Thunderbird. Finally, autos had pulled in on both sides of the vehicle. Victorio went to the rear of his Nissan, opened the trunk, and tinkered with the spare tire for a moment. Satisfied no one was paying him any attention, he closed the trunk, bent low, and slid under Will's car. After taking a small flashlight from his breast pocket, he found the brake line on the driver's side. A tiny wrench was taken from the same pocket and used to loosen the fitting. As fluid began to pour from the line, Victorio screwed the fitting back on, precisely one-and-a-half turns. Fluid continued to drip, but at a much slower rate. Then he slid over to the passenger side and did the same. With a pair of wire snips, he severed the emergency brake line. The entire operation took thirty-five seconds.

The jukebox blasted in the background, so Will waited until the rock song ended before he attempted conversation with Gabbie.

"So, what's on your mind, Cadence?" Gabbie sipped through her straw while she waited for his answer.

"Anthropology. I was wondering about a person's skull. It doesn't really change shape over time, does it?"

"Only the nose, Major. It gets fatter, particularly on snoops." She flashed another smile. "I have a knack for sarcasm. If you want conversation, it's part of the package." Then she softened. "Go on."

"Did you have time to examine the images I left?"

"Yes. With decent resolution, I could tell if it's *not* the same person. The Polaroid copy you gave me is too badly focused, but I did some rough measurements and can't rule anything out." Then she reached into her handbag, retrieved an envelope, and handed it to Will. "Your photos."

"Thanks for the effort," Will said, deciding that she had not gone to Bustamante; otherwise why would she still have the photos? He held the envelope for a moment, then quickly laid it on his lap when he spotted Colonel Bustamante approaching.

The music started again as the colonel arrived. He grinned at Will, offered a quick "Greetings, Major," then immediately turned his attention to Gabbie. "Ready?"

"Ready." Gabbie slid her chair back. A shower-fresh scent of jasmine tinged the air. "Thanks for the drink, Will. If you'll excuse us?"

"Sure."

As Gabbie led the way to the exit, Bustamante turned his head, catching Will's attention. Bustamante's glance seemed to betray his annoyance over seeing Will and Gabbie together. After watching them pass through the door, Will nursed his beer for a few minutes, wondering if Gabbie was filling the colonel in on their recent conversation. After a few calm minutes passed, Will headed for the exit.

He found his car in the darkened parking area. The small puddles that stained the pavement where the car had been went unnoticed as he backed out. Will drove through the gate and swung left. More fluid squirted to the pavement each time Will used the brakes.

Victorio wore one driving glove. The other sat ready on the passenger seat beside a cellular phone as he followed Will.

The T-Bird accelerated down Halawa Heights Road until Will approached a red light. He stepped on the brake pedal. It went to the floor. Will was momentarily stunned, then realized his problem as the automobile careened toward the intersection. He pulled the emergency brake. The handle came out with no resistance, and the car kept accelerating. He down-shifted into second while swerving around a car that was slowing in front. Horns blared and tires screeched. Will wheeled to the right, his engine screaming in protest as he tried to align with the cross traffic. Too tight a turn. He overshot into the oncoming lane. Headlight beams danced dead ahead. The T-Bird skidded toward a three-foot-high cement barrier that loomed to his left. The front fender hit the barrier hard, with a grinding metal-on-stone sound that went right through Will like an electric shock. He hurled forward against his seat belt, but the car had no shoulder strap. His chin struck the back of his hand as it gripped the steering wheel. The left front tire bounced up and over the barrier and Will wedged his knee to keep from sliding along the seat. The chassis slammed against the side of the cement slab. Sparks showered from under the car. They sprayed onto brake fluid that had drenched the wheel cavity. The T-Bird went grinding along with the one wheel hooked over the top of the barrier.

The scraping stopped.

The T-Bird's one remaining beam shone up at an abutment twenty feet ahead. Will read the words *Die, haoli* scrawled in red paint across gray steel. He waited until his breathing slowed, staring ahead at that ominous native-Hawaiian instruction to foreigners before he reached out a trembling hand to turn off the ignition. He tasted blood, then smelled gas fumes.

Across the street from the wreck, the Nissan came to a stop. Victorio put the other glove on over a needle that poked from a thimblelike device on his middle finger. The needle had a tiny syringe mounted behind it that contained .2 cc of ammonium zyntalin, a vasodilator that rapidly lowers blood pressure, inducing shock and heart seizure. He got out and hurried toward the wreckage.

Will tried to open the driver-side door, but the impact had jammed it. He undid his seat belt and slid down the inclined seat to the passenger side.

Smoke began billowing around him as another car pulled to a stop behind the Thunderbird. The car's high beams came on. Seconds later, two men were beside the passenger door, trying to open it. Will shoved at the door. Then another man pushed his way past one of the men who had managed to crack the door open. Will shifted a leg out. He looked up. The new man was inches from his face. His breath smelled antiseptic. His eyes were almost fully dilated, their coal-black centers betraying nothing, staring with detachment at Will through yellow lenses, as though he were simply a valet helping someone out the door. The man took Will's arm in one hand, then reached for his leg. Will felt the man's hand bump the leather strap of his knee brace and catch on his trouser as he tried to pull Will from the wreck. The man withdrew his hand.

Flames appeared in the rear window. Someone yelled, "It's gonna blow!"

Will squeezed out, and all four of them ran from the burning car.

The rear of the Thunderbird lifted as the fuel tank exploded and everyone dove to the pavement.

16

A FIRE ENGINE BLOCKED the roadway near where Will sat on the curb, staring at the accident form he had been handed, a handkerchief pressed to the side of his mouth. A few feet away, a police officer leaned against his squad car while filling out a report. The T-Bird remained lodged against the barrier, steam rising from its blackened hulk as a fireman continued to hose down the rubble.

Victorio watched the proceedings from his car until certain from Will's continued mobility that the needle's potion had indeed failed. He dialed his cell phone. The receiver was picked up at the other end. "Hello."

Victorio spoke. "This is the store manager."

"Has the order been shipped?"

"Not yet. The credit card was rejected." He listened for a moment, then asked, "You want to try another transaction?"

"No, suspend my purchase for now." The phone went dead.

A headlight glared in Victorio's mirror as Gabbie's motorcycle rolled by the Nissan, then slowed to a stop.

Gabbie lifted her helmet, taking in Will and the remains of the T-Bird. "Good God, Major, are you all right?"

Will looked up from the form he was filling out and watched as Gabbie got off the Harley.

As she approached, Will started to get up. "I'm fine . . . now."

He nearly tripped backward over the curb in his effort to stand. Realizing he had reinjured his bad leg, he steadied himself, trying to ignore it. They stood apart, almost at eye level. He had thought of her as towering over him in height, but she was actually shorter by a few inches.

"Let's have a look," she ordered. She took out a handkerchief and wiped at the injury, then turned to look at the car. "I think you'll live, but the car's a goner. What happened?"

"Brakes went out." Will stared at what was left of his T-Bird. "Was my father's car."

The Nissan drove by slowly, then merged into traffic.

"Some guys helped pull me out." Will looked around. "Didn't even hang around long enough for me to thank them."

The policeman, still working on his report, noticed the blood on Gabbie's handkerchief. "You sure you don't want me to call an ambulance?"

"No, I'll be okay," Will said.

The officer shoved his clipboard in front of Will and explained that a release was necessary so the car could be towed. Will signed the paper. The policeman gave him a card that listed the location where the wreck would be hauled.

Gabbie reached into her saddlebag and set another rider's helmet on the seat. "Need a lift somewhere?"

Will stared at the motorcycle.

"That's if you don't mind riding *sissy.*" She got on the bike and crossed her arms in front. "I'll go nice and slow, if you like."

He strapped on the helmet, threw his leg over the rear of the machine, and plopped into the seat behind her.

Gabbie started the engine, then moved off at an easy pace, as though testing his comfort level. When he placed both hands on her waist, her head turned slightly. She took her right hand and peeled his from her waist and placed it lower on her hip. He moved his left hand down without her help. At the corner, she turned to face Will. "You going to tell me where you live?"

"Nanakuli," Will said.

Gabbie nodded. "Ready?"

Will stared into her clear visor, so close, a distant sensation being communicated from those dark, mysterious eyes. He noticed the stoplight turn green. "Cleared for takeoff."

Gabbie started out carefully, as though conscious of his state of mind after the accident, but minutes later her motorcycle eased onto the H-1 Freeway. Immediately Will felt like they were rocketing along, though in fact he noticed they were simply matching the traffic flow. He peered over her shoulder, trying to anticipate the dips and curves as she wove through traffic. He got the feeling she was enjoying demonstrating her skill as a biker, making the ride a little more dicey than if she were traveling alone. Taut muscles in her hips shifted as she maneuvered the machine, and Will's hands began to feel like land mines. Should he enjoy her physique too obviously, he was sure she'd pull to the side of the road, get off, and flatten him.

As they passed a pickup truck, she twisted around. "Nanakuli's a big town. Which exit?"

The pickup accelerated alongside, away from her line of vision, and started into her lane as she had her head turned.

"The first one." Then he saw the truck. "Watch out!"

Gabbie leaned away, and Will gripped her tightly as they bounced across lane reflectors in the highway. He squeezed his inner thighs against her legs as she adroitly straightened out and accelerated.

"You owe *me* one, now!" he shouted as soon as his heart slowed to a point where he could speak. Then he released the vise-grip his legs had on her thighs.

She took one hand off the steering bar and patted his thigh. He suspected the touch was designed to assure, but instead it served to excite him in spite of the peril, or maybe because of it. He wondered if the danger gave her the same sensation.

They came to a stop on the dirt driveway of Will's wood-frame bungalow. He stayed seated on the cycle, awed by the ride until Gabbie shut off the engine and glanced at Will's hands, still firmly attached to her hips.

"Oh, sorry," Will said, then slid backward to get off. As his feet hit solid dirt, his trousers hung up for a moment on his knee brace until he gave a tug. Once firmly grounded, he returned the helmet.

Gabbie reached up, took his chin in her hand, and checked his cut lip.

"The bleeding stopped," she said. He felt a rush at the firmness of her touch, so in control, and the way her gaze washed over him as though she were inspecting more than the status of his injury. "I don't imagine you have anything to put on that lip."

"No." Will blushed as the possibilities crossed his mind, then wondered if she could detect his embarrassment in the dim light, then caught her unsuccessful effort to suppress a grin.

Gabbie pulled her hand away, dipped it into a saddlebag, and produced a small medical kit. She tossed it at Will. "You can manage with this. Please get it back to me in the morning."

She restarted the cycle, then roared from the driveway.

Will was left standing in a cloud of dust. He watched until she turned the corner, wondering why she had come upon his accident so soon after she had gone off with the colonel, but glad she had, and glad she knew how to smile, no matter how hard she wanted to appear detached.

Once inside, he tended to his bad leg and noticed a small tear near the knee on his trousers, then remembered it had hung up when he dismounted the cycle. He checked his knee brace but saw no damage to it that might indicate the cause of the tear.

He considered getting some rest but was too keyed up to try sleeping. His thoughts shuttled between the accident, its possible cause, and Gabbie. Was all of it connected? She knew he was headed for the Sunset Club. Had she notified someone who then sabotaged his car? Did she show up at the scene to check on results? He again recalled what the marine aide had said about the army being unable to "tame" her. *What did that mean?* Finally he wandered into the den the owner used for an office and turned on the computer. He saw the AOL icon appear on the monitor and clicked on it. Using the GUEST option to gain entry, he typed in *google.com.* When the search page appeared, he entered the name *Gabrielle DeJean.* The results showed seventeen items. The first two were about a French author by that name. The third entry caught Will's attention. Its log line read: "Cause of Death Under Investigation For Fort Huachuca Soldier Found in Desert. In a bizarre twist, investigators have pieced together disturbing facts surrounding the August 14th disappearance . . ."

Will clicked on the URL-cached feature and up popped an archive page from the *Fort Huachuca Scout,* the post newspaper at the "Home of the U.S. Army Intelligence Center." The words sent a chill up Will's spine as he considered the possibility that Gabbie was part of some intelligence organization. He did not have to scroll far to encounter the name DeJean. It appeared in the headline story. Will read the article.

Dateline: Friday, August 18, 1995 . . .
In a bizarre twist, investigators have pieced together disturbing facts surrounding the disappearance and subsequent death of Corporal Lamar N. Combs. The blossoming scandal involves Sergeant Paul

Kingston, Corporals Robert R. Wilson, and Leonard J. Triston, all decorated members of the Army's Infiltration/Special Operations Unit. The disappearance of Combs was originally classified as an unauthorized absence when he failed to report for duty on Monday, August 14. Combs had been having disciplinary difficulties with his superiors. On August 16, his remains were discovered by hikers who observed birds circling above a desert mesa two miles from the nearest dirt road. The staff judge advocate's office has now placed charges against the deceased's immediate superior and two other soldiers for alleged hate crimes.

Information provided by post authorities indicates that Kingston and two members of the C Company belonged to a white-supremacy organization. Combs reportedly was the object of resentment because his mother was white and his father an African-American. Kingston was aided by Private Gabrielle DeJean, a mortuary affairs specialist on the post, in obtaining a Western Diamondback rattlesnake to be used in an attempt to intimidate Combs. The snake was placed inside his barracks room. The prank turned deadly when Combs returned from a night of drinking at the enlisted mess and did not detect the snake. He was fatally bitten. Upon discovering that Combs had died, the members of the conspiracy took his corpse deep into the desert and abandoned it. The following Monday, Kingston reported Combs missing. The alleged homicide might have gone undetected except for the testimony of Private Gabrielle DeJean, who provided information that led to a confession by one member of the trio. DeJean, who claims she was unaware of Kingston's true intentions with the snake, had reportedly received death threats demanding silence regarding her role. Angered by the threats, she instead went to the authorities and detailed suspicious findings she had observed while assisting in the Combs autopsy. Meanwhile, Private DeJean has been provided round-the-clock protection and is expected to testify against the accused.

Will checked to see if there were any later articles on the subject, but found none. He tried the local Arizona newspapers, but none had an accessible Web archive that went back that far. After he shut off the computer, he sat wondering about this woman who apparently was threatened with death but did not become submissive; when they crossed this woman, she came at them.

17

WILL DROVE A RENTAL car to work the next morning. A memo summoning him to the colonel's office was sitting on his desk when he arrived. At least this time the note had not been taped to the office door for all to see. Will entered Bustamante's office and stood at attention. The colonel shifted in his chair, studying Will for a moment from behind his desk until apparently satisfied that the injuries were more to Will's pride than to his physical being.

"I've been informed about your little mishap. I should think proper auto maintenance would be second nature for someone with your training."

Will tensed. "Maintenance?"

"I understood you were driving a vehicle that was almost fifty years old. Time has a way of wearing things down."

"Wear and tear could have caused my brakes to fail, but I don't think so."

The colonel raised an eyebrow. "I guess we'll never know, from what I hear about the wreckage." Bustamante opened a manila folder. "Anyway, General Stoner and I want you to get your feet wet. We've located a cave in Laos where POWs may have been held, may *still* be held if you believe this report." Bustamante tossed the folder across the desk. "Courtesy of the daughter of a former MIA. It seems she had serious personal problems. They found her yesterday." Bustamante delivered his next words with a blank stare. "A suicide." His face remained expressionless.

"She was apparently despondent over a failed romance combined with frustration over a delusional theory regarding her father's continued imprisonment. A classic case of severe depression, I'm told."

Will pulled his eyes off the colonel, moved a step closer, and lifted the folder. Inside was a sheaf of papers and a photograph. His legs went weak as he recognized the picture of the two alleged POWs that Pam Robbins had shown him. Will dropped the envelope. He put out his hand to steady himself, touching the colonel's desk.

"Cadence?"

Will's head snapped up as he withdrew his hand.

Bustamante rose from his chair. "Are you all right?"

"Pam Robbins is dead?"

"Most assuredly." The colonel sat. "You knew her, then?"

"Yes."

"The Polaroid?"

Will nodded, trying to make sense out of what he had just heard. "She killed herself?"

"With a handgun registered in her name."

Will remembered seeing the gun in her purse at the academy.

The colonel had a wary look about him as he went on to explain how two days ago federal agents arrested the owner of a graphics shop that was in the business of making fake driver's licenses, IDs, and the like. Miss Robbins's name showed up on their customer index. The agents went to question her, but when they arrived, the police were already on the scene. Seems her mother had called the Denver precinct from her home in Wichita. Her daughter had not been answering her phone. The police were there checking on her and found the body.

"Looks like the young lady had gotten wind of the arrest. The agents found that some files in her word processor had been erased. They used a DOS retrieval program and enough was recovered to put new light on this photograph and the one you showed me." He indicated the alleged picture of Pam's father. "It leaves little doubt about her complicity."

Will was numb with confusion. For an instant he had to consider:

Had he been taken in by Pam? He immediately rejected the thought. "Complicity in what?"

"Faking MIA photos."

"What could she gain from that?"

"The launch of a new and expensive search effort? Money? Notoriety? Who knows? If her father survived the war for some period, his back pay with interest would be substantial. You see, Major, some people are just greedy, others so strongly convinced about their cause, they feel no remorse in fabricating evidence. The Communists, you'll recall, were very good at that."

"She may have been a zealot, but stooping to fraud? I can't believe it." Will's words sounded hollow, even to him. That he could have been drawn into a scam added to his queasy feeling.

"You *better* believe it." The colonel let slip a little grin of contempt. "Anyway, because of the sensitivity surrounding this affair, General Stoner has now taken a personal interest in putting the Robbins case to rest. I had already assigned Dr. DeJean and a team to investigate her father's crash site in Laos and a cave where POWs may have been held at one time. You'll join her on a flight that leaves Saturday at 17:30 for Guam, connecting in Bangkok for Vientiane."

"Yes, sir." Will barely heard his own words as he placed the photo back in the folder. He still could not accept the death or duplicity of Pam Robbins. He found himself trying hard to remain calm, to keep from bursting with outrage over what the colonel seemed to treat as a routine turn of events. *What if I'm wrong?* This was neither the time nor place to get more emotional, so he moved to leave.

"One more thing," Bustamante said. "The *doctor* is in charge of this operation."

When Will paused to consider what Bustamante had just said, the colonel added, "She's a GS-14, the civilian equivalent of a lieutenant colonel. Any questions?"

"None, sir."

Bustamante stood. "Look, if you need some personal time off, why don't you call it a day and go home."

"I'm fine, sir." Will turned for the door, then had a change of heart. "But I may take that time off. Thank you."

After Will closed the door, Bustamante used his private line to place a call to Washington.

When Will made it back to his office, he pointedly ignored Major Chase, who had arrived during Will's absence. A flippant remark from the marine was all it would take for Will to explode. Will went to his desk and sat staring at the wall, too stunned to think of anything except the fading memory of Pam Robbins, standing there, shivering in the cold at the Academy Cemetery. He pictured her wild, childlike eyes in the coffee shop and remembered her saying, "If you can't do it for my father, would you do it for yours?" Had she practiced saying that? Was it a setup? It certainly drew him in like a hooked trout. The possibility made Will seethe.

He considered what to do now. How could he, sitting three thousand miles from Denver, hope to prove one way or the other whether Pam Robbins was a fraud? Without a word to Chase, he headed for his rental car in the parking lot and drove toward Nanakuli. Thoughts about Pam dominated his consciousness. He had seen the gun in her purse. Had she bought it for protection, or was she already contemplating suicide? He wondered how many women used guns to kill themselves. Not many, he decided. Sleeping pills, razor blades, jumping off buildings seemed in his mind to be the more common methods. Many women just did not have a bent toward handling firearms. But she had had one.

Will wondered whether his aircraft accident and the leg brace he wore had drained the warrior out of him as surely as it did his strength. Had he lost ambition, assertiveness, aggressiveness, the qualities that made for a successful fighter pilot? Did he have less spunk than Pam or Gabbie? Both of them got angry when the opposition got in their faces. He was angry all right, but his ire had no real focus. *Who was to blame and for what exactly?* He was baffled.

Will saw a car parked alongside the freeway. A rear tire had blown and the vehicle looked abandoned. He remembered his own car, then fished around in his wallet until he produced the card the policeman had given him and read the address where his Thunderbird had been taken. He exited at the Farrington Highway off-ramp near Barbers Point Naval Air Station. From there he headed leeward to the Campbell Industrial Park.

Driving along the main road, Will looked for some sign indicating the auto dismantler's location. He rolled slowly past a manufacturing facility and a storage area filled with shipping containers. Ahead were smokestacks of the electric power plant. Then he checked his mirror. A vehicle with hazard lights strung above its windshield was bearing down on him. Will eased into the right lane to let it pass. It was a tow truck pulling a derelict car. Will followed as the tow truck turned right at the next intersection and then swung immediately right again, through a gate. A sign read, ALL VISITORS REPORT TO THE SALVAGE SHED. THIS MEANS YOU!

Will drove inside and down a blacktop road toward a one-story frame building. A sign over double doors read, KAOMI AUCTION AND SALVAGE, INC. He spotted his T-Bird as soon as he turned into a parking space. The hulk was sitting inverted on top of a heap of metal piled alongside the shed. Will swallowed hard as he recognized the distinctive taillight assembly. The blackened chassis sat baking beneath a molten sun. Heat waves rose from the metal into dead-calm air.

Will got out and went inside the building where a heavyset man was using a wrench on an engine block. He was shirtless and had a tan that looked as if it went all the way to the bone. The man was sweating and cursing as he tried to remove a valve cover.

"Excuse me," Will said.

The man was working on a Ford 302 engine block, identical to the one in Will's T-Bird. He looked up. "Yeah?"

"That T-Bird you got outside on the pile—it's mine."

"Not no more, it ain't. You signed a release." The man gave Will the once-over. "Was you in that sucker when it blew?"

"Until just before it went up."

"Wow, man! You one lucky haoli."

"I know. Mind if I take a look at the chassis?"

"Go ahead, but the only thing worth any money is sitting right here." He tapped the engine block with his wrench.

"Have you done anything to the brake system?"

"Nothin,' but I think most of it melted, man. Had to cut the engine mounts with an acetylene torch just to get this much off." The man waved his hand, then went back to work.

Will went outside and moved a car door aside, stepped around a refrigerator and a pile of nondescript metal all twisted together. At the top of the heap, he checked the T-Bird's rear end. Both brake lines had burned through. When he touched the fender, he nearly burned his hand on the sunbaked surface. He took out his handkerchief and tried to loosen a line nut where it attached to the brake assembly. The nut would not budge. Then he eased his way around the trash to the front of the car. The brake cylinder showed some heat damage but no cracks. The lines were still intact. When he twisted the nut at the brake assembly on the driver's side, it resisted, then came loose in his hand. The one on the passenger side did the same. Will stared at the fittings. They had been loosened in a manner that he was sure caused them to leak each time he had applied the brakes. When all the fluid had drained, his brakes had failed.

Will returned to his bungalow wondering if he should take his suspicions to the police. He felt he needed to find out more before anyone else knew what he had learned. If, as he now believed, suicide was not the cause of Pam's death, then could he discover the true cause? It might have a connection to the attempt on his life. To make his case believable, though, he had to act quickly, before JTF sent him halfway around the world to poke inside a Laotian cave.

Will used the computer in the bungalow to check airline schedules. American Trans Air had a charter rate direct to Denver. The return flight would arrive back in Hawaii a bare hour and a half before his scheduled departure for Asia with Gabbie. He checked his watch: 11:15 A.M. He was forty minutes from the airport and his takeoff time was at 1:45 P.M. Traveling light, he might make it through security in time.

Will hurriedly packed a change of clothes in a hang-up carry-on and stuffed a large B-4 bag with his passport and things he would need later for his Asian TDY. He snatched a coat from his closet as he headed out the door, then drove to Honolulu International Airport. Before he checked in, he rented a storage locker for his Laos baggage.

Two hours later, American Trans Air's Boeing 767 climbed east of Honolulu. Will glanced out the window. Below, a thin cloud bank spread like a sheet across Molokai, halting beneath its craggy peaks. On the north side, tiny Kalaupapa Peninsula jutted clear. He wondered if lepers still lived on that peninsula, away from the eyes and consciousness of the rest of Hawaii. He smiled wryly at the thought that the people at JTF were acting like the cloud bank and being sent to Laos was their way to quarantine him.

He settled back in his seat to think as he toyed with his dinner. Time was a factor. He had to be back at the Denver airport at noon the next day for the return flight to Honolulu. That left about ten hours on the ground to find out what had happened to Pam and where she had gotten that photo. The task was daunting. Not sure where to begin, Will considered going to the Denver police first. At midnight? No. All he knew was the address where she had lived. He would start there. In the meantime, he must get some sleep, in spite of his anxiety that his dream might return along with a migraine. From experience, he knew that circumstances were ripe for a recurrence, and he had forgotten to pack his pills. If he had an attack on the plane, the crew might elect to return to Honolulu. He finished his meal, pulled a magazine from the seat back in front of him, and began to read. After an hour, his forced concentration began to wear him down. His eyelids got heavy. He tried to breathe deeper, getting more oxygen to his brain. After a while, the magazine lay open on his lap, and he drifted off.

Guided by computers tracking satellite signals, the plane bore through heavy clouds, wing spoilers out, the whole plane creaking and groaning as turbid airflow rocked the machine while descending over the Rockies toward the mile-high city.

Will slept fitfully but was spared the dreaded dream. He was awakened by slight lifting as the flaps were lowered. He blinked, not sure of where he was. Moments later he felt a light bump when the landing gear extended. As the cobwebs cleared, he squinted out the window and saw a misty blur of bloodred light as rays from the wing-tip beacon reflected off the cloud mass. It all came back to him. He imagined the death scene at Pam's house, then forced his mind off the subject. He focused instead on other possibilities in his future, wondering if wrestling airliners was his future once his military service ended. Aviation had been his passion, but his mistake—the midair collision—had made him turn inward, unsure of his flying skills. The thought of never again being at the controls of an agile fighter plane weighed heavily on him. Like getting knocked off a horse, he wanted to get back on and rebuild his confidence. That would never happen, though. It was unlikely commercial flying could take its place. But once his stint at JTF was finished, what other skill did he have to offer civilian employers? There would always be questions about his accident, about his competence in the air. Like demons, the unspoken doubts, the inquiring eyes of other pilots would always haunt him.

Nonetheless, absorbing thoughts about flying occupied his mind. His hand gripped the armrest as if he were up forward with the pilot wrestling the controls. A minute later, the plane swept beneath thick swirling coils of murky stratus that hung above the airport.

Snow flurries whipped in sheets through the beam from the landing light as Will tried to gauge when the pilot would start the flare, prior to touchdown. He tensed, breath held in suspension, as the nose of the plane rotated upward, the pilot feeling tentatively for that first brush of rubber on concrete.

Instead of relief, Will felt a twinge of uneasiness as the plane settled on the runway. He glanced at his watch: 11:15 P.M. The late show was about to begin in earnest.

Twenty minutes later, Will left the terminal in a rental car. Once away from the airport, traffic into the city diminished quickly. The late hour and the snow probably kept even the hardiest Friday-night partygoers indoors. Faraway lights from the downtown area reflected off the cloud cover like a halo. Maybe it was the weather, the barren trees, the thin layer of snow covering the lawns and roofs of the houses, the lone pedestrian braced against the wind, but the street scenes seemed to have a tough, mule-and-hardtack feel to them. As Will turned up Niagara Street, its weather-beaten clapboard homes gave evidence to the hardy construction of the 1890s.

He found the house on a corner lot. Number 1290, Pam Robbins's home, was a white two-story with appealing dormers and Victorian latticework. A white Toyota was parked in the driveway. The same one he had seen at the academy. Soft light reflecting from the snow and from a streetlamp gave an almost daylight quality to the hour. He parked across the street beside a posted sign with a figure of a doggie detective displayed beneath the words NEIGHBORHOOD WATCH AREA.

The interior of the Robbins place was dark.

Will did not like the feel of it as he glanced about. The neighbor's house where he was parked still ticked with life. A shadow drifted in front of a TV set, interrupting the blue glow that seeped past a frosted windowpane.

Will remained riveted in the driver's seat, paralyzed with indecision. He checked his watch: 1:40 A.M. Had he come all this way to sit and stare? He sucked in a deep breath, then stepped from the car, walked across the street and up the drive to the sidewalk that led to the front door. Caked ice on the front steps made the footing treacherous. The cold made his bad knee stiffen. He leaned against the doorjamb, rang the bell, and wondered what on earth he would say if anyone answered.

No one came.

At the house across the road, the TV was no longer on. A light now shone from an upstairs window.

Will tried the door. Locked. He had no idea what he might find even if he could get inside, but felt compelled to try. He moved off the porch to the driveway, making his way to the rear. He noted no tire tracks from Pam's car in the snow.

The yard was fenced in, but the gate was unlocked. Once inside, Will stepped past a snow-covered evergreen and found the rear entrance. Bolted shut. At ground level, he noticed a pair of padlocked basement doors that extended from the foundation wall. They obviously led to a space below the house. He could tell by the corrosion on the lock and the hasp that the opening had not been used in years. The wood frame around both doors was badly split and rotted. Will noticed the butt of a hinge sticking up on one side. He slipped two fingers under the edge. The wood crumbled as he worked for purchase. He pulled. The hinge came up, its wood screws held for a moment, then slid free. Too freely, he thought. He moved nearer the house and pulled at the top hinge. It popped loose just as readily. He felt certain he was not the first to use this method of entry. The door panel conveniently folded atop the other half.

Will peered inside.

The basement loomed below in total blackness. He took a deep breath. If he got caught breaking and entering, especially under these circumstances, it would mean the end of life as he knew it. Well, his life wasn't all that spectacular, he decided. He felt his way down concrete steps, cursing his lack of foresight in not bringing a flashlight. A strand of spiderweb caught on his face. His foot slipped, plummeting into a puddle that had collected at the bottom of the steps. Icy water filled his shoe and sent chills through his body along with a sharp twinge in his knee. He stuck his other foot forward, feeling for higher ground, found it, and crouched forward into the basement, waiting for the pain to subside. The heavy odor of damp wood hit his nostrils. Will reached above for the ceiling. His hand thudded into a stout beam mounted inches above his head. With his other hand he reached out, groping at the air, wondering if a horde of basement denizens, angry at this nocturnal disturbance, were swinging their feelers and slithering toward him. One step at a time, he made his way forward, groping for the steps that he knew had to be somewhere out there waiting in the darkness.

Outside, a truck rumbled down the street. The ground under Will's feet shook as the vehicle approached. Headlights swept the corner and across the yard, illuminating the snow-covered evergreen.

Enough light bounced through the opening behind Will to give a momentary glimpse of the basement. A wooden stairway materialized off to his left. Then as though a camera's lens had shut, the basement was plunged again into solitary darkness. He moved toward the now unseen steps. Two paces and his toe bumped into the base of the staircase.

There were five steep steps that led to a door. Will put his hand on the doorknob, then stopped to listen. The *plop-plop* of water dripping into the puddle where he entered was the only sound. He twisted the knob and the door opened into a pantry off the kitchen. Suddenly Will could see again as light, pouring in through all the windows, invaded the house. A peculiar odor filled his lungs—antiseptic, as in a hospital. He stepped into the kitchen, wondering if Pam had died right here.

Will eased around a small dining table and moved through an alcove into the living room. The scene seemed as if from a black-and-white photograph: murky stones surrounding the fireplace, a TV and VCR cabinet, a sofa against the wall, framed images above it, all in muted shades of gray or ebony. Pam Robbins had spent her days here, burned logs in the fireplace, hung the pictures, sat on the sofa, watched the TV. He could feel her presence still as he stepped on the carpet, edged around a coffee table and through the room, then found the staircase to the second floor. It was cold here. He could see his breath as he ascended the steps.

The top of the stairs ended perpendicular to a hallway that ran in both directions. To the far left, at the end, a bathroom door was ajar. To the immediate left, a door stood shut. He opened it and stuck his head inside. He could make out a four-poster brass bed against the far wall, its overstuffed pillows arranged neatly above a lace-trimmed bedspread. Her bedroom, he guessed, then carefully closed the door and reversed direction.

Two doors were closed along the other extension of the hallway. Inside the first one was a desk with a computer and monitor. Pam's office. An antique barrister's bookcase was against the wall, the kind with glass doors that lifted up, allowing access to books on each of three shelves. The middle door was propped open. A file cabinet stood next to the desk. He went in, closed the door, then took another long breath.

Was the neighbor across the street still up? He crossed to the window and looked out through tree branches, beyond the streetlamp. No lights were on. He went over to the desk, found the surge suppressor, and turned on the computer. Will returned to the window, shut the blinds, and pulled the curtain closed. Back at Pam's desk, the room came to life as Pam's Windows display lit up the screen, but a prompt indicated he needed a password.

The desktop was neat, tidy. A Post-it note was fastened to an oak disk-holder set beneath the monitor. Will tipped the note up to the light. It read, "Call Toy, 424-0673." He noticed a wicker wastebasket beside the desk. He glanced inside. It appeared empty until he nudged it and noticed another, nearly invisible, note stuck to the side near the bottom. He pulled it free and read the words, "Order Benedetto for JD." Beneath the sentence was added, "Archtop Guitar, $39." The note had been lined through as though the task had been completed. He looked around the room for a guitar, then went over to the bookcase. It was crammed with Asian war books, Jack Broughton's *Thud Ridge,* Tim O'Brien's *The Things They Carried,* Haing Ngor's *A Cambodian Odyssey,* Spike Nasmyth's *2355 Days, A POW's Story.* There were no books about music.

Will heard a *click* behind him. He stuffed the two notes in his pocket, snapped off the power switch, and froze. A beam of light leaked underneath from the hallway.

The police? No, he would be hearing more than delicate footfalls approaching. A shudder went up his spine as whoever was out there padded softly past and on down the hall.

Will was at the door in an instant. He pressed his ear against the wood and listened to the sound of a door closing. He shut his eyes. He had broken into an occupied house! If discovered, he might get himself shot, or cause a coronary to whoever was living here. Either way, the outcome was too awful to contemplate. He eased the door open and glanced down the hall. The bathroom door was shut. He debated staying put. Having not yet heard the toilet flush, he decided to get the hell out of there. He slipped into the hall, eased the door closed, then tiptoed toward the stairway. His eyes were riveted on the bathroom doorknob, its white porcelain unmoving, like the eye of a dead fish.

Two more steps and Will reached for the banister, then turned down the stairs. At the bottom of the staircase, he heard the rush of water as the plumbing surged. He scurried through the living room and kitchen, turned into the pantry, then pulled the door to the basement closed as he went down. At the last step, he paused to listen, thankful for the black security blanket that enveloped him.

18

THE SUN POKED THROUGH the windshield to wake Will. His rental car was parked three blocks from Pam's house. He had turned on the engine and heater periodically to keep warm, had even managed to get a few brief periods of sleep. Thankfully, there had been neither dreams nor migraine to interrupt his rest.

The local time was after seven. Will felt stiff and groggy. He looked at himself in the rearview mirror. A lined and tired face stared back at him. It reminded him of the computer image Sergeant Larson had made, one that was not supposed to appear for another dozen years.

Will drove to a convenience store, got some coffee and a sandwich, changed clothes, and used his electric shaver in the rest room, then went outside to the pay phone. All he had were the notes from Pam's office. He punched in "Toy's" number, and his concern about how to handle the conversation was solved after two rings. An answering machine identified the phone's location as the Toyota dealership whose weekend hours were announced as 10:00 A.M. to 9:00 P.M. Will considered that a dead end, so he plucked Pam's card from his wallet and dialed her home number. After four rings, he heard a soft, feminine "Hello."

"Good morning, my name is Will Cadence. I was a friend—"

"Cadence?" The voice at the other end seemed to brighten a little. "You're the air force major?"

"That's right."

"Pam mentioned you and your father several times. I'm Dora Robbins, Pam's mother."

"Mrs. Robbins, I was so sorry to hear about Pam."

"Thank you." The brightness was gone.

Will struggled to find something to add, something with the right feeling. Nothing came. "Ahh, look, I'm in town on business, but don't have to be at the airport for a little while. I wonder if I might stop by?"

"Well . . . right now is not a good time. I don't know—"

"Did she tell you we were working together, trying to resolve your husband's case?" His comment was greeted with silence. "It's important that I talk with you. I won't stay but a minute."

He could hear her sigh over the phone. Then she answered.

"All right. Do you know the way?"

"I have a map."

The doorbell was answered this time. Mrs. Robbins, a wisp of a woman, appeared. She wore a tan skirt and a wool sweater that covered a pale yellow blouse. A pair of reading glasses dangled from her neck. A flesh-colored hearing aid poked from an ear. Will assumed one does not sleep with a hearing aid on and now understood why no one answered the doorbell the night before. But it was her face and hair that struck Will. She had Pam's same intense, childlike eyes, the narrow chin, the red hair. Will guessed her age at sixty-five. She could have been a retired teacher, a librarian, or just what she was—a sad woman with a head start into old age.

"Nice of you to come by," she said as she extended a delicately veined hand. Will shook her hand, then stepped inside and felt the rush of furnace-hot air that escaped past his face to the outdoors. A steam radiator hissed in the foyer.

The living room now seemed alive with color—the hearth stones of red adobe, the beige sofa with its floral-pattern pillows, the burnished oak of the entertainment cabinet, the coral green figures in the Oriental carpet.

"I hope you didn't take my reluctance to see you personally," Mrs. Robbins said. "Under the circumstances, you must understand—"

"I do." The room was stiflingly hot. Will took off his coat, but she didn't offer to take it, so he folded it over his arm.

A smile flickered as she bid Will to sit on the sofa, close to another radiator. "I've made some tea," she said, then disappeared into the kitchen.

Pam's likeness beamed down at Will from photographs above the sofa, her facial expression as he had never seen her in life. In one, she was no more than three or four, bubbling with laughter as her father—Will was sure of it—carried her on his back. In another, she was older, probably in high school, posing with teammates decked out in soccer uniforms and smiles, a trophy at their feet.

Mrs. Robbins returned a moment later and placed a silver tray with an old English teapot and two china cups and saucers on the coffee table. "Cream or sugar?"

"Neither." Will sat and watched her pour. Her hand was steady, sure. She seemed composed, not a trace of perspiration although still wearing the sweater. She seemed to enjoy the heat. When she finished, she handed Will a cup and saucer. He took a sip, expecting the temperature to be scalding hot, but to his surprise it was not. "Thank you, it's just right."

She poured a cup for herself, then looked at the noisy radiator. "Do you think it too warm? I can't seem to get the heating system to work. First it's bitter cold, then too hot."

It was hot, but he didn't want to belabor the matter. "Feels fine, really. I came in from Hawaii."

"Oh? All that way." Mrs. Robbins raised her cup and took a sip, then set it back on the saucer, prim and proper. Her eyes remained fastened on Will, concern showing in them.

"Yes, a long trip." Will held her stare. "Mrs. Robbins, I was wondering if you could help me. You see, Pam gave me a photograph, one that may be of my father." He took the copy of the Polaroid from his pocket and laid it on the coffee table.

Mrs. Robbins picked up the picture and studied it. "I'm sorry, I've never seen this. Pam rarely discussed these matters in recent years, the mention of your name being an exception. You see, I finally came to accept the loss of my husband, but she didn't, so we mostly avoided those issues."

"Well, would it be possible to check her files—"

"I'm afraid they won't allow it."

"They?"

"Why the police, of course. They put those awful yellow crime-scene tapes around the place."

Will glanced about, wondering where the tapes were, then noticed smudged footprints in the carpet where his dirty wet foot had stepped the night before. He felt his pulse rate jump.

"I took them down, couldn't stand the sight of it." Then her gray eyes sparkled like silver needle points, and for a moment she emitted that same hardness he had seen in Pam. "I'll put them back before the police return." She seemed to revel in the thought of putting one over on the Denver Police Department. "They let me stay on if I promised not to begin packing her things—that's why I'm here in Denver—until after the autopsy. Officer Wilson is coming by today to advise me on that. In fact, I thought it was him when you called."

Beads of sweat appeared on Will's forehead. He had already literally stumbled into dangerous territory. If he stuck around for the arrival of the police, not only would he miss his plane, he could find himself in trouble explaining his purpose here. Also, his footprints were on the carpet, his fingerprints in Pam's office, and her notes missing. If the police concluded Pam's death was not a suicide, they would not appreciate his having removed possible evidence. He would become a suspect. Time was running out.

"Mrs. Robbins, there is something I'd like to find out. My questions may seem intrusive, so I'll apologize in advance. You see, Pam and I were working on a theory about the disappearance of our fathers. I believe she was committed to resolving the matter. Now I'm told Pam was despondent and committed suicide. I find that hard to believe."

Mrs. Robbins tensed. "She was going through a very difficult period." Her expression changed, seeming a little less settled. "Tell me, what makes you think otherwise?"

"I think she felt that my being at JTF was a big step toward getting closer to the truth. Pam had asked me to get assigned there. Would she take her life before I had a chance to prove . . . or disprove her suspicions?"

"She had more on her mind than chasing after fantasies."

Will remembered Pam mentioning a canceled engagement. "A failed relationship? Was it that devastating?"

"Indeed." Mrs. Robbins frowned, the message clearly being that this subject was off-limits.

Will chose another tack, remembering the note about the guitar. "I recall Pam once mentioned music to me, guitar, I think. Did she play in a group, or sing?"

"That was some time ago, but actually she did neither." Mrs. Robbins turned away, teacup held in midair. She seemed to be considering the incongruity of her answer as the hiss of the radiator filled up the silence. Finally, she met Will's stare. "Her fiancé was a musician, a drummer in a rock group." She put down her cup. "I never approved of that relationship. Tad was so much younger than Pam, so immature. Anyway, the band broke up a year ago, and they scattered. Eventually Tad left town. Pam never got over him, though."

"Do you know where I might contact him?"

"No, he was as wild as the prairie wind, claimed the whole world was his address."

"Was anyone in the band named Benedetto?"

"Tad's name was Emerson. Never met any of her other friends from here."

Will remembered that the archtop guitar note had what looked like someone's initials. "Do the initials JD belong to anyone Pam might have mentioned?"

"Can't think of anyone." Then Mrs. Robbins looked out the

window. She seemed to sense his uneasiness. "The funeral is Tuesday. Will you be staying over?"

"No, unfortunately." Will would have liked to see who showed up but he had to weigh that against what he might learn in Laos. "I really should be heading back to the airport. I have a plane to catch, then another in Hawaii bound for Laos." The word *Laos* dangled in the air like a worm on a hook. When there came no nibble, Will continued. "They've asked me to visit the site where your husband's plane went down."

"I wonder what for? They sent us his bones, ashes really."

"Yes, but Pam raised some new questions, and I've been asked to try to answer them."

"Questions?"

"She maintained that your husband is still alive."

"You must be referring to that photo with the two men."

"Yes. Do you know where she got it?"

"A Laotian refugee forwarded it to the National Alliance of Families. They sent it to me."

"Is it possible that the other photo came from the same source?"

She shook her head. "No. I would have remembered it." Mrs. Robbins folded her hands in her lap. "I'm really tired this morning. I did not sleep well last night."

Will stood. "Again, my condolences over your loss."

"Thank you." Mrs. Robbins led the way to the front door. As Will stepped gingerly past her into the brisk morning air, she spoke again. "She was lonely, like me. At times, I, too, thought life was becoming unbearable."

"Do you really believe Pam took her life, Mrs. Robbins?"

She smiled, bitter futility showing in her eyes as she held out her soft, pink hand for Will to shake. "I don't really know," she said, then closed the door behind him.

Will drove two blocks up Niagara to Colfax where he turned right, heading west toward I-225, which would eventually lead him to the airport

He spotted a gas station so he pulled in to fill up.

As he pumped gas into the tank, Will felt that he had learned little for his effort. He considered staying over for the funeral. Something tangible might surface if he hung around long enough. Of course, he would be AWOL, and the colonel would not think kindly of his missing the flight to Asia. After refueling, he went to the pay phone and looked in the White Pages. Maybe Tad Emerson or whoever Benedetto or JD were could give him a lead. There were seventeen Emersons. Twelve answered his call. None of them knew a Tad Emerson. He thought about calling the nightclubs that touted live music in the Yellow Pages, but it was way too early to try that. Then Will looked up music stores. Maybe the owner or one of the employees might know about a rock group with a drummer named Emerson. He found one nearby that provided a map and listed its hours. Will checked his watch. The shop was just about to open and was on the way to the airport. Four minutes later, he pulled in front of Barham's Music Outlet.

He parked, crossed the sidewalk, and pushed open the door, a bell above the doorframe announcing his entry. The place was empty, but behind a counter at the rear was an open alcove. While he waited, Will glanced around. Barham's was one of those specialty shops that sold violins, guitars, and cellos and did repairs. Instruments, old and new, hung from hooks along the length of one wall. Next to where he stood was a bookcase lined with hard- and softcover music books, song sheets, and magazines. Toward the rear, Will noticed a partly assembled cello clamped to a gig on top of a table that was covered with a fine layer of sandpaper dust. The place reeked with the smell of rare woods.

A woman wearing a denim coverall came out of the alcove. Her gray hair hung to her waist, and she had a round, full face that shouted Earth Mother. She stopped beside a computer monitor that sat on the counter. "May I help you?"

"I'm not sure. I'm trying to find a Tad Emerson, drummer with a rock group."

"Don't know of him, but then I don't always know my customers' names."

Another dead end. Will pulled Pam's note from his pocket and read it again. "Is there anything unique about archtop guitars?"

"The neck design. We sell them, but I don't have any in stock. We're trying to reduce inventory at the moment, but I could order you one." She looked under the counter and produced a catalog.

"Well, right now I'm just trying to get smart on the subject. Does the name Benedetto mean anything?"

"Benedetto is *the* name in archtop. Handcrafted in Pennsylvania."

"Ah, so thirty-nine dollars wouldn't buy one of those."

"Not hardly, but it *would* buy Benedetto's book."

Will guessed the note was for the book. "Could I see a copy?"

She went to the monitor and typed on the keyboard. "It's so specialized we don't carry it, but in this case maybe we should." She flashed a smile. "You're the second person this week to ask about it."

Was it possible he had found the place where Pam had ordered a book for someone with the initials JD? Will tried to think of how to find out without spooking the clerk. He could not see the monitor, but he saw the woman's name tag with a smiley face next to the letters.

"Rifka, would the other interest have come from a woman named Pam Robbins?"

"You know Pam?" Her eyes dropped, and she cleared the query from the monitor.

"My father is missing in action, like hers." There, he had said it. *My father* is *an MIA*. For the first time he truly believed it. The number of coincidences had exceeded any reasonable threshold of randomness. The photographs, the reaction to his efforts at JTF, the sabotage of the T-Bird, and now Pam's death. The only possible explanation was that he and Pam were on to something, something sinister and so important that committing murder to protect it had become a necessity.

Suddenly Rifka seemed uneasy. "Mr. . . ."

"Cadence, Will Cadence," he uttered, coming out of his thoughts.

"Mr. Cadence. Since you seem to already know, Pam did order that book."

Finally, Will thought, *a nugget, something to go on.* "Did she mention what use she intended . . . a gift perhaps?"

"I'm afraid I can't give out information like that. I suggest you ask Pam herself."

"I would, but Pam passed away a few days ago."

Rifka froze.

"I'm trying to straighten out her affairs." A stretch of the truth, but it was all Will could think of to say. "Was there anything about this order you can tell me? I know she didn't play guitar herself. Did she have a book sent somewhere?"

Rifka's mouth opened but nothing came out.

Will could tell that she was becoming very uncomfortable.

"Look." He pulled out his wallet and showed his military ID card. "I'm an officer in the air force."

Rifka leaned around the monitor to glance at the ID card. Then she studied Will's face but retreated behind the machine before speaking again. "She used to place orders over the phone, mostly sheet music and the like for the band she was connected with. Hadn't seen her for maybe a year until last week."

"She came in to order the book? Did she say who it was for?"

"Whoa." Rifka put up her hand. "What's this all about?"

"Pam's dead and I'm trying to find out what happened to her. I really think it might be important to know who or what was on her mind before she died."

"This sounds like a matter for the police," Rifka said.

"Fine," Will bluffed. "Call them."

Rifka bit her lower lip, then with a fussy movement she typed on her keyboard, after which she turned the monitor so Will could see it. "Yes, she came in this time to order it."

He read the shipping address. "Is that all? No name?"

"That's the way she wanted it sent, except she penned a message and put it inside the package."

Will noted the date Pam placed the order, then jotted down the data entry for the book's destination: U.S. Embassy, (PC), Box 422, Moscow, CIS.

PART II

19

AT DENVER INTERNATIONAL AIRPORT, Will called information and got Gabbie's number in Hawaii. There was no answer, so Will left a message on her recorder stating that he "might be a little late getting in." He asked her to let the passenger agent know that he *was* coming.

On the return flight, Will kept trying to make sense out of the fragments of information he had. He remembered that Pam had highlighted the mention of his Russian studies at the academy when they had first met. Was this expertise one of the reasons she chose him? On the day she probably died, Pam ordered a book and had it shipped to Moscow. Why? The only connection he could make at this point was with the Polaroid Pam had given him. At the Academy when they met, she had said that to reveal the origin of that image would place someone in danger. Pam was open about the photo of her father, claiming it was made in Laos. She refused to say where the other one came from. It could mean that the source for the Polaroid was still located near the site where it was made. If he could locate the source, he might know where to begin looking for information about his father and Pam's as well. Maybe she ordered the book in person because she suspected her phone was being tapped and meant to keep the book's destination secret. The note she included in the package could be intended to warn or possibly get more information from the source. Might knowledge by others of the recipient place that person in danger? Even the box number might give away the person's identity. He guessed there would not be many guitar players at the U.S. embassy associated with that box number. A connection between the guitar book and his father was a long shot, but it was all he had to go on.

Show time for his flight to Guam was two hours before departure. Will's plane from Denver was scheduled to land thirty minutes *after* show time—at another terminal. His trip off-island had not been authorized. Technically, he was AWOL the minute the plane left

Hawaii for Denver. If he missed his Guam flight, there would be questions he did not want raised.

To his relief, Will's plane landed at Honolulu on time. He got his belongings from the locker, then sped—leg be damned—coattail flying, through the terminal. He found his rental car, then drove to the long-term lot at Hickam on the military side.

Will left his winter coat in the trunk, then humped his B-4 bag toward the Air Mobility Command Terminal. By the time he reached the entrance, he was breathing hard, and his world had that overexposed look that comes with staying up all night.

He stepped inside the terminal, a one-story glass-fronted building with an open waiting area behind a pair of automatic doors. At the rear, two separate departure lounges were cordoned off. To the right was the processing counter. Will saw military personnel and dependents exiting through final security before loading onto a bus. He spotted Gabbie boarding. She paused at the top step and turned back toward the terminal, a dour look on her face as she squinted, trying to see through the tinted glass. Will waved from across the terminal, but she apparently did not notice.

At the processing counter, Will handed a set of orders to a passenger service agent, who seemed to take his late arrival in stride. While he waited, he noted the airplane's routing continued to Bangkok and beyond, making a circuit of the globe on a military courier route. The agent tagged Will's bag, then tossed it on the conveyor belt as a computer spit out a boarding pass. Will raced for the bus.

He was the only passenger aboard as the bus drove across the tarmac to a waiting C-141, a four-engine transport, painted mottled gray. One man in a flight suit scurried about the front entry, helping board the last passengers from the previous busload. At the rear, a man in fatigues maneuvered a forklift into the open tail section. He raised a pallet loaded with large canvas mailbags onto the airplane's cargo ramp.

Deafening sound from a power unit roared near the plane's wing root as Will exited the bus. He covered his ears to fend off the din and went up the steps into the plane.

Passengers had filled the front half of the windowless interior, sitting in airliner-type seats. The aft section had three loaded pallets positioned in tandem. Cargo stretched all the way to the ramp, which was now closing.

Will proceeded down the aisle looking for a place to sit. He spotted Gabbie seated against a bulkhead, a grade-school aged boy seated beside her. A protrusion from the bulkhead prevented a third seat in that row. Gabbie looked up as he passed, her expression showing a little surprise. Will gave her a tiny wave of greeting, and she smiled back.

There was only one space open, across the aisle, one row behind Gabbie. Will headed for the vacant seat beside an older couple whom he guessed were retired and riding Space-A. Before he sat, his paranoia running full speed, he noticed in his peripheral vision a man two rows farther back who seemed to be showing a bit too much interest in his arrival. Will caught his eye, and the man immediately looked away. He was dressed in a navy blue sport coat and dress shirt open at the collar.

Will settled in, having avoided one crisis, but felt no respite. A sensation of claustrophobia descended as though he were being shunted down a tunnel with no way out. The more he learned, the farther from a resolution he seemed to be getting. He wanted to find out who received mail at box number 422 in Moscow, yet here he sat, headed for the jungles of Laos.

The C-141 took off and climbed into the afternoon sky. When the plane leveled off, the loadmaster came through the cabin handing out box lunches and blankets as the plane's air conditioner cooled the interior. Will had a sandwich and carton of milk, then felt the weight of fatigue descend on him. He put his box lunch under the seat in front and covered himself with a blanket. Sleep came the moment he closed his eyes.

An hour later he was abruptly awakened by droplets of cold water splashing on his head. Condensation had begun dripping from an air conditioner duct that hung above him. He shifted his position to avoid the intermittent drops, then noticed the man in the jacket, who had eyed him earlier, pass by going forward. The man carried an attaché case fastened to his wrist via a short chain. Couriers were a common sight on airlift missions, so Will thought little of it as the man entered the lavatory.

Two minutes later, he came out.

Will stood. As he moved into the aisle, Gabbie noticed him. She took a Snickers bar from her box lunch and handed it to the boy seated beside her as Will proceeded up the aisle and into the lavatory.

While he locked the door, Will's foot bumped something. On the floor sat the man's attaché case, its chain dangling from its leather grip. Then he saw the door handle being jiggled and heard an agitated voice from outside.

"Open up, please!"

Will opened the door. "Lose something?" He held the attaché case toward the man.

"Thanks," the man said as he checked to be sure it had not been tampered with, then spun away.

Will shut the door, wondering how a courier, if that's what the man really was, could forget something so important.

When Will came back down the aisle minutes later, the boy who had been sitting next to Gabbie was now in Will's seat across the aisle. He had a Snickers in hand and flashed a smug little grin of contentment when he saw Will. The seat next to Gabbie had a blanket on it, upon which a box lunch lay, his own, he presumed.

Gabbie pointed to the seat beside, a visual command to sit down.

Will glanced at the boy, then turned back toward Gabbie. "A seat upgrade for a Snickers. What a deal!" He picked up his things and slid beside her, a smile on his face.

Gabbie looked up from a sheaf of papers she was reading. "A Snickers is no laughing matter." She turned the pages facedown. "I know, pretty old and lame."

"Lame is something I've gotten beyond. Old, I'm still fighting."

"Well, before we turn gray, I thought we might as well start getting used to each other's company."

After a long look, Will said, "You're the boss."

Gabbie smiled. "Right you are."

She put the work sheets back in a folder, then reopened her box lunch and removed a ham sandwich. "You cut it pretty close at the terminal," she said as she squeezed mayonnaise from a packet onto the bread.

"I got hung up on personal business."

"It's a good thing you called. If you hadn't, your seat would have been given to a Space-A passenger. Guam is a popular destination this time of year."

"Thanks to you, my luck held."

"I'll say, arrive from the mainland with five minutes to spare." She turned to face him, head tilted back, scrutinizing him. Her eyes seemed to bore holes right through him as she spoke with the calm, cool confidence of the sure-minded. "When you called, they were making a flight announcement in the background—a final call. It was faint. I had to play the tape over a few times before I figured out what it was."

"I plead guilty. What's the punishment?"

She turned away, seemingly pleased with her cleverness. "You get to drag my bag all over Laos."

"A sherpa, then."

"Porter. Sherpas do the snow country."

"Right."

She took a bite of the sandwich, chewed for a moment, then asked, "Thought it might be Washington, but you'd never have gotten here in time."

For Will, the conversation had sped from the getting-to-know-you stage to a clear-cut interrogation. "What made you think I was in D.C.?"

"Scuttlebutt has it you're close to a certain senator, soon-to-be president."

She seemed to know a lot more about him than he realized. Maybe she *was* in league with JTF in this cover-up operation. Her current role may be to ferret out what he knew, then pass it on. If that were the case, though, she was being awfully direct. He decided to keep the question exchange going. "Scuttlebutt? From the colonel?"

"No." She said it with a note of irritation.

"Major Chase, I take it."

"Bull's-eye." She bit into the sandwich again, but the quiz session was not over. She swallowed. "Now, do I have to name every city on the mainland or are you going to fess up?"

He felt certain she already knew where he had been, even though they don't usually mention the departure city during airport announcements. "Denver . . . personal stuff."

Gabbie looked down as though disturbed that his answer was intended to shut off her line of questioning. Then she faced him again. "I hope I'm not getting too personal, but how old were you when your father died?"

Will had to stop and think. He was no longer certain his father *was* dead, so the assured finality of Gabbie's words unnerved him.

"I was almost four the last time I saw him."

"So, you never really knew him."

"I have little memory of him, but there are the pictures."

"And then you grew up, joined the air force."

"Not exactly. I had no money and surviving sons get a free ticket to college."

"You mean the Air Force Academy."

"That's one option," Will said. "Be a sole survivor, have a heartbeat, get decent grades, and you're in."

"Maybe so, but I used the GI Bill and still had to work my tail off at a civilian university to get my degree. The academy had to be harder."

"Than anthropology school? It only took four years of push-ups and book learning for me, plus another year in pilot training. Then off to the hundred-hour war."

"Kuwait?"

"I got to see only ten hours of it. Seems like a lot of expense and effort for not much payoff. Never even squeezed a trigger."

"Why not?"

"I flew on another pilot's wing."

"And he squeezed the trigger?"

"Twice. They painted two stars on his plane."

"And you?"

"I got to watch one hell of a fireworks display. That was enough for me. You see, for years I was angry with my father. He didn't have to go off to war, didn't have to leave us behind and get himself shot down. Joining the air force and getting a taste of battle was my way of trying to find out what made him do it."

"And did you find out?"

My dead wife would say so, had she lived, he thought. "There is a certain intoxication to combat."

"And from what I've read, doing a good job as a wingman is just as important as being the shooter."

"That's the rhetoric, and according to the colonel, I'm still someone's wingman . . . yours."

A hint of a smile altered her mien as though she considered the statement accurate. "By the way, how is your leg doing?"

"Ah . . . back to lame subjects."

Her abrupt changes of direction were keeping him off balance. *How much did she know about my knee?* His leg had been dinged in the car wreck, but only his cut lip was noticeable. His knee ached from his stumble in Denver, but usually only stiffened in the cold these days. Hawaii had been anything but cold. He may have limped his way into the terminal, but she had not seen him. Gabbie must have caught his puzzled look.

"Saw you slip after your pileup and felt the metal of the leg brace bump me while we were on the Harley."

"The knee's coming along," he answered, convinced now that damn little went unnoticed by this woman. He was intrigued that she was sensitive to his touch, even if that touch was from a metal leg brace. By now, he knew the next question would be about how he had managed to injure the knee in the first place—and it was. Will hesitated, wondering if the anthropology department at CIL-HI had access to air force accident reports. He suspected they did, given the nature of their work. If she had read the report, then her question was a test of whether he was the type who rationalized mistakes. "I bashed it doing an unscheduled exit from an F-15."

"You ejected?"

"My plane shed a wing after I ran into my flight leader." He tapped his knee. "Got a permanent reminder."

She asked if he looked forward to eventually getting back to flying fighters. Of course he wasn't going back, but Will sensed that she already knew the answer to that question, too. In fact, he got the feeling she knew all the answers. He made a mental note to find out how much of *his* life was available on the Internet. "I'd like to fly again someday." Then he had a thought, a diversion. He hoped to work the conversation toward her Fort Huachuca incident. "How have you managed to stay in one piece riding that Harley, especially with guys like me running stop signs?"

She finished her sandwich and dabbed her face with a paper napkin. "I had a good teacher. My father sat me on the gas tank of his Indian Chief on my third birthday, then went zooming around the neighborhood to show me how nifty it was. That's all it took to hook me." Gabbie chuckled at the recollection. "He'd get arrested if he did that these days." She put down the box lunch. "He took me on the bike to hunt, all over the High Desert. He was Cajun French and one-quarter Native American, which is why he thought he should own an Indian ride back then." She glanced at Will. "I'm part Blackfoot, which is why *I* don't own something called an Indian and *do* have something called a Harley. Some politically correct things happen to be just that way with me."

"I'll have to remember never to let on that I might be a Cleveland fan."

"You're not serious."

"Right, I never was anywhere long enough to settle on a hometown favorite. What about you? Where'd you grow up?"

"Victorville, Cee-A. Great place to roam the High Desert. Took my first serious spill when I was ten." She stretched her arms out in front. "Headfirst over the handlebars."

"Oh?"

"There I was howling with pain, the fingers of my left hand bent back double. My old man popped them back in place and in two minutes had me calmed down. I had no broken bones, but the tendons were stretched all to hell and gone." She raised her hands like pilots do when talking flying. "Better not hangar-fly with me at the bar." Her right-hand fingers, like the barrels of a gun, began tracking the other hand. Then she arched the fingers of her left hand back like a Thai dancer as though her hand were doing a high-G break-turn. "This hand can pull nine G's!"

"What do you know . . . wounded in action at ten."

"Yeah, I was a terror."

Will decided to push a little deeper. "You mentioned the GI bill. You were in the military once?"

She didn't answer right away, and Will wondered if she were thinking like he had, wondering what her companion already knew.

"Army. Liked it, too, which is why I later applied for the job at CIL-HI."

"If you liked it, how come you left?"

"I was enlisted then, and here I am, not too long after, getting to tell majors what to do."

"Like your very own jungle porter," he said in agreement.

She smiled at him, a friendly grin, but Will could sense that she wanted to go no further regarding army life.

To Will, she apparently kept much about her early life private, much as he had never fully opened up to anyone about his past. He had to find a way to connect, to find the one solid confidant who could bolster his determination. He would keep trying with Gabbie.

Four hours later, the pilot made a bumpy approach to a smooth night landing at Guam for refueling and a crew change. As the front entry opened, the glow from yellow floodlights leaked in and the warm, humid smell of a recent rain shower rolled through the cabin. The loadmaster announced that they would have to deplane while the C-141 took on fuel. They could leave their belongings onboard.

Outside, the wet ramp reflected a glossy sheen in the light of a half-moon and the floodlights. The weather was clearing rapidly with wisps of dirty-looking cirrus clouds sailing across the night sky.

Off to the southeast a thunderhead rose ominously. Lightning flashed inside it, momentarily illuminating it like a frosted bulb. When it darkened, moonlight muted the cloud's billowy creases into all the grays of a ghost.

The passengers filed onto buses for the ride to the terminal, a beige building at the east end of the tarmac. Once inside the air-conditioned interior, everyone except CIA agent Garcia, still posing as a courier, remained in a closed-off area. Garcia boarded a staff car and went to report his status. An hour later, he rejoined the passengers and boarded the plane.

As Will stepped inside the plane, he paused a moment in thought, then turned and climbed carefully up the short ladder onto the flight deck. The crew area was more spacious than Will had imagined. The pilot and copilot stations were well forward. Behind each of them was a jump seat. To the right was the flight engineer's position. Two bunks were stacked one above the other at the rear. He hoped he might recognize someone, a classmate from the academy perhaps, in the new crew.

The pilot was seated, head turned away. A female sergeant sat in the engineer's seat, and a baby-faced lieutenant stood behind the copilot's seat. The lieutenant saw Will enter.

"Hi, come on up."

Will read the lettering on his name tag which read NELSON, and embossed below was his nickname, NAILS.

"Thanks, Nails."

Then Will heard someone coming up the ladder. Thinking that the loadmaster was coming forward, he moved to the side to get out of the way, but heard Gabbie whisper behind him.

"My God, they look like teenagers."

The pilot, in the left seat, swung around as though he overheard Gabbie. He wore lieutenant colonel's leaves and sported a rakish-thin mustache whose length was barely regulation. When his eyes lit on Will, his expression changed as though someone had just announced a death in the family. In a deliberate movement, like a cobra rising to a threat, he started to get out of his seat. Then he saw Gabbie standing in the entryway, and he seemed to catch himself. His attention returned to Will and though his tone was subdued, there was no mistaking the authority behind his words.

"Sorry, no passengers on the flight deck these days."

Will held his stare for a moment, then spoke. "Fine." He bumped into Gabbie as he started out. Once untangled, she led the way to their seats. As soon as Will plopped down heavily beside her, she asked, "What was that all about?"

"It's a two-beer story . . . to borrow an expression."

"I'm not going anywhere."

Will sighed. "*That* was Tom Boyd, the aircraft commander and my former boss." Though Will was taken aback by the encounter in the cockpit, he was not totally surprised. The embassy run involved a handful of experienced crews who deal with sensitive diplomatic pouches and delicate issues such as the insertion or retrieval of spies. Since Senator Dalton had helped arrange a flying assignment for Boyd on Will's behalf after the accident, Will considered the odds high that he might run into Boyd somewhere along the route.

"Boyd and I used to be paired in the air. I was his wingman during the Gulf War, when he got those two MiG kills."

"So?"

"It was Boyd's plane I collided into last summer." Will went on to explain the details, ending with the accident board's conclusion blaming Boyd. "A lot of controversy erupted from the board's decision. Most of the squadron pilots agreed that as a wingman my first responsibility was to stay clear of my leader. The guys felt I should have kept my eyes on Boyd's plane, period. The board didn't see it that way, placing fault squarely on Boyd's shoulders for calling for the formation rejoin before I had time to complete my cockpit checks. The wording stated that Boyd 'task-saturated his wingman during a critical phase of flight.' So my former friend and flight leader, Tom Boyd, got reassigned to transports where they gave him cockpit duties while denying giving him a senior command position in the unit."

Will did not want pity. He simply wanted Gabbie to understand what he felt. "I blew it, the board blew it, and Tom Boyd has despised me ever since."

20

Back in Washington, President-elect Henry Dalton found himself an incredibly busy man. Janet Mills ran his transition team from a suite of offices in the Blair House where the task of changing the White House guard had been staged for the last eleven administrations. Dalton, however, preferred familiar surroundings and favored the view from his Senate office where he continued to spend a part of each day. More important, he felt a greater sense of seclusion in his old office. Not counting his Secret Service detail, the only staff member still with him was his secretary, Arline Haske, who received his incoming calls.

Dalton gazed out the window as snow flurries dusted the capital. A storm system that chilled the Midwest had finally shoved its way east, and Dalton enjoyed the look of it. Like the storm, he was almost on scene, nine more days until the presidency. Another huge, new beginning. Nothing could stop him now, or could it? He swung his chair from the window and stared once more at the air force lieutenant general promotion roster before him on his desk. The list was normally sent by the Service to the Senate for confirmation before being released to the rank and file. If any objections were to be raised, the Senate could redline a name and that officer would not receive promotion. One name on the list had triggered Dalton's current absorbed mood.

He put his initials in the block provided, then reached for his private line, dialed, and waited for the party to answer. After one ring, he heard a familiar voice.

"General Stoner's office. May I help you?"

"Cath? This is President-elect Dalton. Is Brad in?"

"Oh, my gosh, yes, I'm sitting in up here today, I mean, yes, the general is in . . . congratulations!"

Dalton smiled to himself, still relishing the effect he was having even this long after the election. He waited a moment for Cath to settle down. "Thanks, Cath. Now, about Brad."

"Sorry. Yes, I'll get him on the line."

A moment later Stoner's voice boomed through the earpiece.

"Hey, cell mate, haven't they told you you're supposed to have your secretary call and make *me* hold the line?"

"Oh, hell, Brad, you know I've never gone in for that protocol drivel among friends."

"That's one of the things I liked about you in the slammer, Hank. You didn't mind if I went first to the quiz room!"

They both had a good laugh.

"Okay, next prez, what can I do for you?"

"Just wanting to see how Will Cadence was coming along."

Stoner hesitated a moment. "Fine, he's doing fine. As a matter of fact, he's gotten into the business so fast, I decided to send him to the field with one of our anthropologists."

"Really?"

"Yes, his immediate boss recommended it, and I agreed. What we call the dollar tour. He should be in Bangkok in a few hours. Then we fly him up to Vientiane and from there he gets a helo up-country. I have a team in there right now working a cave in the karst that may have been a prison. He'll get to see how we do witness interviews and the archaeology stuff. Should be back in about a week."

"How safe is it?"

"Laos is quiet right now," Stoner was quick to answer. "Only when we go poking among our former allies, the Hmong hill tribes, is there much concern, but we've got plenty of armed security with the team."

As Stoner spoke, Dalton stared up at the Vietnam Memorial photo that he and Will had discussed during Will's visit.

"There's nothing to worry about," Stoner said. "In fact, I'm flying out there tomorrow for a no-notice inspection. I'll look in on him, pull the plug if things aren't ironclad."

Dalton glanced back out the window, taking in the view while he thought. "That's fine, Brad. Keep me posted, and by the way, I just initialed the promotion list."

"The three-star bump sheet?"

"I can't reveal the results," Dalton said, "but you might consider taking a bottle of champagne along."

"Thanks, Hank, I mean Mr. President-elect. Getting a sendoff like that from you means a hell of a lot."

Dalton hung up and swung his chair around to stare long and hard out the window, lost in thought.

21

STILL IN DARKNESS, THE C-141 settled onto the runway at Don Muang International Airport, Bangkok. The plane taxied to the Thai air force military terminal on the south side. Its cabin door opened to the dank smell of wet vegetation mixed with a faint odor of incense drifting in from a nearby temple whose stupa was visible as Will and Gabbie exited the plane.

JTF personnel were helped through customs by Lieutenant Colonel Lantis, a U.S. embassy officer who then led Will and Gabbie outside the terminal. A white van with diplomatic plates was parked in a VIP slot, motor running, and a Thai national stood by the open rear hatch. He piled their gear on top of other bags. The Thai slid the panel door open, then went around to the driver's side.

"Hop in," Lantis said as he opened the other front door, then took the seat next to the driver. Will looked around. He noticed the man who had left his attaché case in the rest room approach a lone Mercedes parked in a lot across the road.

Will followed Gabbie into the van and saw the loadmaster, spotter, and copilot already seated in the rear. Boyd was against the window in the middle seat. A glance at Boyd, who stared straight ahead, convinced Will that conversation was not on his mind.

The van pulled away, passed the Mercedes—which showed no sign of intended movement—proceeded through a military gate, then jerked to a halt at an intersection. A motorcycle came alongside and stopped by the curb, where a family of four untangled themselves from the back of the machine. The father paid the driver, who then sped off.

Will nudged Gabbie. "Your favorite mode of transportation provides gainful employment over here."

She glanced outside. "And when you see the downtown traffic, you'll know why."

Lantis, in the front seat, spoke over his shoulder at Boyd. "After we hop off at the hangar, my driver will take you and your crew to the Intercontinental Hotel. How long is your stay?"

"Two days, then off to New Delhi, Moscow, and home," Boyd answered.

Lantis turned his attention to Will and Gabbie. "I'll be piloting the two of you to Vientiane in our turboprop, an hour-forty hop."

Gabbie winced. "Tonight?"

"This morning," Lantis corrected Gabbie, after checking his watch. "Sun should be popping up in another two hours. A helo is waiting in Vientiane to take you to the dig site." When he saw the tired look on Will's face, he added, "That's what JTF ordered."

The van turned onto a road that paralleled the ramp for a quarter of a mile, crossed an inky-black canal, then swung right to a row of hangars, stopping beside a twin-engine C-12 aircraft. One prop was already spinning. Two maintenance men came trotting from the hangar and headed for the back of the van while Lantis got out and went straight for the plane's entrance. "Point out your luggage to the ground crew, then climb aboard," he shouted. "The guys will take care of the bags."

Will pushed open the van's side door. Gabbie covered her ears and moved past Will.

The cabin was noisy and dimly lit, so Gabbie and Will had to work their way forward carefully. There were no other passengers. They took seats right behind the cockpit. By the time they had strapped in, the second engine was running. As the plane began to taxi, Will looked out the side window. Headlights from a car flicked on along the road that led to the hangar. Will tried to see if it was the same Mercedes he had seen by the terminal, but the C-12 turned, blocking his line of vision.

Minutes later, the plane took off and climbed in smooth air. After leveling off, Lantis twisted around in his seat. "You change clothes in Vientiane, leave your bags, then head north by chopper. Nobody overnights at the dig site—too dangerous."

Gabbie leaned forward. "What's the danger?"

"Government troops are still fighting the Hmong highlanders nearby. You don't want to get caught in the middle of a cross fire."

"Good plan," Will said.

"The security team is on its way in now. They'll do a sweep, check for mines, then set up a perimeter watch while you and the recovery team do the pick and shovel work."

Vientiane Airport's single runway lay just north of the Mekong River. After landing, the C-12 taxied past a row of Russian Mi-8 helicopters and a single-engine AN-2 Colt transport, then stopped at the ramp as a thin band of gray light on the horizon signaled the start of the new day.

Inside the terminal, Will and Gabbie were led to the VIP lounge where they changed clothes in the rest rooms. Ten minutes later, in fatigues and jackets, they boarded a UH-1 helicopter crewed by a U.S. Army pilot, copilot, and crew chief. After liftoff, the crew chief handed headphones to Will and Gabbie, who donned them.

The crew chief pressed his mike button."We dropped the security team off an hour ago. A guide is waiting for you at the dust-off. Word is, it's a three-mile hike up to the site." He gave an apologetic shrug.

Gabbie nodded while the UH-1 helicopter wound around towering karst ridges that looked dark and foreboding in the half-light. The helicopter lurched from turbulence, and the rotors picked up a waffling patter as the machine climbed. Then the pilot steadied onto a northeast heading as darkness ebbed over Laos.

Will looked out the open side door to the east as the orange glow of the sun spilled across the Laotian hilltops like the touch of a warm hand. He peered down into a valley, trying to find some semblance of life stirring in the lowland as it lay shrouded in darkness.

On top of a ridge, a company commander in green jungle fatigues, wearing a beret with a red star pinned to it, answered a field phone. A coded message had been received on the shortwave radio at his headquarters. Instructions were relayed by land line to the company commander. He listened intently, then gave orders to a helmeted soldier, who looked no more than fourteen. His fatigue uniform was at least two sizes too big. The recruit moved out into a clearing and readied a shoulder-fired missile.

The cadre officer soon joined his soldier. The two of them stood silently watching the still-dark sky to the southwest.

The officer saw it first, sun glinting off something moving in the air, just above a ridge four miles away. He pointed. "See him?"

"Yes." The boy raised the missile launcher. Inside the tube was an American-made Stinger missile. Now expanding in its aiming sight was a target this weapon was never intended to track, a U.S. Army UH-1 helicopter.

The boy touched the activation switch with his thumb, and the launcher's infrared seeker immediately relayed a weak, low-pitched warble. He moved the sight off target and the tone muted. The target was still out of range but closing steadily. When the helicopter filled the inner ring of his sight, he uncaged the missile's seeker. The rotating seeker jumped slightly, centering on the target. The soldier heard a new sound, a high-pitched whine that got his heart pumping. He had practiced before, using the launcher sight on friendly helicopters, but had never fired. His arms began to shake.

The officer saw the boy sway. He moved closer and grabbed his shoulder. "Steady!"

The boy swallowed hard, then jammed his cheek against the conductance bar and snuggled his eye into the rubber sight-ring.

The helicopter was almost abeam their position. A moment later it passed, and the aircraft's exhaust stack was exposed. The Stinger's infrared tracker squealed in eagerness.

The boy eased his shaking finger inside the trigger guard. The missile roared from the launcher before he could consciously be sure he had squeezed the trigger.

Inside the UH-1, the impact of the Stinger at first felt like a bump from turbulence. Then the sound of an explosion rocked the craft. Parts from a flaming turbine wheel cut through the roof and sliced into the crew chief's chest.

Gabbie stared, wide-eyed, as the crew chief tried to stand, but his seat belt restrained him.

The copilot whipped his head around and peered into the cabin. The crew chief, his hand clutching at his chest, twitched in spasms against his seat belt. After one second's worth of that horror, the copilot snapped his head forward and began transmitting on the radio.

Both fire warning lights were on. The left engine rpm was winding down, and the needle on the right fuel-flow gauge jumped from zero to maximum as its engine surged in response.

In the cabin, Will took off his jacket and swiped at the flames. Then he saw a fire extinguisher on the rear bulkhead. He unbuckled his lap belt, tore the extinguisher from the mounting and began spraying at the flames. Fuel gushed in from a hole above Gabbie's seat. "Get away from the gas!"

Gabbie popped her lap belt loose, too. Then Will pulled her by the collar toward him with one hand as the helicopter began spinning wildly to the left. He lost his balance and grabbed hold of a bulkhead fitting, but the fire extinguisher slipped from his grasp, bounced once, and flew out the open door.

Up in the cockpit, the pilot and copilot wrestled to control the helicopter. The warning panel was aglow with flashing red lights.

Smoke filled the passenger area. Flames torched down from above Gabbie's vacated seat. Will held on to the fitting with one hand while clinging tightly to Gabbie, who was on the floor, rolling away from the flames and toward the open door.

The ground rushed up and the pilot made a last-ditch effort to autorotate as the UH-1 dropped into the trees.

The rotor blades went thrashing through foliage, hacking away at the upper branches until they slammed into solid wood, where they shattered with a crackling report.

The chopper dropped, hitting hard with a glancing impact on the side of a shallow ridge. It then spun beside a stout tree trunk, where the tail section ripped away.

Will and Gabbie were flung out the door. They rolled down the incline. Farther up the slope, the chopper was wrapped around the tree. One engine still surged, each shriek of power sounding like some prehistoric animal bellowing in fury. The rotor hub, its wings clipped, spun madly above the fuselage as fire crackled and black smoke boiled upward.

Will tried to stand. His knee throbbed, pain shooting up his leg, as he took a shaky step toward the helicopter. Flames roared from the machine. The heat bore down on him, and he covered his face with his forearm, trying to see if anyone was within reach. He decided that whoever was still inside that inferno was beyond help.

Will dragged Gabbie behind some protective brush. He slid beside her, then noticed two armed men in uniform, one wearing a red-star cap, standing on the crest of the ridge. They seemed intent on the helicopter as Will crouched behind the foliage. The helicopter engine abruptly quit running. Gabbie was breathing on her own, so he kept his hand near her mouth, ready if needed to stifle a moan, and watched.

The soldiers waited until the flames abated. Then one of them slid down the incline and began working his way around the smoldering wreck. He stuck his AK-47 inside and nudged something, then shouted to the man above.

The man on the ridge suddenly became alert to the sound of an approaching helicopter. He yelled at the soldier, who scrambled up the ridge. Both of them moved out of Will's sight.

An HH-53 Jolly Green Giant helicopter appeared overhead. A minigun swiveled from a port on the aircraft as the chopper sideslipped to a point above the column of smoke that rose from the wreckage. The huge rotors whipped the smoke and what was left of the treetops into a swirling frenzy. Will watched as a man was lowered by cable on a tree-penetrator device. As his feet touched the ridge, the man hopped off the penetrator and unshouldered his M-16. He made a visual sweep of the area, spoke into his helmet microphone, then slid down the incline to the UH-1 hulk and peered inside.

Will came out of cover and yelled, but the noise from the helicopter's powerful turbines was nearly deafening. The man did not respond, so Will grabbed a stone and threw it in the man's direction. It pinged off the UH-1.

The startled airman swung around, leveling his gun at Will.

Will put his hands up as the man spoke into his mike. A moment later the airman lowered his rifle, then waved for Will to join him.

Will pointed to where Gabbie lay unconscious. The man slid the rest of the way down the hill. He checked Gabbie's pulse and looked for signs of injury. He then loosened her waistband and Will noted she was wearing a money belt beneath her fatigue blouse. The airman tapped her knee to ensure she had proper leg reflexes. She was still out as he lifted her into a fireman's carry and trudged up the slope.

The airman strapped Gabbie onto the lone leaf-seat that already extended from the penetrator housing. Will and the airman pulled down the other two seats and got on. The hoist began reeling all three of them up through the trees to the helicopter.

Once safely inside, Will pointed at the burned hulk. "What about the three crewmen?"

"Beyond help, all three," shouted the pararescuer. "Were there any more passengers?"

"No."

"We'll come back for the crew later."

When the HH-53 leveled off well clear of the crash site, the airman took off his helmet. "You're damn lucky," he shouted. "If we hadn't been flying just across the Mekong in Thailand for a joint exercise at the time we heard your radio call, it might have been days before you'd have gotten out."

"Thanks," Will said. He looked at Gabbie, who was regaining consciousness but looked to be in shock. He put his arm around her and held her as the helicopter headed south toward safety.

22

THE JTF DETACHMENT IN Vientiane was quartered in a walled-in compound. Because of the danger from land mines, the unit included a medical section housed in a tent, complete with surgical facilities for trauma injuries. Will and Gabbie were airlifted there. Upon landing, they were separated to undergo medical examinations. After treatment, both were kept overnight for observation, and Will was given medication to help him sleep.

The next morning he was told that General Stoner had arrived from Hawaii and wanted to see them as soon as they felt well enough to discuss the incident. After a quick session with the medic, Will waited outside for Gabbie.

Though the shoot-down may have been a chance occurrence from hostile action, Will was not ready to believe in coincidences. With this second near-death experience in a matter of days, he felt confident Gabbie would be in his "conspiracy" camp now, especially since her own life had been jeopardized. Moments later, she appeared dressed in a white blouse and khaki trousers. Gabbie swayed stiffly, her hand going to her bruised forehead, as though she was still recovering from shock. She greeted Will politely, making no mention of the ordeal.

Will tapped his temple as they walked. "Wonder what that stuff was they knocked me out with?"

"Thorazine. They were considering using it on me until I told them I'd been unconscious. Anyway, it's a long-term tranquilizer."

"It's given me a long-term headache."

"They can probably give you something for that."

"No, thanks. I'll suffer in silence. No more complaints. I'm just glad to be alive."

"You're limping."

"Knee is a bit swollen, but as I said, no more complaints."

They arrived at the detachment commander's office, a converted French villa on the other side of the compound. At the door to the office Gabbie brushed past Will. They entered a reception area, and a pair of arms wrapped themselves around Gabbie. Poking over her shoulder was the face of none other than Major Byron Chase, the general's aide.

"Byron," she said, "we're fine."

Chase flashed a grin at Will. "How you doing?"

"I'm doing."

At that moment General Stoner emerged from a rear office with the detachment commander, an army major.

"Ah, you're looking better," the general said. "I checked on you both a few hours ago. You had quite an experience."

Will glanced at Gabbie. "I'll say—"

"Come inside," the general cut in. "Have a seat, and tell me what happened."

They followed the general into the office. Chase headed for a credenza to pour coffee as Will and Gabbie took chairs.

The general went behind a gray metal desk and sat. "Before you start, let me say that I've shut down our effort here for the time being. We'll need to fully investigate the accident."

Will leaned forward in his chair. "Accident?"

"I don't like to speculate," the general said, while raising his hand to cut off any interruption, "but the crash may have been caused by engine failure."

Will felt his eyebrows lift. The general reacted.

"According to the written report from Dr. DeJean, the first indication of a problem was when engine parts came ripping through the ceiling of the helicopter. Do you have a different version, Major?"

Will turned to Gabbie. "You wrote a report already?"

"I had a concussion," Gabbie said. "I guess they were concerned I might go into a coma during the night, so they kept me busy on a laptop for a while."

Will stared, unable to determine what to make of that, so he decided not to pursue the issue. Instead, he answered the general's question. "Yes, my version is different. I felt something hit the aircraft first, and the suddenness of the engine failure makes me believe the cause was hostile fire."

"Oh?" The general perked up. "That's the first I've heard of that possibility. That jolt you mentioned could have been nothing more than turbulence, severe enough to be that last bit of stress a flawed turbine could take. Did you see ground fire?"

"No."

"And you?" The general looked at Gabbie.

"No."

"Then we are in the conjecture mode, I take it."

"Not quite," Will countered. "After we crashed, I saw two Asians in uniforms, Pathet Lao–type garb, with red stars on their caps. They checked the helicopter for survivors."

General Stoner looked at Gabbie. "Did you see that?"

"No, but I was pretty much out of it by then."

"Well, Major, I'm not doubting your word. All I can guess is that it may have been some local militia scavenging the crash site. Wouldn't it make sense that if an unfriendly force was in the area, the rescue helicopter that picked you up would have encountered strong resistance, too?" The general tapped his finger on an open folder on the desk. "The only ground fire the rescue crew reported was from a rock you threw that endangered the P. J."

"Rock?" Will was incredulous. "Pebble would be more descriptive."

"Pebble, then," the general snapped.

Will decided the general had a point about the lack of ground fire, unless, of course, the armed group had received instructions to target only one specific helicopter. An allegation like that, without anything to back it up, would probably bring the curtain down on Will's effort to find out about missing prisoners of war. He held his silence.

"Fine," General Stoner said as he closed the folder. "In case they haven't told you . . . the crew did not survive. We're bringing their remains in this morning, and let me assure you, we'll look into every possible cause. In the meantime, I want you both to go back to Camp Smith."

For Will, that meant the end of his hope to uncover any tie-in between Pam's missing father and his own. "But shouldn't we check out the cave? It may contain the answer to—"

"It'll have to wait. Much as we'd all like to continue that inquiry, prudence dictates caution." His eyebrows rose. "After all, you're the one claiming hostile action in this incident."

The phone rang, and the detachment commander moved to answer it. A moment later he hung up. "The C-12 just landed."

"Good," the general said, then addressed Will and Gabbie. "You two gather your things, go to Bangkok. Major Chase will arrange tickets for you on a comfortable commercial flight back to Hawaii. Then I'd like a complete report, and if you need time off, you've got it." His gaze drifted to the window, and his tone softened. "Sometimes it takes a while before the mind accepts the reality of a harrowing experience and is able to recall what really happened. Don't be afraid to ask for help in that regard, either."

Will shifted uncomfortably in his chair at the subtle suggestion that maybe his mind was off in never-never land and that a shrink might be what he needed.

The general stood. "In the meantime, I have three families to notify and an investigation to conduct."

The session was over.

Will and Gabbie found their bags and headed for the C-12 turboprop.

"Actually," Will said, "I'll be glad to get out of here. Inside of seventy-two hours, I nearly wind up dead twice! I'm surprised no one finished us off last night."

Gabbie stopped, seemed to be trying to focus on what he just said. "Are you thinking your car accident in Hawaii and this helicopter mishap in Laos are connected?"

"Accident? Mishap? Connected? That engine didn't come unglued by itself."

"Frankly, I don't remember much of what happened. You're jumping to conclusions."

"Jumping? Try pole-vaulting. It has to do with the Polaroid I showed you, of my father."

Gabbie shook her head. "I'm sorry, I told you all I can about that."

"Oh, right, you and your buddy Bustamante . . . God's gift to national security!"

"Goddamn it, Major." Gabbie halted. She started to say more but stopped herself.

A Laotian worker helped load their baggage, while the two pilots, both new to Will and both in civilian clothes, handed out immigration and customs forms. They mentioned they would stop on the civilian side of Don Muang in Bangkok so Gabbie and Will could transit to a U.S.-bound flight.

As their plane taxied to the runway, Will noticed the Pacific Command's Boeing 707 sitting on the ramp. General Stoner had obviously used it to get here so quickly. Will wondered about that. Certainly that plane would also be used to bring home the remains of the helicopter crew in the next day or so. Will and Gabbie could have gone back with the casualties. Maybe it was his perceived paranoia reasserting itself, but Will sensed an underlying urgency in the way the whole post-crash period was going. Then again, maybe the general wanted to avoid a scene with flag-draped coffins and survivors traveling together. The general, Gabbie, all of them, could be right about the helicopter crash. Could it be just a matter of coincidence? But the loose brake lines back in Hawaii had been no coincidence.

The C-12 landed in Bangkok and headed for the civilian terminal. As Will and Gabbie carried their luggage inside the building, the pilots indicated they should proceed to the crew processing line with them.

The C-12 pilots flashed passes and were waved through along with Will and Gabbie. They proceeded down steps to the baggage and customs area. The two pilots led the way to a NOTHING TO DECLARE processing line that had a CLOSED sign in front of it. The sign was removed by a man wearing an inspector's uniform as the pilots approached. Will noticed two Thai military guards, armed with M-16s, standing behind the Thai customs agent. The pilots were waved through after handing over their customs form, but instead of being treated likewise, Will and Gabbie saw the Thai inspector put up his hand for them to stop.

"Wait, please."

Will and Gabbie halted. Will noticed that the crew was gone and one of the guards replaced the CLOSED sign. The inspector pointed at their baggage and smiled. The bags were placed on the counter. The nearest guard unshouldered his rifle and set the stock on the ground by his foot. The inspector put aside the customs forms and opened Will's B-4 bag. He began rooting around the bottom of each side pocket. Suddenly, he withdrew a plastic packet containing a powdery substance.

Will reacted. "Whoa now, that wasn't in there two hours ago." The agent opened his find and sniffed the contents. He turned to the guards and shouted in Thai what Will assumed were the words, "Arrest them!" because the closest guard began to raise his rifle.

"What!" Will looked at Gabbie, who stood with mouth open, obviously dumbfounded.

The guard swung his rifle up, leveling it at Will, then looked down as he fidgeted with his hand for the safety switch.

It may have been the aftereffects of the Thorazine or the accumulation of harrowing events, but something snapped inside Will. He lunged toward the guard, shoving the barrel of the gun away. The startled guard lost his grip on the weapon. Will spun clear, holding the rifle by the barrel. He flipped it around and pointed it at the other guard, who was still trying to bring his gun to bear.

"Hold it!" Will bluffed, not knowing whether the gun would fire even if he squeezed the trigger.

The other guard froze. Will watched the man's eyes, wide open, full of fear. If he raised his gun, Will intended to lower his weapon.

"Drop it." Will motioned with his gun toward the floor.

The guard let go of his weapon. It clattered to the ground. Will swung his barrel around at the customs agent. He dropped the white package. It spilled across the counter as the agent slowly raised his hands.

Gabbie backed away. "Are you crazy?"

"Crazy? No. Mad? You're damn straight." Will stepped to where the other rifle lay, bent low, removed the ammo clip and stuffed it in his pocket. "None of this lunacy is accidental, and in case you haven't noticed, taking you out, too, is part of the program."

"There's some mistake—"

Will pointed to the spilled powder. "No mistake. That stuff can get you the death penalty here." He turned to the inspector. "She's innocent. Consider it all my fault."

He started for the exit. "Stay here, Gabbie. I'm sure the embassy folks or General Stoner can get you released." He turned to the inspector. "Follow me, and I'll shoot."

Gabbie plucked their passports from the counter, stuck them in the back pocket of her khakis, then ran past Will, bursting through the door and down a short corridor that led outside. Will pressed after her. "What the hell are you doing?"

"Leading. You're not qualified to cross the fucking street on your own."

She took the rifle from him as they ran down a short enclosed hallway that led deeper into the terminal. When they reached the opening to the main concourse she removed the clip and stuffed it in her back pocket with the passports, then dropped the weapon.

"No running," she said. "We have to catch up with the crew, get to the embassy."

Will glanced behind. No one was following. They walked at a good pace into the crowded terminal reception area. As they made their way toward the exit doors, police cars roared to a stop outside.

"They've raised the alarm," Gabbie said.

Will saw a sign for the Amari Hotel near an elevator and stairway. "Quick, this way."

They took the steps and came out on the next level where they entered a highway overpass that connected to the airport hotel. Halfway across, an exit descended to the street below. Will saw a group of men loitering around a cluster of parked motorcycles.

"Let's go."

He led Gabbie down the steps. A thin man with a short stubby mustache sat on the nearest bike, smoking a cigarette.

A siren could be heard, its clamor increasing. Will approached the man on the cycle. "Can you take us to the American embassy?"

The driver made no effort to go. He removed his cigarette, then slid his tongue under his lip as though trying to dislodge a bit of bothersome tobacco. Finally he spoke. "Three hundred baht."

"Fine," Will said. "Let's go!"

The driver put out his hand. Will pulled a ten-dollar bill from his wallet. The driver took the ten and held it up to the light. "Okay!" Then he kick-started the machine as Gabbie jumped aboard and Will squeezed on behind her.

The motorcycle lurched away from the curb. Will held onto Gabbie. "Déjà vu," he muttered without the slightest hint of humor.

A police car, its siren blaring, appeared behind them as the motorcycle curved around a corner and began to wend its way past jammed vehicles on the side street. Will's thigh smacked a car fender, then shoved against Gabbie, nudging the ammo clip from her pocket. As it came free, Will brought his hand back in reflex to snatch it. The clip tumbled away and the passports came free with it, all of it scattering onto the pavement.

"Hold it!" Will yelled.

Gabbie and the driver whipped their heads around to see what was going on. The clip spun along the asphalt, rounds spilling out, and the passports flipped through the air as the police car came in sight.

"Forget it!" Gabbie shouted. "Go!"

The motorcycle driver got the message. The cigarette that had been dangling precariously from his lips was flicked away, and he began to slalom through bumper-to-bumper traffic onto a highway. The sound of the siren fell away, but Will knew that the police could be radioing ahead for other units to pick up the chase.

Will had an acute feeling that maybe he had made the wrong choice back at the airport. The police were in pursuit, and this was rapidly becoming a nightmare of the real variety. If caught, he knew without a doubt that whatever he told them now, it would not be believed. Then there was the matter of Gabbie and what they might do to her. The "death penalty" might be carried out before the arrest.

Ten minutes later, the motorcycle driver left the highway and swung down a narrower street, a Thai *soi* that was barely able to accommodate one lane of traffic. Vendors lined the sidewalk. Pedestrians shuffled along, shouldering teak yokes from which hung baskets full of vegetables, the whole arrangement bouncing in rhythm as they walked.

The cycle driver leaned left, then right, weaving between the people and carts and onto another main road. The motorcycle negotiated between the slow-moving cars, then zipped down another cramped *soi.* Will rubbernecked, looking for signs of the police. Nothing. After thirty-five minutes of this the driver turned onto a divided avenue and came to a stop. He pointed at the other side of the street, where a long, high wall ran the length of the block.

"Embassy," the driver said. Clenching the filter of a fresh cigarette in his teeth, he grinned and patted his motorcycle.

A white, nearly windowless building peeked above the wall. Midway down the block, the wall was interrupted by a steel-gated driveway and a pedestrian entrance, both of which were blocked by three Thai police vehicles.

The motorcycle driver pointed. "No good."

Will checked the scene. "There's no way to get inside."

Gabbie nudged the driver. "Get us out of here!"

The driver smiled. "Three hundred baht." The hand came out.

So did another of Will's tens. "Go!"

The motorcycle zoomed off, but two blocks later the driver pulled to the side of the road. He parked the machine and indicated for Will and Gabbie to follow him inside a small, open-air restaurant.

Two chicken carcasses hung behind a glass enclosure at the entrance. Steam rose from a large cauldron filled with a heavy broth, set above a charcoal stove. The place reeked of garlic and was crowded with Thais, most of them bent over bowls of noodles or rice. Businessmen with Mekong Whiskey faces, Singha Beer faces engaged in rapid, high-spirited conversation while sipping from tall glasses filled above the brim with ice. The locals took little note of the trio that made its way toward a pigeonhole in the rear, where a flimsy table and four metal chairs sat vacant.

"Dangerous now," the motorcycle driver whispered. "They look for us." He motioned for them to sit. "My name Sunchai. We eat now. Go later when no more police."

Sunchai ordered fried rice. They ate, Will and Gabbie keeping a wary eye out for the police as they picked at their food. After a half hour, Sunchai left, indicating he would return soon. Will had held back telling Gabbie all that he knew, partly because he had not trusted her. Right or wrong, Will decided that since Gabbie had become a target, too, she was not a knowing partner in any cover-up. He took the opportunity to tell her the details of his suspicions, explaining first about the tampering with the brake lines on his Thunderbird. She listened without comment. He sensed she was rationalizing away every word he said, but when he mentioned the death of Pam Robbins, her eyes held his for a moment.

"I spoke to her," she said, "about some material at JTF."

"What material?"

Gabbie hesitated. "I'll lose my clearance if I discuss it."

"The people who have sworn you to secrecy have been trying to kill you. Keeping quiet about this only serves their purpose."

"No, I can't go through it . . ." Gabbie stopped in mid-sentence, her eyes flitting about the room.

Will leaned forward. ". . . Again?"

Gabbie met Will's gaze head-on, but said nothing.

"Getting booted out of your job . . . *again?*" Will turned away, punching his fist into his other open hand. Then he faced her. "Look, I know about Fort Huachuca. There, you were only threatened with death, and you went after those responsible. Here, you've nearly been killed twice, and you're blowing it off! What's with you?"

"You son of a bitch!" She stood, as though to leave, then seemed to realize she had no place to go. She spent a long time glaring at him until, finally, her shoulders sagged a bit. "I loved that job. I love what I do *now,* too." She sat, then spoke in a low, controlled voice. "What do you want to know?"

"Everything."

"Everything?" She sucked in a long, deep breath, then began. "The first incident involved an out-of-channel rush job, a top-secret, compartmented request direct from the CIA. They wanted to know if we could match one of our MIAs to a man in a photo. That was unusual in itself. When I took the image to the records section for an aging composite, the package got pulled. I never heard another thing about it until Pam Robbins called me, all bent out of shape. She claimed it came back altered, along with a note stating that the picture was a fake. She had no way to prove that JTF, or the CIA, or whoever, had modified her photo to make it appear bogus. She told me she had another photo, a Polaroid, that she'd be sending, but this time she was taking pains to make sure it didn't get altered. I never got it, though."

"Is that why you hesitated, then offered to help when I showed you the copy of the Polaroid?"

"Yes. You don't run into those much anymore, so I wondered if that was the one Pam had mentioned."

"Finally, I get some information that tracks," Will said, then spent a few moments contemplating what to do next. "If I could convince President-elect Dalton to look into these incidents, he could order a full investigation. I see no way to get through to him this week, though. But once he's in office—"

"You're right," Gabbie said, "and if this is a cover-up, it will take more than our say-so to bring it out in the open."

"Did any documentation come with the Robbins photo?"

"Yes," Gabbie said, "the photo of the two men had been turned in at the embassy in Vientiane."

"Laos," Will said, "is a dead end for now."

"I found something interesting in the Polaroid you gave me, something I didn't mention."

"And that is?"

"Do you still have the photo?"

From his wallet, Will produced his now tattered version.

"See the bushes in the background? I tried an enhancement process on the vegetation. From what I could determine, there are no leaves on the bushes."

Will stared at the picture, not yet convinced. "Meaning?"

"Wintertime. They don't really have a winter in the jungles of Laos or Vietnam."

"But they've got plenty of it in Russia," Will added.

"Russia?"

"Pam Robbins got this from someone who would be put in danger if the source were known. She was extra careful about sending a gift, a copy of a guitar maker's book to a Moscow address." Will went on to explain about the book and the music store. "She seemed to be delighted with my Russian-language background when she reviewed my past. Could she have thought Russia, where they have real winters, holds the answer?"

"That's a pretty long shot, Will. They have winters all over the globe."

"Maybe so, but Russia is my guess for where people need to start looking." Will thought: *And if things were different I'd know just who to ask for a lift.*

Sunchai returned again. He had checked the embassy, but the place was still cordoned off.

Gabbie turned to Will. "Any ideas?"

Will thought for a moment. "There had been a time when Tom Boyd and I had been closer than blood kin. We knew each other's ideas before we even thought them. When I flew on his wing, it was as if we were just one man flying two planes. I guess I'd better take a shot at resurrecting an old friendship." Will tapped the driver on the shoulder. "You know the Intercontinental Hotel?"

Sunchai shrugged.

"Right," Will said as he held up three fingers.

The Thai laughed and moments later off they went down the divided, tree-lined avenue. At the intersection Sunchai turned right and soon roared to a stop at the top of the drive that curved in front of a sprawling hotel. Will got off the motorcycle. He reached for his wallet.

Sunchai grinned. Then he put his hand up in a stop motion. "Free," he said.

"Ha!" Will said. "I'm starting to like this guy."

Will and Gabbie were ushered through a lavish foyer that opened to a tropical garden. The registration desk was to the left. A female clerk, wearing a traditional Thai silk dress, looked up and smiled as Will approached the check-in counter.

"Do you have a Thomas Boyd staying here?"

The woman checked the registry and nodded. "He is a guest here. Would you like me to call his room?"

"Yes," Gabbie said, sliding in front of Will. "Tell him a Dr. DeJean and her friend, Mr. Cadence, are here to see him and would like to come up."

The clerk made the call. When Boyd gave his okay, she gave Gabbie the room number. They took the elevator and a minute later stood outside Boyd's room. Will knocked.

Boyd cracked open the door. He stared with a blank expression past the chain lock at Will. Finally he said, "You lost?"

"No. We're in a hell of a jam."

"Oh?" Boyd then noticed Gabbie. His eyes stayed fixed on her, but he did not move to unlock the door.

Gabbie smiled. "Could we come in?"

"Please do," Boyd said. The door closed and Will heard the chain slide free. "Come right on in." Boyd reopened the door and stood holding it open as Will and Gabbie entered.

"Look," Will said, "I don't like being here any more than you like having us, but we need help. The Thai police are after us. We've been framed."

"You mean like being blamed for something somebody else did?" Boyd's smile was heavy with irony as he turned to Gabbie. "I don't suppose he told you about our little midair collision?"

"He told me you caught the blame for his mistake," Gabbie said. "Does that about cover it?"

"Not quite. Your buddy here didn't see it as his mistake, so he called in a heavy, got himself off the hook at my expense."

Will kept silent.

"Go ahead. Deny you had the good old senator put the squeeze on," Boyd said. He folded his arms across his chest, then returned his gaze to Gabbie. "He figured I wouldn't find out that the senator phoned the board president, but I did."

"I didn't ask the senator to help me."

"Oh, right. You'd best stop the bullshit before I even the score right here in front of your girlfriend."

"Gabbie's my boss."

"So was I, and you sure fucked me!"

Will grabbed Boyd's collar.

Gabbie shoved her way between them. "Knock it off!"

Boyd stood his ground, eyes glittering with sustained anger.

Gabbie turned on Will. "Now!"

Will let go of Boyd's collar. "You want the truth?" Will glowered at Boyd but got no answer. "Fine. I'd found out from the board secretary that they were going to recommend taking your wings away. I knew I couldn't change the accident verdict, but I could do something about the sentence. I called the senator and asked him to intervene. That's where your assignment to fly transports came from." Will tapped his leg. "The board didn't have to deal with me on the flying issue."

Boyd fixed his eyes on Will as if trying to decide whether to believe him or not.

"If you find that hard to swallow," Will continued, "you can ask the next president once we're out of here. I'll arrange that, too."

"If you're so tight with the prez-to-be, why aren't you calling him for help?"

"I can't. It's a little complicated . . . about my father, but until I can prove what really happened to him in Vietnam, I can't involve Dalton. My inquiries have some folks really upset."

Boyd could not conceal a little smirk. "What? The Vietnamese and I have something in common."

"I'm talking about our side."

Boyd rolled his eyes.

"He's telling the truth," Gabbie chimed in.

"And now you're here to put me in charge of saving his ass?"

"And mine."

"Humph. Willy boy has a habit of dorking up people's lives, doesn't he?"

"The way I see it, he was your friend and still is, so you need to shelve your personal problems." Her resolve seemed to catch Boyd by surprise. He made no move to speak.

"Good," she said, "because right now we need your help getting out of the country before the Thais arrest us."

Boyd backed toward the desk. "Why are they after you?"

"Drug trafficking," Will said.

"Whoa, I want no part of this."

"Listen, somebody tried to kill us in Laos! Our helicopter got shot down. When we didn't buy the farm, they stuck drugs in our bags on the C-12 we flew into here."

Boyd gaped at Will. "I heard about a chopper going down. You were in that thing?"

"We both were," Gabbie said.

Boyd dropped his arms to his side. "Okay, I hear you." He went and unlocked a briefcase that was lying on the bed. A folder lay on top. He opened it and checked a schedule. "In two days there's a C-130 to the Philippines. You can try for duty-passenger seats on it."

"No good," Gabbie said, "unless it continues on to the States."

Boyd shook his head no. His hand moved down the schedule, stopping partway. He studied the schedule another few seconds.

Will picked up on Boyd's hesitation, but Will remembered the C-141 mission routing he had seen while waiting for his ticket in Hawaii, plus Boyd's comment days before about going to Delhi and Moscow. "What else?"

"The courier mission, tonight. It stops in Delhi, then Moscow for a crew change, and on to Washington."

Will caught a look from Gabbie. In that split second, a sense of foreboding was communicated. He knew from her expression that she suspected he might try to solve the riddle of the MIAs once he was on Russian soil. Will felt as though the same force he had sensed upon leaving Hawaii was propelling him onward, inexorably toward resolving the cover-up allegations. Well, if fate was dealing these cards, he was ready to ante up. And if sometimes fate needed a little shove, that was okay, too. "We go tonight, but how do we get aboard?"

"You get a little help."

"From who?"

Boyd smiled. "It's *my* mission." He put his hand out. "I'll need your passports so I can work the manifest."

"We lost our passports," Gabbie said.

"Time out! I can't get you past immigration. Go to the embassy and get temporary ones."

"We can't," Will said. "The Thai police are checking everyone who tries to enter."

"All bets are off," Boyd said.

"No they're not," Gabbie said. She tapped her side where her money belt rested. "Just tell us how much time we have until the plane leaves."

Sunchai was standing beside his motorcycle as Will and Gabbie exited the hotel. Will approached and used both hands in an open-close manner. "Passport, you know passport?"

"Ah," Sunchai said. "Passport . . . go States?"

"Right, except we have no passports."

"No have?" Sunchai stuck his hand out for another payoff.

Fifteen minutes later they were posing for the camera in a small photo-processing shop. Then it was back on the motorcycle and a ride that ended under an overpass beside a row of plywood shanties. Sunchai led them toward one of the huts. Electric power lines dangled precariously above their heads and were connected to each hovel. Inside a shanty, a Thai boy, who Will guessed was no more than fifteen years old, was watching a kickboxing match on television. Sunchai spoke with the boy, who then produced two stacks of passports from a carton. The boy looked at Will first, then Gabbie. He flipped through the stacks, removed one passport from each, and went to sit at a table near the wall that had papers, bottles, pens, and pencils lumped together in a pile. The boy used what smelled like an alcohol solution to peel the photograph from the first passport. Will's photo was laid against that picture, and the boy used scissors to make Will's photo the proper size. Will's image was laid facedown on a flat piece of rubber; the real passport photo was inverted on top. The boy took a ballpoint pen and used it to press a tracing onto Will's snapshot of the embossed embassy seal that was indented on the genuine photo. When he was through, he glued Will's altered print to the passport. Thirty minutes later and after payment of two hundred dollars by Gabbie, the passports were handed over. Will checked his. It looked genuine. The alteration was somewhat crude, but an inspector in a hurry might not spot the forgery.

"I'm Robert Craig," Will said to Gabbie. "And you?"

"Carol Banister." She looked up from the passport. "Great, not only am I nearly broke, I've gained ten pounds and two years."

"I think I've aged that much in the last two days, but mine has me a year younger."

"Surely these have been reported lost or stolen."

"Probably," Will said. "But they haven't expired. We might be able to get out if the Thais don't check crew members too closely. Back home is where it will get interesting."

"Who cares once we're back in the States?"

"Right, boss."

The embassy van, driven by the same Thai who had taken them to the C-12 two days ago, pulled up outside the military terminal at Don Muang Airport. Boyd got out and went to the rear of the van while the driver unloaded four duffel-like mail sacks onto a forklift. Then he and Boyd followed the forklift through the freight-access gate.

In the distance, a C-141 transport sat on the ramp, its rear cargo door open.

Will and Gabbie, wearing flight suits like the ones the crew wore, remained inside the van, watching for any sign of the drug-bust agent or the guards they disarmed. Twenty minutes later Boyd returned with the driver and got in the van. Boyd handed over copies of the crew manifest. "It's set. Show these as you go through and act bored. The manifest serves as your visa. Let's hope the shift at the immigration counter on the military side hasn't gotten the word on you two."

Gabbie took a copy of the manifest. "Thanks."

Boyd handed another set to Will. "The manifest was made up by Sergeant Ritter, our loadmaster, old buddy. Try not to foul up another career. If you get caught, you're to say you got the forms from me. As far as my part in this, you get the chance to rip me another good one." Boyd flashed a grin.

"I appreciate this, Tom. Look, I—"

"Let's just say I'm doing it," Boyd nodded toward Gabbie, "for her and leave it at that." Boyd held Will's stare. "One more thing. You don't have name tags. I hope these inspectors don't notice. If they do, think of something believable."

The driver looked over his shoulder at Will and Gabbie.

Boyd slapped his hands together. "All set, crew?"

"Let's do it," Will said.

Boyd led the way across the street and into the terminal. As Will slipped through the door, he glanced back in time to see the van driver pull away, a cell phone at his ear.

Boyd went first through the immigration line, flashed his passport, and showed his copy of the manifest to the inspector, a frail-looking Thai. The man ushered Boyd past with a bored flip of the hand, then took a big smile from Gabbie. He barely glanced at their passports as, eyes still on Gabbie, he waved them both through.

Once inside the plane, Boyd led Will and Gabbie to the cockpit. The copilot and the loadmaster gave them wary looks. Boyd motioned for Will and Gabbie to take the jump seats behind the flight deck. Then Boyd took the pilot seat and began rattling off checklist items. After the plane was ready, Boyd received word from the ground crew that passenger loading was being delayed. No reason was given. Boyd shrugged as Sergeant Ritter headed out onto the ramp.

A half hour later, Will leaned toward the open crew door, watching, as a man, sweating heavily and in need of a shave, hurried into the cabin, carrying his suitcase with him.

At that point, Sergeant Ritter poked his head in and asked for the passenger manifest. The flight engineer, Sergeant Carla Jefferson, passed it to Will who handed it over. A minute later it came back. Will scanned it as he gave it to Carla. A new name, James R. Connors, was penned in at the bottom. The form showed that he was going all the way to Washington.

Will leaned toward Gabbie. "They've added someone at the last minute."

"So?"

"Our van driver made a call as he drove away. Then we get delayed until this guy shows up in a sweat, five o'clock shadow on his face, no time to check his bag. I don't think he had this trip on his schedule an hour ago."

"You really are getting paranoid."

"That I am."

Forty minutes later, the plane reached altitude and began cruising west of Rangoon. Boyd turned control of the plane over to copilot Nelson, then took his headset off. He stepped around the center console, pulled a *Stars and Stripes* newspaper from his lower flight suit pocket, and moved onto the flight deck. He glanced at the front page before tucking the paper under his arm, then swept his other hand through the air, indicating the airplane to Will and Gabbie. "These come in handy when you need one, huh?"

"You'll get no complaints from me," Gabbie said, "but I won't feel totally cozy until it gets us back to the States."

"With a little luck, you'll be in D.C. in eighteen hours. To tell you the truth, I wish I was going with you." Boyd held up the newspaper. The headline read, PRESIDENT-ELECT EAGER TO TAKE HELM. Below the bold letters was a picture of Dalton speaking at a preinaugural news conference. He held up both hands with seven fingers extended, indicating the number of days before he would become president. "I get to wait on a specially equipped C-141 that's being sent to haul a crowd of Russian VIPs to the inauguration."

Will looked at the newspaper, then saw something else. To the right, in a sidebar, was a picture of General Bradley Stoner. "Could I see that?" Will reached for the paper then read, Ex-POW To Get Third Star—Gen. Stoner Next Deputy, Air Combat Command.

Will showed it to Gabbie. "Stoner was a former POW?"

"He doesn't advertise it," Gabbie said. "His aide told me the general didn't want to be accused of using it to advance his career. Around JTF, the general's past is a nonsubject."

"Right, no personal agendas." Will snorted, then read further. Stoner had been an electronic warfare officer (EWO) on an RB-66, an aircraft that was used to jam Soviet-made radars. Stoner's plane was shot down in 1966 by a SAM missile. Will remembered his conversation with Russ Whitten on the tennis court at Hickam Air Force Base. Whitten had memorized the names of all the POWs, yet had failed to mention Stoner's name when he recounted the number of EWOs who had been released at the end of the war. Stoner flew as an EWO in RB-66s, so it was possible Whitten had not included him in the count because he was not part of an F-105 Wild Weasel crew, like the others. Still, it was an intriguing omission. Will read on, then pointed at the last paragraph. "Says here that his new assignment puts him in the direct chain-of-command of the U.S. nuclear arsenal."

Boyd shook his head. "Hope he doesn't carry a grudge against those former Commies we're about to overfly."

Gabbie and Will exchanged curious glances.

23

Back at the JTF compound in Vientiane, a heavy-eyed General Stoner was on the phone in the detachment commander's office. The local time was 5:30 A.M. and the general was visibly upset, but not by the early hour. Colonel Bustamante was on the line.

In the outer room, Major Byron Chase was busy cleaning up. A promotion banner showing three stars hung across a wall and read: CONGRATS, CHIEF! Spent champagne bottles sat on a table beside the remnants of a two-layer cake.

General Stoner got up from the desk to close the door for privacy. Then he went back to the phone. "You're saying it was in the embassy driver's report? . . . The mission includes two stops . . . . We *can't* allow foreign security to board in Delhi! The plane has diplomatic immunity . . . . What the hell's going on with those two. They had no time to find drugs here in Vientiane." Stoner hung up, then buzzed in Major Chase.

"Get the flight crew out of bed. I need to get back to Hawaii."

"Yes, sir," Chase said, then left.

After the door closed, General Stoner sat alone, deep in thought.

The C-141 crossed the Bay of Bengal and continued above the vast expanse of India and on to the capital. Both Will and Gabbie stayed aboard in New Delhi while the plane was refueled and cargo was transferred. Will watched the loadmaster heap the diplomatic pouches from the plane onto a forklift. The airman then accompanied the mail as it disappeared into the customs area, returning minutes later with outgoing pouches. Will also noted that four armed men stood guard near the plane whereas no security personnel were anywhere around a U.S. C-130 cargo plane nearby where maintenance men were replacing an engine. Will assumed the guards were present to deter terrorist threats against U.S. interests.

It was still dark when Boyd and his crew returned an hour later to continue on to Moscow. Once safely out of India, Will and Gabbie took to the double-deck bunks at the rear of the flight deck. The C-141 winged its way northwest at forty-one thousand feet over Afghanistan. Will, asleep in the lower bunk, began tossing and turning, deep into an all-too-familiar nightmare.

Once again, Will felt himself losing his grip on the garage rafters. He awoke, gasping, one eye open, terror gripping his face.

"What is it, Will?" Gabbie rolled off her bunk and knelt beside him. "You're shaking!"

"Oh, God, not now," Will moaned. He put his hand out, reaching up for the edge of the top bunk. Bolts of red and yellow light danced in his head. His quivering hand wrapped around the frame of the bunk as he tried to sit up.

Gabbie stepped back. "What's wrong?"

"Migraine," he stammered.

His temple started throbbing as heartbeats began hammering inside his skull. He was out of the bunk now, on one knee, holding the numb side of his head in one hand. Only his left eye was open. He grabbed Gabbie's arm. "Water, aspirin, anything, please."

Carla had heard the commotion. She moved from her station and pulled a canvas medical pack from a cabinet. "Hang on," she said. "We've got some Tylenol." She got out two pills, tossed them into a paper cup, then filled another with water.

Will reached for the first cup, fingers fumbling as he wrapped his hand around it. He closed his eyes and swallowed the pills, next drank the water. Inside his brain, Technicolor flashes rippled like lightning. Each heartbeat brought a hammerlike jolt of searing pain. He fell back against the cot frame and sank to both knees. Then he started breathing deeply and slowly as he clamped both arms around his waist and rocked back and forth, fighting off the nausea.

By now the whole crew was aware of his problem. Boyd glanced from his seat as Will finally struggled to his feet and sat on the edge of the bunk. Will opened both eyes and saw Boyd staring, so he tried to smile, but his lip contorted. The right side of his face was still tingling.

Boyd watched for a moment as Will attempted to get himself under control. "You okay?"

Will nodded. "Give me a minute." He took a few more breaths to gather himself, then spoke. "Whew, when I get this dream, bam, I wake up to a thundering migraine." He looked at Carla. "Sorry to be such a bother."

"No problem, sir." Carla held up the first-aid kit before putting it away. "That's why we carry these."

Gabbie sat next to Will on the bunk. She leaned close so the others could not hear. "What's this all about, Will?"

"It's a dream, touching on something that really happened." Will rubbed his temple. "The morning my father left for the war, I hid in the garage rafters. Almost four years old and I thought hiding would keep him from leaving. After he drove off, I fell. Landed on my head. Was out cold for half a day. Never got to tell my father how sorry I was for doing that."

Gabbie touched his arm. "Maybe it's time to let it pass."

"Wish I could." Will put his hand over hers. "Finding out what really happened to him may be the cure, and I can't help but feel that Moscow holds the answer."

"No way are you getting off in Russia."

"Look, everything that's happening is tied together. All I want to do is talk to whoever came up with that photo. The only way I can do that is by finding out who gets mail at box four-two-two in the U.S. embassy in Moscow."

"If you're right about Moscow, whoever is trying to stop you will be waiting there!"

"I'll work something out."

"Not without my okay." From the look he gave her, she added, "I'm still in charge, remember?"

Halfway over Afghanistan headed toward the Russian border, Will looked out the cockpit windscreen as the sun rose in the east. Shadows marched across the reddish-brown crags of the Hindu Kush Range. Snow capped the mountains and long white tentacles reached deep into valleys where rust-brown swatches of plowed earth stood out like wine stains on a crumpled carpet. As the snow cover grew more dense to the northwest, Will soon began to feel uncertain about where he was. The peaks resembled whitecaps as far as the eye could see. Will felt a shiver, a sense of secrets held in the land beyond.

Something powerful was drawing him ever closer to the answers he sought. He listened to the slipstream sweeping across the Plexiglas panels of the cockpit. A memory stirred. He sensed a voice whispering as the wind had on that cold day in Colorado at the cemetery when all this had started. He looked in the distance. His lips parted. A word hissed from his mouth.

Russia.

He had studied the history and the language and been mesmerized by the land of the czars, cossacks, and rugged peasants, all imbued with a fierce love of country. They had beaten back the likes of Napoleon and Hitler.

As the miles slid beneath the nose of the plane and the sun rose higher, the land grew brighter, beautiful in a haunting, perilous way. Then a narrow band of high cirrus, icy-white clouds, stalked across the sky and blurred the sun. Below, the mountains softened into shadowy gray masses, while ahead the terrain became flatter, monotonous, seemingly infinite. Winter had curled her talons into the huts and farmhouses that dotted the landscape alongside mud-brown threads of nearly obscure roads and lanes.

Will went over again what Gabbie had said. She was right about Moscow. Whoever was after them might be waiting there, just as it seemed they were in New Delhi. Then there was the presence of the late-arriving passenger out of Bangkok. Was he connected to the downing of the helicopter and the planting of drugs in their luggage? If Will stayed onboard, would he be grabbed in Washington by the same element that had tried to silence him in Asia? If he got off in Moscow, would they try to take him there?

As the C-141 crossed over the Aral Sea, Will reached forward and tapped Boyd on the shoulder.

PART III

24

On a gray blustery afternoon, the C-141 made a smooth landing at Moscow's Sheremetyevo II Airport. The plane cleared the runway and rolled down a taxiway that had early-winter snow piled alongside in ragged drifts. To Will's surprise, the amount of snow was less than he had imagined. The airport sat on a windblown plain with great patches of bare brown earth wherever the surface showed the slightest vertical development.

Their transport eased around an Ilyushin IL-76 cargo plane. The design for it was copied from the C-141 Will was now in. At the Air Force Academy, he had learned how the Russians went about cloning foreign products. "In Russia," his teacher had said, "they think *bigger* is *best* and that *better* is the enemy of *good enough.*" To the Russian mind, the biggest of anything is regarded as the ultimate triumph. Quality is secondary. Inside the aircraft, the designers had not bothered to install many of the backup systems that were integral to the C-141. They would put in a few safety features, until management declared, "*Poidyot.*" Good enough.

Boyd brought the aircraft to a stop in front of a new but Spartan-looking terminal.

As the last of the passengers departed, refueling began. Boyd turned to Will and Gabbie. "Show time, folks."

Will led Gabbie down the cockpit ladder, and the two of them disappeared aft, toward the still-closed cargo ramp.

Inside the terminal, the late-arriving C-141 passenger, no longer in a sweat, followed the other travelers into the transient lounge, a glass-enclosed area with a view of the tarmac. The passenger went to a window to keep an eye on the C-141 and its crew. There he exchanged glances with CIA agent Phil Garcia who had flown commercial, nonstop from Bangkok and who was waiting nearby to see if Will or Gabbie got off. As the two men watched, Boyd and his crew, minus the loadmaster and spotter, emerged from the plane with their baggage. They headed inside the terminal to an adjacent arrival area.

Two Russians dressed in leather coats and looking exactly like the Foreign Intelligence Service agents that they were, monitored the immigration proceedings. They directed their attention to an official at the crew station where Boyd, his copilot Nelson, and Carla, the flight engineer, were being processed. After the trio was again waved through, the FIS agents approached. The taller man's coat bulged forward at the waist, unable to fully cover the hard-drinker's belly beneath. He flashed a badge while the other agent, a wiry-looking man with bad teeth, hung back.

"Documents, please," the tall one said.

Nelson put down his B-4 bag, then started to hand over the crew manifest sheet when Boyd put out his hand. "Hold it." Boyd snatched the page. "What's this all about?"

The tall one straightened, his eyes full of dare. "A routine check, heightened security, yes?"

"No." Boyd pulled out his passport. "This you can check." He pointed to the lettering on the cover. "Diplomatic immunity."

"What about the other members of your crew?"

"My loadmaster and spotter will be following shortly."

"Any more?"

"No." Boyd hesitated, wondering if they knew about Will and Gabbie, then continued. "None getting off."

The tall agent looked out the window at the plane. The cargo ramp had been lowered and a forklift approached. "Good," he said, without looking at Boyd. "You may go now."

"*Da svedahnya,*" Boyd said, then stuffed his passport in his pocket as he walked off shaking his head.

The crew left the terminal and went to an embassy van parked near the freight entrance. All but the front windshield were tinted over, a counterterrorism requirement that made it difficult to see inside. The driver, a Russian, helped load the bags. A fourth rear bench had been removed to provide cargo space and a second luggage tier had been installed. The driver stowed bags on the upper cargo deck before closing the rear hatch. Boyd got in the van and moved to the rearmost seat with the copilot. Carla went around and got in the front passenger seat. No one sat in the middle seat.

On the tarmac, four Russian militiamen in gray overcoats and fur hats were positioned at the front and rear of the plane. A wooden pallet with four canvas duffel bags marked DIPLOMATIC, were loaded from the C-141 onto the steel fingers of a forklift. Then the loadmaster and spotter walked beside the Russian lift-operator as he drove to the cargo inspection area.

Inside the terminal, the two FIS men gazed at the plane like a pair of caged gorillas looking at the outside world. Garcia and his recently arrived CIA compatriot watched them and the unloading operation from nearby.

A few minutes later, the loadmaster and spotter reappeared, walking alongside the forklift as it came out of the inspection depot and exited the ramp. Once outside, the van driver saw the pallet coming and reopened the hatch. The whole load, pallet and all, was eased onto the lower cargo tier in the van. The driver shut the hatch as soon as the forklift was clear. Meanwhile, the loadmaster and spotter boarded and sat in the middle seat.

The van pulled away from the terminal and soon was on the main thoroughfare into the city. The road, a four-lane divided highway, soon broadened to six lanes, then ten lanes.

"Just like in America," the driver announced. "Good road, but only in Moscow." Traffic was heavy and moved at breakneck speed. "We have kick-ass mayor. Fix a lot of problems. The rest of my country not so good."

While Carla kept up the conversation with the driver, the loadmaster passed keys to Boyd, who reached behind and unlocked two of the bags.

Will's head popped into view. He wriggled out, stretched his right leg, then helped Gabbie exit from the other bag. They stayed low, opening the rest of the bags, then shifted some of their contents into the empty ones before replacing the locks.

Boyd glanced to see that both Will and Gabbie were ready. He nudged the copilot who eased forward, around the middle seat, and slid next to the loadmaster.

Boyd looked behind again at Will and Gabbie and whispered. "Crawl around to my row."

Gabbie went first and wriggled up beside Boyd. Will followed and settled next to Gabbie.

Will looked outside. A billboard announced the newest BMW. Then one appeared advertising Versace fashions. He sensed a sad immortality in the model's eyes as she looked on in style as darkness descended on the landscape.

The van moved through a flat area with birches and pines, small trees, mostly in stands. A black sedan flashed by. The driver pointed at it. "Mercedes. Used to be Russian Volgas carry Party big shots. They upgrade to Mercedes, but the ones in fancy cars are Mafia now. *New Russians,* same people."

Will and Gabbie stared at an outline of prefab apartment houses. The driver pointed again. "Khrushchev neighborhoods, built by fat Nikita." At an intersection that led to the apartments, a militia member directed traffic with a light baton. A sidewalk with a postearthquake look led to the first row of buildings. A few people made their way along the rippled, icy pavement. Although the driver seemed to paint a discouraging portrait of the city, Will felt it looked much like New York in winter except for the odd lettering on the billboards.

On the side of the road, someone was leaning inside the open hood of a Russian Lada, trying to repair it. Inside the vehicle, a woman hurled invective and shook her fist.

A half mile later, a huge masonry ediface loomed out of the descending darkness. "One of Stalin's buildings," the driven said. "That one is the Hotel Ukraine. There are seven alike, so they are called the Seven Sisters." Beneath the hotel, shadowy figures bent against the wind. Traffic was heavier now.

As they rolled onto a bridge that crossed the Moskva River, the driver bobbed his chin at a Marxist ice-cream cake of a building. "Our White House," he said. "Seat of Russian parliament." He pointed to a place on the street. "Over there Boris Yeltsin climbed on top big tank to roar defiance during the coup attempt."

The van crossed over and turned left. Piled snow by the curb was covered with soot, but the street, though wet, was clear. Two blocks later, the driver turned into the south gate of the U.S. embassy.

"Let them see you have passport," the driver said.

A Russian militiaman stepped outside a dim kiosk that stood beside the entrance. He flicked on his flashlight and shone the beam inside the van. Another security guard began checking for bombs under the vehicle, using a mirror on a pole.

Everyone got out of the vehicle and went inside the security section. The crew showed their diplomatic passports. Will and Gabbie produced their forged tourist ones.

Outside, the gate opened as the guard waved the van through. Once they were issued passes, Boyd led them past a cafeteria to the post office. A long bank of postal boxes extended from the service window across the length of a wall. Several people stood in line waiting for service. Will and Gabbie moved to the area of the boxes looking for number 422, but all the boxes were marked with a letter and four numbers. Then Gabbie noticed the clock—five minutes until closing.

Will got in line. At his turn, he approached the clerk. "Excuse me, but I'm trying to locate the owner of a postal box here in Moscow."

The civilian clerk, a pale woman in her thirties, looked over a pair of reading glasses at Will. She glanced at his flight suit, then his face. "Are you part of the mission here?" From her lack of accent, Will asumed she was an American.

"No, we just got in, and while here I had hoped to locate someone whom I believe *is* part of the mission."

The woman hesitated. "I'm not sure I follow—"

"A gift was sent by a friend of mine to a buddy working here. My friend wanted me to find out if it arrived. I lost the note with the recipient's name on it but do recall it was sent to box number four-two-two."

"Four-two-two is not a letter box, it's a mail drop, a general-delivery number for an off-station unit."

The woman checked a wall list. "Used to be for one of the Peace Corps postings in the Ukraine. They have their own embassy postal service in Kiev now, but we forward them any of their mail since a lot still comes here." She glanced at the list again. "Four-two-two is for the Peace Corps English Language Center, Room 109, Municipal Ministry, Kharkov."

"Kharkov, you say? And their mail is delivered from here?"

"Once a week through Kiev, along with the diplomatic stuff that goes there from here. Last batch had to go yesterday because their winter festival starts tomorrow and most of the embassy shuts down. Three days worth."

"How long a drive is it to Kharkov?"

The clerk gave him a glance, then answered. "About ten hours this time of year."

"Do you have a phone number for that language center?"

"No, only for the embassy post office and it's closed by now."

"Right." Will shook his head and smiled wanly. "Thanks."

They went outside and started walking toward the van. "There's still time to get you back to the airport and on the C-141," Boyd said as he walked beside Gabbie and Will. "Ain't much point hanging around here unless you want to stay with us at the Rossiya Hotel and do some sightseeing."

Will was in no hurry to leave. He had tried to get Gabbie to stay aboard the C-141, but she would have none of that. To get her okay to slip into Moscow, he had agreed to simply talk to whomever had gotten Pam's book. He still felt that way, but didn't want to unnerve Gabbie into thinking he intended to pursue the issue beyond that if new information warranted it. "Seems like we have little choice. We'll stay."

Gabbie homed in on Boyd. "I'm curious. Why are you taking such risks?"

"I might ask you the same thing." Boyd paused, but when Gabbie did not offer to respond, he answered, "After what a bunch of bureaucrats did to me, I love every chance I get to pay 'em back." Boyd hesitated a moment, then looked over at Will. "Maybe I was wrong about some things, too." He saw the driver returning. "If you're ready, so's our chauffeur."

The driver gave Will and Gabbie a quizzical look, shook his head, then hopped in the front seat. He smiled as his passengers boarded. "There are interesting places to see on the way."

The van moved off, turned several corners, and drifted past Number 2, Lubyanka Street, former home of the KGB. Will gave it a long look, wondering what appalling secrets it held.

They headed for Red Square in the center of Moscow. Just off the square, on Tverskaya Street, they drove past a mix of Russian and foreign stores, Christian Dior, Estee Lauder, even a Pizza Hut. The onion domes of St. Basil's Cathedral peeked above the walls of the Kremlin, the centuries-old stronghold of the Russian czars.

The driver accelerated the vehicle and soon jerked to a stop in front of the Rossiya Hotel.

The group got out, grabbed their things, and went through a double-door entry. Inside, small shops were spread left and right. Young Russians sat at slot machines, smoking Marlboros and plunking down coins with the efficiency of Las Vegas retirees. The crew headed for the registration desk. Will noticed a currency exchange and another shop that offered car rentals. At the registration counter, Will discretely picked up a train schedule. Minutes later they all had room keys.

As Will headed from the elevator to his room, he glanced back. Boyd had put down his bag by his door and yelled after Will, "We're outta here in three days. Wheels up at ten hundred hours on the next C-141, with or without you, Will."

"I'll be ready," Will shouted over his shoulder. He noticed Gabbie watching from her own doorway.

Once inside his room, Will leaned against the door, trying to put together some semblance of a plan. He looked over the train schedule, but Kharkov was not listed. He waited until certain none of their entourage was still in the hall, then headed back to the lobby. He used his credit card to obtain rubles and U.S. dollars. Will noticed a large map on the wall outside the rental car agency. He found the word

Moskva. From it, a road and rail line wound their way south. No train went direct to Kharkov. Will then walked inside.

The attendant, a man about forty, eyed his new customer as Will approached.

Will smiled and greeted the man in Russian.

"Hello," the man said. "I speak English if you prefer."

"Fine. I need a car."

The agent pulled out a form. "Going where?"

Will heard the door open quietly behind him. He turned. Gabbie stood with arms folded, not a bit of amusement showing on her face. She shook her head. "We have to talk."

Will sighed. "Please, I've put you through enough. Go shop, sightsee, dine."

"Now you're giving *me* orders?"

"I'm sorry. Look, all I want is a chat with whomever Pam sent the book to, okay?"

"Going by car? The train too slow?" When Will remained speechless, she continued. "I saw you snatch the train schedule. What do you plan to use for money?"

Will's hand made a reflex to cover the pocket where his money was stashed.

"Oh," Gabbie said, "already been to the money exchange. Used your credit card, I'll bet, so now they'll know where to look for you."

Will stepped closer to Gabbie. "Keep your voice down."

"More orders. Where the hell do you think you're going?"

Will realized she already knew it had to be Kharkov, but he wasn't going to say it.

"Total crap," she said. "You don't even know if the right person is there."

To Will, she had become like Boyd had been to him, both of them knowing the other's thoughts.

"Gut feel," Will said, "but that's where I'm starting." He turned back to the attendant. "I want to tour Moscow."

The attendant stood silently for a moment as Gabbie's stare bored icicles through the back of Will's head.

"*We* want to tour," Gabbie corrected.

"Ah, you have your medical and driving insurance from your host Russian travel agency, yes?"

"No," Will said.

"Then I must have a deposit. Seven thousand U.S. dollars. Cash or credit card?"

"Whew. Seven thousand?"

"They are having an auto theft ring here. They like new cars."

Will thought about how much cash he had.

"What can I get for three hundred?"

The agent laid on a disdainful look.

25

THEY WENT FROM STORE to kiosk to store inside the hotel where Gabbie picked out a light backpack and cold-weather clothing, which they wore after trying them on for size. Will explained his plan as they shopped; Gabbie continually shook her head. At least she had stopped with the "this is crap" routine. At the little grocery, Will paid for food, flashlight, Swiss Army knife, a thermos, and a map while Gabbie tossed the items into the backpack. They filled the thermos with hot, sweet tea from the hotel restaurant.

As they left, Gabbie looked up at the ceiling. "Let me summarize. By now, whoever is after us already knows where you used your credit card, so they probably have someone on the way here. That someone was probably waiting at the airport—an hour away—trying to figure out where we are. That means they'll be here in about ten minutes. If we move our asses, they will find us no longer here. With me so far?"

Will nodded.

"Then they'll determine how we got here and find the van driver.

From him the trail will return to the embassy post office where the good letter lady will reveal your interest in the Ukraine. Another two hours max for all that to connect. And you still want to try this?"

"Yes."

"Oh, my," Gabbie sighed, then let slip a smile seemingly laced with irony. "Your master plan just better work. Let's go."

They left from the alley behind the hotel on an English-made Norton motorcycle that had seen better days. Will rode behind Gabbie, both helmeted, on the best set of wheels the rental agent could find for their money. At the first red light, Will referred to the map.

Gabbie, bundled up in a parka, lined pants, and gloves, turned her head. "Which way?"

Will pointed to the right where a street led away from the inner ring around Moscow. Gabbie swung onto the avenue and turned her head again. "I hope you learned to read and speak Russian well enough to keep us out of Siberia!"

"Da!"

Gabbie wheeled through traffic, driving less fanatically than the Thai driver had in Bangkok, but the dips and leans still threw Will around and were unnerving to him. He preferred being at the controls, as he had been over Baghdad. The passenger role gave him too much time to think about the hazard of the moment. He had, however, come to a small appreciation of what his father must have felt over North Vietnam, riding six feet behind Henry T. Dalton as he yanked the plane left and right in response to enemy gunfire. The outcome there had proven dire indeed. But what had his father's fate really been? The question drove Will now.

Outside the center of the city, the night closed in. Stars appeared. Gabbie kept their speed down, citing the danger of frostbite, even though winds were light. The road was unlike the one from the airport. Intermittent patches of hard-packed snow filled potholes that looked like mortar craters with chunks of asphalt scattered around the depressions. They were headed south now, passing through rural plains. Vehicles rumbled along in both directions, hauling everything from coal to cinder blocks.

Will spotted a huge truck stuck just off the shoulder of the road. A man was shouting from the driver's window. Gabbie maneuvered the cycle around it.

A gigantic cloud of diesel exhaust belched from the slithering, ice-bound vehicle as heavily clothed women threw sticks under the wheels. The whole scene had a prehistoric eeriness to it, like a clan of Cro-Magnons attacking a mammoth that was mired in a pit.

"I'm not the only woman who's doing the dirty work around here," Gabbie said.

"We'd be hopeless without you," Will agreed.

There were few passenger cars on the road. Will saw a directional stone off the shoulder. He had Gabbie point the headlight on it. Will recognized the Cyrillic and Roman letters for Podolsk. They passed a grim-looking limestone quarry that was marked on his map. Those were the first firm indications that they really were on the right road. Next came a cluster of log houses, then dilapidated tenements. They crossed a river on a combination rail and auto bridge. Once within the city, Podolsk had a scattering of streetlights and buildings of older architecture, most in need of restoration. Everything looked weather-worn. A lone police car was parked near an intersection in the center of town. The traffic light did not work. As Gabbie came closer, she edged around a pothole and her headlight illuminated the driver, leaning from the window of the car. The officer lowered a radar gun that he had pointed at the motorcycle. He stared with the cold analytical eyes of a shark as Gabbie and Will rolled by.

Will nudged Gabbie. "Nice priorities they have here. The red lights don't work, but their radar guns apparently do."

"At least they aren't aiming the kind that throw bullets," Gabbie shouted.

"Point taken," Will said.

Besides being stopped by the police, Will also feared they might skid on ice or slam into a pothole, but the road was surprisingly clear of snow. He watched to see that the police car did not follow, then hung on as Gabbie accelerated out of town, the big-lugged tires occasionally churning snow in a giant rooster tail behind the machine.

As Will and Gabbie rolled farther south, the villages got smaller.

Most of the houses were made of logs whose window frames were painted a garish blue that looked carnival-like when lit by the motorcycle's headlight. The temperature dropped rapidly, and soon Will felt Gabbie shivering. She pulled over and drank tea from the thermos.

Ten kilometers from Serpukhov, the next major town, Will saw a pair of headlights reflecting in Gabbie's handlebar mirror. He watched as the vehicle held its distance. Then when Gabbie increased speed, he saw that their follower stayed with them.

"We may have a tail," Will shouted.

"That policeman?"

"Probably not. He wouldn't have taken so long to catch up. You could be right about the credit card. Ain't technology great?"

The road went straight south past an endless progression of empty fields and an occasional stand of pines on either side. The other vehicle stayed just far enough behind to keep the motorcycle illuminated.

Gabbie turned her head. "My heart can't stand too much more of this."

Will saw lights ahead. A narrow bridge loomed out of the darkness, arching high over a river. He noticed the outline of another span off to his right, about a quarter mile away.

Gabbie started across in the center of the confined roadway. They passed the halfway point and dropped toward the far riverbank when the headlights from their follower went out of sight, blocked by the curve of the roadbed.

"Can't turn a car here," Gabbie said. "Maybe I can lose him if we backtrack." She braked the motorcycle and switched off the headlamp as she swung around. Then she accelerated in the opposite direction. Seconds later, they approached the vehicle. Gabbie steered toward the tight space to the right. She flipped on the headlight to the high-beam position.

"Holy shit!" Will yelled and hung on.

A black sedan, horn blaring, swerved in the blinding light. Gabbie started for the space opening to the left now, then swung back into the right lane as the car whipped the other way, the Norton barely squeezing past the vehicle as it reversed its momentum.

Once clear, Gabbie accelerated to the end of the bridge where, with lights out again, she turned off the road, rolled down an embankment, and stopped under the bridge abutment. She shut off the engine. They listened to the hum of the steel structure as their pursuer's car rumbled to the other end. Then headlight beams swept across the top of the far bank. A minute later the car zoomed overhead and continued searching north.

"Nice head fake," Will managed to say when his heart rate got under control. "But I wish these things had ejection seats."

"You don't do well leaving vehicles." She tapped his leg brace.

"Right. One more thing. I saw the driver's face," Will said.

"You did?"

"When the headlight swept across. I can't be sure, but it looked like the guy I ran into on the C-141 to Bangkok. He forgot his attaché case in the rest room." Will stared after the long-gone car.

"The horror show continues." Gabbie started the Norton and gunned the engine. "What now?"

Will checked his watch. "Back over the bridge," he yelled as the Norton surged up the embankment to the road surface. Gabbie gave him a look of disapproval, then roared south across the bridge. At the first intersection, Will had her turn right.

They came to a railroad crossing. Five minutes later, a train station appeared out of the gloom. Gabbie bounced across a field to a dirt road, then rolled to a stop by the station.

The building looked old, made of brick, with a gable roof and a long wooden platform that stretched in both directions.

Gabbie shut off the engine. "I may be mistaken, but your plan seems to lack a train." There was no humor in her voice.

"Have faith. We're early." Will slid off the Norton and stepped to the platform. An enclosed waiting room was dimly lit and devoid of people. No light was on at the ticket window, but across the street a nearby restaurant was open.

Gabbie parked the motorcycle. They crossed the street and went inside the restaurant. A handful of tables surrounded a coal stove. One man, bearded and burly, sat alone, holding a glass. A woman appeared from the kitchen. When she saw her new customers, she wiped a table with her apron and bade them sit.

Will greeted the woman, took a quick look at the menu, then said in Russian, "I need some information about the trains."

The woman tilted her head toward the man drinking alone. "Ask him," she said in Russian, then added, "You want eat?"

Will ordered sandwiches and hot bean soup, then began considering how to approach the man without being too abrupt.

The man at the other table looked them over with bloodshot eyes, then muttered something. The woman disappeared into the kitchen. A moment later, she returned with two shot glasses and a vodka bottle. She placed the glasses on the table and poured.

Gabbie looked at Will. "Did you order these?"

The woman seemed to get the message. She pointed to the bearded man.

"*Americanski, da?*" the man said, displaying a mixture of yellow and black teeth. He mumbled again.

"Says he's buying," Will said to Gabbie, then faced the man. "*Spasibo.*" Will thanked the man, but neither he nor Gabbie raised a glass.

"*Nyet?*" The man stood on two shaky feet and began staggering like a careful drunk toward them while waving his nearly empty glass. He slurred in heavily accented English, "You want beer? Is insult to offer beer!" Then he plopped down beside them. A whiff of vodka mixed with the sour smell of the man's clothes hit Will full force.

Will pulled out the schedule. "We're trying to find out about the train."

"Ah, traveling. Better to travel with something to keep cold off, yes? I am Anatoly. Now, where you come from on that motorcycle?"

"Moscow," Will said since no convenient lie came to mind. He decided that no matter how drunk, the man was observant enough to have heard the motorcycle and might be able to help. "I am wondering if the next train is on time, and how do we get tickets?"

The man stifled a burp. "You ask station manager." He thumbed his chest, then looked at his watch. "In nineteen minutes, train is come. You want soft or hard car?"

Will looked at Gabbie. She closed her eyes in resignation. "Soft," he said.

Anatoly clinked his glass against Will's. "*Nostrovia!*" Will repeated the toast, then downed his vodka, so Gabbie did the same.

Anatoly pointed outside. "You pay a little extra, I put motorcycle in baggage car. Where you go?"

Will thought a moment, then decided their pursuers seemed to know where they were headed and Will needed some help getting to his final destination. "Kharkov," he said.

"Get off, Belgorod," Anatoly said, as the woman reappeared with the sandwiches. "Ride motorcycle across border, no customs, no tax."

After they ate their soup and sandwiches, Will and Gabbie headed across the street to the station with the manager.

As if from nowhere, a dozen people appeared, all of them stamping their feet in the cold outside the darkened ticket window. Anatoly opened the office and issued vouchers to Gabbie and Will. Then he turned to serve the Russian passengers. Just as he finished, the building began to shake. "Train is come." He used both hands like whisk brooms to shoo them toward the boarding area. "Go car six, compartment four," he said, then disappeared down the platform with the motorcycle as the train pulled into the station.

Will checked his watch as the train came to a stop—11:45 P.M. He checked the voucher and noted that the train made eight stops before arriving at Belgorod at noon. Time was slipping away.

People began climbing aboard the train before anyone could get off. A woman in a long military-style coat and fur hat pushed her way off the train. She strode about, crunching among footprints whose icy molds made the place look like a frozen beach. Her breath puffed out in clouds of mist as she watched the proceedings. Then she spotted Gabbie counting cars. She said something in Russian to Gabbie, then switched to English when she got no response. "Yes, you have question?"

"We are trying to find car six."

"Car number six is now number five," she announced. "Please, go car number five and give voucher, thank you."

"Thank you," Gabbie said.

They found car number five, climbed the steps, let another woman remove a stub from each of their vouchers, then walked into a scene that took them both by surprise. It looked as if they had entered a narrow English pub. The floor had a wine-colored carpet. Polished brass door-grips were lined up along the corridor; each shone beneath Roman numerals that glistened on varnished-wood frames of the compartment doors. A Victorian samovar simmered above a brazier of glowing charcoal and filled the car with warmth and the scent of fresh tea.

"We've got compartment four," Gabbie said, then glanced into the lavatory and gave an approving nod as they moved into the car.

"What if compartment number four is now compartment number three, thank you?" Will grinned as he opened the door to number four.

Gabbie stepped inside. "Who cares? I'm in heaven." There were two cushioned benches across from each other. Between them was a built-in side table with a glass lamp that had a beige shade with tassels around the bottom. Green velvet curtains dipped across the window from above the lamp and were tied off to each side.

Suddenly, a stout, leather-faced woman appeared. She muscled past Will and pulled open the two benches, revealing made-up beds. Then she opened a cabinet above one of the beds, pulled down two goose-feather pillows, fluffed them up, and placed them at the head of the beds. Without a word, she bustled from the compartment.

Will crossed to the window. He looked out onto the platform as the last of the passengers boarded. "That was an amazing piece of riding back there on the bridge."

"Someone has to keep you out of harm's way. You certainly can't do it." Gabbie came and stood beside him.

"Can't argue that, and now that all of my Harley-Davidson fantasies have been satisfied in your presence, I have no plans to expand my experience once this is over."

"Good," she said. "What about the man in the vehicle that was following us?"

"If he finds us, he'll have to leave his car. The way things operate around here, that ought to give him fits." He looked toward the rear of the station. "Wonder if we'll ever see our motorcycle again." Then he closed the curtains.

Suddenly the train lurched. They bumped together. She lost her footing and grabbed onto him. He reached to steady her. The train began to pull from the station.

"The trains just go," she said. "No bells, no whistles."

They stood close, looking at each other. "Without any warning, a person could fall," he said. "I'm already off balance."

Gabbie hesitated, then pulled away. "Vodka does that, too." She sat on one of the beds, then began pulling off her shoes. Their eyes met again. She turned away and took off her jacket. "We'd better get some rest. I saw a shower nozzle in the W. C. at the end of the corridor. You first. I plan to be a while."

When Will came back from the W. C., Gabbie eased past him, walked down the passageway carrying her towel, and locked the door behind her. She looked at herself in the mirror, pushed back her hair, splashed some cold water on her face, and took a deep breath.

Her leggings had suspenders that attached at the waist. She slipped the straps off her shoulders, then took off her blouse and bra. She undid the front zipper on her pants, finished undressing, used the toilet, then removed a handheld shower nozzle, mounted above the floor drain. Hot water splashed on her face, missing her hair. It ran over her shoulders and down the long curve of her back. It splattered on her chest at the neck and dashed between the rise of her breasts. She took soap and lathered; her hands seemed almost detached from her body as they made swirls that covered her with white circles of foam from the neck down. She bent over and dabbed each foot, and ran her fingers between her toes. Then she stood up and rinsed.

After toweling off, Gabbie slid the pants back on, then put on her blouse but did not tuck it in. She folded her underthings into a small pile, then carried her things to the cabin.

Will lay under the covers, staring at the ceiling.

Gabbie put her folded items under her bed and pulled back her covers. When she got under the quilt, she grabbed the zipper on her leggings and pushed down. The zipper hung up. It wouldn't budge. She looked down at it. Part of the pant fabric had caught under the zipper slide. Try as she might, she was unable to make any headway. She tried to squeeze out of the opening, but the fabric wouldn't give as she tried to work the material past her hips. She gave up on that idea and went back to tugging at the zipper. Then the zipper tab came off in her hand. After a few minutes, her frustration level seemed to peak. She threw the zipper tab on the floor.

"My zipper's stuck," she said. "And the damn tab broke."

"Can I help?" He lay motionless, eyes riveted on the ceiling as the train rattled along the rails.

"Well . . . maybe you can get it started." She slipped out from under the covers and stood.

Will pushed aside his blanket and rose, wearing only his white cotton underwear. He saw her glance down, then divert her eyes as though hoping he hadn't noticed her interest.

He moved toward her with the curl of a smile rising at the corners of his lips.

She stuck her index finger in the center of his chest. "No funny business!" Then she parted the tails of her blouse, exposing the top of her pants and her bare waist.

"I'll give it my best professional shot." He bent low to get a better look, then took hold of the waistband with his left hand. His fingers pressed against her firm abdomen as they slid behind the offending zipper. With his other hand he took hold of the zipper slide. He felt his heart begin to race.

As he shifted closer, Will's lungs ushered in a salivating breath of woman-shower scent. The sensation merged with the excitement he felt blossoming. His shoulders tensed as he readied to pull. When he did, her hips rotated as though she was reacting to something else.

The zipper budged.

"There, it gave some." He pushed down and it moved a little in the other direction.

"Okay, I can get it the rest of the way." She grabbed nervously at his hand, and her fingers felt warm and inviting to him. He gave way as she found the zipper, her fingers unsteady.

Will stepped back for a moment and watched as she turned away, struggled, obviously making no more progress.

"Here, let me finish the job." He touched her shoulder and she turned to face him. Then he slipped his hand past hers and this time it slid deeper. He felt the tips of his fingernails run over pubic hair. He wondered if she had felt it too, and the answer was immediate. She inhaled, drawing her lower abdomen in.

The muscles in his upper arm flexed as he pulled up. She was so close to him now that her breath warmed his chest. He moved his fingers around behind the zipper and with his other hand gently wiggled the slide as he drew it up. It moved, then jammed again, so he pushed down. This time the zipper broke free, pants parting to the floor in an abrupt motion. His hand bumped her thigh.

She twitched at his touch.

"No," she said, her breath coming quick and heavy, but she did not draw away. She turned her face up to him, her big brown eyes troubled but inviting.

He rotated his hand and it melted into the hot wetness between her legs. She kissed hard and drove her tongue into his mouth as he cradled her onto his bed. He lifted her blouse up and over her breasts. Then he pulled away, eased his shorts off with one hand, then moved between her legs. They kissed again.

"You make me want so much more!" The words gushed from her lips, then she wrapped her legs around him, squeezing those long, lean limbs tight as she drew him toward her.

The heat inside Will rose to an intense hunger for her. He had gone too long without a woman, and never one the likes of Gabbie. As he entered her, he felt as if he were breaching great physical and mental dams.

26

In Washington, the time was 5:00 p.m. The Christmas tree lights had just been turned on at the ellipse in front of the White House for the last time of the season. Lights were on in the Oval Office, too.

The president, with but four days remaining in office, had summoned CIA director Thornton Bishop and JCS chairman General Richard Ellis for discussions. General Ellis arrived at the White House first. The president's private secretary informed him that the secretary of state was out of town and that the CIA director and the president's chief of staff would be the only other attendees. She asked the general to have a seat until CIA director Bishop arrived.

Thornton Bishop was still outside the White House, sitting in his car, listening on his mobile phone. He did not appreciate the no-notice roust from dinner that invariably meant that an unbriefed and vulnerable session lay ahead. The summons to the White House had come with only the words "the Ukraine," giving a clue to the agenda. Bishop was trying to get word from the U.S. embassy in Kiev regarding whatever was going on over there. His sensitivity was high given the fact that one of his agents, who had gone from Hawaii to Bangkok to Russia, had only hours before been instructed to proceed by car from Moscow to Kharkov in the Ukraine. The urgency of the agent's mission was well known to Bishop. It had risen to number one priority, but Bishop could not get through on his secure phone. He checked the time. Any further delay would cause a flap. He grabbed his briefcase.

Bishop, looking tired and agitated, entered the White House and bustled up to the president's reception office. As he hung his overcoat on a coat rack, he eyed a smug and confident-looking General Ellis. "What's up, Richard?"

Ellis shrugged. "I haven't been briefed either."

"You may go in now," the president's secretary said.

The president, his sleeves rolled up and his tie loosened after what had been a long day for him, too, leaned against the front of his desk reviewing a situation report as the men entered. The sit-rep indicated the Ukrainian government had taken a turn against the Russian federation, threatening to abrogate their military treaty. This could place at risk the long-range missiles in the Ukraine—the Russians might lose control of them.

Standing at the president's side was Terry Hanson, the president's chief of staff and political pit bull. Six feet in front of the president was a walnut coffee table where blank pads and pencils for note taking were laid out on the polished surface. A straight-backed chair was positioned at the end of the coffee table, centered above the dominating presidential seal that was woven into the blue circular carpet.

Bishop had worked issues here many times over the years. He strode past a grandfather clock by the door toward one of two yellow sofas placed on each side of the coffee table, then dropped his briefcase on one of the cushions. General Ellis entered more cautiously. Ellis had met with the president here before his JCS confirmation, but since then his encounters had been in the Situation Room, three floors below, or in an anteroom outside the Press Room. All he remembered about the Oval Office was the admonition not to step on the presidential seal.

The president shook hands with the new arrivals, then moved to his chair. Ellis sat on a sofa across from Bishop. Hanson remained standing.

"An hour ago, I got a call from the Russian president. He advises that the Ukrainian government is being bullied into breaking the SALT agreement. There have been demonstrations. My primary concern at this point is that the anarchists in the Ukraine are decidedly anti-American. If the demonstrators don't get their way, a coup is not out of the question."

Bishop winced. He was in the awkward position of being unable at the moment to lay his cards on the table. His own staff could be dead wrong about what they suspected was going on in the Ukraine. He needed time. He also sensed his agency would become the focal point for criticism, having not predicted this latest potential disaster. He was in a lose-lose position with a handful of disconnected but mounting clues to work with. If only he could have gotten word from Kharkov by now. Meanwhile, ever the bureaucrat, he needed to cover his ass. If there had been an armed confrontation, that might throw the ball in the JCS court. "Mister President, have you heard of any violence?"

"No," the president said. "At this point, things appear tense but not critical."

Bishop glanced at General Ellis, who sat stoically with notepad and pencil in hand, showing no willingness to take the pressure off him and the CIA.

The president continued. "The Ukrainian General Staff has cut off all discussion with its own government. The military has at the moment a firm hold on the Russian-made, but jointly operated, ICBMs. What I want to know now is what the Ukrainians have that might threaten us."

That question was clearly military in nature, though the information was gathered by both CIA's and DIA's analysis divisions. Bishop leveled his gaze on the general, who again abstained from entering the discussion. He then opened his briefcase and began searching through his data sheets.

General Ellis watched for a moment as Bishop fumbled on the hot seat, then waded in. "Fifteen percent of the ballistic missiles allowed under SALT are positioned there. They were to be destroyed during the next reduction phase."

"Give me hard numbers," the president said to both of them. "How many missiles, warheads, that sort of thing?"

"About sixty ICBMs," Ellis said. "None have nuclear warheads, though. The Russians removed them."

Since Bishop was still looking through his papers and didn't challenge the statement, the president focused his attention on Ellis. "So why am I worried?"

"The treaty allows the Russians to fire the missiles or chop them up. They fire the missiles since it is cheaper, one at a time, with a dummy warhead. The missiles are programmed to impact inside Russian territory. The Ukrainians could take control of these missiles if there's a coup and replace the dummy warheads with either chemical or biological weapons."

The president considered that statement, then asked, "What does the CIA have to say about Ukrainian chemical or biological capability?"

Bishop knew the answer, so he gave up on his data search. "During the Soviet era hundreds of tons of high-grade anthrax, plague, and smallpox were stockpiled all over the Soviet Union. The program was called *Biopreparat* and involved some sixty thousand employees, many of them Ukrainian." Bishop paused, deciding finally to stick his neck out. "We have indications that some of these employees have been working in secret at a medical institute in Kharkov. That's in central Ukraine."

The president snorted. "Indications? Wonderful. Can they put that stuff inside an ICBM?"

Bishop nodded. "With the nuclear warheads removed, it's an easy engineering task to replace them with chemical or biological dispensers. These could activate in the air upwind of our cities, infecting millions."

The president shook his head. "And what do we do about these ICBMs, gentlemen, just sit around and wonder what's inside them and who'll win the standoff?"

General Ellis doodled with his pencil for a moment. "We can retarget our missiles to blanket the probable launch sites." Then he took the pencil and jabbed the point into the paper. "Then if things get out of control, we'll be prepared."

Bishop made a face, not at all sanguine, about the suggestion to reverse concessions hard-won from the Russians since the end of the Cold War. "Can we stand the heat once word gets out?" His eyebrows came up. "And it will get out. The Russian federation will then likely retarget our cities with their nukes."

The president let out a grunt. "I can handle the heat for four more days, Thornton. Then it's Henry Dalton's problem." He kept his eyes on Director Bishop, whose strained look had not abated. "Yours, too, until you are replaced," the president said, "but I'm sure General Ellis can come up with something to take the sting out of it with Congress."

"I can call this an exercise," General Ellis said. "We could use the old target folders, updated, of course."

The president looked from Ellis to Bishop, then to his chief of staff, Hanson. "Do I have a choice?"

Hanson nodded toward General Ellis. "I think the JCS approach is the safest option. I can work the congressional notification end. An exercise. I'll send a note over with the slush pile, and it'll be months before anyone asks a question."

General Ellis's look of satisfaction went undisguised. "We might want to consider bringing the president-elect up to speed on this issue soon, too."

The president sighed, then turned to Hanson. "Terry, isn't Hank Dalton penciled in for a session here tomorrow?"

"Yes, sir, late lunch in the family dining room to talk cabinet issues, then the first ladies . . . I mean—

"I know who you mean," the president snapped.

"Yes, sir. Then Mills to tour the White House."

"How late for the luncheon?"

"One o'clock."

"Fine, I'll be cranky enough by then to give a real sparkler of a brief on the Ukrainian situation." The grandfather clock struck the hour. The president waited until its last peal. "You hear that, gentlemen? Woodrow Wilson put that clock there. It has faithfully ticked through five American wars. We will do what is needed to ensure that it doesn't melt while tolling the start of an ICBM exchange." The president sighed heavily. "So now, Thornton, tell me about this idiot I may have to deal with . . . this Marshal Slava Podvalny?"

27

THE SUN WAS ALREADY well above the horizon when Will heard Gabbie stir. He had been awake for some time. Finally she stretched and reached for her clothes, noticing that the tab had been reattached to the zipper pull on her leggings.

"Thanks for fixing my zipper."

"I'm handy that way."

"Very."

He brushed aside an errant strand of her hair. "Sleep okay?"

"Best night's sleep I've ever had on a train."

"How often have you snoozed on the railroad?"

She smiled. "Enough to know a good night from a bad one."

The train was *ca-clicking* along past a vineyard. Its vine stakes were painted white, all lined up like unfinished grave markers. Two whitewashed sheds nearby had the look of dilapidated mausoleums. The ground was wet and brown, with only small patches of dirty snow in shady spots. The train topped a rise. A marker by a road that ran alongside the tracks read 624 KM. Beneath the numbers was a Cyrillic word and an arrow aimed at a rutted trail that headed west.

Gabbie peered out. "Where are we?"

Will pointed in the distance to where a tank was mounted on a giant stone pedestal. "The battlefield at Kursk," he said. "The Russians named a sub after it."

"I remember. It sank."

"Yeah, in the North Sea. Hitler's war machine sank here. When you say *Kursk,* it sounds like you're hocking something up, which I'm sure were the sentiments of every German soldier who bled here."

Spread before them was a wide-open area of gently descending terrain that sloped toward the confluence of two rivers.

Will pointed. "Those are the Seym and Desna Rivers. Right here in July 1943, during Operation Citadel, Hitler was taught his first real lesson in the absurdity of German invincibility. It was a bit ironic. For once Adolf pleased his generals by waiting for good weather. That gave the Russians time to field their new 122mm gun on a T-34 tank. Seventeen German armored divisions with twenty-seven-hundred tanks took on four-thousand Russian tanks in the largest mechanized battle in history. It turned into a rout. The Germans hauled ass." He looked at Gabbie. "These Russians know how to build big guns, and they know how to put up a good fight, though they may need some finesse building cities."

Gabbie shivered. "Could you try Italy or France next time? It's warmer and *I* can finesse some of the language."

"Next time? You must be starting to like hanging out with me."

"You have your good points."

Two hours later, the train pulled into the Belgorod station. As they stepped from the car, Will pointed down the platform. "We're still in business."

A woman was wheeling the Norton toward them.

The road south from Belgorod was clear of snow, and the sun shone brightly. Will felt warm, but was not sure it was from the solar rays or from the feelings that drifted through his mind about Gabbie. He felt revitalized, more alive than he had since his midair collision. Now, with his destination at hand, he felt a buzz, excitement mixed with apprehension about what he might find ahead and about what he might be bringing down upon the woman whom he gripped as she steered the Norton on the way to Kharkov.

The earth flattened after they crossed another river. Mile after mile of fallow fields stretched in both directions. Cattle appeared in small herds. The animals looked thin. Off in the distance a trio of factory chimneys poked above a long, low collection of metal buildings. Like a battleship steaming into action, the stacks pumped dirty clouds of smoke into a blue Ukrainian sky.

Except for the occasional sign of industry, Will had seen little indication since Moscow that this part of the globe had ever been the site of a world power. It was hard to imagine that anything much more complicated than farming was happening here.

Toward sunset, they reached the outskirts of Kharkov. The layout seemed like every other town or city they had passed. All had parks, cultural buildings, apartment houses, statues, and a central square.

Gabbie slowed as she approached a crowd on the sidewalk. Pockets of people swelled into the street—yellow faces, Slavic faces, Aryan faces, Armenian faces—all surging toward the center of the city. A militiaman ordered Gabbie to stop at the entrance to a square. Will checked his map as they got off the machine. He moved closer to a reviewing stand, one of two that flanked a speakers' platform; both were filled with people. Stark buildings, dominated by one colossal skyscraper, encircled the scene.

Will and Gabbie remained standing beside the reviewing stand, close to the speakers' platform. A barrel-chested man with a solid gray mustache stood at the podium, which was ablaze in floodlights. He wore a bemedaled marshal's uniform and was surrounded by military officers and a garish arrangement of black-on-red banners and glowing torches. The sun was just setting behind the assembly. Pinks and purples from a thin cloud deck gave off a macabre radiance above crimson pendants that fluttered in the wind. A brass band struck up a march. Spectators looked in unison at companies of soldiers. Jackboots thundered against the cold pavement as columns of troops close-marched in from three of the roads leading into the square. Row after row of soldiers began to fill the open area in front of the marshal. With white-gloved hands they thrust rifles forward. The tip of each fixed bayonet extended menacingly beside the neck of the man in front. After the soldiers came athletes dressed in training suits, followed by a large crowd of Ukrainian workers moving arm in arm, many of them carrying banners or torches.

A shout rang out. The band stopped with a flourish.

The marshal strode to the microphone, chin thrust forward, his movements imperial. The partisan leader who in 1944 had executed wounded Germans and a doctor named Kraus outside Radenberg still emitted a brawny power, and he was still bitter. He surveyed the crowd as though reviewing his minions, then began his address. His words were in Ukrainian, but there was no doubt about the angry, chilling tone.

Will and Gabbie watched as the throng roared its approval every time the aged though vigorous marshal pounded his fist.

"My God," Gabbie said. "Looks like we've done a time warp back to the brownshirt era."

The thought had also flashed through Will's mind, along with what he knew of Gabbie's experience with the neo-nationalists at Fort Huachuca, but he kept silent about it.

As Marshal Podvalny's speech ended, the troops began to march off.

A tall man in a colonel's uniform climbed the steps to the podium. He had a pale, bony face and narrow, penetrating eyes that peered from beneath a shiny-visored cap. When he spoke, his upper lip moved unnaturally, exposing his teeth on one side so that he looked like he said everything with a sneer. He handed the marshal a mobile phone. Then, as they descended to a waiting staff car, the marshal spoke on the phone for a few moments. He hung up, and in an agitated voice, gave orders to the colonel who listened intently while letting his gaze settle on the strange pair standing near a motorcycle.

Will caught the officer's glare. Apparently, so did Gabbie. She nudged Will. "Let's get out of here."

They hopped on the motorcycle and rode back in the direction they had come. At the corner, Gabbie pulled to the curb near a couple who were standing away from the crowd. The man was clean-shaven, wore wire-rimmed glasses, and had on a charcoal gray overcoat. The woman had a well-groomed Irish setter on a leash and filled a black sable coat that appeared extravagant beside the thick parkas, mittens, and rubber boots of nearby babushkas.

Will pulled out his map. He thought about trying his Russian on the man, but this was the Ukraine and Russians were probably not too popular here. "Do you speak English?"

"A little," the man said with a slight accent.

"I'm trying to find an American who volunteers here. Where would I find the municipal ministry?"

The man perused Will's map. "You have an old one. They left out many of the details." He spoke to the woman in what Will guessed was Ukrainian. A lively discussion followed with the woman seeming adamant about her opinion. Finally, the man indicated one of the unmarked routes. "I think you can find it here along this road, but they are closed today."

"I'd like to find it anyway," Will said.

He pointed to a street that led away from the square. "Go that way." He gave Will a knowing look. "It is safer."

Will noted the point on the map, gave his thanks, and they pushed off. Two minutes later they rolled into Tevelev Square.

Four-story buildings, all of them constructed in the same post-Stalinist style, wrapped around an open expanse of concrete. A bronze statue of Maxim Gorky in a thoughtful pose stood in its center. A few people bustled along the sidewalk paying no attention to the motorcycle or its riders.

Gabbie circled the square, stopping when Will pointed at a building with a sign that indicated it was the local city hall. A heavy green door next to the sign stood ajar.

They dismounted. "Well," Will said, "looks like they're open for business after all."

Gabbie put down the kickstand while Will went ahead to the entrance. The frame had shifted so that the door could not be moved. "Looks like they never close."

They squeezed inside. A sign taped near the entrance read, ENGLISH LANGUAGE CENTER, RM. 109, in English and Cyrillic letters.

"Bingo," Will said.

As they wandered along a dim hallway past darkened doorways, the only sound came from the clicking of their shoes. A bare bulb midway down the hall provided lighting except for a pale glow that showed through a frosted door pane at the end of the passageway. Room 109.

Will went to knock but heard the sound of a latch being worked on the other side. The interior light went out and the door flew open. The front wheel of a bicycle appeared out of the blackness, pushed by a man whose hair was loosely pulled back in a ponytail and whose right ear sported enough gold rings to hang a shower curtain. Will focused on the top of a guitar case that protruded above a strap over his shoulder. As soon as the man saw Will, he halted, then began retreating back inside.

"We're Americans!" Will said.

The man hesitated, saw Gabbie standing beside Will, then swung the door open. "Whew! You scared the crap out of me." He glanced down the hall as though making sure no one else was around. "The crazies are out looking for blood."

"We just want to talk to you," Gabbie said. "I'm Dr. Gabrielle DeJean and this is Major Will Cadence."

"Dansky, Jim Dansky," the man said, offering a tentative hand.

Will smiled as he shook the hand of the man with the initials JD. He felt certain he had found Pam's source for the Polaroid.

Dansky turned the light back on and invited them inside. The room was small, with a high ceiling that accentuated the smallness of the space.

Dansky set the bike against the wall, then leaned his guitar against a bookshelf. The shelves were made of pine boards and cinder blocks. The boards bowed in the middle from the crush of heavily bound books stacked there. Two straight-backed chairs and a cluttered steel desk were the only other furniture. Dansky sat on the edge of the desk. "It's late." He folded his arms across his chest and smiled. "You guys tourists or what?"

"In a way," Will said as he sat. "We're trying to find a friend of an American named Pam Robbins."

Dansky quit smiling. "Are you friends of, ah, this Pam Robbins?" He took note of Gabbie.

"Yes," Will said. It was hard for him to imagine straight-laced Pam Robbins and this young Bohemian as being close friends who exchanged gifts. "And I take it you're the one she sent the guitar book to."

"Which book would that be?"

"Making an Archtop Guitar by Benedetto."

"Haven't seen it."

Will decided the book may not have arrived yet, and if so, then Dansky wouldn't know about the note Pam put inside. He thought for a moment about how to proceed. "We'd like to know if you ever sent a photograph to her—"

"The guy with his hands up?"

"Yes." Will produced his copy of the Polaroid.

"That's it, no shit." Dansky gave Will a penetrating look. "You're the second American to ask me about it today."

Will and Gabbie exchanged glances. Gabbie asked, "Who was this other person?"

There was a moment of silence, then Dansky shrugged. "Embassy guy. Said his name was Garcia, but said he didn't have the picture. Only knew about it."

Will had a puzzled look. "Can you describe this Garcia?"

"About six feet, average-looking guy. Drove an official sedan."

After a moment's reflection about the car on the bridge, Will said, "Could be our watchdog."

Now Dansky had the puzzled look. "Friend of yours?"

"No," Gabbie said, "but we know the man. Can you tell us any more about him? What you told him, where he went."

Dansky looked from Gabbie to Will. "I can, but what's this all about?"

Will browsed the bookcase again. "It's quite a long story, a bit of intrigue that we're trying to unravel."

"You mean like spy stuff?"

"Like spy stuff," Will said.

"And who are the good guys?"

"We are," Gabbie said.

"Right," Dansky said, making no attempt to disguise his cynicism. He glanced furtively at the door, his only way out. "Hey, you hungry?" He rose slowly, as though trying to create the impression that he really wasn't in a hurry to get out of there. "I could use a bean or two, and I got a date." He slung his guitar over his shoulder, grabbed his bicycle, and headed for the door before waiting for an answer. "Come on, I'll take you where I told the embassy guy he could get strong coffee and a meal."

The decor at the Tsentralny Restaurant was vintage Greenwich Village. An espresso machine gurgled behind a dimly lit counter near the back. On a tiny circular stage lit by a single track-light, a man with hair halfway to his waist sat on a stool and played John Denver's *Poems, Prayers & Promises,* each chord rolling off the frets with an ache. He took notice as the three Americans entered.

Small, intimate tables were jammed in every available space with two or three patrons sitting around most of them. Will scanned the room but saw no sign of the man they had seen on the C-141 and again on the bridge.

Dansky found an empty table near the stage as a burly waitress with lumberjack arms approached, giving both Will and Gabbie the once-over as Will hung his pack over the chairback. She took an order from Dansky for a pitcher of beer, some bread, and borscht.

When the musician finished his song, he put down his guitar and stepped to the table. Dansky introduced the college-age man as Josef. Dressed in jeans and a T-shirt with a Hard Rock Cafe logo in need of a wash, Josef looked to Will like a throwback to America's hippie generation.

Josef slid a chair over from another table as four couples bustled noisily into the restaurant. Dansky looked them over. "I don't see the embassy guy, but it doesn't surprise me. The cat looked like he'd been awake for three days. Probably went and bagged some z's."

"If this Garcia is the man we know," Gabbie said, "he drove all night to get here."

Will made no comment. He was undecided about whether to continue the conversation with Josef in attendance.

Dansky was quick to notice the silence. "It's all right. Josef is on our side."

The beer, mugs, borscht, and a loaf of black bread arrived. Dansky took the pitcher and began filling mugs. "So now," Dansky said, "why all the sudden interest in the photo I sent Pam?"

Will leaned forward. "Because Pam's dead, Jim."

Dansky stared right through Will's chest, almost as though he were trying to figure out if he had a role in Pam's death, and was not liking the answers he was getting. Finally, he refocused. "Dead?"

"A week ago."

"How?"

"The police say it was suicide. I have my own opinion, and we're here to try to resolve the issue."

Will went on to explain how Pam had recruited him to help find out about her father. "I believe she was killed because she learned something about POWs that certain elements within our government want suppressed."

Dansky leaned back to stare at the ceiling. "Dead? That's heavy." He sighed. "She used to hang out with a guy in our band back when I was doing gigs in Denver." Dansky put his elbows on the table, intertwining his fingers together beneath his chin. "That's how I met her." Then his lips twitched into a wry smile. "We were both in love with the same guy." He eyed Gabbie. "How's that for a romance wrinkle?"

Gabbie held his stare. "Sometimes love can arrive at the most unexpected times, in the most unexpected places, between the most unexpectant people."

"Yeah," Dansky nodded.

Will felt the comment applied not only to Dansky but to Gabbie and himself as well. He decided to change the subject. He mentioned his father's background and asked where the Polaroid had come from.

Dansky took a sip of his beer. "A woman I know brought it in. Old lady Trinkler."

Will asked, "Does she live here in town?"

"No," Dansky said, "she's got a place over by the airfield."

"Did she say how she got the picture?"

"She's an old *balabusta,* a granny, a little demented now. Rattled on about 'Americans' and somebody taking her goddamn shovel. I took down her ravings, thinking at first she was talking about a World War II vet, but she wasn't, not with that Polaroid. The snapshot was made from the kind of film that didn't come out until the sixties or seventies. I got one of those cameras as a kid, so the guy in the picture wasn't an old-timer. I'm thinking maybe he was somebody like Francis Gary Powers, the U-2 pilot, right?" He shrugged. "Anyway, Pam's the only one I ever met who gave a shit about that stuff—always going on about missing in action, so I included the picture when I wrote asking her to get me the guitar book . . . to give Josef for Christmas. He makes guitars on the side."

Gabbie asked, "Did you tell Garcia, the embassy guy, about all this?"

"About the photo, yes. The book never came up. He wanted to know where the old lady lived, too." Dansky thought for a moment, looking as though he had decided he might have done something wrong. "Wonder why he didn't say anything about what happened to Pam."

"He may have had something to do with her death," Will said. He looked around the room. "Can you take us to Mrs. Trinkler?"

Josef put a cautioning hand on Dansky's arm. Dansky took a long draft, all the while watching Will over the edge of his mug. Then he lowered it with a noticeable bang that startled a woman at the next table. Dansky waited until she looked away. "Look, my father's Polish, my mother's Jewish, and as you have figured out by now, I'm gay. I'm not going anywhere tonight with those Uke fascist psychos on the loose."

Will lowered his voice. "You talking about the guys playing storm trooper?"

Dansky nodded.

"We saw the demonstration in the square," Will said. "Who was the loudmouth in the marshal's uniform?"

Josef piped in. "Has to be Marshal Slava Podvalny."

"He's a hard-wired Ukrainian," Dansky added, "weaned on an icicle, and hates anything Russian or American."

Gabbie asked, "What's he got against Americans?"

Josef answered, "You people supported Stalin in the Great Patriotic War. Podvalny fought for the Germans, and he's Muslim on his mother's side."

"This Podvalny," Gabbie said, "sounds like he's got the populace riled up about something."

"Yes," Josef said. "There's talk of civil war."

Dansky inched forward. "The old fart has the local military backing him, which means at the moment he has his trigger finger on all the ICBMs in the Ukraine." He leaned back again and grinned. "Ought to make you sleep well tonight!"

"I thought the Russians had removed the warheads," Will said.

"Maybe so, but folks around here are real jittery about what might have replaced those nukes," Dansky said.

Will took a deep breath. "I can only deal with one crisis at a time. Tell us how to find the woman."

"Lives alone on a farm near the airfield. You'd never find it in the dark, plus you'd scare the shit out of her this time of night." Dansky looked at Gabbie. "You two got a place to stay?"

"No."

Dansky's eyes swept the room again. "Well, there are only a few decent hotels, and you may run into your embassy buddy at any one of them."

"We'd rather find him on our terms," Will said.

Dansky seemed to drift off, taking a long slow sip from his beer mug. "You know, Pam went a little psycho when she found out her true love was a switch hitter. In the end, though, we both lost out and wound up consoling each other." He turned to Gabbie. "It isn't anything fancy, but you can stay at my apartment, not far from here . . . both of you, if you want?"

Will noticed Josef shut his eyes momentarily at the invitation. Then Josef got up and headed back to the stage, shaking his head as he went.

Will caught Gabbie's attention as her eyes shifted back from Josef's display.

Gabbie gave Will a hint of a "Why not?" shrug, then she turned to Dansky. "Thanks," she said, "we'll take you up on that."

"Good," Dansky said. "I'll draw you a map to Trinkler's in the morning."

They ate and drank at the Tsentralny for another hour. Dansky even went onstage to play a duo. Then, after the crowd had thinned, the four of them left the restaurant. The embassy visitor never showed.

Dansky and Josef led the way on bicycles while Will and Gabbie followed on the Norton.

Ten blocks later, they stopped at a high-rise apartment. Flowerpots with withered foliage ringed the entrance. The doors to the building had been torn off. All the glass had been broken in the foyer. It looked as if it had been that way for a long time. There were two elevators inside. One was littered with cardboard scraps and seemed more likely to serve as sleeping quarters for transients than as transportation. The other, a freight elevator, had cheap plywood sides, one panel of which someone had apparently tried to remove, without success. Dansky and Josef rolled their bicycles into the elevator.

Dansky pointed to the Norton. "You can't leave that out here. In an hour, your headlight, saddlebags, everything not welded on, will be stripped clean." He motioned for Will to follow with the motorcycle into the elevator. Everyone squeezed in. Instantly, the strong smell of urine hit Will's nostrils. The elevator cables creaked in protest as they rode up.

The bicycles were placed against the wall by the door, but the Norton would block entry and exit so Will rolled the Norton inside the first room. It was small, a combination kitchen–living room in front that had a pullout sofa, two overstuffed chairs, credenza, and a throw rug cast over a polished hardwood floor. The oily Norton seemed terribly out of place.

Dansky opened the sofa bed, then pushed past hanging beads that served to curtain off a hallway to a back area. A few seconds later, he returned with two quilts, sheets, and an electric heater that he plugged in.

"You guys can camp out here." He pointed at the curtain. "Bathroom and sink are just on the other side, turn right."

Josef grabbed a vodka bottle from the credenza.

Dansky joined him, and they headed for the bedroom. "Josef and I are going to argue the merits of Ukrainian poetry."

"Goodnight," Josef said. "Please turn heat down before you sleep. It is not so cold tonight."

Gabbie circled the room, maneuvering her way carefully around the Norton. A black-and-white print of two doves, one fallen in an attitude of death, the other faithfully standing by, graced the wall above a neatly filled bookcase. A window looked out onto the street. She moved to the sofa bed and checked the quilts, sniffed, then raised her eyebrows. "Clean." She spread one out, placed a sheet on top, and folded it over. She did the same with the other set and positioned them side by side like sleeping bags on the open sofa. Then she placed two of the sofa cushions at the head of each quilt. Satisfied, she stepped around her achievement and moved toward the bathroom.

Will perused the books, leather-bound tomes, only a few in English. Two minutes later, Gabbie nudged his arm. "Better use the bathroom. I left the light on, and by now Josef is probably near beside himself over the waste of electricity."

As he moved down the short hallway, Will heard angry voices,

Dansky and Josef, ratcheting away as he stepped into the bathroom. The toilet extended from the wall. The wash sink was in an adjacent room. Everything spotless.

When Will returned to the front room, Gabbie had wrapped one quilt tight around her, the opening to her sleeping arrangement facing away from the center of the sofa. Message received. He turned down the thermostat on the heater, then switched off the light. Hazy moonlight filtered in from outside. He went to the window and pushed aside the drapes. The buildings looked like something out of a George Orwell novel. Across the street, two men weaved along the street, arguing.

Suddenly he felt Gabbie by his side.

"Don't tell me the brownshirts are surrounding the place," she said.

"Not at the moment." Will frowned and indicated the two drunks. "People from these republics put men in space, supplied and financed a horde of world conflicts, and manned the second largest nuclear arsenal in the world."

"How? Half of them move as though they're going drunk to a funeral. The rest look as though they're coming from one with a hangover."

"*Rodina,*" Will said. "The motherland. Threaten it and these people do their finest work. Russians, Ukrainians, Chechens, Georgians, they all pulled together when they were part of the Soviet Union. These Ukrainians, by the way, bore the brunt of the Soviet losses during World War II, around ten million. After the war, the communist system weighed them all down like an oppressive religion, so their frustrations focused on the socialist state. With that suddenly gone, the people in the republics have turned to hating each other again. What bothers me now are generals who drink vodka like water and look for something to do when there is no enemy at the gates."

"People like Marshall Podvalny?"

"He's one," Will said, and thought again about Gabbie's problem at Fort Huachuca. "We've got like-minded idiots in the States. Ever run into any?"

Gabbie looked at Will, as though gauging just how much he knew about that episode, then answered. "Once, a long time ago. I knew someone who turned out to be a little too far to the right for my taste. But from what you said in Bangkok, you've led me to believe you know all about that."

"I only know you got caught in the middle of something and did the right thing."

"Not everyone would agree with that." She stared ahead, lost in thought for a few seconds. "I dated a man who was well thought of in the Army. I'd done some taxidermy work for him and his buddies—rednecks all—and one of them wanted to know where they could quickly get a rattler. Said they needed it for a Monday morning survival training exercise. I took them into the desert, to a natural spring where I'd spotted a kangaroo rat colony. You'll always find snakes close by that setup, and we did. They did the capture.

"What they really wanted it for was to terrorize another soldier whose parents were biracial. They put the snake in his room and it found its way under the man's army blanket. He staggered in pretty well lit from partying late and collapsed on his bunk. The snake bit him through the blanket. The next day was a Sunday. They went checking on him and found him dead. They killed the snake, then argued all day about what to do next. That night they carried his body and the snake out. They drove into the desert, then trekked a few miles off the road. Thought it'd be months or years before the remains were found. Wanted it to look like the rattler hit him there. Anyway, as luck would have it, a few days later some hikers saw birds circling and went over to check. They found the corpse and the dead snake nearby. I was present for the autopsy, and when I saw the snake I pretty much knew I'd seen it before from the size, coloration, and number of rattles. I found my boyfriend and his cronies at the mess and asked what they'd done with the snake they caught. They knew the body had already been found, so they were spooked. That's when they threatened me."

"And got your dander up."

"Oh, yeah. I'd been around their kind most of my life, but this one trooper was way over the top with his bigotry. I turned them in."

Gabbie paused for a moment. "Not sure what I'd done if they hadn't said they'd slit my throat." She shuddered. "Then when they got hauled in, they claimed I was in on it from the start. Said I knew the whole gig. Anyway, I got the benefit of the doubt and took the army's offer of an early out. Left with a clean slate, honorable discharge, full bennies. The GI Bill got me into school, and sure enough when I started looking for a position, up popped the army slot at CIL-HI. I applied and the rest is history, as they say."

"What I'd say is that it took guts and determination to do what you did." Will turned to face her. She had her sheet wrapped around her like a sari. Her hair flowed onto her shoulder.

"Thanks," she said. "That's kind of you." She shivered. "But it's cold in here. The floor feels like ice under my toes." Gabbie turned and moved toward the sofa bed.

Looking at her movement in the soft light suddenly made Will feel awkward. Their lovemaking on the train was one thing. Spontaneous. Here with other men in the next room, he wondered if their togetherness had made her feel ill at ease, thus the earlier message with the quilt. Will asked, "Should I sleep elsewhere?"

"Elsewhere?" She stifled a laugh as she looked toward the hallway and the other bedroom. "I think not."

He stripped to his shorts and T-shirt, took off his knee brace, then placed his things on a chair next to hers. He took his sheet and blanket, opened it wide so it covered her as well as him, and slid beside her.

The two of them lay side by side, not saying a word.

Will peeked in her direction. Her eyes were flitting around the ceiling as though she were feeling an earthquake. Finally she spoke. "And about last night—"

"Vodka and perilous times," he said, cutting her off, "the one helping make the best of whatever calm you find during the other."

She turned away, toward the window. "Ever since that brush with the law, I've been leery of men with overinflated egos, Special Forces types, Seals . . ."

"Fighter pilots."

She let slip a hint of a smile. "I've always thought of myself as being pretty rock-solid when it comes to the real world out there. Now, I don't know if I'm ready to open up again in a more personal way, to care about someone . . ."

". . . with an overinflated ego."

She rolled toward him. "I guess it's a little late to be worrying about opening up again." Then she touched his arm. "And you? Why aren't you married with two-point-five kids and a three-bedroomer in the suburbs?"

"How do you know I'm not in that situation?"

"I checked."

"I checked on you, you checked on me. Why not? Everyone else is checking on us these days." He had not meant to change the subject, but instantly he knew he had. He felt her body shudder. "Upset?"

"No, a bit scared," she said. "Someone from back home is after us. The town is full of neonationalists, and by now whatever replaced the KGB is probably on our case, too."

"A fair recap."

She relaxed, rolling away, onto her back. "Boyd's plane leaves in thirty-six hours. Let's get back to Moscow."

He mulled the thought over, pushing aside guilt over exposing Gabbie to more danger. "After I find the old woman. Once I sort out the business of the photo, we can grab the train and be back north with time to spare."

Gabbie sighed.

"Look," he argued, "all we have is rumor and innuendo. The woman could provide real answers. How can I stop now, given the possibility my father might be nearby feeling the same chill of the night."

"Will, I'm really trying to understand."

"I know."

Her eyes washed over him, like the time in the officer's club in Hawaii, mysterious, the haunting way that she had looked at him then. She closed her eyes, just for a moment. When she opened them, he found a certainty there.

"It *is* getting colder in here," she whispered.

He pulled her to him, blankets shifting. They kissed, lips touching lightly, exploring, arms, legs moving and fusing, searching for comfort, then finding warmth and passion in the cold winter night.

28

JANET MILLS APPLIED THE final touches on her makeup, being careful not to get any on her blouse. Then she put on a red, belted herringbone jacket, smoothing it over a black wool skirt.

A guided tour of the White House conducted by the first lady, she thought, *for me!* She put her compact away and left her private washroom. This and other new accoutrements had been provided in the Rayburn Building after the election, but they would pale in comparison to what lay ahead. Five minutes later, she met the president-elect and together they headed for the pickup point in front of the Senate building.

Cameras rolled the instant they stepped outside. Janet had become the darling of the dailies. Her performance in the women's seminar and the prospect of having an intelligent, single woman run the distaff aspects of the social scene at the White House had placed her on the front page of every newspaper and magazine in the country. Of course, for Janet, her vision of her role in the administration was far more than just that of a social secretary. For months she had been getting more ink than even the president-elect, but hers was a tenuous position. She had been careful with interviews, turning down one from *60 Minutes* while accepting one with Barbara Walters. That appearance had gone over well. Now, in Henry Dalton's presence, she astutely kept her profile low, avoiding the barrage of questions that were thrust upon her as she left the Senate Building.

When they were seated in the limousine, Janet looked at Dalton. "How do I look?"

"Terrific. Just the right touch of conservatism and style."

"Thank you, Sen—" She put her hand to her lips. "My God, how long it will take to feel comfortable calling you Mister President?"

Dalton chuckled. "Three days from now would be a good time to have it down. Of course, I've got to learn to call you the White House hostess. What a mouthful. Wonder if you can come up with a shorter title—and hostess won't do."

"It'll be a pleasure to work on it," she said.

"By the way, this tour we're getting is traditional."

"I know. They've been doing it since 1909 when Mrs. Teddy Roosevelt took Helen Taft through. I looked it up." She beamed. "Lord, here we are on our way to the White House, and my boss is going to be the next president of the United States. I still pinch myself every morning."

Dalton turned to her and smiled. "Me, too."

Henry Dalton and Janet Mills were driven to the south portico. As their limousine pulled up the curved driveway, they looked out at the home of all since John Adams who had ever led the country.

The president and first lady were standing to greet them just inside the entrance to the Diplomatic Reception Room, a large oval chamber centered under the portico. Dark shadows under the president's eyes reinforced the gloomy image that the newspapers had been reporting since the election. There would be no second term for this president, whose plans to embellish his legacy during the years when reelection politics no longer mattered for him personally had been dashed. Rumor had it that he was becoming increasingly testy toward his staff. He forced a smile, shook hands, and bid them enter.

Janet walked in and took in the rich carpet, plush furniture, and pastoral mural that went completely around the reception room. The first lady smiled and extended her hand. "If you didn't feel the thunder of history while walking in here, you wouldn't be human."

"I've got shivers already."

Hanson, the incumbent president's chief of staff, came forward and shook hands with Dalton, then Janet. "We're all set for a photograph."

Janet caught the look of resignation on Hanson's face that said he knew he had only three days left in the castle.

The foursome lined up in the center of the carpet while the official White House photographer snapped away.

The group, consisting of the four "primaries" and assorted Secret Service agents, the president's chief of staff, and a number of hand-wringers, headed out of the room.

The first lady indicated a man keeping pace to her rear. "Janet, this is Enrico Françoise, our executive chef." Enrico moved forward and bowed slightly as he shook Janet's hand. A hint of perspiration was on his forehead.

"Hello, Enrico," Janet said. "And what are we having today?"

Enrico cleared his throat. "For this luncheon, madam, ginger fruit cocktail followed by poached salmon-peppercorn with asparagus spears."

"Sounds delicious," Janet said. She wondered how much of her hard-ass reputation had preceded her arrival—all of it probably—and every member of the staff felt vulnerable. The slightest miscalculation and *poof,* they could become part of that thundering White House history. Not lost on Janet was the fact that she, too, was in the same position. One critical mistake and replacement by Dalton was just a raised eyebrow away. But Janet had learned the art of button-pushing well, especially regarding that air force major—Cadence—who had showed up during the campaign. The director of the CIA had gotten back to her. There was some indication that Dalton might be beholden to the officer, but he would not share details. Maybe he didn't have them yet. In any case, just knowing that Dalton was vulnerable empowered her. Janet smiled inwardly at the difference between herself and someone like Chef Enrico. She would never show her insecurity. Not ever.

The president led the way into an elevator. Only the four of them got in. As the door slid shut, the president grumbled, "The only thing private about luncheons at the White House is that they're not televised."

"I suppose," Dalton said, "you never quite get used to the cast of thousands."

"You do get numb to it after a while," the president said.

The first lady caught Janet's ear. "Your staff numbers one hundred three."

"My God!" Janet said.

"You'll get used to running things," the first lady said. "Especially the sixteen maids and housemen, seven butlers, nine cooks, and five ushers. You'd have to be crazy not to like this place."

They took the elevator to the second floor, then were led by the president into the dining room. A modest table was positioned near a marble fireplace. The walls were adorned with a mural depicting the Revolutionary War, set above beige wainscot paneling that wrapped around the room. On a cherry credenza nearby were a stack of briefing papers, all in blue folders with the presidential seal atop each. Through two huge windows at the end of the room, the sun cast a warm glow, unlike the mood the president had been suppressing.

Moments later, Hanson reappeared.

"I've asked Terry to join us today," the president said. "He'll be giving a foreign affairs update at the end of the luncheon. He'll also note for the record our final discussions regarding Cabinet assistants that you may want to retain."

The president, no doubt, still smarted over Dalton having bolted the party to run as an independent and defeat him, not to mention the rumor that the first lady was privately miffed at the thought of being replaced by an unmarried staffer. That contrast could reduce the first lady's own vision of her place in history. Janet assumed that the traditional invitation to the White House for a personal tour had been arranged to offset those rumors, ensuring that their departure would carry no hint of sour grapes.

The group chatted over champagne cocktails, until Enrico appeared, signaling that all was ready for the luncheon.

The table was set for five, with the president at the head. Dalton, then Janet were seated to the left of the president. Across from them were the first lady and Hanson.

The meal progressed smoothly, and Dalton's proposed retention of four current Cabinet assistants seemed to delight the president.

After dessert, Janet began a tour with the first lady, while the president and Dalton went with Hanson and several aides to the Cabinet Room for coffee. Once the group was seated around the head of the oval mahogany conference table, Hanson began the foreign affairs briefing. He started with the situation in the Ukraine, presenting satellite photographs of a number of military installations in and around major population centers.

"The problem, as we see it," Hanson said, "is that the government is run by crooks, who have kept the country close to Russia politically. As a result, Russia has left their de-armed ICBMs in place awaiting destruction under SALT. These weapons in the wrong hands could be launched against us with either chemical or biological warheads."

Dalton put up his hand to interrupt. "Who is supposed to control the ICBMs in the Ukraine?"

"It's a joint effort," Hanson answered. "Both sides maintain the silos and mobile launchers. There is a flaw regarding launch control, though. If the nuclear warheads are removed, the missiles can be fired without submitting the normal launch codes. In other words, the Ukrainians can launch without Russian clearance, and there are indications that a coup is in the works, headed by a loose cannon, one Marshal Slava Podvalny."

"As a matter of fact," the president interjected, "the situation is at issue right now because Podvalny is anti-Russian and anti-American and may be intent on taking full control of the ICBMs. A man with no apparent conscience could become an instant power-wielder in command of more than sixty mobile and fixed missiles, each capable of delivering multiple warheads filled with chemical or biological agents."

Dalton asked, "Do the Ukrainians have chem-bio weapons?"

"During the Cold War," Hanson said, "they used a number of medical institutes, one in the Ukraine, for developing those capabilities. The Ukrainians control that institute and presumably have access to all the research data."

Hanson slid a photo in front of Dalton. "This is the latest satellite photo of Kharkov Airfield, seventy miles from Kiev. These planes are controlled and flown only by Ukrainians."

Dalton appeared lost in thought, his eyes focused on something near the edge of the photograph.

Hanson waited a moment, then pointed to the revetments, U-shaped mounds that ran along both sides of the taxiway and served to protect the aircraft from bombing attacks. "Only a direct hit could damage the planes. You can see live ordnance on dollies next to the aircraft, suggesting this is not mere preparation for a training exercise." Hanson indicated one of the planes. "Here, air-to-air missiles are being loaded on a Sukhoi Su-30, the latest version of a Russian-built interceptor."

"I'm familiar with that type," Dalton said, his gaze returning to the airfield. "It has no air-to-ground capability, only air-to-air missiles and cannon. Where are the tactical bombers, the kind needed to support a coup?"

Hanson was slightly taken aback by the question. "We feel the interceptors are being readied to make sure no interference comes from across the border in Russia." When that statement kept everyone waiting for more, he riffled through his papers. "The fighter-bombers are staging out of Kiev." He slid another photo in front of Dalton.

Dalton studied the new photo, then asked, "Why does Podvalny consider us his enemy, too?"

"The fact is," the president said, "his mother was Muslim. He grew up to despise the old Soviet atheists, and in the course of time came to condemn the Christian world as well."

"Some folks need a villain, anyone handy, to justify their mischief," Dalton said. "What are our options if there is a coup over there?"

"We . . . you'll have to work closely with Moscow on this. It's as much their problem as ours, but I've let them know I will increase our alert posture to DEFCON Two if there's trouble." The president gave a signal for coffee to be served. "The important thing to remember here is that if the Ukraine goes belly-up on the Russian agreement, all the other CIS member states will get their hackles up, too. The whole damn European stability that we worked so hard at may go down the drain."

29

The next morning, Will, Gabbie, and Dansky exited the elevator together and maneuvered the motorcycle into the street. The sky was overcast. A chill wind brought with it a sense of oncoming snow. Josef had gone off earlier to get gas for the motorcycle.

Dansky gave a hand-drawn map to Will. "Left at the corner, then straight up Sumskaya to Gorky Institute." He pointed to a gray stone structure in the distance. "The medical facility."

Gabbie glanced at the map. "We turn right, there?"

"Yeah. The rest of the route is on the map. Mrs. Trinkler's daughter told me her family moved here from Germany before the war. Her mother taught English in Berlin, but I find her a little hard to follow. Anyway, there's a big tree with a split trunk by the house. You can't miss it."

Josef rolled up on his bicycle, a plastic container strapped above the rear wheel. He undid the restraints and handed the fuel to Will who began pouring it in the Norton's tank.

When Will finished, Josef pulled a revolver from his waistband. Will and Gabbie froze. Josef glanced at Dansky, a look of disapproval on his face. "Jim belongs to Peace Corps, but if Podvalny's goons come for us, they'll have war to deal with." He took the gun by its six-inch barrel and thrust it toward Will. "You can borrow."

Will took the gun, a portable cannon. There was nowhere to comfortably stow it on his person. He thought about putting it in his backpack, then decided it might not be readily accessible there. He put the weapon in one of the Norton's side bags.

"Thanks," Will said. "I hope we don't need it." Gabbie got on, then Will swung his leg over, sliding behind her, and they were off. A few minutes later, they passed the Institute, a walled fortress of a building with a gated drive-through for ambulances. Across the avenue was a park where people were strolling in spite of the cold weather.

Once outside the city, Gabbie and Will moved south along a paved road. It quickly narrowed, with barely enough pavement for two vehicles. The shoulder was rutted with ice-hardened tire tracks. Gabbie slowed to a crawl when trucks approached.

The land was flat, with thick birch forests scattered among fallow fields. There were few landmarks, a twist in the road, a lone withered pine, an old log farmhouse surrounded by whitewashed fence posts.

They stopped to check directions, eventually turning down a dirt road past stark, frame houses. They saw few people. The road split. Will pointed right, to a lane rutted with tracks from cars and wagons. Gabbie had to snake her way along. As they crested a small rise, they spotted a wagon coming toward them, drawn by a pair of straining horses whose nostrils chugged out clouds of vapor. Gabbie waved at the driver. A boy, dressed in layers of ragged clothing, gave no acknowledgment but pulled his team to a stop and set his wagon brake. The horses trained a watchful eye on the smoke-belching Norton as it passed. The wagon was loaded with yams in bushel baskets, tucked in front of a pile of hay.

Overhead, a jet fighter descended on landing approach to a runway somewhere out of sight. A helicopter rattled above the treetops in the distance as the Norton rolled to a stop in front of a log house.

Halfway between the road and the house was the split tree trunk Dansky had described. Another motorcycle, a large one, lay against the tree. The shade in the front window was drawn, but a thin wisp of smoke seeped from the chimney.

"Somebody's home." Will slid off the cycle. He scanned the area. Set off behind the house was a large toolshed. Its heavy door was ajar, but no one was in sight. Gabbie set the kickstand, and they started for the front door.

Gabbie grabbed Will's arm. "What about the gun?"

Will stopped. "We can't go toting that cannon in front of an old woman. If I stick it in my belt, I can't sit. I don't see the embassy car around, but let me check something first."

Will crossed the yard to the tree and put his hand against a cylinder head of the big motorcycle. The engine was warm to the touch. Will had no time to contemplate the meaning of it as he heard a door creak. He looked up.

A man stood in the shadow of the doorway. He was dressed in a black leather coat, worn over a thick turtleneck. The coat was open and hung low on one side as if weighted down. The man had his thumb tucked into his waist. Will was certain he was the rider of the other motorcycle. The coat told him that. He must have heard the noise from the Norton as they arrived.

"Good morning," Will said. He took a step away from the motorcycle. "You speak English?"

"Yes," the man said.

"I wonder if you could help us. We're looking for Mrs. Trinkler." Will took off his glove.

The man moved to better light and frowned as though wondering why Will had gone to look over the motorcycle. His face was pale as milk, and his pupils were black dots that stared out like cougar eyes. He spoke with a sneer as the side of his lip lifted. "She doesn't live here anymore."

Out of uniform now, Will suddenly realized he was the Ukrainian colonel they had seen in the square talking with Marshal Podvalny. A shiver of pure fear ran up Will's spine. "Do you know where she is now?"

The man paused as though considering his options. "She left an address here somewhere. Why don't you come inside. I'll look for it."

Will glanced toward the pouch on the Norton, yards away. Too late. The man was obviously armed, and a move by Will to leave might force his hand.

The colonel held the door as Will and Gabbie entered. A heavy brass menorah sat atop a waist-high bookcase to the left. Books were strewn on the floor, a hasty search interrupted. Chairs, a table made of rough-hewn logs and covered with papers, added to the clutter. A corner cabinet of ornate cherry was tucked away by the window to Will's right. Inside the curved-glass enclosure, delicate porcelain figurines halted their dances in fixed poses—the life's treasures of an elderly recluse.

The colonel went around the table and began poking through a stack of papers, his tone casual, smooth. "I am Karl Stayki, and you are?"

Will hesitated. Should he give their real names? What if the man wanted to see their passports? If he already knew who they were, then lying should not make any difference; the man would try to do whatever he had been ordered.

"Robert Craig," Will said, but his mind drew a blank trying to remember Gabbie's new name.

Gabbie stopped just inside the door and eased it closed.

"Carol Banister," Gabbie blurted after an obvious pause.

Stayki smiled as he looked down, shuffling aimlessly through the papers in front of him. "Is there something I can help with? Why it is you want Mrs. Trinkler."

Will looked past Stayki to where light spilled from an archway that led into the kitchen.

"We're from the Peace Corps," Gabbie said. "Mrs. Trinkler had an interest in one of our projects."

"Peace Corps?" Stayki tilted his head to one side. "And what project would that be?"

A faint sound, like an animal whining, leaked from the kitchen, then a *thump.*

Will glanced toward the sound, his senses fine-tuned, as he struggled to stay calm.

"To teach English." Gabbie said.

Stayki's smile was gone, all business now, his hand moving inside the coat. "English? You're not here to see her about that." His hand reappeared, gripping the butt of a pistol.

"Run!" Will shouted at Gabbie as he snatched the menorah, then flung it toward Stayki who ducked. Will lunged toward him. Stayki's gun came up just as Will's hand shoved the barrel aside. The weapon, a machine pistol, fired wildly. Rounds peppered the corner cabinet, shattering the glass and scattering the porcelain statues. Stayki fell backward to the floor with Will on top, each struggling for control of the weapon.

Will noticed the slide full aft on Stayki's gun. Empty. Will swung his free fist at the man's jaw, then felt something hit him from behind.

A glancing blow. Everything went gray. Stunned, he felt himself being flung sideways. He was aware of his peril, but felt no sensations in his body. As he struggled to regain control, the sound of gunfire penetrated his consciousness. For a moment, he thought he had been shot, but he felt no pain. Then his vision cleared. He lay alone on the floor. He tried to stand, but fell back, so he crawled to the open door and peered out.

Gabbie stood by the Norton, both hands wrapped around the butt of a gun. Smoke wafted from the barrel. She swung the weapon toward Will, then lifted the gun clear. "Come outside and stay down!" she ordered. "The other one ran back inside."

"The other one?" Will got to his feet, stayed low, eyes looking behind him as he moved outside and to his right. He bumped into something and spun. A man was propped against the wall in a sitting position. Blood poured from a gaping wound in his chest. A pair of glasses tumbled from his nose and clattered to the porch deck.

"Whoa!" Will yelled. The man's eyes were rolled back in death. He was not Stayki. Lying in the man's hand was a pistol. Will wrenched it from his grip.

Seconds later, Gabbie slammed her back to the wall between Will and the door. She pressed against the structure, her breathing forced and clipped, gun at the ready.

Will checked to see that the weapon he now had was not empty. "The one inside is out of ammo, or I'd be dead." Will slipped his backpack off, then stepped around Gabbie and threw the backpack inside. No sound came from within.

"Forget it," Will heard her say, but he had already slipped inside. He crept forward, feeling edgy, nervous, seeing no movement. Gabbie followed. Will signaled for her to stay put, then continued on, listening, looking, moving past the bookcase—no sound but his own rapid breath. He swallowed, then sprang across the open arch, glancing into the kitchen as he disappeared on the other side. An entrance to the pantry was visible in the background. An oil lamp hissed on a table near a stone hearth. A water-pump handle angled above a sink next to a chopping block that dominated the center of the room. A chicken, recently butchered, lay on it. Will peered around the arch, then moved past the wooden block and a set of gleaming knives hanging overhead. He was nearly in the pantry when he heard a scratching sound. He whirled. A small dog lay on the floor, its body twitching, blood streaming from an ear, eyelids fluttering. Will held his fire, then slowly turned toward the pantry, moving closer to stare inside. On the wood floor he saw a bloody knife, a body, a woman—Mrs. Trinkler no doubt—her throat cut. A cold draft blew through an open rear window.

"Damn," Will said. Then from behind he heard the staccato sound of a motorcycle starting. He turned. Gabbie stood right behind, covering him. Both of them rushed to the front of the house and onto the porch.

Colonel Stayki was on his motorcycle, churning out of the yard. He had run his machine over the Norton.

Gabbie fired once. The bullet apparently missed as Stayki roared down the road and disappeared out of sight.

Gabbie turned, her hands shaking as she looked back toward the house. "Is Mrs. Trinkler? . . ."

"Dead." Will glared down at the other gunman's corpse. "This one must have been hiding in the back. He slugged me while I fought the other guy, then came outdoors after you. Out of ammo and with his buddy dead, Stayki slipped out that rear window." Will nudged the corpse with his toe. "This is one son of a bitch who won't be marching in any more parades." He looked at Gabbie. Her hands were shaking."You okay?"

"No," she said. "Have you ever shot someone?"

"I only got to watch the shoot-downs, remember."

"You may get to see a lot more." Gabbie looked at Will. "You don't look too steady, either."

"Got a knot on my head, but I'll live."

Will retrieved his backpack, then together they examined the motorcycle. The back wheel was bent. Spokes had separated from the rim.

"Let's see if we can ride it," Gabbie said. She lifted the Norton and started the engine. They climbed aboard and rolled from the yard. The rear wheel wobbled from side to side as they made their way over ice-hardened ruts.

"We have to stay off the main road," Will said. He pointed to a stand of pine trees a short distance away. "Head for cover. Let's see if there's a path we can use."

Gabbie turned the machine in that direction. When they were about a hundred yards from the grove, the rear wheel collapsed.

Gabbie emptied the saddlebags into Will's backpack. Josef's gun still had five rounds in it. Will checked the dead man's pistol. Nine rounds left.

The two began hiking back toward Kharkov. Will kept an eye to the sky and the main road in the distance. Stayki would likely be back soon with troops, so Will urged Gabbie along the forest edge while they tried to keep the road in view. The grove was thick with spruce. Dead branches poked at them like sabers. They snagged on the side bags that Will carried over his shoulder. He was breathing hard, stepping gingerly with his aching leg over dead logs—everything was slippery and covered with snow as they made their way through the thicket. They passed a cluster of deserted farm buildings and crossed an open field. Somewhere in the distance a dog launched a chorus of angry barks.

Will and Gabbie, guns in hand, scampered down a shallow slope, moving through a stand of birch when, to the west, they saw the wagon and boy they had encountered earlier. The boy's horses were struggling along the road in the distance as flashing lights from vehicles appeared over a hill beyond the wagon. In the lead of the caravan were two police cars, behind them a jeep and two canvas-covered army trucks. Will and Gabbie watched from cover.

The procession drove out of sight as it descended behind a knoll for a few seconds, then came around a curve and slowed as it came abreast of the wagon. The police cars moved past, but the jeep and the trucks behind it ground to a halt. Colonel Stayki got out of the jeep. Immediately two soldiers and a German shepherd jumped from the rear of the first truck and headed for the wagon.

One soldier let the dog sniff around the wagon while the other soldier poked his bayonet into the hay. The boy sat and watched. When the dog showed no interest in the hay, the colonel pulled his revolver and fired twice into the pile. The horses bolted, startling the boy who fell from his perch onto the yam baskets. He struggled to his knees, shouting at the horses, as the wagon lurched ahead out of control. Meanwhile, the colonel and his convoy moved off toward the Trinkler farm.

A quarter of a mile in the opposite direction, the wagon careened into a curve and finally came to a stop, mired in a snow drift off the shoulder. The boy, flailing his arms in defiance at the disappearing convoy, climbed down and went to calm his horses.

As soon as the military vehicles were out of sight, Will rose. "Let's go." He started heading deeper into the woods.

Gabbie protested. "With dogs, they'll be on top of us before we get another mile."

"You got a better idea?"

"Stow the artillery." Gabbie put her gun in Will's backpack while he stuffed his smaller weapon in his pocket. Then she angled off in the direction of the road. "The wagon. Let's go." Will watched her for a moment, her stride strong and purposeful. She never looked back, scrambling through a tangle of branches and vines toward the road below. Will followed as snow flurries began drifting down from a ragged overcast.

Gabbie reached the road surface first. "Come on," she shouted. "Just ahead."

The boy stood in front of his team, reins in hand, urging his horses forward, attempting to get the wagon out of deep snow.

Gabbie ran faster. "Let's give him a hand."

The boy peered, wide-eyed, from behind the horses as Gabbie neared the back of the wagon. She began pushing. Seconds later, Will was beside her. They shoved together, and the wagon slowly moved through the snow, back to the road surface.

The boy climbed onto the wagon. "*Da Kuyu,*" he said with a grunt.

Will pointed ahead toward Kharkov as he tried his Russian on the boy. "*Can you give us a ride?*" Will motioned with his hand toward the back of the wagon, then pointed at himself and Gabbie.

The boy turned away, looking over his shoulder toward where the soldiers had gone. He spat. Then he faced Will and Gabbie. "*Da!*" he roared as he pointed to the haystack.

Will and Gabbie climbed aboard. They began to pull straw over themselves. "How sure are you that he won't turn us in?"

Gabbie wiggled into the straw. "In the hierarchy of needs, there's one much overlooked drive . . . the urge to get even."

After ten bumpy minutes, an army vehicle approached from the rear. It slowed as it came up behind. Will gripped the gun and waited beneath the straw, but the vehicle swung left, passed slowly, and went on ahead.

An hour later, as the wagon lumbered into the outskirts of Kharkov, Will heard the wail of approaching sirens. He peered from the hay. The horses began to rear, then lunge against the reins. Up ahead, the Gorky Medical Institute was framed by great clouds of black smoke that billowed into the air. The top floors were in flames.

Fire engines streaked by. People ran by shouting as the boy steadied the horses.

"Time to hit the streets," Will said as he hopped off, then helped Gabbie down. He stuffed rubles in the boy's hand and got a huge gap-toothed smile in return.

Will and Gabbie moved with the crowd past the fire and on to Tevelev Square. They cautiously approached the ministry where they had first found Dansky. No vehicles were parked out front. Room 109 was locked, lights out. They headed for Dansky's apartment. By the time they arrived, darkness had descended, but the lights were out in Dansky's apartment window. They waited out of sight across the street for Dansky or Josef to return.

Twenty minutes later, Will spotted the dim lights of two bicycles bobbing up the street. Dansky and Josef materialized out of the gloom and braked to a stop. Dansky flicked off the battery-powered light on the handle bar above a basket filled with wrapped packages. "Ah, you're both still in one piece. Any luck with Mrs. Trinkler?"

"We got there too late," Will said. "She's dead. So's one of Marshal Podvalny's goons."

"The war's on," Josef said.

"A skirmish, maybe," Will said. He tossed the saddlebags into Josef's empty basket. "Your gun is inside."

Dansky stared at the bag as though it contained the plague.

"You mentioned Mrs. Trinkler had a daughter," Will said to Dansky. "Do you think she'll talk to us?"

"You break the news that her mother is dead, who knows? But she is one of my students, so it's worth a try. She lives in the newer part of town near Luxem Square."

Gabbie interrupted. "Will, let's start figuring out how we're going to get the hell *out* of this place."

"Gabbie, we are on to something important. Stayki and the others are scrambling to erase everything. Mrs. Trinkler's murder, the attempts on our lives. It's all connected. Leave now and they win."

Gabbie clasped and unclasped her fists, her eyes riveted on Will, like in Bangkok the time when she tried to get up and leave but had nowhere to go.

"Time's running out," Will said as he turned back to Dansky. "Can we go now?"

"We can walk." Dansky gave his bicycle to Josef, then grabbed two of the packages he'd brought, producing a wedge of cheese and a loaf of bread. As Josef headed for the elevator, Dansky looked at Will and Gabbie. "Anyone hungry?"

"Famished," Will said.

Dansky offered the loaf to Gabbie, who tore a piece off without a word, then took a savage bite.

The Khodorovs were in their thirties and both spoke English. Minna had small eyes, a finely sculpted nose, and hair short as a schoolboy's. Her husband, Mikhail, was a contrast, with a broad Slavic face that had traces of black stubble under hollow, pale cheeks. Their apartment was scrupulously clean, warm, and had the kind of appointments—matching easy chair and sofa, Oriental carpet, artwork—that signified that the residents made a good living. A child's doll lay on a chair.

After Will explained what happened to Minna's mother, Mikhail led Minna to the sofa. She began to sob. Gabbie approached, her manner sympathetic, yet to the point. "Mrs. Khodorov, I know this is a bad time, but I think your mother was killed because of a photo she gave to Mr. Dansky."

Mikhail said something to Minna in a voice that was razor thin. Then he turned to Will. "Please—"

Minna put out her hand. "No, no, it's all right. I know about the photo. Mother told me about it when I mentioned that the new American volunteer was Jewish. She wanted to know if he could be trusted." Minna looked through tear-filled eyes at Dansky. "It happened twelve, maybe fourteen years ago. My mother awoke one night to gunfire and barking dogs. She hid in the root cellar, then heard the boots of many people above. She heard them mention '*Americanski.*' From the sound of their movement and voices, they seemed in a great hurry. Lots of shooting. They didn't find Mother, and the next morning she noticed a shovel missing from the shed. She went looking, found a hole dug under the fence that surrounds the nearby airfield. On the other side, she saw her shovel, so she slid under the fence, picked up her tool, and saw the crumpled picture caught in a bush. She took it. The next day, she noticed soldiers had come back, from the airfield side this time. They brought their own shovels and filled in the hole. Then they fixed the fence."

"That photo was of my father," Will said.

Mikhail flicked his hand, as if to dismiss the notion. "Her house is also near a gulag. They kept deserters there. Maybe one escaped."

Will leaned forward, focused. "Could they have held Americans there?"

"I never heard such a thing," Mikhail said.

Will was not dissuaded. "Where is this gulag?"

Minna dabbed at her eyes with a handkerchief. "Four kilometers east of my mother's house."

"Forget it," Mikhail said. "That gulag was closed by Gorbachev along with a lot of other military things during the Soviet breakup."

Dansky spoke. "That's when the Russians started pulling out. Left were some planes, their well-guarded missile sites, and the Gorky Medical Institute."

"The one on fire tonight?" Gabbie asked.

"That one," Dansky replied.

Will wondered if there was a connection to their search. "What was it used for?"

"Plastic surgery research," Mikhail said. "But it has a reputation for other things, too. There were *incidents*— quarantines, deaths. The rumor was the Soviets were testing germ weapons there."

Gabbie shook her head. "It's starting to look like someone didn't want anyone nosing around there, either."

"Sweet Jesus," Will said.

In Washington, D.C., the time was 12:45 P.M. as Director Jarret Kraus arrived at the Pentagon after a morning session at DIA's main headquarters in Crystal City, Virginia. He passed security and took the executive elevator to his office on the third floor. There, he greeted his secretary and went to his desk where the overnight message traffic and DIA's activity log were waiting for him along with the rest of the day's agenda. He scanned the highly classified messages first, stopping when he read a report coming out of the Ukraine. He read it through. Next he picked up the log, noting a one-liner about an EMT team that had swept his office for electronic bugs during the night. His eyes darted around the room. He reached for his intercom button, then withdrew his hand, deciding instead to step to the outer office. There, he asked his secretary to find the logs for the past two weeks. Kraus then returned to his desk. She brought the logs in and left them with his afternoon cup of coffee. After a few minutes' search, Kraus found what he was looking for. EMT had come only a week ago. Unless he had personally requested it, a security check of this nature was unlikely to have been repeated so soon. Something was up. Curious about who had ordered such a search, he went back outside and asked his secretary for a copy of both sweep reports.

30

WILL, GABBIE, AND DANSKY hurried down the dark cobblestone street away from the high-rise. The city seemed deserted, no drunks, no vehicles, just one man walking briskly in their direction, about a block ahead.

"Something's up," Dansky said, glancing around. "Where the hell is everybody?" Then a woman appeared from a side street. Dansky relaxed. "Is this stuff making me jumpy or what?"

"You should be jumpy," Will said. "They're trying to destroy evidence."

Dansky looked from Will to Gabbie. "What evidence?"

"About American prisoners of war. I don't know where he is right now, but my father was one of those brought to the Ukraine. Of that I'm now positive. And someone is trying to wipe out any trace of that presence."

Dansky shook his head. "Someone burned an entire hospital to destroy records?"

"Arson is not above these folks. The Ukrainians killed Mrs. Trinkler and tried to kill us," Will said. "And that embassy agent you met nearly ran us off the road. Arson may have been the quickest way for either him or the Ukrainians to wipe out the evidence." He stopped walking. "Jim, that military prison, that gulag, where is it?"

Dansky nodded. "You plan to just walk right in?"

"Mikhail said they closed the place. Shouldn't be too much trouble getting inside." He gave Dansky his best imploring look. "You know where I can get a car?"

Dansky laughed. "You've seen *my* wheels!"

"Okay, can I borrow your bike?"

"Can *we* borrow it," Gabbie corrected.

When they got to the apartment, Josef was already asleep. Dansky offered his and Josef's bicycles, then followed Will and Gabbie out of the building. Will tossed his backpack, with the gun and flashlight inside, over his shoulders. Once they were out of sight, Dansky headed back to the apartment.

Will and Gabbie pedaled in the cold, still night. From time to time, Will turned on his bicycle light in order to improve his chances of missing potholes. The clouds began to scatter and the moon appeared. Almost immediately, the institute rose out of the gloom. The top floors were scarred by flame. Around the structure, men from two fire trucks and an army personnel carrier held vigil. Water that had been sprayed from the fire trucks now hung in long, frozen tentacles down the side of the building. The glare from the ice gave off a sheen to the otherwise lusterless cement walls. Only a few scattered lights were on in the lower part of the building. A fleet of ambulances was parked near the emergency entrance, where a gurney was being wheeled from the hospital to one of the waiting ambulances.

Will and Gabbie pedaled on. They got on the main road out of town, and had gone about a mile when Will signaled for a stop. He straddled the bicycle and craned his ear.

"Listen," Will said. "You hear it?"

Gabbie tilted her head to the side. "Sounds like heavy machinery." She listened again. "Coming toward us from dead ahead."

They rolled the bicycles off the road and over a small brush-covered berm where they laid the bikes down. After crawling back up the small rise, they crouched, trying to see what was coming toward them. A minute later, an army truck appeared, moving at walking speed. Its lights were mere slits—headlights taped—and the noise from its engine was not what Will and Gabbie had heard. Moments later, another shape appeared out of the night. Its engine whined at high rpm. The front wheels had huge lugged tires on them. The vehicle's lights shone in two dim beams that barely illuminated the road in front. A crimson glow seeped from the cab, revealing the grim faces of two men who were straining to see ahead. Behind the cab, a nose cone of a missile moved into view. Attached to it was the long tube of a missile booster, all of it strapped to a rig whose tires were immense.

"Jesus, a mobile ICBM," Will whispered.

"ICBM!" Gabbie repeated. "They can carry nuclear weapons! What are they doing running around in the dark?"

"Maybe a coup is under way, and these guys are either hauling ass or joining the party."

Once the ICBM had rumbled off into the night, Will stood and picked up his bicycle. He looked down at Gabbie, who had not moved. She pointed in the direction that the missile had taken. "Are we going to ignore what we just saw?"

Will shrugged. "For the time being. Could be this is the way they move the damn things around. They don't call them mobile for nothing."

"So why are they moving missiles around that aren't supposed to have warheads?"

Will stared at Gabbie, dumbfounded.

"I know," she said. "You can only handle one crisis at a time."

"Right."

They pushed off again. Will was surprised his knee had not yet reacted to all the strain and now to the cycling. A half hour later they came to an intersection where Gabbie pointed to the right. This turn brought them onto the route that led back to the Trinkler farm. The progress was slower as they negotiated their way over frozen ruts in the road on their thin tires, past the Trinkler place and eastward.

After twenty minutes, they approached a point where the road dipped underground to a tunnel passage. At ground level above the tunnel, a chain-link fence crossed and curved away in both directions. Beyond the fence lay an open strip of bare ground that extended to a huge walled enclosure in the distance. The underpass appeared to provide the only access to the place. What looked like electrified wires topped the fence. A rusted warning sign written in Cyrillic letters was attached to the barrier.

Will looked around for some sign of life. Seeing none, he took the flashlight from his backpack and flicked it on for a moment, illuminating the sign. *IЦШФdФЊТФ IПТЮ.*

"Danger, mines," Will said, "if I'm remembering that vocabulary lesson correctly."

Will and Gabbie rode the bicycles down the slope to a barricade. It was made of iron bars that were locked tight, completely blocking the tunnel entrance.

After pedaling back up the incline, Will glanced at the wires that topped the fence. "Power is probably off, but it doesn't matter. That wall in the distance is too high to scale anyway."

Guard towers that appeared to be empty stood at each corner of the fortress. "It looks deserted, but I'll bet there's a safe way in," Gabbie announced. "I've seen enough abandoned forts in Vietnam to know that you can't abandon anything of value for long and not have it picked over by the locals." She looked down, then pointed to wagon tracks that turned from the road, reversing direction on the shoulder.

Will checked around again before bending over the wagon tracks. He turned the beam on for a few seconds. "You might be right. The tracks go deeper here, as though the weight had increased." He checked along the fence line and found a faint trail that disappeared into the brush.

They hid their bicycles in the undergrowth, then began working their way along the trail around the perimeter of the cleared area. Will's foot bumped into something solid. He picked it up. It was a brick with mortar still attached on one side. "Looks like they dropped some of their booty." Periodically, Will used the flashlight to follow the trail as it paralleled the fence line. The tracks stopped two hundred yards from the road.

Will checked the fence. Nothing indicated people had climbed over or cut through the fence there. He clicked on the flashlight and swept the beam across the ground on the other side of the fence.

"Hold it," Gabbie said. "Shine it where you just had it."

Will moved the beam back.

"There," Gabbie said. The beam illuminated the exposed pressure plate of a land mine.

"Forget that route," Will said. He swung around and checked on his side of the fence. Nearby he spotted dirt clods. Moving closer, he saw footprints frozen in the soil.

Gabbie followed. "Maybe they went under, Viet Cong–style."

"A tunnel?" He continued sweeping his light in ever-widening circles. "You might be right. If prisoners somehow managed to tunnel out, maybe the locals found the exit and used it as a way in."

Gabbie pulled at every substantial piece of foliage that sprung from the ground. "But the photo showed your father as a captive," Gabbie said. "If there were a tunnel, the bad guys would certainly have discovered it after the escape or recapture. They would have filled it in."

"You'd think so, but it looks as if someone is still getting in and out. These frozen tracks seem reasonably fresh." Will's light illuminated another bit of brick mortar that lay on the surface. "It's somewhere near here." He moved a few yards deeper into the brush and tugged at a thick clump of dead scrub. A branch came loose. He grabbed more, and the whole bush came out of the ground, exposing a hole.

Will aimed the light down the opening that was no more than eighteen inches wide. The hole descended about a yard, then turned toward the compound. "This is how they got out," Will said. "And how I'm going in."

Gabbie grabbed his sleeve. "Will, this is—"

"Necessary," he said.

"And if you blow up?"

"Look, those bricks didn't grow here. Someone's been using this tunnel to haul junk out of there. No escapee would be interested in taking any bricks with him."

"Wait," Gabbie cautioned. "I've got experience with mines." She indicated the open area between the fence and the wall. "These people use pressure *and* magnetic mines. You don't have to step on the magnetic kind to trigger them." She pointed at Will's gun. "The light may not set one off, but that heavy steel gun might get you blown to kingdom come."

"All right." Will took the gun and handed it to her. "Wait here." He dropped into the opening, bent over, and clicked on the light. The tunnel headed off in the direction of the compound. There were scrape marks on the tunnel floor. "Looks clear," he called out, "and well used." Then he took a deep breath and started to crawl forward.

Gabbie dropped in behind him. "You're not doing this alone." She began covering the entrance with brush.

Will turned his head. "What about the gun?"

"I left it topside."

"Sure you want to do this?"

"Hell no, but get going before I change my mind."

"You want the lead?"

"I'll let you have the honor of blowing us up."

Will inched forward. The tunnel was narrow. They could crawl, but could neither stand nor turn around. Roots dripped from the ceiling. He hadn't gone more than a dozen yards when the tunnel seemed to close in on him. The air had been crisp near the entrance, but deeper inside the tunnel the atmosphere was dank and smelled of rot and mold.

A little farther on, the tunnel widened, with enough room to turn around. Will shone the light on the sidewall as Gabbie moved near. "Whoever dug this used a small garden trowel. You can see the marks it left, and from the way the cuts were made, they started the work from this end. They were tunneling in!"

Gabbie ran her glove over the marks that Will had indicated. "So the prisoners didn't escape this way."

"Not unless they had outside help."

Will swung the light forward and pushed deeper into the tunnel. The way seemed blocked not far ahead. He made his way another ten yards, and then the tunnel swung abruptly downward. He poked the light down the opening.

"Probably went deeper to avoid the mines you mentioned," Will guessed.

The tunnel dropped two more feet before moving on. Will put the light in his mouth, then eased arms forward, headfirst into the opening. His hands hit the lower surface, and he began sliding forward. His right knee let him know it wasn't enjoying the crawl.

"Will," Gabbie said in a quavering voice. "I cannot describe the feeling that is gripping me. If that light goes out, I'm going to freak out."

"You won't be the only one," Will said. "You want to go back to the entrance?"

"Do you?"

"I can't turn around here."

"Then let's keep moving ahead," Gabbie said.

He inched forward, his shoulders scraping the side walls and knocking soil loose. He felt panic rising now. If the tunnel were blocked at the other end, he was not sure they could do the slow awkward crawl backward needed to get out. His knee ached, and he was sweating. With no light of her own, he knew it was worse for Gabbie.

Will moved another twenty yards. The air felt a little cooler. He moved the beam of light around. A small hole in the side wall, large enough for a burrowing animal, arced away toward the surface. A cool draft hit his face, and he sucked in fresher air. "You doing okay back there?" He heard her rustling along, closing the distance.

"I don't want to think about how I feel. Just keep going. Don't stop, don't talk, just move."

The tunnel took a slight curve to the left, where it widened again and went deeper. He lowered himself into the next section and pulled himself forward. In the beam of his light, he saw that the tunnel went straight for another five yards, then began to curve sharply upward. Will started forward again. "I think we're getting close to the end."

"Then go!"

The upward curve was really a shaft where it was high enough to stand. Will found footholds carved into the sides as he pointed the light upward. Stonework rose up the sides and granite slabs covered what appeared to be an opening above his head. He jammed his foot into a notch and made his way up. As he checked more closely, he could see that the stone slabs were fitted together side by side over the hole. A metal rod crossed in the center under the slabs and disappeared into concrete in the sidewalls. A small niche or pocket ran off to the left where another metal rod crossed perpendicular to the center one. The second rod touched the stone slab above it. By this time, he heard Gabbie moving underneath him and, sensitive to her blooming claustrophobia, he said nothing. Then he heard her ask, "Why have you stopped?"

"I'm checking something."

"Hurry."

Will shoved his forearm against the stone slab directly above him. It would not budge. He doused the light, put it in his breast pocket, and tried both hands against the stone. Suddenly, his knee gave way. "Watch out!" he shouted. His feet slid past Gabbie's head, jamming his legs against the upper part of her torso. "Oh, God," she screamed and began to claw at his legs. "Get me out of here!"

Will grappled in his pocket for the light. "Calm down!"

"I can't stand it!" she screamed. Her thrashing became more intense as her nails dug into his thighs.

Will got his hand on the flashlight and flicked it back on. "Calm down!" he shouted as he reached above, found a handhold, and heaved himself up. "We're okay!"

He looked below. Gabbie was staring, frenzied, breathing through flared nostrils as dust filtered down in the beam from his light.

"We're okay." Will fumbled for the words to tell her that they might have to back their way out.

"Leave the light on," she pleaded.

He passed the light to her. "Here, you hold it."

She took it and pointed it past Will and onto the slabs. "Oh, God, no. Don't tell me we're not going to get out of here."

"We'll make it . . . somehow." He said the words with a lot more confidence than he felt. Will eased up to the top of the shaft. Then, with one toe jammed in a foothold and his good knee hard against the wall of the tunnel, he gave a mighty shove with his shoulder. Nothing moved. "Shine the light up here."

Gabbie moved the beam to the side so it shone past Will. She asked in a calmer voice, "What's that rod for?"

"Don't know yet, but there's two of them." Will shifted his foothold and ran his hands around the stones above the center rod until he found a small rectangular one fitted next to a larger slab. He put his hand against it, then looked down at Gabbie. She was trying to hold the light steady. "Be ready to move out of the way in case I lose my footing again." He turned, set his knee into a notch, took leverage using the metal rod, and gave another shove. Still nothing. Then in the faint light, he saw a wedge of wood jammed between the smaller stone and the large slab. He pulled at the wood, and it came free. He placed the wedge inside the cavity just as the smaller stone started sliding down.

"Watch out!" Will yelled. The stone clanked to a stop against the center rod, leaving a gap in the slabs above. Will pushed on the end of the nearer slab. He heard a grating sound. He moved aside and saw that the slab had rotated around the second metal bar. He inched closer and shoved again. It gave way, swinging upward, the second rod acting as a fulcrum. Cold air rushed in, and Will inhaled a huge breath. "Douse the light."

She turned it off. Then he began to shiver as the chill invaded his sweat-covered head. "We're in," he whispered.

They listened a minute for sounds before Will rotated the slab far enough for him to squeeze through. He poked his head out and found himself inside what was left of an abandoned building. One wall still stood. In the moonlight, he made out what looked like scorch marks around the remnants of a windowsill where twisted iron bars snaked into the air.

"We just broke *into* a prison," he whispered.

"Fine," Gabbie said. "I want out of this hellhole, now."

Will shoved his way up. When he stood, he could see beyond the shattered wall to where a road ran along the inside of the enclosure. Dark one-story buildings stretched away in both directions. In the moonlight, everything had a ghost-town look.

Will reached down to help Gabbie. When she was on the surface, he took her by the shoulders. "You okay?"

"I am now, but I can't go back in there."

He pulled her to him and they held on to each other. In the tunnel,

Will had seen her lose that fabric of strength she had shown all along. Now, knowing full well that he had no idea how to get out of there without returning the same way, he wondered how she was going to overcome that fear. He would deal with that crisis later.

"They trashed the place," Will said. He stared for a long moment at the stone floor surrounding the escape hole. "Notice, there's no handle. No way could anyone remove that slab from up here. Someone broke in to spring whoever was here. I'm betting the rescue targets were American POWs."

"But what proves Americans were here?"

"Maybe we'll find some evidence, writing on a wall, a note, something." Will led the way. When they got outdoors, he saw the opening for the vehicle tunnel that ran under the minefield. The access looked foreboding and had a locked iron gate on this end as well. The entry road rose past the gate and into the compound, then branched left and right, running at least a quarter mile in each direction along the wall. They took the right branch and walked with only the whisper of an icy breeze for company, moving quietly as though any extra sounds might cause the place to come back to life. The buildings looked like military barracks, row after row with peeling paint, missing windows and doors. They entered one structure and found that the electric sockets had been removed and wiring ripped out.

"Anything that can be hauled off has been taken," Will said.

"Except the mines."

"Yeah, and the portable stuff went out of here down the hole we just used."

Gabbie was still skeptical about the POW angle. "The locals may have tunneled in after the compound tenants pulled out."

"Except they came up inside a gulag," Will said. "Kind of odd, don't you think?"

Gabbie shrugged. "Maybe they didn't want their comings and goings to be noticed by a caretaker."

A block from the entrance, they came to an intersection and turned the corner. Farther along, another wall appeared, a high interior one that seemed to surround a circular compound. It had a metal double door, chained shut. The lock was rusted, and when Will gave a tug, it fell open. "I think someone wants it to look as if the place is locked up tight." He shoved one door open enough to squeeze through and peered into the half-light from the nearly full moon. Gabbie slipped inside. "What is this?"

"Not sure. Let's take a tour."

The wall enclosed an area the size of a small stadium. A road ran from the gate to a cul-de-sac in the center. Cables ran twenty-five feet above the ground from one side of the enclosure to the other. Torn remnants of camouflage netting hung from the cables like a heavy valance, high against the wall. The webbing stretched in tattered shreds from cable to cable. They stepped past street-lamps that stood dark and corroded except for one that had been pulled down across the road. Off the pavement, bits of brick, smashed window frames, roofing tiles, and Sheetrock were piled in heaps around the cul-de-sac. Beyond the rubble, an open area with a few bare trees extended to the edge of the wall.

"People used to live here," Gabbie said.

"They sure liked their privacy," Will said. "That netting looks as if it could be pulled over the entire place so satellite cameras couldn't get a look."

They walked around the debris, skeletons of structures, foundations, and overgrown weeds. He shined the light on tread marks. "Some kind of tracked vehicle has been here. Looks like they used a tank to bulldoze the buildings." The rusted remnants of a car lay flattened in the driveway.

Near the second pile of rubble, a rusted convertible, minus wheels, sat in the next driveway. Will checked the rear of the vehicle with his light. Not a bit of paint remained. "They burned it," he said as he stooped to check the license plate. It had rusted, but the raised letters CALIFORNIA were readable. Will straightened. "What's this doing here?"

Then Will shone the beam on the holes where the taillights had been. "I know this car model!"

Gabbie bent over to see what Will was looking at.

Will squinted at the chassis. "This is what's left of a '56 T-Bird. It's like the burned-out hulk of my own car in the salvage yard in Hawaii!" He stood, then walked to where the front of a house would have been and shoved away a piece of doorframe. Next to it were splintered pieces of two-by-four studs. Most of the bricks were gone. Only broken sections of masonry remained where the steps had been. The Sheetrock panels, crumbling at his touch, were disintegrating from exposure to the elements. He stepped around, tracing the outline of the structure by following the foundation slab. Will made his way through the rubble, looking around, trying to sort it out as pain started to build inside his head.

Will touched the side of his face. "I have this strange feeling." He felt a slight numbness. "Oh, no!"

"What's the matter, Will?"

"A migraine coming on." He took a couple of deep breaths and felt a little better. Then Will's foot bumped something in the leaves, so he turned on the flashlight and saw a small, flat piece of wood. He stared at it for the longest time, then picked it up. "This is what's left of an address plaque." The brass numerals had been removed, but the outline of the numbers were still readable. He showed it to Gabbie. "Five-one-one-seven."

"So?"

"That was our old house number, at McConnell Air Force Base!" He pointed at the car. "First, a T-bird like my father's." He moved farther around the debris. "Now, even our garage is here." The structure had been shoved over, sidewalls crushed, garage roof upside down but nearly intact. Cross members of the rafters cast a shadow on the underside of the roofing panels as Will shone his light there.

Gabbie reached out and grasped his forearm. "They built a replica of your house here?"

Will kept staring at the rubble. The pounding in his head increased. Pain flashed through Will's brain like a lightning strike. He fell to one knee, dropping the address plaque.

Gabbie held on to his arm. "What's wrong, Will?"

"That day, the house. It's like it just happened—my dad drives off, and I'm hiding in the rafters. My mother comes looking for me, but . . ."

Will reached out a shaky hand. As he wrapped his fingers around a wooden beam, he jerked as though an electric shock had jolted him. He moaned. "Damn!" Will grabbed at his temple with the other hand. "Oh, it hurts." He fell to the ground, releasing his grip on the timber. "Not now . . ." he groaned, rolling onto the grass.

The next thing he knew, he heard Gabbie's voice as if from far away. "Hang on, Will. It'll pass." He opened his eyes. She was cradling his head in her arms, gently rubbing his temple.

Slowly, he turned his face to her. He felt drained, but calmer. For the longest time, he stared into the night. Finally, his breathing slowed. He focused on her face and brought his hand up to touch the side of his jaw. Feeling had returned. "I need another minute." Finally he stood, a little unsteady. "We have to figure out what the hell went on in this place."

Gabbie stepped in front of Will. "Give me the light and look straight ahead. I want to check your irises." With her hand, she steadied his head, and her touch felt good to him. He gave her the light. She continued to talk, matter-of-factly, as though saying one thing while thinking another. "Espionage would be my guess. The Soviets were known to be fanatics about that sort of thing." She moved the light on and off each of Will's eyes while he gazed at her. "Normal," she said. "I read once, they even built a U.S. style neighborhood near Moscow, complete with a high school, Coke machines, the works. If they brought your father here, they may have used the place to train spies."

"You think he was a turncoat?"

"I don't know what to think."

Will considered the possibilities. "As the war dragged on, the Soviets might have been able to brainwash some POWs. Maybe they were part of an experiment that included the Gorky Medical Institute in Kharkov."

Will and Gabbie had no more time to concern themselves with what lay at their feet. They froze at the sound of an engine roaring in the distance followed by the clang of metal on metal.

Will looked in the direction of the noise. "Oh, shit. To the tunnel, let's go!" he yelled. They started running for the interior exit.

Suddenly, another crashing sound was heard. Will got to the doorway ahead of Gabbie. He peered through a crack in the door. He could just make out the opening to the underpass visible beyond the rubble of a collapsed barracks. At the entrance to the underpass, an armored personnel carrier sat idling. Its diesel smoke drifted past oversized tires to where it swirled in the beam of the vehicle's headlights. Behind, the gate lay open, one side knocked off its mount. A soldier poked his head out a top hatch and began shining a floodlight on the area. He also manned a machine gun, mounted beside him. Two soldiers emerged from the rear of the vehicle to take up posts near the gate.

"They've cut us off," Will said. The floodlight swung along the road between the barracks heaps and onto the partially open doors. "Back!" Will whispered. He pulled Gabbie to the side and they held their breath as the beam of light remained steady on the entry. The engine noise increased.

"They're coming," Gabbie said.

Will took a quick glance around the cul-de-sac. All the houses were flattened. Debris might offer cover for a limited time, but if the troops were a search party they would have little trouble finding them. A few leafless trees stood behind the foundations, but they were of no use. Then Will spotted the camouflage netting. Its suspension cables hung parallel to each other from the top of the wall, over the foundations of the houses. The netting was gathered high against the wall, like heavy bunting, dipping from one cable to the next. They ran along the wall from cable to cable until, at the third one, Will found a torn portion whose webbing dangled within grasp. "Quick, up we go!" With a boost from Will, Gabbie grasped at the webbing, going hand over hand upward until she got a foot into the netting, enabling her to continue on her own. Then Will leapt. His weight stretched the webbing as he pulled himself upward. The netting separated and Will hung suspended, swinging from just one cable. He reached higher, pulling himself up, hoping the webbing would not tear free. He stepped his way, rope-ladder fashion, up to where he could reach for the top of the wall. Gabbie sat on the rim and was looking from Will to the ground on the other side.

Will could see the entrance to the underpass, a block away. The guards were fanning out, using flashlights, but heading away from their location.

The drop to the ground from the wall was too far to jump. Will began pulling on the webbing he had climbed until he had enough to toss over the wall. As he did so, the personnel carrier clanged through the doors and roared into the cul-de-sac.

"Go," Will said, and the two of them scrambled down the webbing, then dropped to the ground, Will taking most of the impact on his good leg. He led the way, crouching low, as they moved along the interior wall, then used a standing barracks as cover while they worked their way to the street. From there they crawled across the road to the outer wall and made their way back to the stockade.

Gabbie stayed right beside Will as they moved across the stone floor. "Will, I don't know if I can handle the tunnel."

He gave her the light. "Take the lead." The beam from a guard's flashlight swept the corner of the stockade. "Now!" Will whispered.

Gabbie took the light and slid into the tunnel, feetfirst. A soldier shouted something nearby. Will scrambled into the shaft. Once inside, he shoved the slab into its original position, then pushed the smaller stone into place.

"Douse the light," Will said, but Gabbie had already switched it off.

Seconds later, he heard faint footsteps above. The sound came closer. He needed the wooden wedge. He felt around inside the cavity until his hand bumped against it. Then he gently slid it into place between the stone and slab.

"Move out," Will whispered.

Gabbie ducked into the tunnel as Will dropped to the bottom of the shaft and began crawling behind her. He suddenly realized he was alone. Gabbie had already climbed into the higher section up ahead. He crawled in the dark, oblivious to the pain in his leg, bumped his head where the tunnel turned upward, then pushed himself headfirst into the upper section. There, he saw Gabbie again, well out in front, moving with abandon. Seconds later the tunnel darkened as she disappeared into the next elevated section. It was tight going and Will's shoulders constantly rubbed the walls as he crawled and clawed his way forward in the dark. He bashed his head again, reached above, found the upper level, and pulled himself up. Gabbie was near the exit.

"The brush is still in place," she said as he came up behind her. "If they're waiting for us, we'll find out soon enough." She turned off the light. They listened for a moment. Then she shoved the brush aside and poked her head outside. "It's clear." She climbed out, spun, and reached a hand to help Will.

Gabbie got the gun from the bushes and began replacing the brush over the hole.

"No," Will said, stopping her. "When they don't find us inside the compound, they'll check the perimeter. Once they see the hole, they'll waste time making sure we're not still inside."

They moved cautiously toward the road until they found their bicycles, undisturbed, in the brush. Gabbie went to pick up Josef's bicycle.

"Leave it," Will said. "If they find it, they'll think we're still around. Hop onto my handlebars. As long as they don't know we've left, we can put more distance between us and them. And if we get out of this alive I'll buy Josef a Mercedes."

Gabbie dropped the bicycle and got seated on the handlebars as Will steadied the bike. He pedaled off, straining hard against the pain in his knee, trying to get his legs to pump faster. Occasionally he glanced over his shoulder.

"Once we get a few miles away," Will gasped, "we'll ditch this bike, too, and go cross-country."

Twenty minutes later, he looked ahead. The sky was changing to the pale blue that hovers before dawn. In the distance, he saw the tree that stood in front of the Trinkler house. As they got closer, Will saw something else. He pulled off the road and pointed. A black sedan, like the one that nearly ran them down on the bridge, sat off the road in front of the house.

"Look familiar?" Will asked.

"Very." Gabbie hopped off.

Will laid the bike down as Gabbie got the gun ready.

He reached for the weapon. "Maybe I better take that."

Gabbie held on to the gun. "That was the first person I ever killed, not the first *thing* I've ever killed. I'm okay with this."

"That's fine," Will said, "but I'm tired of watching all the shooting." Gabbie gave him the weapon.

The place was still shrouded in darkness. They stepped around shrubs to the back, then peered into the pantry. Nothing moved. Then Will heard a faint scraping noise well off in the distance. They crept over to the shed where they heard the sound again. It came from out in the field. They edged around the shed toward a shallow rise. As Will led the way up the incline, he saw a fence in the distance. It made him think of the one in the photo Pam had given him. On the other side of the fence, silhouetted against the gray half-light of daybreak, was the figure of someone digging.

Will moved on pure adrenaline now, but for once felt he was on the offensive. They crept across the open ground, gun at the ready. A hissing sound was heard and became more prevalent as they moved closer. The person was focused on his labor, oblivious to their approach. When Will and Gabbie reached the fence, they noticed it had been cut and laid open. A few yards beyond the fence a man bent low to his work, grunting as he dug with a shovel into the brittle ground beneath his feet.

31

"Freeze," Will yelled, "or I'll blow your goddamn head off!" Will slipped through the opening in the fence, the gun pointed at the man's back. He moved to where the man stood motionless as Gabbie eased through the fence.

"Drop the shovel!" Will repeated the order in Russian.

The man hesitated.

"Now!" Will shouted.

The shovel clattered to the ground beside a suitcase and a pair of long-handled wire cutters. The man turned to face them. Unmistakably, he was the one who had left his briefcase in the rest room on the C-141, the man Will had seen in the car chasing them on the bridge near the train station.

A piece of electronic gear was beside the suitcase. At the man's feet, a blowtorch hissed, its dim blue flame flickering in the dawn.

"Okay, nice and slow, face down on the ground, hands behind your back."

The man slowly raised his hands over his head. "Take it easy, Major. I'm on your side." He remained standing.

Will cocked the weapon. "Do you have a hearing problem? Hit the dirt."

He dropped to his knees, then flattened onto his stomach near one of several holes that he had apparently dug earlier. The man put his hands together behind his back.

Will held his weapon near the man's head. "Gabbie, see if he's armed."

Gabbie bent over and began to frisk the man. She pulled an automatic pistol from a shoulder holster and slipped it in her pocket. Then she moved to pat him head to toe, removing his wallet.

"Listen," the man said, "I'm on your side—"

Gabbie stepped forward to jam her foot into his neck. "No, you're not."

Will placed the muzzle of the gun to the man's temple. "We recognize you." Will felt him twitch, the vibration being transmitted up the barrel of the gun.

"Who do you work for?"

"The embassy."

"Bullshit," Will said. "You were assigned to watch us from Hawaii to Bangkok. When we left there, another of your ilk got aboard at the last minute to continue watching us. Meanwhile you flew ahead, probably by commercial airliner, to Moscow to continue tailing us, none of which sounds like embassy work. Have I got it about right?"

The man made no sound, so Will leaned lower. "Give us any more bullshit and I'll splatter your goddamn brains all over the Ukraine."

Gabbie flipped through his wallet. "Everything here shows he works in Washington. Goes by Phil Garcia."

"Works for whom?" Will placed the gun against the man's temple.

After a long moment, he spoke. "CIA."

"That I can believe," Will said.

"I have orders," Garcia said, "and time's running out. I was just about to leave. Help me gather up what I've found here. We'll drive to the embassy in Kiev and clear up this whole business together."

In the distance, two Ukrainian fighter jets took off, their afterburners carving a crimson gash across the morning sky until the noise melted away.

Will looked at the holes Garcia had dug. He noticed some tattered clothing, and he spotted what looked like remains in the one Garcia was last working on.

Gabbie must have seen it, too. Will watched her as she moved to the hole. She bent over the suitcase beside the hole, reached in, and picked up a skull. The flesh had decomposed, but patches of hair still clung to the crown. A small black hole was visible in the center of the forehead. Gabbie shifted her position, and Will could make out two partly clothed skeletal forms exposed in the ground. A hand was raised on one, the fingers bent, the bones locked in a position Will knew instantly.

Will felt as if a fist had slammed into his stomach as he focused on the grisly spectacle that lay nearby. He pulled the gun away from Garcia's head, stood, and took a step toward the grave. Even though Will still had the gun pointed at Garcia, his interest was on the contents of the grave. "Who is buried here?"

"I don't know yet," Garcia said. "I followed you and came here two days ago for the same reason you did, to find out more about the Polaroid and what happened to Jack Cadence. The old woman told me where she found the photo, that someone had dug under the fence and something was buried out here, but it was too dark to search, and I didn't have the right equipment. This stuff," Garcia indicated the paraphernalia around him, "was shipped in tonight."

Gabbie looked up from the skull. "What made you come to this spot?"

"I used the black box to search for underground disturbances along the fence." Garcia pointed at the electronic gear, then gave a quick glance at the blowtorch as though irritated that its sound had masked Will and Gabbie's approach.

Gabbie picked up the electronic device. "It's a terrain scanner, a radar, like the kind we use at CIL-HI to locate burial sites."

"It registered positive at this point along the fence," Garcia said. "Someone had dug here, which tallied with the woman's account, so I cut through and located the grave the same way."

Gabbie picked up a second skull from the suitcase. "You mean graves." She compared the two skulls, side by side, then put one down and opened the jaw of the other one, turning the skull toward the brighter light in the east. After a moment, she shook her head. "Let me have the flashlight, Will."

"I wouldn't use that," Garcia said.

Will handed it to her. "Why not?"

"There's an airfield tower about a mile away. They'll probably notice even that amount of light."

Gabbie used her free hand to shield the light, then turned it on to examine at the jawbone. "How did you know you'd find remains here?"

"I wasn't sure what I'd find," Garcia said.

Will nudged the blowtorch. "Were you planning to burn whatever you did find?"

"No. You ever try digging frozen ground?"

Will noticed mud piled near the hole while he watched as Gabbie continued to shine the light inside the open jaw. She turned the skull over to inspect what looked like an exit wound, giving it a good, long look. Then she picked up the first skull again and did the same, pausing even longer.

"Look," Garcia said, "we don't have time to go into details. There's more to this, and I can explain what I know as soon as we're in the car and on our way out of here."

Gabbie looked up. "Why the hurry?"

"It's getting light and we'll probably be spotted by airfield security. There's a runway not far to the east."

Gabbie set the skulls aside. She began checking the skeletal remains that were still in the grave. She looked closely at an extended hand, then reached to touch it.

Will saw the shape of that hand again and finally accepted what he somehow already knew. His father was dead. He had risked their lives to prove something the government had already told him, only this death had not quite happened the *way* they claimed. Will heard himself speaking, but it seemed as though his voice was different. An angry, frustrated rage was building as each word slipped out. "Who did you expect to find buried here?"

Garcia kept silent.

Will cocked the gun.

"Wait!" Garcia spread his hands out in front. "I'm a field officer. They don't tell me everything. I might be compromised. You've got to understand that." Garcia was shaking.

"That's my father buried there, you son of a bitch!" Will's eyes teared up. "Now you know!" The gun wavered in his hand.

Gabbie looked up from the grave. "Will, don't . . ."

Will took a deep breath, then ran his sleeve across his face as tears began running down his cheek. "We came all this way and bastards like you had already killed him!" He took another step toward the grave. His shoulders sagged as he walked to the hole, knelt, and put his own hand around the fingers of the crippled hand that lay there.

He realized his father had been alive the day Will threw the rose on the casket, had been alive when he graduated from high school, when he learned to drive, and done all his growing up. "Damn it."

"Will," Gabbie said, "I'm so sorry." Tears filled her eyes.

Will stared at the remains, then flicked a momentary glance at Garcia. "He's the son of a bitch who should be sorry."

Gabbie faced Garcia. "Why did you try to kill us in Laos?"

Garcia thought for a moment. "None of that was my doing. My orders were to stick to your tail, hoping you'd lead me to the source of that photo and try to find out what it meant."

"Then what?"

"Then report back. Can't you understand we're trying to solve this puzzle, too?"

"Or destroy the evidence," Will added."Why did you burn the medical clinic in Kharkov?"

"I don't know anything about that. Look, we've got to get on the other side of the fence before we're spotted."

Suddenly they heard a roaring sound. Will looked up as an armored personnel carrier swung around the wooden shed behind the Trinkler house and came rushing toward them. Will raised his pistol.

A blast of machine-gun tracers sprayed the ground nearby. Garcia started to get up when a flaming ricochet caught him in the chest, knocking him back.

Will considered shooting it out with the gunner. He glanced around, but there was no immediate cover and both of them would likely be killed, so he held his fire and raised his hands. Gabbie did likewise as the vehicle came to a stop.

Colonel Stayki emerged, gun in hand. A soldier trained the vehicle's machine gun on Will as the driver peered through a slit in the vehicle. Stayki waggled his weapon in signal. "Drop your weapons . . . carefully."

Will dropped his pistol. Gabbie dropped Garcia's.

Stayki slipped through the fence opening, a mocking smile on his face as he glanced at Garcia who lay motionless, blood bubbling from a smoldering chest wound. "I admire you all. Very persistent." He waggled the gun at the remains in the grave. "Your new friends, the Russian government, wanted them dead, demanded proof of it. One of them was caught just as he crawled under the fence. The other one I got a little later." He looked at Will. "These men were an unexplainable embarrassment to the Russians." He turned and yelled something in Ukrainian. Then he faced Will again. "Sorry about these delays. I had to leave a few men behind to make sure you weren't hiding in the tunnel." The driver appeared seconds later, lugging a jerry can.

"When I was here back then," Stayki nudged the suitcase into the grave, "I had a Polaroid camera." As Stayki spoke, the soldier began dousing the skeletons with gasoline. "Useful in my line of work—no negatives—but it was still a little too dark when I made the first attempt. I was careless, hadn't set the flash. I threw the snapshot in the bushes thinking it would not develop. Unfortunately Mrs. Trinkler came upon it." He said something again in Ukrainian and the driver moved to the side. "A friend in your country sent me a copy of it, so I suspected she was the one who found it, her house so near." He walked over and picked up the blowtorch, moved clear, then tossed the torch into the grave. "No mistakes this time." The gasoline burst into flames.

Above the roar of the fire Stayki shouted, "You nearly ruined everything" Then he raised his gun toward Will.

A shot rang out.

In his peripheral vision, Will saw the machine gunner slump forward. The barrel of the machine gun swung upward and the gun launched a fiery burst into the sky. Stayki ducked, then he looked at Garcia, whose hand held the gun that Will had dropped. Garcia swung his arm toward Stayki.

Stayki fired, hitting Garcia in the shoulder. Garcia's pistol fell from his hand.

Will shoved Gabbie aside and dove for the gun she had dropped. He rolled as he got the weapon in his grasp. Another blast reached his ears. He felt stones pepper his leg as a round creased the ground beside him. Then it was Will's turn as Stayki took a moment to recover from the recoil of his own weapon. Will squeezed the trigger. The gun bucked in his hand.

Stayki's eyes were suddenly like pale glass, wide, dazed.

Will fired again.

Blood squirted from Stayki's neck as he pitched forward, into the flames.

The driver ran for the fence opening as Will swung and fired another round, dropping him in his tracks.

Gabbie was beside Garcia. She lifted his head.

"I'm finished," Garcia whispered, "but . . . want you to know . . . I never did or meant any harm—" Then Garcia's eyes rolled back and his throat rattled one final breath.

Gabbie pressed her finger to his neck feeling for a pulse. "He's gone." She laid his head down and checked his pockets, pulling out a set of keys. "We can use his car to get back to Moscow."

Will looked north, toward Kharkov. A set of flashing lights appeared over the far rise. "We'll never make it that way." Vehicles were moving along the road. "That bastard must have radioed ahead for help before he got here."

Will glanced at the armored personnel carrier, idling on the other side of the fence. "Come on!" he said as he slipped through the opening, gun in hand, then ran to the side of the machine. He climbed to the top, pulled the dead gunner over the side, then dropped through the hatch. Inside, he moved to the driver's seat and perused the levers and controls as Gabbie scampered in, too.

32

A MILE AWAY, MORE than two dozen interceptors sat in horseshoe-shaped revetments that opened onto a taxiway at Kharkov Air Base. Six planes were being refueled while four others were already crewed and running. At various points, troops manned 37mm antiaircraft guns that poked from sandbagged bunkers.

Inside the airfield tower, two uniformed men shared control of taxi and runway operations. The junior controller handled the movement of four Sukhoi Su-30 interceptors as they made their way out of the revetments and onto the taxiway. The route curved to a wider arming area that connected to the runway. The heavily loaded fighters turned, lining up wing tip to wing tip near the end of the runway. As each plane taxied to a stop, the pilot and radar operator, sitting in tandem, raised their hands, indicating to nearby maintenance men that the crew was no longer touching any switches. Now that it was safe to arm the weapons, the armorers scurried under the high-wing jets and began pulling red-flagged safety pins from the missiles carried by the twin-tailed jets.

As the interceptors were being armed, the junior controller in the tower spotted a column of smoke in the distance. He trained a pair of binoculars on it. A fire was blazing near an armored personnel carrier that was sitting just outside the security fence. The man spoke urgently to the senior controller, who took the binoculars. One look and he reached for the telephone.

Gabbie studied the layout inside the APC. "We had a demo course in Russian equipment during army basic." Gabbie pointed to one of the controls next to the driver's seat. "Try shoving that one forward."

Will put the gun aside and pushed the lever forward. The APC lurched ahead. "We're rolling," he shouted.

Through the viewing slit of the APC, Will saw exhaust spewing from the tails of jets beyond the fence, several hundred yards from his position. He glanced at his watch: 8:15 A.M., then back at the planes, marshaled near the runway.

Gabbie moved beside him and peered through an adjacent slot. "Are you thinking what I'm thinking?"

"Yeah. And I'll bet it was what my father and whoever he was with was thinking when they came near here, too. The only way out is to fly."

"Then why are we sitting here?"

He accelerated straight for one of the stanchions in the fence. The front of the APC slammed into the metal post. It sheared off at its base, collapsing with a crack. The fence flattened as the APC's tires rolled over it.

Will heard something slapping at the side of the vehicle, followed by a popping sound. Gabbie rushed to a side port. "They're shooting at us!"

Will accelerated ahead, aiming for the marshaling area and the four planes. Two of the jets began taxiing onto the runway.

"The army teach you how to use a Russian machine gun?"

"Yeah, we got to do that, too," Gabbie said as she climbed the ladder and poked her head outside.

The APC rumbled across the open ground and onto the pavement as rounds from the antiaircraft guns kicked up dirt around the vehicle.

The maintenance men near the jets took one look at what was happening and bolted for cover. Will swung behind the two remaining planes and drove between them, blocking the gunner's aim. "Point the machine gun at the cockpits," Will yelled. Gabbie swiveled the weapon on its mount.

In the tower, the senior controller picked up his microphone to alert the aircrews to the APC's presence. The first two jets, already on the runway, began their takeoff rolls to the deafening roar of their igniting afterburners.

Through the driver's slit, Will saw the pilot of the third plane stop what he was doing and look out at the APC. Then the pilot's arm shifted and the engine noise increased. The plane began to move. Will shouted, "Stop him!"

An instant later he saw a stream of tracers sail in front of the jet's nose. The plane jerked to a halt.

Will grabbed his gun, opened the tail hatch, and dashed outside. Sirens wailed in the distance.

The pilot and radar operator stared motionless as Gabbie trained the barrel of her gun on them.

Will sprinted to the side of the lead plane. He laid his gun on a missile pylon while he hoisted himself up, then picked up the gun and scrambled across the wing. Once on the fuselage, he darted along the top of the engine inlet to the canopy sill. Will gestured with his gun to the dismayed crew for them to open the canopies.

The pilot and radar operator reached forward and pulled levers. Both canopies opened. Will jerked his thumb, motioning them to get out. The pilot undid his harness and slowly began to rise with his helmet still on. The radar operator, who had dropped his helmet on the cockpit floor, was already unstrapped and standing. Will looked over his shoulder. Security vehicles were fast approaching from the tower area. Will motioned for the pilot to remove his helmet, then pointed the gun at the pilot's head. "Now!"

The man set his helmet on the canopy rail, then scrambled over the other side, after the radar operator. Will waved for Gabbie to join him. With no one holding the brakes, the plane started rolling. Will grabbed the canopy rail to steady himself, then stepped onto the front seat as the crew sprinted away.

Gabbie swung the machine gun at the remaining jet. The crew ducked as she unleashed a burst beneath their plane. Pieces of rubber flew out across the tarmac as bullets shredded the tires. Gabbie climbed out the top of the APC, jumped to the ground, and raced for the plane as Will settled into the front cockpit.

She used a missile to chin herself up, got a leg over the pylon, then leapt to her feet and sped across the wing. She almost lost her balance when Will slammed on the brakes.

Will jammed the pilot's helmet on, then looked for Gabbie. "Hurry!" he shouted while pointing to the rear cockpit. Security vehicles were bearing down. Will fired his pistol, then threw it away when it ran out of ammo.

Gabbie half jumped and half fell into the rear seat as Will released the brakes and shoved the throttles forward. The plane lurched ahead, then veered toward the runway when Will stepped on the right brake. He still wasn't strapped in as he reached for the canopy handle and shoved it forward, then brought the throttles to midrange.

As his canopy closed, Will checked his mirror. Gabbie was just getting her helmet on.

"Can you hear me?"

"Yes, what do I do now?"

"The yellow-striped handle, probably by your right arm. Shove it forward!"

"Found it!"

In his headset, Will heard excited Ukrainian chatter. He glanced behind. The vehicles were being outdistanced as the plane rolled down the runway. Then, from the corner of his eye, he spotted an Mi-24 Hind helicopter taking off near the tower. Under its nose, a turret with a four-barrel cannon began swiveling in Will's direction. Mounted under its stub wings were two rocket packs. The big camouflaged gunship swung its nose immediately toward Will's plane.

"Damn!" Will checked the mirror again and saw Gabbie's canopy slam shut. "Hang on." He shoved the throttles into afterburner just as the interior of the cockpit lit up. Will looked left. The Hind pilot had turned on his laser illuminator. "They're lasing us!" Suddenly he saw the whole nose of the helicopter erupt in muzzle flashes. Will had no idea what his speed was, but he pulled the stick toward him and the plane sprang into the air. The jet shuddered from bullet impacts while the stall-warning horn blared.

"We're hit!" Will lowered the nose to the runway. The fighter skipped along the surface gaining speed. Then Will hauled back on the stick. The plane leapt into the air again. Will snatched the gear handle up and looked over his shoulder. The Hind fell away and ceased firing. Seconds later, a string of tracers sailed across the nose. They exploded above the jet, leaving black puffs that were swept behind as the plane accelerated. Will banked the jet. Tracers rose from the ground toward the plane. "Hold on to your socks." He pulled the stick aft, gritting his teeth against the sudden G force that pressed him deep into the seat. "Got to spoil their aim," he said with a wheeze.

"Oh, my God," Gabbie gasped. "I can't . . . hold my head up!"

Will eased forward on the stick, relaxing the G force. He saw more cannon fire rippling from antiaircraft guns that ringed the airfield. Rolling level now, he pulled the nose up. A second later, the world turned gray as the plane went into the overcast.

"My whole body is shaking," Gabbie managed. "Are we safe?"

"For the moment." Will scanned the instruments. "We've taken some hits. Don't know what half of these gauges are telling me, so I don't know how badly this tin can is damaged." He pulled the throttles out of the afterburner range, then looked around the sides of his ejection seat, found the lap belt, and snapped it together. He located the attitude indicator and leveled the wings. Next he determined which gauges were the altimeter and airspeed indicator. Another gauge near the throttle quadrant looked like a fuel gauge. To the right of it, two amber lights were lit on the warning panel. Will guessed they were hydraulic pressure gauges, and he hoped the Russian designers had done a good job copying U.S. backup systems. If not, he would know soon enough when the flight controls locked. He decided not to add this possibility to Gabbie's concerns. Behind the throttles was what looked like a radio control panel that had only channel selections but no manual frequencies. It was set on channel one. Next to it, Will recognized a U.S.-style transponder, a system that transmitted a code that appeared on the scopes of ground radars. The transponder was on, meaning the Ukrainian radars were displaying his position. He turned off the switch.

Will heard chatter on the radio channel. He wondered what the two fighters that had taken off ahead of him were up to as he checked on Gabbie in the mirror. "You strapped in back there?"

"Hell, no!"

"This is no motorcycle. There's a lap belt by your side."

"Soon as I get it hooked up, you can tell me where the barf bag is located."

"I like that. Still got your knack for sarcasm."

"No, Will, this time I'm dead serious."

Will produced a nervous, unseen grin. "Put your mask on. Then find a green toggle switch. In my cockpit, it's by my right elbow. Push it forward and you'll be getting hundred percent oxygen." He heard the sound of her breathing change. "That's it. Should make you feel better." Then he noticed a small scope next to the radar and turned on the knob. Above the scope, a yellow warning light illuminated. Three concentric circles appeared on the display, looking like a bull's-eye. At the lower portion, the six o'clock position, a strobe appeared. He heard a low-pitched warble in his headset followed by a nervous query from Gabbie.

"What's that noise?"

"We've got company."

"Who?"

"A radar is locked onto us."

"Which means?"

"We have to do something before we get a missile stuffed up our tail."

"Then do it!"

Will rolled into a turn, still in the clouds. The strobe drifted to seven o'clock, then quickly slid back to six o'clock, which meant to Will that it came from an airborne radar. A plane had turned with them.

Will shoved the nose over, and the altimeter started unwinding rapidly. The gauge read in meters, so he had to do a little math conversion to figure out how much altitude he had to play with. One thing he knew for sure, zero meters and zero feet above ground meant the same thing. Unfortunately, his altimeter read in meters above sea level, not ground level. He had not noticed the altimeter reading during taxi, and although the terrain around Kharkov was fairly flat, he didn't know how high above sea level it was. What he did know was that low altitude played havoc with radars, and he stood his best chance of losing the interceptor if he could mask his airplane behind a ridge or hill.

"Gabbie, keep looking behind. If you see a missile smoke trail coming our way, holler."

"I'll scream."

"Fine." Will checked the altimeter again: twelve hundred meters. "Look, if I don't break out of the clouds by five hundred meters, we'll try to get on top of the weather to fight it out there. If I can figure out how—"

"How? You don't know how?"

"Not yet, but I'm working on it."

"Oh, Will!"

As he passed through a thousand meters, he slowed his descent, hoping to break into the clear before he ran into the side of a hill. At eight hundred meters, a gray soupy mist still whipped past the cockpit. He saw the ground for an instant, just as the tone in his headset went to a high pitch and the strobe elongated to nearly half the radius of the scope.

"He's launched a missile!" Will banked the plane sharply, turning in a descending arc. Seconds later he broke into the clear. A field, with snow-speckled furrows, was rapidly rushing up. He pulled back on the stick, then eased off a little, delaying the last of the dive recovery so as to bottom out close to the ground. A second later he heard a roaring sound. A missile rocketed by, just off the left wing, then dove into the ground and exploded.

Will checked his six o'clock. Nothing. Then he scanned the whole horizon.

He saw them far to the left. Two Su-30 Sukhois popped into view headed in the same direction as Will. They cruised in hazy air below the clouds, banking left and right, apparently trying to spot their target. They could be seen by Will because they were silhouetted against the cloud deck, whereas Will's plane blended with the ground. If he pulled up into the clouds to hide, the ground radars would be able to track his plane and the Sukhois would be vectored on him in seconds. His options were to stay low, trying to avoid detection, or go on the offensive. As Will considered his decision, he spoke to Gabbie. "We've still got company. Two bogies, nine o'clock."

"Where's that?"

"The left side!"

"I see them."

Will made his decision. "Keep them in sight." He pulled the power back and turned well behind and below the Sukhois, staying just above rolling hills as he glanced inside the cockpit. There was a red cover guarding the trigger on the control stick. He flipped it open with his finger and squeezed the trigger. Nothing happened. Then he moved a thumb switch on the throttle to the aft position. In the head-up display, a glass prism above the instrument panel that served as a gunsight, he saw a red circle appear with an aiming dot in the center. Will eased back momentarily on the stick and the circle moved. "Okay," he said, "we're in the gun-tracking mode of the firing system." He squeezed the trigger again. Still nothing. "Now I have to figure out how to arm the trigger."

"They're moving in front!" Gabbie said.

Will peeked at the Sukhois. They were sliding from ten to eleven o'clock, drifting forward but holding their distance, precisely where he wanted them. He looked over the switch console on his right side. All the toggles were forward. Then he checked the front console between his legs. A single, yellow switch was in the down position. He moved it up, then squeezed the trigger once more. The plane shook as the cannon fired a few rounds, one a tracer that hit the ground not far beyond the nose.

"What was that?" Gabbie asked.

"Our cannon. We're in business." Will picked up the Sukhois, now three miles distant at eleven o'clock. "Tighten your seat belt, Gabbie, the fight's on!"

Will shoved the throttles into afterburner and felt the smooth acceleration as the engines responded. He scanned the sky one more time in every direction, then banked toward the enemy planes. Familiar sounds and sensations surged over and through him, engines roaring like great cats, the rush of air past the canopy, the heavier feel to the stick, the push at his back from the engine acceleration—like a giant hand hurling him into the fray. Sonic shocks lifted from the engine intakes like thin shimmering heat waves that blurred the air. Will was reacting to training now, his left hand wrapped around the throttles, right hand gripping the stick, thumb trimming out the control pressures as airspeed wound up tighter and tighter. His index finger rested lightly on the trigger, his mind's eye lining up the target. His only thoughts were on what lay ahead. He became one with the machine, instinctive, mechanical, a part of it, fusing into a completeness he could never explain.

The Sukhois were still holding formation, spread wide so they could watch behind each other. The wingman was a half mile to the side and slightly behind his leader's wing line. Will would get one chance. *Take the closest one, the wingman. Flame him, then turn into the leader's flight path.* The leader might get one chance to down Will.

The Sukhoi expanded above the canopy bow of Will's front windscreen. Closing to within three thousand feet, he lined up below and behind the wingman. Then he pulled up. If the enemy leader was sharp-eyed, Will might not get close enough before being spotted. He had it worked out, though, power pulled to midrange to keep speed under control, aiming dot sliding toward the target. He eased in a little rudder—feeling pain in his knee for the first time since the bike ride—slipping the aiming dot to the right of the target as it zoomed into range.

Suddenly, the Sukhoi snapped into a right turn—warned by his leader—just as Will anticipated. He rolled to stay with the turning wingman as the target slid under the aiming dot. Will squeezed the trigger, heard a sound like a deep-throated hum and felt his plane buck from recoil as his cannon opened fire. The aiming circle wiggled as tracers leapt in front of his plane, each round arcing toward the maneuvering Sukhoi like a red streamer. The Sukhoi flew into a withering buzz saw of cannon shells. The canopy shattered. Flames flickered from the aft fuselage as a fuel tank ruptured. Pieces of aluminum skin ripped clear. Then the plane tumbled end over end, wings tearing free to release a huge eruption of flame.

"You got him!" Gabbie shouted.

"The other one! Where is he?" Will rolled left, toward the leader who was moving into firing position at Will's eight o'clock. "Tally ho." The snout of the Sukhoi moved forward, revealing the white belly of the plane. "He's pulling lead. Hang on!" Will's neck muscles went taut as bowstrings from tremendous G pressure just as the underside of the attacking Sukhoi lit up like a sparkler. Red fingers of death snaked toward Will and Gabbie's jet as Will shoved bottom rudder, snapping his plane upside down. He pulled the nose toward the ground. Tracers flashed by. The ground rushed up as Will rolled wings level and began a pullout. Then he saw the Sukhoi overshooting, moving rapidly from seven o'clock high to six, then to five o'clock on the other side of Will's tail. He reversed his turn.

"What's happening?" Gabbie asked, her voice registering the dread over being the passenger on another wild ride, this one totally unfamiliar.

"A scissor," Will shouted. "He's trying to stay behind me, and I'm trying to turn behind him. Aerial chicken!"

The Sukhoi banked toward them as Will pulled hard in the direction of his opponent. Moments later the enemy plane streaked behind with guns blazing, narrowly missing Will's plane.

"Damn, he's good!" Will shoved full left rudder. The plane snap-rolled left, both planes reversing direction again, back toward each other, the maneuver resembling a giant scissor crisscrossing in the sky. But Will's Sukhoi rolled a little faster. In full afterburner, his airplane shuddered like a wet dog as he flew just above stall speed. Will slid his finger back on the trigger while applying light pressure on the stick. The other Sukhoi started moving rapidly across his windscreen, sliding out in front on this pass. Will got set, no tracking shot this time. Instead, he planned to aim well ahead of the target, then squeeze the trigger and hope the Sukhoi would fly through the cannon stream. It would all be done on instinct. If he got lucky, one or two shells might hit the target.

Will kept the enemy plane in sight at the top of his canopy. Condensation trails streamed from the other Sukhoi's wing tips as the pilot tried to match Will's turn. For an instant Will thought they might collide. He pulled the stick aft. The shuddering increased. Any more back stick and the plane would snap into a spin. Will pressed the trigger and held it down as the Sukhoi swelled in the windscreen. Tracers sprayed as if from a fire hose. The Sukhoi pilot rolled level to avoid the curtain of fire. Will saw a bright flash on the side of his opponent's fuselage.

The two fighters separated. Smoke began boiling out of the Ukrainian's right engine. The pilot rolled out of his turn, then pulled up. Moments later the Sukhoi disappeared into the overcast.

"He's had enough, and so have I." Will dove for the ground, leveled off above the treetops, and checked his heading indicator. It showed him going west. He pulled the throttles out of afterburner and scanned the sky again. Well off in the distance, he spotted a column of smoke. He turned toward the smoke and, as he got nearer, saw chimney stacks like the ones at the factory they had seen on the road to Kharkov. He followed the road that headed northeast from the complex. Minutes later a town appeared in front of the nose of his plane. "I hope that's Belgorod dead ahead." He noticed his clothes were drenched in sweat. Then he saw a telltale ribbon—railroad tracks headed north. His heart leapt. "If I'm right, we're in Russia," he announced. Feeling no pain, he unhooked his oxygen mask from one side and wiped perspiration from his face. Banking the plane to follow the tracks, Will became aware of an enormous high flooding over him.

33

At Moscow's Sheremetyevo Airport, Boyd joined copilot Nelson as he did the walk-around inspection of the C-141. The rear clamshell doors were open. Boyd stuck his head inside and saw the VIP pallet, a container shaped like a windowless mobile home that fit inside the fuselage.

"I'll check the box," Boyd said. He hopped up onto the tail ramp, then moved forward to the side of the pallet, opened the door, and peered in. The loadmaster was placing pillows and blankets on each of the two dozen seats. The appointments were plush by air force standards—a galley, and a small conference table with seating for four. Along both sides of the wall were fold-down bunks that had pull-around curtains. Up to eight passengers could sleep at the same time.

Satisfied that all was in order for the VIPs, Boyd continued forward to begin readying the cockpit. He checked his watch as he climbed into the crew compartment: 0915 hours. Outside, around the tarmac, he noted what appeared to be the heaviest security he had ever seen at Sheremetyevo. Armed soldiers were positioned at points all along the tarmac. He knew the extra security had to do with VIPs he was taking to the United States. His group was not part of the official entourage; these were guests the president-elect had invited for the inauguration.

"I'm going back inside the terminal," Boyd told Nelson as the copilot stepped onto the flight deck. "I want one more look for our two wandering crew members."

As Boyd entered the terminal, a group of Russians in tailored suits and carrying overcoats were being ushered from the VIP lounge toward the C-141.

Will studied what he thought was the fuel gauge. The needle was halfway toward zero. He looked out, keeping sight of the railroad tracks, his primary means to navigate back to Moscow and the C-141. Estimating the distance he had to fly, he concluded there was barely enough fuel to reach Sheremetyevo if he continued at low altitude. Climbing higher would give him greater range but would also give ground radar a better chance to locate his aircraft.

Now that he was on the Russian side of the border, Will doubted Ukrainian jets would continue the chase. Since the weather was improving the farther north he went, he could climb and still keep the railroad in sight.

"We're getting low on fuel. I'm going up a few thousand feet," he said, adding power and raising the nose.

"If we climb," Gabbie asked, "won't the Russian radar see us and scramble fighters?"

"Maybe, but radar coverage is heaviest on the border, so they'd be on us already if we'd been spotted coming over."

"If we run out of gas, we can still eject, can't we?"

"No, we're not wearing parachute harnesses."

"You mean if that fighter had shot us up back there, we'd have had no escape?"

"If this thing held together, we could crash-land."

"Humph. I vote we fly low and slow."

"You're the boss." Will leveled the plane.

Back inside the terminal the Foreign Intelligence Service men who had accosted Boyd days earlier walked toward him. The tall, imposing one spoke into a cellular phone, then called out to Boyd. "Your passengers are loaded. You are to depart now."

Boyd looked at his watch. "We have a few minutes yet."

"Now, leave now."

Boyd had heard enough. "Excuse me, just who are you?"

The man leered at Boyd. "Security. There is a sercurity problem. We want your plane out of here!"

Boyd hesitated. The agent pulled a gun. Boyd stared at the weapon as he backed down the corridor, boiling inside.

Moments later, Boyd thundered into the cockpit and dropped into the pilot seat. He glared out at the security activity at the airport as he put on his headset and turned to his copilot. "Read me the damn checklist!"

Will glanced at his fuel gauge again. The needle stood two index marks above zero. Another yellow light was lit on the warning panel, which Will assumed was the fuel low-level alert. "We have no choice but to climb," he told Gabbie. As he pulled the nose up, he reached over and turned on the transponder so the Russians would immediately see his radar return on their scopes. He dialed in 7700, the international distress code. "They'll be a little confused when they see us on their radars. We'll land and taxi beside the C-141 while they're trying to sort it all out. Once we get inside Boyd's plane, they can't touch us."

"I just hope your buddy Tom Boyd didn't oversleep!"

Will leveled at eight thousand feet in clear air. Then he heard Gabbie shout for him to look forward.

Moscow lay dead ahead.

Inside the control tower at Sheremetyevo, the tower chief watched as Boyd taxied the C-141 toward the runway. A phone rang. He answered it, listened for half a minute, then spoke to his assistant in Russian. "An unidentified aircraft with an emergency is approaching. Advise security to be prepared to shoot it down."

The assistant reached for his hot line while the tower chief took a pair of binoculars and scanned south. A plane appeared just below the cloud deck. "Here he comes. Let security know that deadly force is authorized if the pilot makes any show of aggression." He picked up his radio mike and spoke in English. "Air Force two-one-three-three-zero, you are cleared for immediate takeoff."

Boyd heard the call from the tower. He glared at his copilot. "You call for takeoff clearance?"

Nelson shook his head, so Boyd keyed his mike. "We're not quite ready, tower."

"We have inbound traffic. Take off immediately or clear the taxiway."

"Jesus, Nails," Boyd said. "That asshole is long on arrogance and short on courtesy." Then he saw emergency vehicles heading across the tarmac. "Tell him we're out of here."

Nelson keyed his mike. "Roger, tower, three-three-zero is rolling."

Will saw the airfield and the C-141 moving onto the runway at the far end. "Damn, he's taking off."

"Can you talk to him on the radio?"

"This radio has only channels, no individual frequencies. It's a Soviet design meant to keep pilots from defecting."

"So try those anyway!"

He looked at the radio control panel. Surely military authorities were monitoring the channels. What if one of the channels was the same one Boyd happened to be on. It was a slim, perilous chance regardless of whether he was overheard by Russians. He decided to use Boyd's old call sign.

"Ajax, if you read, acknowledge."

Will waited a moment, listening to the dry hiss in his ear phones, then rotated the control knob. Channel number two appeared in the viewing window. He tried again. Nothing. He tried all four channels and found only empty static.

Will pulled his power to idle. "There's only one way to stop him." He lowered the landing gear as he banked abruptly to line up with the runway. After he rolled out on final approach, he put down the flaps and muscled the plane onto the asphalt. The jet landed long and hot. Will put on the brakes.

Boyd had already lined up the C-141 for takeoff when he saw a jet fighter bearing down on him. "What the fuck?" He pressed his mike button. "Tower, you've got traffic landing into me!"

"Roger, three-three-zero, hold position," the heavily accented reply came back.

"Horseshit," Boyd muttered. He added power and turned the plane to the side of the runway before stopping, allowing scant room for the other plane to pass.

The crew of the C-141 watched as the jet careened directly at them, smoke pouring from its wheels. At the last second, the fighter veered to the side and came to an abrupt stop next to the big cargo plane. Boyd saw the pilot begin to unstrap as emergency vehicles approached.

"Jesus," Nelson said, "half the rudder on one tail has been shot away. That's a Sukhoi Su-30, one of Russia's hottest fighters, only that one doesn't have Russian markings."

The tattered remnant of a rudder looked frightening, but that's not what worried Boyd. Smoke continued to pour from under the Sukhoi. Boyd shook his head. "Hot indeed. Those brakes may blow any second. What a friggin' circus!" Then he heard the tower call, "Air Force three-three-zero remain clear of the fighter!"

Boyd turned to Nelson. "That's fine with me." He shoved the throttles forward.

The plane jumped ahead as the copilot radioed. "Roger, tower, we're rolling."

Will saw the C-141 begin moving. "No, Tom! Wait!" He took off his helmet, watching incredulously as the big transport gained speed down the runway. Over the engine noise, he heard a shout. He turned around and saw Gabbie pointing. Smoke was drifting up from under the wings, but Gabbie was not pointing to that. Will looked toward the parking ramp. An armored car was closing in. A soldier, manning a machine gun on the rear of the vehicle, took aim at Will's plane.

Will put his helmet back on. He swung the nose of the fighter around, pointed it down the runway, and added power.

"What's going on?" Gabbie yelled.

"Our ride's leaving, and so are we."

The C-141 lifted off as Will accelerated down the runway. The Sukhoi shuddered in jet wash caused by the big cargo plane. As he pulled the nose up, Will heard a loud pop and the plane seemed to settle on the left side.

Gabbie heard it, too. "What's that noise?"

"The tire just blew."

Will wrestled the Sukhoi into the air, reached for the landing gear handle, then hesitated, thinking, *Keep the gear down to cool the brakes or they might blow the wings off.*

The C-141 turned west and disappeared into the clouds. Will continued straight ahead toward the cloud bank. Once his plane was surrounded by the thick gray blanket, he, too, turned west. There was a circular display, like a small TV screen, centered on his instrument panel. It was not illuminated, and there was no on/off switch.

"Gabbie, is there a round scope in front of you?"

"Yes."

"That's the radar. Are there any buttons near it?"

"A whole bunch."

"Start pushing them until the display comes on."

Moments later a repeater scope in Will's cockpit lit up. "That's it. Don't touch anything." Will watched as the edge of the screen filled with numbers and a line swept back and forth across the screen. "Great. Now all we have to do is find Boyd."

"Then what?"

"Get him to turn back and land."

"Can we land with a flat tire?"

"We'll find out."

Will turned the plane to the right, then glanced down at the scope. A small white spot appeared ten degrees from the edge and about halfway up the scope. "See that blip? That's got to be him." He turned to center the radar return while shoving the throttles forward to more quickly close the distance. Then he checked his fuel gauge. The needle was sitting one notch above zero. He raised the landing gear handle. A second later he heard a loud *thunk*. A red light in the handle remained on.

"The gear is jammed, and we're operating on fumes. Can't use afterburner."

Slowly the target moved down the scope until it was barely above the bottom of the display. Will looked ahead, straining to see something, anything to focus on, a wing, a rudder, a light of some kind. The Sukhoi bucked in the churning cloud mass and intermittent rain pelted the canopy, its sound slapping the Plexiglas. He was sweating, tense with the knowledge that he was risking another midair collision with Boyd. His mind raced back to the night over the ocean and the horror of the explosion whose image remained hauntingly vivid.

Will gripped the stick tighter as his eyes tried to penetrate the dense gloom that surrounded this borrowed plane. Demons of guilt—the thought of endangering all the people aboard Boyd's plane—got the best of him.

"I can't do this," Will said. "It's too chancy."

He pulled the throttles back and eased forward on the stick, feeling a sense of defeat. There was so much more he needed to know about his father, so many things he needed to bring to light back in the United States. If he could at least talk to Boyd, he could pass on what he had seen and maybe something could be done, but there was little chance for that. Then the clouds became veil-like compared to the thick spirals of gray fury he had been wrestling.

"There!" Gabbie yelled, "Above . . . to the right."

Will peered up. Like a ghostly ship, the C-141's wing, then its fuselage appeared out of the murk. "Got him." He glanced down at his fuel gauge. It fluttered near zero. Will pulled back on the stick and added power. Carefully, he eased toward the left wing of the cargo plane.

"There's not enough fuel in this thing to go any place to land, Gabbie."

"What can we do?"

Will looked at the huge transport, all sleek and buttoned up. Safety was mere yards away, but might as well be on the other side of the planet. Then he had a thought.

"There's one chance."

"What?"

"Take your helmet off and keep it off only until you're sure they recognize you."

There had been a time when Will and Boyd had been closer than blood kin. Bound by the brotherhood of airmen, the leader and wingman, they had anticipated every move, every thought of the other as they entered each flight maneuver. A slight wing dip, a rudder waggle, a gentle bob of the plane's nose had all transmitted silent meaning. Now, as Will slid the fighter forward, he muttered, "Okay, buddy, pay attention, and let's not have a heart attack."

Boyd caught sight of something in his peripheral vision. He looked left. "Holy . . . what's going on!"

Boyd grabbed the control yolk and disconnected the autopilot. Both planes bobbed slightly, so Boyd banked away trying to distance himself from the intruder, but the fighter rolled to stay with him.

Nelson leaned left to see. "What's going on?"

"We've got company, and I don't have a clue what that idiot wants." Boyd leveled the plane slowly, his eye flitting from the fighter to his instruments as he rolled. "Nelson, give Moscow Control a call and find out what the hell he's up to."

Nelson reached for the radio button. "That's the same Sukhoi we saw on the runway."

Boyd looked closer. "Hold it, Nails. Don't call yet."

Part of one tail was damaged and the left landing gear was partially closed. Pieces of tire tread flapped in the breeze.

Carla unlocked her seat belt and leaned forward for a view. "There's a woman in the backseat of that fighter."

Boyd saw the woman, then looked again at the front cockpit. A man was waving. "Christ almighty, that's Cadence and the anthropologist."

"He's signaling something," Nelson said.

Boyd stared at Will, who was pointing rearward, then opening and closing his hand.

After a few seconds in thought, Boyd said, "He wants us to open the back end."

Nelson gulped. "The clamshell doors? Is he planning to drop the gear and taxi up the loading ramp?"

Just then the leading edge of the rear canopy on the Sukhoi lifted up. It caught in the slipstream, peeled away, and sailed between the two tails of the plane. "Watch it," Nelson shouted. "They're going to eject!"

"Negative," Boyd said. He saw Gabbie hunched over, staying out of the wind blast. "They want in." He turned on the autopilot, then keyed his intercom. "Loadmaster, is there a LAPES harness aboard?" he asked, referring to the safety harness used by the crew when the aircraft doors were opened in flight.

"In the equipment locker, sir," Sergeant Ritter replied.

"Okay, rig it to the winch and after we dump pressure, open the clamshell doors and reel the harness out!" Boyd looked out at the Sukhoi and flashed Will a circled thumb, an okay sign.

"I see that fighter alongside. What's going on, sir?"

"We're going to try bringing two people aboard."

"Yes, sir!"

Nelson touched Boyd's sleeve. "This is court-martial stuff. We can't open up the back with passengers onboard. You'll end your career in Leavenworth."

"Career? Listen up! Dump the goddamn pressure, engineer!"

As Carla reached for the switch, Nelson spoke up again. "What about the VIPs?"

Carla hesitated.

"We're at nine thousand feet, Nails. They'll all stay warm and cozy in the box. The masks won't even drop." He smiled. "They may even take better naps while we're at this."

Boyd reached overhead and found the emergency pressurization T-handle. He gave it a yank and felt his ears pop. Next, he gave Will an exaggerated thumbs-up. When Will nodded his head, Boyd signaled him to move aft. He watched until the Sukhoi drifted out of sight behind the transport, then he turned control of the C-141 to Nelson. "Keep it level, Nails."

As Boyd got up, he caught a sideways glance from Nelson. "Think of it this way, Nails. Someone has been trying to kill those two. Now, if we save them, you're a hero. If things turn to shit, you can claim duress, 'cause I swear to God I'll rip your ass if you don't get with the program." Then Boyd headed aft.

"Be ready to go when I tell you," Will said to Gabbie.

Crouching low in the rear seat, she had to shout into her microphone to be heard. "Are you serious?"

"Getting hauled aboard is our only chance!" Will saw the clamshell doors open. A few seconds later a line appeared with a harness attached to it. He noticed Boyd with a portable headset on, watching from the edge of the loading ramp.

Boyd watched the Sukhoi slide under the tail of the big transport. The exhaust from the C-141's four engines made Will's jet yaw and sway in the jet wash. He could see Will grappling for control, trying to steady the fighter.

Sergeant Ritter operated the winch from a set of switches on the sidewall. Boyd watched for a moment, then pressed his mike button. "Pull power off the inboard engines, Nails."

The plane began to decelerate rapidly. "Easy, easy!" Boyd shouted. "Keep it smooth. Add power on the outboards." The noise of the engines stabilized, and Will now seemed to be having an easier time of it.

The loadmaster continued to unreel line, which whipped around in the fierce windblast.

Boyd pressed the intercom switch. "What's our speed, Nails?"

"Two twenty, sir," came the answer.

"Bring it back to one eighty."

"Roger."

As the plane slowed, the harness ceased its wild gyrations and began to move in more rhythmic motions, like a kite in a strong, shifting wind. As the harness veered toward the Sukhoi, Boyd saw Will signaling for Gabbie to grab it, but windblast caused it to flutter from her reach.

"More line!" Boyd ordered.

The line extended farther, and Will maneuvered under it again. This time it swung toward Will's canopy, bounced once, and careened toward Gabbie. She reached to snare it, but her hand was flung back by the force of the wind. Gabbie pulled her arm down and waited as the harness came sliding over Will's canopy again. A leg strap flopped inside. She grabbed it and pulled the rest of the harness in.

"Okay, Mike," Boyd said, "give her plenty of slack."

More line played out. Boyd watched as Gabbie worked the harness over her shoulders. Then he saw her undo her seat belt. A moment later, she gave a thumbs-up.

"Reel it in, Mike."

Sergeant Ritter reversed the drive, and the winch pulled in slack until it became taut. Boyd saw Gabbie kick free from the ejection seat as Will eased the nose of the fighter over. In the next instant, Gabbie was spinning in the slipstream.

"Faster, Mike," Boyd yelled.

The loadmaster turned the winch speed to maximum. Gabbie came hurtling into the cargo bay where Boyd grasped her around the torso. Then Sergeant Ritter was beside them. Both men worked to unlatch Gabbie's harness fittings. Seconds later, Gabbie was hauled within the bay. The loadmaster tossed the harness back overboard and began letting line out again.

As soon as Will saw Gabbie pulled to safety, he jettisoned the front canopy. The line reappeared, and Will tried to fly close enough to grasp it. Suddenly, Will felt the plane decelerate. The right engine had flamed out. He knew the other would follow shortly, when the left tank went dry. He shoved the throttle to the stop short of afterburner. The engine responded, and Will came surging toward the harness again. He had to jam in the left rudder to keep the plane under control because of the off-center thrust. The fighter wobbled in jetwash as Will reached with one hand and caught a leg strap. He pulled it down, slid it under his buttocks, and connected the buckles, then hooked his arm through a shoulder strap. In the next second, he felt the plane drifting back as the left engine ran out of gas. He pushed away from the seat, and the slipstream sucked him clear of the Sukhoi.

Windblast tore at his clothes as he began to spin wildly. Will locked his arms and legs together around the harness while the constant rotation brought on the worst dizzying vertigo he had ever experienced. He tried to open his eyelids, but the searing wind burned like sandpaper, forcing him to concentrate on nothing but holding onto the harness. One moment he felt the wind slacken as he rose into the backdraft behind the plane. Then he dipped down to spank against the howling wind that surged under the plane like a raging waterfall. Loose straps flayed like whips at his back while buckles cracked into his helmet.

Suddenly he felt hands on his shoulder and around his waist. As the noise decreased, Will heard a voice.

"You can let go now."

Will tried to relax his hold on the harness but could not. Again he felt hands working at his side. He heard the hiss of the clamshell doors slamming shut. Will attempted to stand but immediately fell over. Strong hands pulled at his shoulders and suddenly Will was on his feet. He saw Boyd's face spinning in front of his own.

Boyd had him in a bear hug as he cheered. "You, Will Cadence, are a fucking maniac!"

PART IV

34

INSIDE THE COCKPIT OF the C-141, Boyd and the crew listened to Gabbie and Will's tale of escape in the Su-30. Will, shirtless and seated on the rear bunk, adjusted a bag of ice that was wrapped around his knee over borrowed trousers from Boyd. Gabbie had on clothes from Carla, who was using a medical kit to minister to Will's scrapes and lacerated arms.

Sitting in the jump seat, Gabbie held a cup of coffee in one shaky hand and a sandwich in the other. Will updated their rescuers on the tangled intrigue they uncovered near Kharkov, heightened by the CIA and Ukrainian pursuit. When Will got to the part about the compound outside Kharkov, Boyd was skeptical.

"Why would the Ukrainians duplicate housing from one of our *training* bases?"

"I can only guess that they planned to move someone in there," Will said, "someone who hadn't lived there before, but needed to be familiar with everything about it."

"Who?"

"I think they wanted to replace our POWs with Trojan horses, doubles of our guys."

"No way they could pull that off," Boyd said.

"Maybe they didn't start out with that in mind. Look, my father knew a lot of high-tech stuff about missiles and radar. Russ Whitten—a former POW I know—told me they separated the electronics guys, like my father, from the other prisoners. Maybe they brought some of them to the Ukraine to beat secrets out of them, and held them in that gulag we found."

"That much I can buy," Boyd said, "but to decide to replace them, no. What's the purpose if they already beat the secrets out of them?"

"Good question," Will said, "the answer to which still eludes me, but we know they had a plastic surgery institute in Kharkov and years to prepare their spies. If their doubles carefully observed American

POWs in the stockade and lived in exact replicas of their homes, they could learn everything they'd need to convincingly switch places."

Carla wondered, "How would they know what the inside of those homes looked like?"

"Every three to four years, the people living in them are reassigned," Will said. "Civilian contract crews come in and get the units ready for the next occupant. Put a spy in one of the cleaning crews and you'd know the layout of every home after a few years."

Gabbie, who had been quietly regaining her strength, joined in. "After the POW release, if Soviet moles stayed in the military and got key assignments, they could gain access to highly classified information and pass it back to the KGB."

Carla scowled. "Wouldn't the real POWs figure out what the Soviets were up to and try to mess up their plan?"

Gabbie answered without a pause. "If our guys were never let out of the stockade area, didn't ever *see* the doubles or the houses, they might not become suspicious."

Boyd shook his head. "Sounds off-the-wall to me. How could the Soviets possibly pull it off?"

"Gabbie is on to something here," Will cut in. "Let's say the Soviets find some of their people who resemble POWs. They bring them to the military compound after doing a little cosmetics on them at the Gorky Institute. It, by the way, was partly destroyed by fire while we were there."

Gabbie agreed. "It's possible the fire was an attempt to destroy evidence about who they had operated on there. In my line of work, we've only lately been learning about Soviet advances in plastic surgery. They've come up with new materials, a tiering technique to build up facial bone mass, and even a way to alter the timbre of the voice box using laser surgery."

"You mean," Nelson asked, "they could make me sound like Pavarotti?"

Boyd gave him a look. "Wayne Newton, maybe."

That got a chorus of uncomfortable laughs while Gabbie was suddenly having second thoughts. "No, switching places wouldn't be practical. So many things would have happened in the Vietnamese camps that these guys would be expected to know; every place has its history."

"That's the most diabolical part," Will said. "POWs were kept in a number of prisons, according to Russ Whitten. A lot of them were kept in solitary for years. It might be possible to slip doubles back into Vietnam without even letting the Vietnamese know about them. If these guys could fool the Viets and real POWs, they could do it back home four or five years later. Don't forget, the POWs weren't grouped together until near the end, in late 1972, when the Vietnamese fattened them up to look good in media photos. The doubles could practice things like the tap codes our POWs used, which the Vietnamese eventually gleaned from tortured prisoners. They'd learn about the guards, the living conditions—everything they'd need to pass muster. All the Soviets would have to do is tell the Vietnamese that these guys were important and should be kept alive. Maybe they even pulled them back out periodically, telling the Vietnamese they wanted to ask more *questions.* Then updated them or just made sure they stayed healthy."

Boyd mulled it over. "So it's possible it wasn't really your father that was in Vietnam just before the POW release?"

"He could have been a double. Maybe he got sick eating fish heads and rice and died. They claimed my father had typhus, said they had to burn the body. All we got back were what the Vietnamese claimed were his ashes."

"This is too much for me," Carla said. "It would have taken your mother about three minutes alone with that guy to figure out he wasn't her mate. The Soviets *had* to know that."

"They figured that out all right." Will slumped back down on the bunk. "They murdered my mother."

Gabbie recoiled. "What?"

Will took a long minute thinking it out. His tone was deadly serious. "My mother was hit by a car two months before the POW release. A hit-and-run. She died from complications ten months after the accident."

"My God," Carla said. "They were that fiendish?"

"*Were?*" Will asked. "Whoever's involved still *is.* They killed Pam Robbins and Mrs. Trinkler, sabotaged my car in Hawaii, and have been trying to finish the job on Gabbie and me ever since."

Boyd thought for a moment. "But what about the ten months before your mother's death. If the Soviets wanted her dead, wouldn't they have tried to finish that job, too?"

"Maybe they decided it was too risky. The double's illness and death may even have been faked so they wouldn't have to deal with his possible exposure."

Boyd didn't seem convinced. "If that's what they decided, why not kill your father and send the real ashes home?"

Will considered that aspect. "That part is troubling. Maybe they needed him alive to cross-check background information they got from time to time from another POW they *did* replace."

"Maybe so," Boyd said. "Any idea who the other POWs in the stockade might have been?"

Will nodded, pausing so long Boyd lost patience.

"Well?"

"Henry Dalton's house was one of the replicas. He lived next door to us." Will looked away, still unable to accept what might be the truth. Then he looked at Gabbie. "His wife passed away long before he went off to combat. They didn't have to kill her."

The sound of the engines and rush of air past the windscreen filled the cockpit as the implications of what had been said sank in.

Gabbie grabbed Will's arm. "Are you thinking our next president is a Soviet plant?"

"That would explain the burning of the plastic surgery clinic, Mrs. Trinkler's death, and a hell of a lot else that's been going on."

"But Dalton's the one who got you the assignment at JTF," Gabbie said. "He wouldn't put you where you might expose him."

"Right. That part doesn't make sense. Why assign me where I might discover the fate of my father and the *real* Dalton."

"I don't think we know the fate of the *real* Dalton," Gabbie said. "One set of remains, the dental work, age of the victim, the malformed hand, all were consistent with your father's profile, but the other skeleton wasn't any Henry Dalton."

"What are you saying?" Will said.

"I examined the skulls before the APC showed up. The second one belonged to a much younger man whose teeth had steel fillings, restorations consistent with Eastern European dental work. Also, the bullet hole was made postmortem."

Will said, "You could tell all that with a quick look?"

"I have a lot of experience with remains, remember, especially with attempts to fake evidence. In this case, the exit wound showed irregular splintering of the bone, unlike what I saw on your father's skull. The skull of the second victim had already begun to decompose before the bullet penetrated it."

Gabbie had the group's full attention. "After death, bones begin drying out. They become brittle and, when struck by a high-speed object like a bullet, you get a wider, irregular bevel at the exit point. There were other indicators. The entry hole had sharper ridges on the outside edge of the skull bone. Linear fractures, the kind you see around broken glass, were long on your father's skull, consistent with live bone and almost nonexistent on the other one. Taken together, my guess is the second skeleton belonged to a cadaver that had been dead for some time, but still had flesh over bone."

"Where would they get one?" Boyd asked.

"Surely the medical institute had a supply," Gabbie said.

"The Ukrainian, Stayki, said the Russians wanted the POWs dead," Will said, "'an embarrassment,' he called them. The colonel needed to send the Russians 'proof,' but he faked at least one of the deaths. Mrs. Trinkler's daughter said 'they came back with their own shovels the next day.' That could have been to bury the other cadaver."

Will waited for someone to offer another explanation but got none.

Boyd leaned forward. "You have any idea when they died?"

"A tougher call," Gabbie said, "but twelve to fifteen years would be my guess."

Will said, "That would be about the time the Soviet Union came apart. It's possible the whole POW replacement scheme had been working fine.

Then along came glasnost. The Russians felt they had to do something, shut down their side of the operation before word got out and America's reaction wrecked Russian political progress. Maybe the Ukrainians didn't cooperate. There is historical animosity between the two countries. They argued bitterly over the Black Sea fleet during the Soviet breakup."

"It doesn't make sense," Gabbie said. "If the Ukrainians helped the POWs escape, then how come Stayki, a Ukrainian, recaptured and killed one of them?"

"I can't answer that," Will said. "The fact remains, whoever caught up with them wanted it to look as if two POWs were shot there. They faked one of the bodies and took photos, but I'm baffled by the deception. If the Russians were the target of the ruse, what did the Ukrainians hope to gain, and if the CIA knows about it, why is our side so intent on covering it up?"

"Maybe," Gabbie said, "our side is really their side. Dalton calls the shots, and the CIA is betraying the country."

Boyd shook his head in dismay. "All guesswork, which won't be easy to sell back home, except in the tabloids."

Will glanced at the clock on the instrument panel. It read ten-thirty. "What time zone is that clock using?"

"Zulu," Nelson answered, meaning Greenwich Mean Time, which is used for navigation reference.

"And Washington is?"

"Minus four hours," Nelson said.

Will did a quick mental calculation. "We have just over two days until the inauguration." He turned to Gabbie. "Not much time to prove Dalton was switched."

Boyd pointed to the radio panel. "We can set up a phone patch on the HF radio."

Will glanced at the panel. "Who would we be talking to?"

"Our military command post."

For a moment Will considered what to do. "If we call in the clear, the Russians, the CIA, everyone will know."

Boyd looked back at Will. "And?"

"They'll try to stop us, might have this plane shot down."

"Bag us?" Boyd said. "Who?"

"The CIA is tops on my list," Will said, "and they'll be listening."

"You can't be serious," Boyd said. He looked from Gabbie to Will. "Yeah, you are."

"We don't know friends from enemies," Will said. "More important, no one knows we're alive or where we are. Let's keep it that way."

Nelson shook his head. "Jesus Christ. If you're wrong about this—"

"Yeah," Will said, "we're court-martialed, ridiculed, imprisoned, but if we're right, the world's in big trouble."

Will stretched out on the bunk, feeling exhausted, as he struggled to fit all the pieces together. The trowel marks in the tunnel that went toward the compound told him that someone helped POWs escape from the stockade. Why had Stayki, a Ukrainian, recaptured at least one escapee, then executed him and buried him with a cadaver? Who in the United States had sent a copy of Pam's photo to Stayki? If it came from the CIA, why would they have, Garcia, their own man, killed?

Will's thoughts shifted as Gabbie crawled into the bunk above him. She had stuck with him, despite all the hazards he had managed to get tossed in her path. How much more could she endure on his behalf? Would it ever end? He closed his eyes for a moment, wanting to clear his mind. There was too much to consider, too little time. He adjusted the ice on his knee, then closed his eyes and thought about how the Ukrainians had caught his father and Dalton, but did not kill Dalton, at least not there. The whole thing was baffling. God, he was tired.

35

DIA DIRECTOR LIEUTENANT GENERAL Jarret Kraus, wearing a sweat suit, entered the weight room at the Pentagon Officers Athletic Center, an elaborate fitness club located deep beneath the exterior grounds of the five-sided building. At 3:30 in the afternoon, the mirrored room was crammed with military personnel who stood, squatted, or lay on their backs grunting through their exercise sets. Kraus scanned the place, which he seldom visited, his own poor muscular development being a prime reason for avoiding the facility. To Kraus, most of the exercisers were more interested in admiring their own reflections than they were with what was happening in the world around them. Many of them he recognized. They used the gym to kill time before carpooling back to the suburbs at 4:00 P.M. sharp, often leaving incomplete work at their desks.

Kraus spotted the man he sought, exercising near one wall.

JCS Chairman General Richard Ellis was doing bench presses, his torso angled upward on an inclined exercise bench.

Kraus tossed a towel over his shoulder and approached Ellis from behind, stopping inches from his head. "You're looking fit."

Ellis looked up. "Oh!" he blurted, totally unnerved. "Good to see you . . . Jarret," he sputtered. Here among the ranks, Ellis had the higher rank, so use of Kraus's first name avoided drawing curious attention. Ellis fingered the weight bar resting above his head. "Care to do a set?"

"No," Kraus said.

"Give me a hand spotting, then?"

"Spotting?"

"Keep an eye on the bar, in case I need help with it."

Ellis began another set of bench presses as Kraus leaned close to whisper. "As I arrived at the Pentagon yesterday, I noticed on my office log that an EMT team had swept my office for bugs during the night. That seemed unusual since I recalled it having been done quite recently. I checked the logs to be sure and EMT *had* swept the office a week prior. This morning I brought in my personal transmission detector. Guess what I found?"

"A bug?"

"No, two," Kraus spat the words out.

"CIA's?"

"They certainly weren't any of ours."

A young male officer squeezed past Kraus to look over the stack of weights. A woman came in and began doing sit-ups on a padded board nearby. She had a Walkman strapped to her waist and was lip-synching to the music coming into her headphones as she carefully laid her towel on the floor.

Kraus gave her close scrutiny, keeping his voice low so that Ellis had to turn an ear to hear above the din of clanking weights, grunts, and moans. "I know your schedule. This is the safest place I could think of to talk on the spur of the moment."

Ellis nodded.

"Things are amiss. Podvalny has taken over the Ukraine, and this morning I learned our problem children are onto some embarrassing details about Shadowmaker."

The woman nearby got off the machine, left her crumpled towel, and moved to a more distant device.

Ellis stared up from the bench. "How much?"

"They made contact with a CIA agent who is now dead."

Ellis's eyebrows flew up. "They killed him?"

"Only detail so far is that they were digging at the grave site of Jack Cadence. Ironic," Kraus winced, "the poor bastard died twice but literally won't stay buried."

Kraus noticed the abandoned towel. He walked over, picked it up, and looked beneath it, seeing nothing. He returned the towel to the woman, who nodded a thanks, then came back over to Ellis. "Got word a jet has been stolen from the Ukraine."

The male officer, sorting through the stack of weights, finally selected two plates and moved off. Ellis reached for the bar again and asked, "Our pair took it, you think?"

"Cadence used to fly F-15s. Word from Moscow is that a jet fighter crashed near there. No remains found yet, but the ejection seats were still in the wreckage. It didn't burn, so it probably ran out of fuel."

"Could they have walked away from it?"

"Doubt it. Pretty mangled, I'm told. I've also learned that the plane tried unsuccessfully to block one of *our* air force transports from taking off out of Sheremetyevo. The fighter took off again after it, but minutes later went down. Our people monitored short and garbled transmissions in English on Russian military channels about that time. They may have had time to radio the crew with sensitive information. The transport lands at Andrews in about three hours, loaded with VIPs bound for the inauguration."

Sweat beads popped out on Ellis's forehead, but he said nothing.

"Goddamn it," Kraus hissed, "don't you have even one useful suggestion?"

General Ellis wrapped his fists around the exercise bar.

Kraus saw the veins swell on the back of Ellis's hands. He looked down at Ellis, whose eyes glared. For a moment he thought Ellis might hurl the weight bar at him.

Then Ellis relaxed his hands. "Once the VIPs off-load, I can impound the plane and isolate the crew."

Kraus sighed. "Give the appropriate orders."

There were no other people nearby, most of them having vacated the room as if on signal, heading for quick showers and the long ride home. Still, Ellis kept his voice low.

"What about the CIA?"

"By now they know their man is missing and can assume he is either dead or compromised. They've learned something about Shadowmaker, but not yet enough to threaten it with exposure."

"How do we communicate from now on?"

"Call this number from a pay phone." He took out a business card and wrote a number on the back, then handed it to Ellis. "Now, you take care of that transport crew." With that said, Kraus headed for the door, followed two minutes later by Ellis.

The woman who had been exercising nearby slid a three-inch directional receiver from her towel's end seam, placed it inside the Walkman case, and left.

An hour later, CIA director Thornton Bishop listened to the recorded conversation to the point where Kraus had returned the towel and the voices were abruptly lost.

"Shit!" roared Bishop.

36

THE SUN WAS ALREADY down, but a thin band of blue still clung to the horizon as the C-141 landed at Andrews Air Force Base in Maryland, outside Washington, D.C.

Boyd taxied to the parking ramp where floodlights lit the tarmac. A line of stretch limos waited near the terminal. Armed soldiers were positioned along security ropes that were being strung in a circle around the plane by maintenance personnel.

Boyd glanced about. "I've brought a lot of VIPs here before, though never seen anything but unobtrusive security. This is excessive." A soldier double-timed to a vacant point along the ropes. "And a little disorganized."

Will watched the man take up his position. "Might be a reaction to what happened leaving Sheremetyevo?"

"Could be," Boyd said as he pointed at an M-16-toting private. "Maybe this time they're going to skip the court-martial and go straight for the firing squad."

Boyd turned to face Gabbie and Will. "Grab a couple of coats out of our hang-up bags. It might be a good idea if you two tried those bogus passports and exited with the VIPs. Chances are, they won't mess with that bunch. Get in one of the limousines and once you're off base, beat feet."

"Thanks, buddy," Will said. He put on a raincoat and added a tie to the shirt he had already borrowed. "I hope you're wrong about the troops. What about you?"

Boyd shrugged.

Will shook his hand. Gabbie hugged Carla after borrowing her blazer. By then, Boyd seemed to have had enough sentimentality. He turned to look outside. Gabbie touched him on the arm. "Thanks, Tom. You were terrific."

Boyd simply nodded. Then, as they were leaving, Boyd glanced their way. "Hey, Will, meant to ask. That clunker you were flying looked all beat to hell. You sorta skipped over how the other guy's jet looked."

Will grinned. He held out his hand, palm up, then flipped it to indicate a plane going down.

"Oh, yeah, how many?" Boyd's eyebrows rose.

Will raised his index finger.

"Good show, wingy, but I'm still one up on you." A faint smile floated at the corners of Boyd's lips as he turned away.

Sergeant Ritter stood by the forward entry door, helping VIPs off. Will caught his eye and pointed at the exit. The loadmaster nodded, and at a break in the flow of passengers, he signaled for Gabbie and Will to fill in.

Outside, a red carpet had been rolled out for the VIPs. Protocol officials waited at both ends. Between them stood the official greeting party, a reception line composed of the base commander, the four-star head of Air Mobility Command, and their wives. As Will and Gabbie exited, a female protocol officer nearest the plane asked for their names.

"Robert Craig and Carol Banister," Will answered.

The woman suddenly looked perplexed.

"We're translators," Will added. "Late adds from Moscow."

The protocol officer smiled, still unsure, but said, "Thank you, Mister Craig. If you'll give me your passports, we'll expedite them through customs." A security officer standing behind the woman held a stack of passports in his hand.

Will and Gabbie handed over their passports and started down the line.

"Wow," Gabbie said. "Don't look now, but the darling of the Washington press is here." In the center, dressed in a black leather overcoat, stood Janet Mills, President-elect Dalton's personal representative. Mills, all smiles, greeted one of the Russian women.

Will froze. "She's probably here because these VIPs are all Dalton's invites."

The protocol officer introduced Will and Gabbie to the first greeters, a two-star general and his wife. Then Will took two more steps and was introduced to Janet Mills.

Mills dropped her smile.

Will shook hands, then stepped to the next greeter. Meanwhile Gabbie grabbed Mills's hand, pumped it, and moved on.

Moments later, as Will and Gabbie were directed toward the VIP limousines, he felt a tap on the shoulder. Turning, he found himself facing the man who had collected the passports. The man gave Will a long look. "Mr. Craig and Miss Banister?"

"Yes," Will said.

"Your passports," the man said.

"Thank you." Will smiled, snatching the passports as he glanced at the receiving line. Mills was staring back, a look of recognition and bewilderment in her eyes, as the last of the visitors moved off.

Two couples inside the limo oohed and aahed about the luxurious interior as Will and Gabbie entered. A wraparound sofa faced a TV and wet bar. A bald, mustachioed Russian produced a bottle of Stolichnaya vodka from his attaché case and began filling tumblers. He looked at Will, then flashed a scatter-toothed smile, as he offered the first two glasses.

Will returned the grin, took the drinks, then leaned close as he handed one to Gabbie.

"Mills recognized me."

"You sure?"

Will nodded. "Sure. Soon Dalton will know we're back!"

Door locks engaged as the procession of cars moved away from the terminal. A motorcycle escort joined at the front and rear as the caravan whisked through the main gate. At each intersection, the lead cop stopped to hold traffic and the trailing cop accelerated to the head of the procession. Soon they were on the Suitland Parkway headed for the District.

By now, everyone had drinks and the bald Russian turned on the TV and began trying to work the remote.

Will looked behind. A motorcycle cop held position twenty yards back. Will spoke to Gabbie in a low tone. "Can't jump ship without causing a ruckus until we get where we're going."

Gabbie looked outside, trying to get her bearings. "Where *are* we going?"

"Let's find out." A phone, placarded for driver contact, hung next to the bar. Will picked up the receiver. "Where we headed, driver?"

The driver looked in the mirror before speaking into his headset mic. "Fort McNair, VIP quarters, sir."

"How much farther?"

"About twenty minutes, just over the river."

Will told Gabbie what the driver said, then added, "If Mills is in on the game, we'll be taken down inside McNair."

Ten minutes later, the limo tires whined over steel grating as they drove across the Frederick Douglass Bridge. Below, the Anacostia River twisted off in the distance like a great black snake, framed against the lights of the city.

Inside the limo, the Russians were in high spirits, offering toasts while fussing over the channel selection until hitting on a Spanish-language soccer game.

"Make like you're getting drunk," Will said as he raised his tumbler. They clinked glasses with the Russians and drank.

"I *am* getting drunk," Gabbie said, eyes rolling as she swallowed the vodka.

Once across the bridge, the caravan descended into the city. The pace slowed as the limo turned onto M Street. Will saw a sign for a Metro station at the next intersection. He grabbed the intercom phone. "Pull over, driver, someone's had a little too much to drink back here."

The Russian with the TV remote suddenly looked offended.

"I can't stop," the driver said. He looked in the mirror again. Gabbie gripped her midsection and began moaning.

"I'm not asking," Will snapped. "Pull over before we're covered with vomit back here."

The driver swung to the curb. The locks popped open as the driver began punching up a number on his cell phone. Will opened the door, stepped out, then turned to help Gabbie as the driver came around the front of the car, his voice low but panicky.

"We have to make this quick or I'm in a lot of trouble."

"Only need a minute," Will said. "She can walk it off."

Will took Gabbie by the arm and headed toward a column marked METRO, centered in a strip mall. As he got close, Will looked over his shoulder and saw a motorcycle cop flailing his arms and yelling as the officer walked toward the limo. The driver had moved out into the street and stood with his arms spread in an it-ain't-my-fault gesture.

"Let's go," Will said. The two of them ran the last few steps to the station escalators and raced down moving steps. Will felt his knee twinge with each jolt. At the bottom, people were passing fare cards through the turnstiles as a Metro policeman watched.

"Oh, jeez," Will said as he fumbled for his wallet and headed for the fare-card dispenser. He slipped a five-dollar bill in, but the machine rejected it. Gabbie grabbed the bill, flattened the edges, then reinserted it successfully as they heard the rumble of an approaching train.

"Hurry," Will urged. A few seconds later they had two fare cards and headed for the turnstiles while the train roared into the station.

"Wait," Will said, grabbing her arm and pulling her back. "Let's see if we're followed. Let them think we got on."

Will led Gabbie out of sight behind a wide concrete pillar near the stairwell as passengers started boarding the train.

Then Will heard feet pounding down the steps.

Someone shouted, "Get aboard! A man and a woman, foreigners . . . I don't know what they look like."

The doors closed and the train began to accelerate. Will stayed flat against the pillar, Gabbie at his side, his heart thundering in his chest.

Will and Gabbie heard radio static coming around the stairwell in their direction. Gabbie gave Will a shove and the two of them moved around the stairwell corner, away from the sound, but now visible to anyone on the northbound side of the station.

Will listened as the cop shouted into his radio, "I don't know what the fuck's going on, Sarge. They exited the vehicle and got on a train." Then they heard footsteps receding and another shout, "I'm on my way," as the cop ran back up the steps.

After things got quiet Gabbie asked, "What now?"

"We go topside." Will looked toward the end of the platform. "They'll set up surveillance at all the stops. Our best chance is to get out of here ASAP."

Together they moved briskly along the platform to the far exit. Once at street level, Will glanced around. A streetlight lit the area, and instantly Will had the sense they were somewhere they didn't belong. Graffiti covered a cinder-block wall nearby. Angry scrawls bore testimony to a part of society that still chose tagging as its bitter art form. Trees, what there were of them, stood barren of foliage in the flickering glow of a mercury vapor light.

Will and Gabbie edged down the sidewalk, past empty shopping carts, piles of trash, seeing no one about but fearing that eyes were on them every step. At the corner, they looked east. A mom-and-pop store was lit up like a tiara in a trash pile.

A female clerk inside the store stood behind a bulletproof enclosure. Will ignored her, found a credit-card ATM machine, and withdrew the three-hundred-dollar limit, knowing full well that they, whoever *they* were, would soon pick up the trail. But he and Gabbie had exhausted their cash and needed more. At a pay phone outside, Will called a taxi. Five minutes later, they were headed south, away from the District.

Will had told the dispatcher he wanted to go to a Howard Johnson motel in Old Town, Alexandria. Gabbie had suggested it, having stayed there during one of her visits to DIA headquarters, but they had no intention of actually staying there. Without doubt their taxi ride would soon be known to their pursuers once the use of the credit card was traced and the clerk at the 7-Eleven was questioned. All of that would take time, however, while the time available before the inauguration was diminishing.

As the taxi drove south, they sat quietly in the back where the air smelled heavy with the lingering scent of stale cigarette smoke. Gabbie's eyes were closed and, even in the chill of winter, her hair lay in matted strands across her sweat-soaked brow.

"I wonder what a normal, ordinary night out with you would be like," Will said softly.

Gabbie smiled. "I'd settle for the enormous luxury of a boring evening at home in front of a TV right now."

Will brushed back an errant strand of hair that lay across Gabbie's forehead. She reached up, eyes still closed, found his hand, and squeezed it.

The cab pulled up to the Howard Johnson's. Will paid the fare, then he and Gabbie crossed the street, walking to the corner, where they caught a bus after a five-minute wait. Two other people were onboard, a red-faced old man with a paper sack that obviously held a bottle and a middle-aged black woman dressed in a heavy brown overcoat. Will led Gabbie to a pair of seats near the rear door. The bus left Old Town and crossed the bridge into Alexandria South.

"What the hell do we do now," Will mused, "ride around all night telling everyone we meet that the new prez is a fake?"

Gabbie started to shiver. "What *I* want to do is find someone who believes in us, has the power to figure out who Dalton is, and can do something about it. I also want to go someplace safe, eat something hot, then take a bath."

The sleep they had caught on and off over the last three days had not been the restful kind, and food had been of the snack category at best. Ahead, Will saw a sign that indicated a motel, one block right at the next intersection. "Would you settle for two out of three of those 'I wants'?"

"No. You owe me all of them and a lot more."

"Yes, ma'am." Will reached overhead and pulled the cord to alert the driver that they wanted off.

They walked back a block, then another west, until they came to a motel, a one-story operation with an office that was still lit and a small coffee shop that was closed.

Will looked the place over. "What do you think?"

"Beats Kharkov all to hell."

A bell chimed when they entered. No one was at the counter, but Will could hear some rustling behind a door in response to the bell. A few seconds later, an old woman with thinning gray hair appeared in a faded yellow bathrobe. She was hunched over, and her head perched on the end of a long, thin neck. She stood behind a glass countertop, beneath which were toilet articles and sundries.

"We're looking for a room with a bathtub," Will said.

The woman looked from Will to Gabbie. "Only got one left with a tub," she said, never taking her eyes from Gabbie. "Can let you have it for sixty-five."

"Fine," Will said. He bought a razor and paid for one day's stay. "Any chance to get something to eat this time of night?"

The woman's dog-tired eyes drifted over to Gabbie again. "I can fry up a couple of steaks and heat some vegetables for twenty dollars."

Gabbie smiled. "We'll take it."

"I'll bring it to you. I ain't openin' up the café."

"Fine," Gabbie said.

The motel room was small, but the tub was not. While they waited for their food, they discussed who to contact and every possibility came up zero. Then Gabbie had a thought. "Hard-copy records of all POW returnees are kept at the DIA facility in Crystal City. If I could get inside for a look, I may find evidence to support our theory, now that we know what to look for and who to look at."

"DIA has probably been alerted to be on the lookout for us."

"I doubt it," Gabbie said. "DIA folks have a long-standing distrust of the CIA. Maybe jealousy would be a better term. Neither agency goes to any length to share information. If the CIA had something to hide, DIA is the last place they'd let know about it."

"Can you get inside DIA?"

"Normally you need a set of orders, but I know some of the people who work there. Maybe I can talk my way in."

"If you can get inside, check the F-105F electronic warfare types. There's one who would probably be real interested in this, but first I'd need to be sure he's not part of the problem."

"Who's that?"

"Russ Whitten, the former POW I told you about. He's probably in D.C. right now for the inauguration."

When the woman brought the steaks, she included a pop-top carafe of wine and two plastic glasses. Gabbie set the plates in the middle of the bed. They sat cross-legged, facing each other, as Will poured the wine. Gabbie took a glass. "I can't help but feel guilty," she managed, "sitting here trying to act normal, as though everything was right with the world."

"Life goes on," Will said as they touched wine-glasses. "Let's put the chase on hold 'til morning."

The smile on Gabbie's face lingered as she got up and walked toward the bathroom. "Do you scrub backs?"

"Been known to."

"Oh, yeah?" she pouted. "How well known?"

"Well enough to know how to do it right . . . I hope."

37

THE SLEEP THEY GOT considering jet lag and the anxiety over the inauguration barely refreshed them. At daybreak they ate in the coffee shop, then took the bus back toward Washington.

Police barricades appeared, stacked in readiness at nearly every intersection in preparation for the inaugural events. Gabbie and Will got off in Crystal City and minutes later stood across from the headquarters of the Defense Intelligence Agency.

Although the head of DIA spent most of his time at the Pentagon, training and fieldwork were controlled from the office building in Crystal City. Housed in a seven-story windowless highrise, it was the place where military and civilian bureaucrats busied themselves gathering and analyzing all the intelligence data that flowed into the system daily. It was also the place were DIA trained its spies.

Cars were lined up at the entry. Two guards walked around, poking mirrors under a vehicle in search of bombs. Another guard peered inside the open trunk.

From across the avenue, Will and Gabbie watched as the morning workforce arrived. Men and women in uniforms from all branches of the services entered the building.

"Most of them are training to be embassy attachés," Gabbie said. "I've given debriefings in their classes after some of the digs I've been on. They learn how to spy here."

"All our attachés are into espionage?"

"Every one," Gabbie said. "And foreign attachés assigned in the U.S. do the same, even those of our allies."

At 8:05 A.M., a stout woman dressed in a chestnut overcoat came walking from the employee parking lot on the other side of the street.

"I know her," Gabbie said.

Even from his position, thirty yards away, Will could see the woman. He watched for another few seconds. "That's Bustamante's former secretary, the one who had the going-away party the day I reported in."

"Betty Winchel," Gabbie said. "I have an idea." She led Will to a busy service station they had passed on their way from the bus stop. Inside the office, Gabbie asked for the White Pages from the attendant. While Gabbie looked up a number, Will glanced around at the shop. Work orders and car keys hung vertically from clips near the door. The service bays were full.

"Got it," Gabbie said, discreetly ripping out the number. Will followed her outside to a pay phone. Minutes later she was patched through to Betty Winchel's desk.

"Hello, Betty, this is Gabbie DeJean."

"Oh, Gabbie!!! How are you? Here in D.C., I hope?"

"I'm fine, and yes, I'm just down the street—"

"Why didn't you tell me you were in town? Oh, God, how I miss you guys and the islands, and Brad Stoner just got his third staaaaar," stretching the last vowel before taking a breath. "Ha! My new boss is a zit. I sure know how to duck out on rising stars, don't I?"

Gabbie cut in. "Me, too, but—"

"And I've lost my island taaaaan—"

Gabbie rolled her eyes. "Betty, I need to see some files."

Betty gulped. "Files? Here? Todaaay?"

Gabbie tried a reassuring tone. "We want to do a skit for General Stoner's going-away party. Need some background poop on the general and his POW cronies."

"Gee, Bob Bustamante came by yesterday to look at those files, too. Maybe he's got all you need."

"Bob was here?" Gabbie caught an inquiring look from Will.

Betty pressed on. "He's over at the Sheraton Carlton, staying for the inauguration. I'm surprised you didn't knooooow." She took another breath. "Don't tell me—"

"No," Gabbie said. "Things are . . . fine with us." Gabbie knew full well that Betty's gossip funnel was always wide open. "Anyway—"

"But the general's already taken over as deputy commander at Offutt Air Force Base. How you gonna do a party?"

Gabbie searched her brain for a response. "The general, he's coming back to Hawaii later this month. We plan to do his aloha then. This happened so fast—"

"Don't I know it." Betty's vocal chords shifted into override. "Listen, I'll notify the front gate. They'll let you in, and I'll meet you at the visitor's window. Gotta tell you all about this new jooooob."

Gabbie hung up. "I'm going in." She went inside the garage office, took the pen from the work order desk, and wrote the pay phone number on her wrist.

Will asked, "Was that Bob Bustamante you mentioned in D.C.?"

"Yes. I'll try to find out why. If something happens while I'm in there, we may need to talk. Wait here. I'll call you." Gabbie hurried off. At the DIA driveway, she stepped around a concrete barrier set up to deter truck bombers. The pedestrian entrance had a booth whose guard operated a door with a buzzer entry. Next to the entry was a one-way revolving security gate that allowed exit. Gabbie waited in line, then showed her civil service ID. The guard pointed to a sign that read, All Visitors Report Here. He buzzed her in and motioned toward a bulletproof enclosure as Betty came out of the headquarters building to greet her.

The guard at the visitor's kiosk, an African-American man built hard as a locomotive, was on the phone when Betty and Gabbie arrived. Betty waded right in. "Listen, Cecil, this here's Dr. DeJean."

The guard put up his hand to have Betty stop talking.

"Cecil, you can talk to your gal friend later. The doctor needs a pass."

Cecil's chest expanded in irritation while he tensed his biceps. "Excuse me a moment, sir," the guard said into the phone before putting the caller on hold.

"*Sir,* my foot, studly," Betty roared as she flicked her eyelashes. "What's her name?"

Cecil's face changed expression not one iota as he slid the sign-in register toward Gabbie and picked up the phone again. "Okay, go ahead," he said into the phone.

Gabbie filled out the log, then pushed her ID under the glass. Cecil took a pass from a slot, slid Gabbie's card in its place, and gave her the pass. "Stand by," he said as he put the phone on hold again. "Stay with your escort, ma'am, and remain on the lower three floors," he said, his eyes following Gabbie as she stepped to the door.

Betty and Gabbie went inside, walked past a small cafeteria to the elevator, and rode to the third floor. Betty continued a running commentary on her job and new grandchild as she led the way down a hall to the unclassified files office where she carded herself and Gabbie inside.

The file depository had rows of manila folders lining the walls behind a workstation with phone and computer monitor.

"The records are filed alphabetically by war." Betty walked along one aisle and located General Stoner's folder, a thick volume. "Vietnam vets are in the gold ones. Who you want to look at?"

"Oh, Stoner's cronies, electronic warfare F-105F guys."

Betty went to a vacant computer workstation. She punched in data, and a sheet of paper emerged from the printer. She handed the page to Gabbie. "Here's the list we have on file. Twelve of them. Find the files, then look them over in here." She tapped the phone on the desk. "Use this to call me when you're done. I've got stuff to do in the adjoining office, so it's okay. Dial three-oh-six. Now, don't wander off."

"Three-oh-six. Promise."

Betty left.

Gabbie found the records and carried them to the workstation. When she got to Whitten's, his folder showed him married with two children when released by Hanoi. A thick sheaf of forms documented serious injuries sustained in captivity. There were two entries about divorces. Nothing seemed out of place or particularly unusual. She flipped to another section entitled "Current Status" and read:

Russell J. Whitten: Head of Aerospace Technologies, Inc.

Company provides highly accurate navigation systems for U.S. Air Force and Navy programs.

Dalton's record was next. She studied his medical history. Nothing seemed out of the ordinary. Then, while checking his debriefing forms, she saw the initials RLB on a follow-up entry in the debriefer's block, dated 1976.

"Whoa, time out." Gabbie stared at the form for a moment. The case officer's initials were familiar. "RLB, Robert L. Bustamante?" She grabbed Stoner's record, and saw that RLB had taken over as case officer in 1976 for him, too. A recheck of Whitten's record and the other folders showed RLB had not been the case officer for Whitten but had worked four of the others.

At the visitor's desk, officer Cecil had completed his call. His mind drifted back to the easy-on-the-eyes doctor. Suddenly, he realized he had issued her pass without querying the restricted-access list. He sorted through the visitor IDs until he found hers, then entered her name on his monitor. His eyes got wide as marshmallows when he read: DENY ACCESS. INDIVIDUAL IS ARMED AND DANGEROUS. DO NOT ATTEMPT TO APPREHEND. CALL 555-224-3733.

Cecil snatched the phone.

• • •

Gabbie took up Dalton's record. She noticed a dental X ray misaligned inside the cardboard folder. She paused, staring at the negative. A shadow covered a corner portion of the right posterior exposure. She slid the X ray out, and when she checked the negative, the shadow was gone, but inside the sleeve, a fragment of another X ray remained. As she removed the fragment, it broke in two and appeared older than the full X ray she had already removed.

She took another look at Whitten's X rays, which appeared older, brittle, and yellow, then went to Stoner's file. His slides were like Whitten's, older-looking than Dalton's.

Holding the largest piece of broken X ray up to an overhead light, her eyes narrowed as she zeroed in on the tooth shown, a molar. Then she took up Dalton's full set of X rays and studied the same molar in them. The teeth were different. Next she looked at Whitten's and Stoner's again. She studied Stoner's for a full minute. Then back to the older Dalton fragment. Slowly her hand reached for the phone. She put it to her ear and listened to the hum of the dial tone while she made her decision. Then she got an outside line and punched 4-1-1. The operator gave her the number for the Sheraton Carlton Hotel. Once connected, Gabbie asked for Bustamante's room. He answered on the first ring.

Gabbie kept her voice low. "Bob, this is Gabbie."

Her announcement was met with a momentary silence, then "Jeez, Gabbie! Where the hell are you? You okay?"

"I'm tired and I'm confused, but what I want to know is if you worked in the POW effort back in '76?"

"Aw, jeez, Gabbie, really. Everyone is—"

"Answer me!" she hissed.

"Okay, yeah . . . my first assignment," Bustamante said, a sudden alertness in his tone. "What's this all about?"

"You were Henry Dalton's case officer."

Bustamante paused. "I'm not sure—"

"Yes, you are. And you were Stoner's case officer, too, weren't you?"

"Give me your location. I'll make some calls. They'll come, bring you in, explain everything."

"Explain it now, Bob."

"Look, I can't." His tone was cool, reassuring. "All I can say is this is a sensitive DIA matter."

"DIA?" Gabbie stammered.

Bustamante held his silence for a long pause, then asked again, "Where are you?"

Gabbie hung up, panic rising. She dialed the phone booth number. Will answered immediately.

"Meet me out front."

Gabbie hung up, then slipped Stoner's and Dalton's X-ray sleeves inside her blouse before stepping into the hallway. No one was in sight, so she hurried down the hall to the elevator and rode to the ground floor, her pulse knocking sledgehammer blows at her temples. As the elevator doors opened, she saw two security guards approaching at a trot. Gabbie mashed the close-door switch on the elevator with her hand. The doors shut just before the guards arrived. She punched the button for the second floor.

Out the door seconds later, she flew down the empty hallway. At the end, the corridor turned. In front of her was an alcove with a door marked EMERGENCY-ONLY EXIT, SECURITY ALARM WILL SOUND. She heard another elevator opening farther up the hall, so she ducked into the alcove, glimpsing the uniform trousers of a guard coming out of the elevator. Footsteps echoed along the hallway and a voice said, "She got off here."

Gabbie noticed a fire alarm mounted on the wall next to her. She pulled the handle and a loud bell began ringing. Gabbie pressed the release bar and threw her shoulder against the door. It flew open and its buzzer joined the fire alarm. She raced down the stairwell. By the time she hit the first-floor landing, people were already streaming through a double door that led outside. She followed them onto the surrounding grassy area, rushed ahead to the corner, turned, then slowed to a lively walk toward the entry gate. Just then, a mass of people burst out the building main entry. She joined the throng and squeezed through the revolving security gate. On the sidewalk now, she looked up and down the street for any sign of Will but saw none.

In front of the entrance, a car was parked in the curb lane. On its roof, a portable police "gumball" was flashing.

More people pushed their way into the street, most of them clustering around the entrance, but Gabbie continued along the street, trying to walk briskly without appearing to run, then flinched at the sound of squealing tires.

A blue Camaro U-turned to the curb in front of her. The passenger window zoomed down. "Get in," Will yelled.

She flung open the door and dove inside. "They're after me!"

Will pulled into traffic. He checked the mirror. The car with the flashing light had not yet moved.

Catching her breath, Gabbie glanced around. "Where did you get the car?"

"You sounded panicky on the phone. I figured walking wouldn't cut it, so I went inside the station, asked to look up another number, then lifted a set of keys." Will picked up a sheet of paper from the seat beside him. "I took the work order, too. The car only needs a tune-up. They may not miss it until tomorrow when it's due to be picked up."

"Oh, God, when will this end?"

"When we get nabbed and sent up the river for life."

Gabbie snapped her seat belt closed, then swiveled to see if they were being followed. "Bob Bustamante is involved," she blurted. "I just called him."

"What?"

"I'm sorry, Will, I just couldn't accept that I might be that bad a judge of character . . ."

". . . still." Will finished the sentence, remembering her adverse associations at Fort Huachuca and irked by the fact that Gabbie had alerted one of the men *he* considered part of the POW replacement scheme.

"Okay, *still,*" she snapped. "I found out from the records that Bob was a POW case officer back in '76. He didn't deny it. Wanted to know my location so someone from DIA could bring me in to explain it all."

"DIA? Where do they fit in?"

"I don't know, but they compete with the CIA in the intelligence business. I thought maybe they're on our side, trying to solve the puzzle of the photos and MIAs."

"You mean maybe *Bustamante* is on our side."

"Okay, I screwed up. Can we get beyond that?" Gabbie glanced at Will, then resumed looking ahead when he nodded. "I've discovered that more than one POW is involved in this switch business."

"Who else?"

"Brad Stoner."

"Son of a bitch!"

"I think I can prove it, too." Gabbie pulled the X rays from her blouse. "You can look at these later, but let me explain. Gold and silver are dense so dental X rays don't penetrate fillings made from them. Some types of amalgam are less dense and X rays penetrate, showing a characteristic called luminescence—a lighter tone. On one of Stoner's slides, I found the bottom part of one filling distinctly lighter in tone. Someone had attempted to replace the filling with silver, but didn't get all the old amalgam out. I'll bet the metal is stainless steel."

"Like used in Eastern Europe and Russia?"

"Yes. The Russian dentist was a little sloppy."

"*Poidyot,*" Will said. "Good enough."

"What?"

"Nothing," Will said, recalling the Russian penchant for replicating things and taking shortcuts in the quality-control process.

"Anyway," Gabbie said, "the dentist replaced the fillings on these guys, then someone switched the X rays in their files."

"Bustamante."

"Probably," Gabbie admitted.

"What about Dalton?"

"I found part of an old slide behind his set of X rays. That's what got me checking the X rays closely. Someone replaced Dalton's dental records with newer ones. The old partial I found showed a molar that is different from the one in Dalton's new slides, but it showed luminescence, too. His replacement slides don't."

Will thought about the other EWO he knew. "Did you check Russ Whitten's folder?"

"He looked clean. Ex-wife, kids, documented injuries that look like the result of torture trauma and no funny business with his dental records. He runs a high-tech outfit that makes navigation equipment for the air force and navy."

"Okay, so Dalton and Stoner will say they had a tooth filled in Eastern Europe some time back, then had it replaced."

"Dalton will have trouble explaining two sets of X rays."

"Right," Will said. He took the envelope from Gabbie and stuck it in his jacket pocket. "Where do we take the info?"

"How about the incumbent president, or why not CNN or the *Washington Post*?"

Will thought for a moment, then shook his head. "If we could even get someone's attention in the White House today, they'd think we're a pair of kooks. As for the media, they'd want to check everything out before going public with something like this. We don't have time. Once Dalton's double is president, he'll have the weight of the whole federal government on his side." Will paused. "Jesus, what if the Russians or Ukrainians have something in mind. With a spy as president and Stoner's double in command of our nuclear strike force, the two of them could handcuff our ability to react in a crisis."

"You think the movement of mobile warheads that we saw in the Ukraine was a prelude to something along those lines?"

"I'd hate to think so, but it has that kind of earmark."

"We can't just sit on this!"

"I don't intend to. Where is Bustamante staying?"

"The Sheraton Carlton."

"Let's go there," Will said. "Your call could have been the right thing to do after all. Might make the colonel panic enough to make a mistake, one that gives us the added proof we need to expose this scheme." Will checked the mirror again—still no sign of pursuit—as he wheeled his way toward D.C., while Gabby produced a tattered map from the glove compartment.

A half hour later, Will parked the Camaro in the Capitol Hilton lot. Gabbie stayed behind as Will crossed K Street to the Sheraton. At the reception desk, he addressed a woman clerk.

"I'm Robert Bustamante," Will said, smiling. "Could you run off my bill. I'll be checking out in fifteen minutes, and I'd like to go over it before I come down."

"Surely, Mr. Bustamante." The woman entered the name in her monitor and a minute later produced a one-page charge sheet.

"Thanks," Will said as he folded it and turned away.

"Oh, Mr. Bustamante?"

Will stopped. "Yes?"

"The courtesy rental car. It hasn't been added to the bill as yet. Just let us know when you'll be returning it when you come down."

"Fine," Will said. He went to the elevator and rode to the second floor, got off, came down the stairs, and hurried out through the garage exit. When he slid in beside Gabbie, he had already studied the charge sheet. "You were inside DIA until about 8:45, so you spoke to him sometime just before that. At 8:37, Bustamante made a local call, then a long-distance call to information, then four long-distance attempts to the same area code and number, 301-422-6541. Those started two minutes after the information call and spanned about twenty minutes. You spooked him, all right." Will grinned. "The clerk said he rented a car from the hotel. My guess is he did that around the time of the calls and was probably fresh on her mind."

"He spent only a minute on each of the four calls," Gabbie said as she looked over the billing. "Probably got no answer, so he went to the location he was trying to call."

"That'd be my guess," Will said, "but where?"

"Call the number and ask. Someone might answer now."

Will mulled it over. "Okay, what have we got to lose?"

At a phone bank in the lobby of the Hilton, Gabbie first called Bustamante's room at the Sheraton to be sure he was gone. No one answered. She dialed the long-distance number that Bustamante had called. Again, no answer and no answering machine.

"I could try the operator," she said, "but they won't give out the name and address."

"True, but you could call information and find out where that exchange is located."

Gabbie dialed and was told that the exchange was for the Brandywine area in Maryland.

"Try the other number he called," Will suggested.

Gabbie dialed. The party at the other end answered by repeating the last four digits of the phone number. Gabbie hung up."That's a CIA or DIA clandestine number. They answer with no names, no 'hello,' just the last four digits."

"We're outta here."

The Camaro rolled from the parking garage and headed south. Gabbie looked at Will. "Where to?"

"Brandywine, where Bustamante called."

Gabbie, using the tattered map in the glove compartment, directed Will onto Suitland Parkway, and when Will told her what he had in mind, she shook her head. "When you were a kid, did you have a do-it-yourself detective manual?"

"Don't scoff, Gabbie, it could work."

"What if this is an unlisted number?"

"Then we're wasting our time, but I don't think so. My guess is that Bustamante called the CIA or DIA and they gave him a code or some kind of clue that prompted his call to information. If the number he was after was unlisted, he wouldn't have gotten it from the operator. But he did get it. Then he called and got no answer, but somehow figured out where to go."

"Would the operator give him the address?"

"Sometimes they do if there's more than one entry under the same name, but if not, he could get it the same way we're going to try, using a local phone book."

Gabbie considered Will's theory. "I take back my sarcasm about the detective kit."

"No need. I had one."

They got off the Suitland at Silver Hill and took Route 5 south, sticking to it until it cut across Highway 381 going east. The wind had picked up, and Will could feel the car bucking in response. Four miles later, they entered the town of Brandywine, a ramshackle burg with grain silos, a gas station, a motel, a video outlet, and a VCR repair shop that advertised a sale on cellular phones.

"Ideal," Will said. He parked a half block away. Once inside the repair shop, he asked the clerk for a local phone directory. When the woman produced two, a local and an area directory, Will signed a contract for a cellular phone and was given the books as a courtesy. For billing purposes, he had to use his credit card. He was back in the car ten minutes later, separating the smaller, half-inch-thick local directory apart at the binding. "Bustamante probably had an easier time of it since it's likely he had a last name to work with." Will handed a section to Gabbie as he put the car in gear and drove off. "Start checking."

They stopped on a side road out of town. With eyes burning for the next twenty minutes, they tried to match the number they had with the 422 exchange until Will got lucky. Under the M's was a listing for Musser with an address: RD 2 Posson Hill Road. Will drove back to the gas station and got directions.

Once out of town, they caught a secondary road and immediately found themselves in rural Maryland, with narrow byways leading off the main road and banks of free-standing mailboxes clustered like spreading mushrooms at each turnoff. The road climbed a slight rise, then dropped, crossing a stream. Just beyond a small bridge, a gravel road appeared on the right.

Three mailboxes were visible as Will slowed. Wrought-iron lettering of the name TATUM sat on top of the first. Next to it, reflective letters were pasted on the side of a box that spelled out the name JACOBS. The flag was up on the Jacobs' box. The third one had no name but tacked to the post beneath was a wooden sign announcing POSSON HILL RD. Will saw a house behind a stand of trees two hundred yards up Posson Hill. The place looked boarded up for the winter. A second house was barely visible through the trees on the other side of the road, which continued over another rise.

"Don't see a third house. What do you think?" Will said.

"Eerie."

"Yeah, and we can't go around knocking on doors. If Musser and Bustamante are out here, they'd be keen on noticing who's coming up the driveway." Will bypassed Posson Hill Road, continuing along the highway until he came to another paved road that ran perpendicular to the small road. He saw no houses to the south, so he went that way, pulling to the side to park between two evergreen trees. A lowering cloudbank cast a darkening gray pall over the area.

"How about if I slip up to the rear of the places on Posson Hill?" Will caught a look of disagreement on Gabbie's face.

"Together," she said. "If nothing turns up, let's get the hell out of here."

Will grabbed the cell phone and led the way, moving among tall oaks and maples to a clearing. The ground was hard and as they crushed matted vegetation, the unmistakable smell of wild onions filled the air. Then they were in brush, moving in silence, stopping every few yards like deer, sniffing the air, listening. A jittery breeze stirred branches above their heads.

Will shivered in the cold. The wind blew right through the thin coat Boyd had provided. At least his knee was holding up. The two houses they had seen appeared through a thick clump of spruce. "Vacant," Will said. "Hang tough. The third one should be over that knoll."

They bent low, working their way over the rise where they spotted the rear of another house. A white two-story lay tucked behind thick brush. An outbuilding, its door wide open, sat well back. Just behind the house was a satellite antenna mounted on a concrete base. A Ford Explorer with a sun shield stuffed behind its windshield was parked near the outbuilding. A sedan sat behind it.

As they moved nearer, Will pointed. "The car has D.C. plates. Maybe we've found Bustamante." He could see the back of the place through thick brush. A light was on in the kitchen, which was partly visible through its door glass and from bay windows on either side of the door. Moving to within yards of the place, they saw no movement but could make out details in the kitchen, a refrigerator, and beside it a phone mounted on the wall. He took out the cellular, dialed the Musser number, then held the phone to an ear as he watched.

Even at that distance, the sound of the phone ringing inside the house was clear. After two rings, a man appeared in the kitchen, shuffled to the wall, and picked up the phone.

"Hello."

Will recognized the voice.

"Hello," the man said again as he turned and faced the window. "Is anyone there?"

Will watched, mesmerized, saying nothing, unable to take his eyes off what he was seeing.

Gabbie leaned close. "Who is it?"

The man hung up, paused, then moved from sight.

"Jesus H. Christ," Will whispered, then lowered the phone. "Henry Dalton is in there!"

38

"IT COULDN'T BE," GABBIE said. "There'd be Secret Service agents all over the place. We'd never have gotten this close."

"I know what I saw and heard." Will stood. "I'm going to find out what the next president of the United States is doing holed up in the boonies—"

"Wait," she said. "There may be two of them."

"I don't give a damn."

"No, you don't understand. Two *Daltons.*"

Will hesitated.

"Don't you see, Will? What if Henry Dalton escaped from the Ukraine? I bet he and his double are both here in the States! We can't rush in to find out which one this guy is. Whoever is in there is probably armed."

They heard a buzzing sound, at intervals, like the phone was ringing again. No one came to the kitchen, but the buzzing quit after two cycles.

Moments later, a shadow swept through the kitchen. The rear door opened. Will and Gabbie dropped flat behind brush.

Bustamante appeared and ran toward the car. He jumped in and started the engine. Then a bearded man wearing glasses came out, locked the door, and limped toward the car.

"Who's that?" Gabbie whispered.

"Dalton. Same clothes, disguise added. We spooked them!"

"Or that second caller did."

Bustamante waited for the bearded man to get in. Gravel flew as Bustamante stepped on the gas, backed onto the road, turned, and accelerated over the rise.

Will gave the house another long look, then started through the last tangle of boughs.

Gabbie raised a cautioning hand. "What if someone else is inside?"

"I'll soon find out. Wait here."

Will pushed clear of the branches and moved to the rear door, climbed creaky steps to the kitchen entry, and peered in. No one in sight. He tried the door. Locked. Both windows beside it had security devices attached. He noticed Gabbie approaching.

"Wired," Will said. "Probably have motion sensors, too." He moved away from the house, checked the upper windows and roof. A mushroom-shaped attic vent protruded from the roof near several intricate wire antennas he hadn't noticed before.

"They may not have motion sensors upstairs," Will said, "and even if they do, my guess is the system isn't connected to the local sheriff." He glanced around. "I need a ladder."

"The barn?" Gabbie suggested.

Inside the outbuilding, Will let his eyes adjust to the darkness, breathed the sweet scent of dry hay, and heard a high-strung whinny deep inside. A stable. A wooden ladder materialized in the gloom, leaning against a loft.

Will hauled the ladder outside and propped it against the rear eave of the house. Once on the roof, he stepped gingerly on grainy tiles, holding on to the antennas for support. Then he sat on the peak. The metal vent by his feet was just over a foot in diameter. Inside its housing, a louvered mechanism spun lazily. Will kicked at the housing with his good leg until the vent came loose and tumbled to the ground. He slid feetfirst into the aperture, wriggled inside the roof, and found himself cramped inside a narrow attic space. While lying on his side across joists, he pulled away insulation, then rammed his elbow at the exposed Sheetrock beneath. After three smacks, he had punched a hole in the ceiling. He peeked below.

Will was above a master bedroom, a sizeable one. He listened for a time, heard nothing, so he swung his feet around and used his heel to enlarge the hole. After squeezing through the opening, he dropped onto the bed and stepped to the floor. Gabbie slipped through moments later.

Dark drapes covered the windows, the whole decor somber. Will flicked on the light. One wall had a built-in bookcase and TV-VCR combination centered in it. Tapes stacked below were labeled by hand and read C-SPAN, CNBC, or CNN and had a date. Will scanned the book titles spotting Bob Woodward's *Veil: The Secret Wars of the CIA 1981-1987.* Next to it was *The Pentagon Papers.* In the row underneath those were biographies of Gerald Ford, Nixon, and retired members of Congress, Sam Nunn, Newt Gingrich, and others. A publication lay open on the night table. Will picked it up: The *Reports of the Comptroller General of the United States Submitted to the Subcommittee on International Affairs.*

"I'd know what to buy this Dalton for Christmas," Will murmured. "Barnes and Noble here I come."

"Kept it tidy, till you dropped in," Gabbie said as she dusted herself off. She moved to the VCR, turned on the power and hit the eject button. A tape popped out. "It's been run but not rewound. Blank label." She put the tape back in and hit REWIND. When the VCR stopped, Gabbie turned on the TV and pressed PLAY. The recording was of a C-SPAN congressional session taken that day. Henry Dalton was being given a salute by his former senatorial colleagues. "Likes to see how his twin looks on the tube," Gabbie said. She turned off the program, then went to the dresser. A jewelry box, shaped like a rolltop desk, sat on top. She opened it. Inside were cuff links, tie tacks, and a set of keys on a ring. She took the keys. "May need these," she said.

Will went to the door and opened it. Across the hallway was a bathroom, door open. Farther down was a closed door.

Inside the bathroom, towels were neatly hung near a bathtub that had an oversized shower nozzle. Gabbie looked at the tub. "Cleanest bachelor pad I've ever seen."

"Seen many?"

"Enough to know a clean one."

They moved to the closed door. Locked. Gabbie looked at the key ring she had. One key was to a Ford vehicle; the others were door keys. On Gabbie's second try, the lock opened. Inside was a desktop computer, printer, fax, scanner, copier, and two black phones that had odd-looking receivers—like surgical or scuba masks—for speaking into. The phones sat on top of cardboard cartons next to a box of Handi Wipes.

"Looks like a poor man's command post," Will said.

"No numbers on the phones," Gabbie said. "Direct lines to somewhere, and I'll bet these buzz. Wonder who's at the other end."

"My guess is the CIA or DIA. The regular phone in the kitchen is probably there so things look normal to visitors. We upset their plans, and either the real Henry Dalton is about to become president or his shadow is!"

Gabbie heard the sound of a helicopter in the distance. "They're on to us!" she said. "Quick!"

They charged downstairs, ran through the kitchen, and as Will unlocked the back door, Gabbie yelled, "Better split up!" She held the keys aloft. "I'll take the four-wheel. You go for the car! One of us might get away."

Will ran outside. The *whup-whup* grew louder but the helicopter was still in the clouds. "No way I'm leaving you!"

"This is more important than you or me. They've got a helicopter, goddamn it, now do what I say! I'll call the number on your cell phone when I'm safe."

Gabbie unlocked the Ford and leapt inside.

Will hesitated, taking a step toward Gabbie.

"Go!" She locked the door and ducked behind the windshield sunscreen as the sound of the helicopter intensified.

Will sprinted for cover inside the stable. The building shook. Straw filled the air as rotorwash swirled in. The horse whinnied in panic, thrashing its hooves against the stall as the aircraft passed overhead. It came to a hover somewhere out in front of the house.

Will ran through the stable and out a rear door. He saw a cloud of dust rise in the field next to the house as the Ford roared across open ground toward the road Bustamante had taken. Will took off, his knee aching in protest as he went crashing through brush, swiping branches, looking back to check for pursuit. Trees flashed by, murky shadows that poked at his clothing. Then he was in the clearing, panting like a spent greyhound. He crossed the field to the road. The Camaro stood undisturbed. He limped the last few steps, listening to the baying sound of the helicopter in the distance.

Will shoved the key in the ignition, started the engine, then sped south, away from Highway 381, until he came to a main road headed west. He made a turn and joined traffic, listening out the open window for the helicopter, wondering what had happened to Gabbie. He saw a sign reading US 301 TO WASHINGTON, 4 MILES. He drove for some minutes, torn by thoughts about what he should have done, could have done, but he had "followed orders" instead. Gabbie could be dead now, her life ended like so many others who had gotten in the way.

As he got closer to Washington, his breathing eased and he began to try to work things out, to make Gabbie's fate, whatever it was, count for something. He remembered Russ Whitten who back in Hawaii had invited him to the preinaugural gathering of former POWs. Will wasn't sure, but he thought Whitten had mentioned staying at the Mayflower. He patted his jacket pocket. It still held the envelope with the X rays Gabbie had given him.

If he got inside the function, Will thought, he could confront Dalton and Stoner, ask them to prove who they were to the other POWs: a little dental checkup to see which X rays their teeth matched.

They'd have trouble refusing in front of four hundred guys who have a score to settle over torture and imprisonment.

Will would need some support, though. Could he really trust Whitten?

39

Will drove to the Springfield Mall, outside the Beltway, parked, and placed a call on his cellular.

"Uncle Russ? This is Will Cadence."

"I'll be gone to hell! Been trying to flush you out for two weeks. Where in blazes are you?"

"Just got in town. Long story. I'm wondering if that invitation to the preinaugural is still open."

"Wide open, but I got to call the committee and let them know. Their security is tighter than a nun's crotch."

Will had a thought. "Is General Stoner on the committee?"

"Hell, no. He's too busy polishing his stars to mess with mundane crap. How come you ask? You on his shit list?"

"In a way, but I'll tell you about it later."

They agreed to meet at Whitten's suite before the preinaugural.

While at the mall, Will bought a travel bag and began filling it with underclothes, socks, toiletries, and casual clothes. Johnson's Formal Wear was his source for a rental tuxedo.

From the store, he drove to a new motel in Alexandria. He paid cash for a room, showered, and dressed, his mood dismal, deflated. These were the first moments he and Gabbie had not been together since leaving Hawaii. His mind flooded with worry as he periodically glanced at the cell phone, hoping Gabbie would call. Meanwhile, he concentrated his study on the dental X rays Gabbie had given him, then placed them in his tuxedo breast pocket.

Outside, he drove to Old Town, Alexandria, parked, dropped the keys on the floor and left. He grabbed the cell phone and joined a throng of couples dressed in formal attire, headed for the King Street Metro Station. A half hour later he got off at Farragut West and walked up Seventeenth to Connecticut, while checking behind for the pursuit he was sure was out there. Limousines wound through traffic. Horns blared. D.C. police were on horseback, on foot, in cars—everywhere.

The front facade of the Mayflower was ablaze in lights highlighting its second-story terrace, adorned with American flags. A long line of guests extended out onto the sidewalk. Uniformed security stood at strategic points near the hotel, their radios crackling with instructions.

On the sidewalk across from the hotel, Will stopped. The air was crisp and the night had softened the wind. People flashed by, most of them jovial, ready to party. A U.S. Air Force honor guard off-loaded from a van. The team proceeded through security, even had their leather flag cases inspected.

The hotel access was cordoned off with two lines, one marked Inaugural Reception Attendees and another Hotel Guests. Whitten had instructed Will to proceed to the guest entry where the management would be alerted to his arrival.

A security guard ushered Will through a metal detector and an explosives sensor before allowing entry onto the promenade with its marble floor, central row of glittering chandeliers, and floral ceiling. He approached the concierge counter and gave the woman his name and whom he had come to visit.

Another security barrier separated the promenade and the elevators. Reception attendees were cordoned off by ropes that led up a staircase past a sign for the Grand Ballroom upstairs.

"Excuse me," the clerk said. "I need to see a photo ID."

Will produced his military ID card. She looked at it and him, made an entry on her computer, then picked up the phone and dialed. "Mr. Whitten, Mr. Will Cadence is here . . . Thank you." She ran a plastic card across a magnetic device, then handed it to Will. "Your guest pass.

Good for this evening only. Show it to security when entering and leaving the elevator. Mr. Whitten is in four twelve. Please pay attention to what floor you exit."

"Thanks," Will said and headed off. A security man at the elevator ran Will's card through a reader, then allowed him to board with two others. Will got off on the fourth floor and proceeded down the hall. At the far end, another guard stood in front of the stairway exit.

Will knocked on the door to 412. A moment later, he heard the chain latch sliding. The door swung open. Russ Whitten filled the space, wearing a formal shirt with the top button unfastened and a brilliant purple bow tie clipped to one side. A matching cummerbund stretched across his paunch. His face broke into a huge grin as he stuck out his hand. "Shit hot from Ko-rat, you made it!"

Will shook hands. "Good to see you, Uncle Russ." Will stepped past Whitten onto a polished marble foyer. Original oil paintings hung in heavy, gilt frames. A built-in teak bar was angled in the corner. Two doors, most likely bedroom entries, remained shut on one side of the room. Floor-to-ceiling drapes were pulled across the windows.

Whitten closed the door, latched the chain, then went to a decanter and set of crystal glasses that sat on the bar. "A little something to warm the belly?"

Will waved him off. "No thanks."

"I hate drinkin' alone. Mind being cold sober even worse." He filled a tumbler with ice, then tipped a decanter, pouring whiskey to the brim, then stared at Will. "Something's up, ain't it?"

Will debated only a second. He had to trust Whitten. "Yeah, there is. I've uncovered a nightmare."

Whitten took a sip from his drink, then placed the tumbler on a coffee table between them as he sat. "I know all about it . . . all about it," Whitten repeated.

Will shifted, looking from Whitten to the chained exit door. His heart sank. *Whitten is part of it?*

"Hang tough, pup." Whitten put up his hand as though to cut off any attempt to leave. "It's not what you think. I'd like you to meet Lieutenant General Jarret Kraus, head of DIA."

The bedroom door opened. Kraus strode in, his eyes darting around as though to be sure nothing were amiss, then settling on Will.

"Delighted to meet you, Major." Kraus merely nodded at Whitten as he crossed the room to shake Will's hand. "We have much in common," Kraus said, his tone soft, full of concern as they sat. "My father was killed by the Ukrainians, too."

Will felt confused. "Your father was a POW?"

"Briefly. He was a doctor, of German ancestry, practicing in the Ukraine. At the end of World War II, when a Ukrainian division under control of the Soviets overran Magdeburg, he was taken from the hospital where he worked and was shot. So were over two thousand of the town's civilians."

Whitten fidgeted with his nearly empty glass, then stood. "A drink, General?"

Kraus seemed to welcome the interruption, "I'll take some bottled water and ice, thanks."

"Now then," Kraus continued, his tone level, though his wandering eyes betrayed his search for the right words to kick off his lecture. "I think it's safe to say I have some idea of what you have been through. I apologize if I seem brusque, but time is precious and we have things to discuss."

While Whitten was at the bar, Kraus forged ahead. "I'd like to start at the beginning, 1976, July twenty-seventh to be exact. I was assistant deputy director of DIA. That morning, a man in a lieutenant colonel's uniform walked into my office in the company of an internal security officer and one of our army attachés, who is now JCS chairman, by the way." Kraus eyed Will, his look taking on a sudden brightness. "The lieutenant colonel's name tag read DALTON, only he wasn't any Dalton. He wasn't even a colonel. He was Major Alex Anderov, former pilot of the Soviet Union. Seems he had left that country by way of Hanoi, disguised as one of our POWs. In the three years after arriving, Anderov fell in love with democracy and out of love with communism. He said all the things he had been told about life here turned out to be false, so he walked in and gave himself up."

Whitten returned, handed a glass to Kraus, and sat. Kraus sniffed at the water as though it were wine, barely sipping it before putting it down.

Kraus shot a glance at the amber liquid that Whitten was shakily bringing to his lips. "He told me they even lied to him about the quality of our liquor."

Whitten withdrew the glass from near his mouth and stared at it.

Kraus continued. "The Soviets didn't initially intend to replace POWs, by the way. They wanted to interrogate electronic warfare crews for the highly classified knowledge they had. Only when the Russians realized that the Vietnam War would likely drag on interminably did they come up with the replacement scheme."

Will could contain himself no longer. "You knew about the POW switches back then and did nothing?"

"Before you pass judgment, I suggest you hear me out."

Will felt dizzy, as though a migraine was in the works. He eased deeper into his chair, realizing that this Dalton, the one Kraus was talking about, had taken him into his home for a brief period while ten miles away in the hospital, life had slowly drained from his mother's body. Then Will had been shunted away on his long journey as an orphan. It all came rushing together, in bits and fragments, none of it fully connected, but each piece now coming into focus. Angry focus.

Kraus continued. "You've discovered, I take it, how the Soviets pulled it off, so I won't go into that. The problem for us back then was what to do about it. You see, the Soviets have a nasty way of being predictable when accused of criminal folly. They simply erase evidence and deny everything. Anderov was sure the Soviets, if confronted, would execute the real Dalton, whom they kept alive in case they needed more background details from him. We then uncovered information that the Soviets held other U.S. POWs, that Anderov *didn't* know about. Those men would die, too."

Kraus hesitated, like a dentist who had touched a nerve and was waiting for the sting to lessen. "Your father among them."

To Will this was incredible logic. "You left them there because you *thought* they'd be killed otherwise?"

"Not entirely. From Anderov we learned why the Russians had sent him in the first place: a singular and very important mission." Kraus rose, as though by standing his next words might have more weight. "The Soviets wanted to get someone in position to pass a warning if we ever decided to strike preemptively—hit first with nuclear weapons, that is. The Soviets didn't want to jeopardize their exposure by giving their double routine espionage tasks, so that one mission was it. Preemptive warning. We didn't want their program jeopardized either, as long as we weren't planning to strike at them. The Russians didn't have to work hard to manipulate the proper assignments and promotions. I made it happen so easily for them. With their double in place, if America ever intends a sneak attack, the Russians think they'll be warned and be able to react first."

Kraus stood and began a measured stroll toward the window. "So, we left Anderov in place. Why? First, to keep Dalton *alive,* while we made certain we had identified all the doubles, then tried to locate and find a way to get our men out. Second, we wanted control over what the Soviets might learn should we someday decide to defend ourselves by actually hitting them first." At the window, Kraus partly opened the drapes. He stood there gazing out at the night. "The hard truth is," he said, then paused to close them and face Will again, "the counterfeit had more value than the original."

"So," Will said, slowly rising to his feet, the venom in his voice undisguised, "you let my father rot while you played politics! And for what? They killed him anyway."

"And others." Kraus said it softly, as though he felt something for them, but his cold brooding eyes suggested otherwise. "We increased our effort to enlist dissidents in the Ukraine, successfully, I might add. During glasnost, they got word to us that the Russians planned to kill our men. You see, the Kremlin was ready to dissolve the old order, but the generals were distrustful of the SALT treaty. They haven't forgotten their history lesson courtesy of Adolph Hitler and the von Ribbentrop agreement."

Kraus lifted his glass and looked through it as though inspecting it for contamination. He took another sip. "In 1988, the Russian generals knew they had a man in place, the Dalton double, who was on our strategic staff and could give warning if we chose to strike Russia while their guard was down. Their general staff was absolutely paranoid about losing that insider, so the order came down to destroy all evidence in the Soviet Union. That included two *camps of silence,* as these gulags are called, that we knew of, in the Ukraine. The Kremlin feared that to do otherwise would allow word of the POWs to get out once the wraps came off the republics. Their spies here would be exposed, and without at least one of them in constant touch with our nuclear intentions, Gorbachev would lose the support of his generals."

Will sank onto the chair. "Gorbachev ordered my father killed?"

"The generals ordered it. How much detail Gorbachev knew is speculation. How much did Nixon know about Watergate?" Kraus paused, to let the question hang for a moment. "We immediately mounted a rescue mission. Unfortunately, we had detailed information from Anderov only on the Kharkov site and little time to get a rescue organized."

"*You* broke into the gulag outside Kharkov?"

"That was our operation."

"How many POWs were inside?"

"Two."

"My father?"

"Yes, and for security, our people moved them separately. The two were to join up at the airfield. Your father was recaptured and killed during that phase. We had arranged with our Ukrainian contact to have a plane ready. The POWs were to slip aboard at night near the runway."

"And Dalton?"

"He was successful in making the rendezvous."

Will understood now why his father may have been captured alone. He did not need to have Dalton, a pilot, along in the escape attempt. DIA had arranged a way to fly out whomever showed up. "Why was another man buried with my father?"

"The Russian staff wanted proof of the deaths of all remaining U.S. POWs. Our people rescued your father and Dalton, then staged a photo session fabricating their deaths. Unfortunately, a search party that included some Russians captured your father. The Russians quickly executed him. In case anyone from Moscow came around later to check, our contact came up with another corpse and buried it the next day at the location where your father was killed so that Dalton's successful escape wouldn't be discovered. They also took care of the Russians who were in the search party that found your father. Those low-ranking men quietly disappeared."

Was Stayki one of their men? Probably, since he knew of the "proof" requirement and the burial of two bodies. Puzzle pieces were fitting together, but the whole idea knocked the wind out of Will. Stayki had tried to kill him and Gabbie to keep the information secret. He reached up, running his hand through his hair, trying to fathom what he had just heard. "What about Pam Robbins's father?"

"The Pathet Lao kept him behind in 1973 as insurance against a return of U.S. forces. He was executed in Laos years later, long after Vietnam, Laos, and Cambodia had fallen, and we didn't react. I can't go into details about how we found out about it."

"So, rumors about hundreds of POWs being kept behind are true!"

"Yes, but not that many were held back. Intelligence reports indicate all were executed before we could locate them. We were faced with what to do about the information. Nuke Hanoi and Vientiane? To reveal that POWs remained behind anywhere would put the Soviet deception in danger of being discovered. The continued existence of the few POWs that were still alive in Eastern Europe would be in jeopardy."

"Did you tell that to Robbins's daughter before murdering her?"

Kraus kept his expression neutral, but from the way he delayed answering, Will had no doubt that behind the calm facade, the man was seething. Finally, Kraus responded.

"Pam Robbins stumbled onto information that put the program at risk. I sent an agent to explain things. He did . . . fully. I'm afraid the realization that her father had died years after the war, and the fact that her government needed her to keep quiet about it, was too much for her. Hence, she chose suicide. We had no idea she had serious personal problems as well and was unstable. I accept full responsibility, however."

Disbelieving, Will looked at Whitten but got no comfort there. "What about the attempts on our lives, on me and Dr. DeJean?"

"I'm afraid that was the work of Brad Stoner's Soviet replacement, whom you already know about. Am I right?"

Will nodded.

"Stoner's replacement learned about the Pam Robbins photos and discovered your connection to her during his routine staff meetings. We suspect he put two and two together to surmise correctly that he was not the only POW replacement. The Russians didn't tell him of others being switched for obvious security reasons, but the photo of your father, an electronic warfare officer captured in a winter setting, gave him the clue that there were others like himself. He knew from his own experience that one of the prerequisites for replacement was for the target POW to be single or widowed. Checking on your father's status back at the end of the war would have revealed the failed attempt on your mother's life and her eventual death. He wouldn't have to spend much time figuring out that the Soviets were involved and why the Cadence double never showed up. From your persistence, however, he suspected you might be successful in uncovering the scheme.

Will stared in disbelief. "Let me get this straight. You let a Soviet spy for over twenty years, then stood by while he tried to kill us?

"Not at all. First, by the time we were certain Stoner's double was intent on murder, we had already lost contact with you in Thailand. Second, the Stoner mole never relayed any of our secrets. He acted like Dalton's double, Anderov, so we assumed he was to communicate only once. Each had a code that would tell the Soviets we were about to launch an attack. As I mentioned, Stoner doesn't know his people switched Dalton, too, but I'll bet he had some idea given Dalton's marital status. When Dalton had you assigned to JTF, that threw him off, of course, since he was certain a Dalton double wouldn't endanger the program like that. In any case, Stoner assigned his aide, Major Chase, to relay anything of interest you uncovered. He intended to sidetrack information that could cause the launching of a detailed MIA probe. Any success on your part in revealing what happened to Major Robbins and/or your father could prompt his exposure. Stoner also employed several stooges in the attempt to silence you."

"On the C-141s, in Laos, and at my father's grave site," Will said.

"Yes, and many died in that effort."

Will took another minute to digest what the general had said. *Had Gabbie died for her efforts as well?* He had to find out, but how? "Where is Henry Dalton, the real Henry Dalton?"

"On the top floor of this building. He is the man who will become president tomorrow."

"You're swapping him with Anderov?"

"We did that in '91 well after we brought Dalton home and had prepared him. We put out a story about Dalton—that is, Anderov—having to retire from the military because of a throat tumor. Three months later, the real Henry Dalton, nicely recovered—in case someone detected any change in appearance or voice—took his rightful place and entered politics, new staff, new life. The rest you know."

"The rest I don't know. What happened to Anderov and the real Brad Stoner?"

"Brad Stoner was executed at a separate gulag in the Ukraine on orders from the Russian General Staff. As for Anderov, we never quite knew if we might need him again, so we set him up in our version of the witness protection program.

"On Posson Hill Road," Will added.

Kraus's eyebrows lifted slightly. "You're even more adept than I gave credit. The fact of the matter is that Anderov is still important to the program. Dalton doesn't speak Russian as well as Anderov does, though we've worked hard on that since his return. The Russians actually contacted Dalton in the mid-nineties to set up a meeting. There, they changed the code word. We used Anderov for that encounter. Stoner's code word was also changed during the same period. We were ready and obtained it, too, which confirmed our suspicion about his mission being similar to Dalton's."

"And Colonel Bustamante?"

"We brought him on-board back in the seventies after Anderov came in. The colonel was involved in compiling oral histories from the returned POWs and had access to certain medical and personnel records which we needed to exchange from time to time. At JTF, he was assigned to make sure Stoner's double didn't stray from his assigned mission. When Dr. DeJean called him today, he passed to me word of her contact, and we decided to bring you both into our confidence once we located you."

"So you have Dr. DeJean?"

"We do not."

Will pondered Kraus's answer. *Did they have Gabbie, or did she escape and the only reason I'm alive is they need to silence both of us?* "Quit the act, General. Tell me where Dr. DeJean is."

Kraus's eyes widened. "I have no idea. I was hoping you might enlighten me on that."

Was Kraus lying? If he already had Gabbie and all this was a facade, then why were they explaining things? Could it have been some other agency's helicopter that dropped in on them? Will wondered. Garcia claimed he was CIA before Stayki came along and killed him. Could the CIA be in cahoots with Stoner's double somehow? By now, Will decided anything was possible.

"Then Stoner's double or his goons have Dr. DeJean."

"If so," Kraus said, "we'll find out where."

Will thought better than to say more on that issue for the moment. Maybe the only reason he was still alive right now was because Kraus needed to find Gabbie, too. He glanced at Whitten again, who looked as though he was hearing all of this for the first time. "Were you taken to Russia?"

Whitten shook his head.

"They didn't transfer all the Wild Weasel crews," Kraus said. "That would have been a dead giveaway. Many were left in Vietnam and received brutal treatment, as I'm sure you are aware."

Will kept looking at Whitten. "So what's your job in this?"

"Russ Whitten," Kraus answered, "was asked to keep tabs on your activity in Hawaii."

Whitten cast his eyes down, clinking the ice in his glass. "Colonel Bustamante and I were to find out what you'd uncovered, pup. There is a hell of a lot at stake."

"Absolutely," Kraus said. "At the moment, the Ukrainians have seized the ICBM arsenal from the Russians. We don't know what their intentions are. The president, I, and all of the Defense Department are watching events there very closely."

Kraus picked up his water glass—a casual gesture—as though stalling for time. To Will, the man was still playing the game: *How much should he tell this meddler?*

Kraus's eyes narrowed perceptibly. "Major, when this program began, we couldn't go blabbing all over town. The CIA is rife with moles. We couldn't even tell the White House, not with every Ronald, George, and Bill writing memoirs. The entire effort was kept close-hold within DIA, as are many of our black programs. Recently, however, due to the actions of Ms. Robbins, the CIA *has* gotten involved. We tried to dissuade their interest after becoming aware of her photographs. We altered the image and copies of the one of her father in Laos. However, the CIA wasn't thrown off and kept intruding. I have, within the last twenty-four hours, addressed the issue with the director of the CIA. They have now pulled their people from the case."

"And I suppose you want me to withdraw with them."

"Should you go public with what I have told you, the new Ukrainian leader might react. You see, not only do the Russians know about the switch in POWs, but so does the Ukrainian leadership. Their boss, Marshal Podvalny, has been in on one aspect of it from the beginning. He worked at the other Ukrainian location where Stoner's replacement was trained. The link between the two has never been broken, as we discovered during the code switch."

"How many others are there?"

"The Soviets began with Dalton, Stoner, and your father. Jack Cadence's replacement was withdrawn from the program when they failed to kill your mother in time. Only two doubles came out, the Dalton and Stoner doubles. We know this from the medical records."

Will shuddered at the thought that he came perilously close to being raised by a Soviet spy. He wondered what kind of man would choose to erase his past, become someone else, ostensibly forever. Perhaps, he thought, spies and the people who pull the strings in the espionage programs have a defect in their souls that allows them to live with what they do.

To Will, the fact that neither Dalton's nor Stoner's replacement knew about each other explained Stoner's agreement to allow Will's JTF assignment. Stoner didn't want to cross Dalton. Will wanted to know why Dalton had pushed the assignment in the first place, but wanted to ask Dalton that himself.

"How do I know you're telling me the truth? For all I know, Anderov might be the man getting ready to be the next president."

Kraus smiled, as though he had watched Will remove his hand from a chess piece, leaving it positioned for a quick checkmate. "Would you like to ask Anderov that question?"

Will looked from Kraus to Whitten. "He's here?"

Kraus nodded at Whitten, who went to the other bedroom and opened the door. A moment later, a man hitch-stepped from the room, removed his fake beard, and was immediately recognized as Henry Dalton.

"Hello, Will." He stared at Will, his right hand instinctively going forward, then halting, as though receiving signals from his brain to offer to shake hands, yet unsure if that was the proper thing to do.

Will gawked for a long time, not knowing whether the man was a mirage, Anderov, or Dalton. Will blinked, yet there the man remained, looking and sounding for all the world like the next president. The man's hand returned to his side. Will stared at it, realizing that if what he had heard were true, then that same hand, Anderov's, had held his at the funeral of his mother. The magnitude of that monstrous deceit made Will's blood churn in fury. He wanted to lash out, to smash his fists into all of them for the pain they had caused. "Are your hearts made of stone?" Will glanced at Whitten, whose eyes were heavy with remorse.

Will brought his attention back on Anderov. He tried to find something in the man's expression that showed feeling, something that would tell him it wasn't all a pretense, that just possibly there was some good that had come from all the violations that had been brought upon him and Pam and all the MIA next of kin.

"Musser?" He nearly spat the word out.

Anderov nodded. "An anagram for *me-USSR.*"

Will smiled at the irony. "But you could also be the man who claims to be president-elect."

"Ah," Kraus said. "We can stay here together and watch Henry Dalton on television an hour from now."

"What if he's Anderov and you are Henry Dalton and for some crazy reason are going along with this scheme."

Anderov smiled. "*Ti dumaesh nastayashy Henry Dalton gavarit po russki takje horosho kak ya?*" (Do you think the real Henry Dalton can speak Russian as well as I do?)

"Not bad, but I would expect a POW who spent two decades in the Soviet Union and, as you indicated, later had language lessons to become fluent."

"Well, then," Kraus said. "Do you have some way of your own to determine which is which?"

Will felt a shiver run up his spine. Someone inside DIA had probably told Kraus about the missing records. *Had they set this all up to entrap him?* As he inhaled, he felt the envelope of X rays against his ribs. If he showed it, they might be confiscated. He had no intention of making it that easy in the event that what Kraus said were lies. "I do, but I need to prove it with the other Dalton first, then this one."

"I'm afraid that's impossible," Kraus said. "A visit by you with the president-elect might generate a flurry of questions that can't be answered right now."

"You mean his staff doesn't know about the switch?"

"As I said, only a few have knowledge of the entire project."

It sounded plausible to Will, as did Kraus's explanation of why they had let Anderov continue in his role, including that one time in the nineties after Dalton had returned. As for letting Will and Gabbie dangle in perilous circumstances, what Kraus had related showed a willingness on the part of the government to permit the sacrifice of anyone necessary, thinking the higher need was to protect the millions who would die in a missile exchange.

Was it all true? Will had to admit, Kraus's being there explaining it added weight to the prospect. Kraus could have come with a gun to end Will's quest the moment he arrived. What Will had to decide was how to prove Kraus's claims and what to do with the information once he had it.

Will said at last, "Surely the son of the man Henry Dalton got shot down with could meet with him privately, especially tonight."

Kraus considered for a moment, then reached for the phone.

40

"MAJOR CADENCE? I'M ANTHONY Ganetta." He showed Will a Secret Service badge as Will left Whitten's suite. Ganetta went to the elevator and held the door. No one else got on as Will stepped inside. Ganetta selected the button for the penthouse.

"The president-elect is expecting you. Have you any cameras or recording devices?"

"No," Will said.

"May I have your phone?"

Will handed over the cellular.

Ganetta tucked it under his arm. "I'll need your pass." He offered a new one, and they swapped. "When we arrive, you'll be met by Janet Mills, the president-elect's . . ." Ganetta hesitated, searching for the right word.

"I know who she is," Will said.

"Fine. She'll take it from there."

The elevator opened. The hall was crammed with security personnel, desks, chairs, coatracks. Will had his new card checked, then wound his way after Ganetta, taking it all in.

Another Secret Service agent had Will pass through a second metal detector before entering the presidential suites.

As Will stepped inside the room, he understood the why of the hallway clutter. Three women were hard at work using desktop computers and monitors. Another wore a headset and was operating what looked like a communications console. A fax machine was spitting out paper to her left. Not a square yard of space remained clear.

Dalton's personal secretary, Arline Haske, turned as they entered. "Hello, Will, good to see you again. We'll get you together with the president-elect shortly."

Standing next to a door that led to an adjoining suite was Janet Mills. She looked out of place, dressed in a bright vermilion off-the-shoulder gown, and was speaking to staff aide Gary Bennett when she looked up and noticed Will.

Janet excused herself from Bennett. She approached Will while putting on a smile like a flight attendant in the midst of brutal turbulence. "Hi, good to see you again."

They shook hands. Ganetta melted into the background as Janet led the way through the room and into the adjoining suite.

"All right," Mills said. "This is highly unusual, but President-elect Dalton will see you shortly. I must ask that you keep it brief. Five minutes maximum, please. The president-elect's schedule is extremely tight."

"So's mine," Will said.

Janet blinked in surprise but held her tongue. "Wait here a moment." She went to a door opposite the one they had entered and tapped lightly on it. Then she slipped inside and closed the door. Janet came out seconds later and motioned for him to enter.

"Come right on in," a familiar voice ordered from beyond the foyer.

Janet whispered, "Please make it quick," then closed the door as she left.

Will moved toward the sound, feeling a combination of anger and awe. The main salon was immense. He strode down marble steps to a sunken, carpeted lounge. Potted trees rose from huge Chinese urns. A columned archway separated the living area from the dining room where a cherrywood dining table was decked out with polished silver and china. An ornate chandelier hung overhead the table, beyond which two milk-white cherubs posed atop a black marble pedestal.

Will tried not to be nervous, but he was. The extravagance was humbling, not to mention who he was about to deal with. The next president of the United States stood looking out the window, his outline a silhouette against lighting that flowed in from outside. As Will approached, Dalton turned, a slow, deliberate move, his leg motion having just the slightest hint of physical impairment.

Will found the sight difficult to absorb. He knew there were two men who looked exactly like Dalton, yet somehow his mind had not yet acknowledged the fact. This Dalton looked just like the man he had left moments before on the fourth floor. But here among the splendor of the Presidential Suite, this Dalton stood apart. Dressed in a gray tuxedo with black trim and gray bow tie, every hair in place, he looked regal, giving the impression of the battle-scarred warrior, the heroic patriarch, the nation's leader.

"Hello, Will. I'm real." He paused, as if to allow Will time to accept the fact. "Henry T. Dalton in the flesh." The president-elect moved to a blue velvet easy chair and had Will take the matching sofa. "I'd like to tell you about your father, but there will be time for that later. Right now, I have to convince you that I am Henry Dalton, and *you* have to accept the fact. Now, I'm told you have a method to accomplish that."

"I do." He removed the dental X rays from the envelope, studied Dalton's old partial negative first, then the full new set. "I'll need to see your lower right teeth."

The president-elect smiled. "Can't you see the headlines: INAUGURATION DELAYED FOR DENTAL CHECKUP." He chuckled, a sound not filled with mirth. He looked at Will as if expecting him to say, "Open wide."

Will approached as Dalton used his index finger to pull his lip back, exposing his teeth on the right side.

Will peered at the dental work, comparing the teeth to those on the newer X ray. To Will's unskilled eye they looked identical. "I can't see the last tooth."

Dalton moved his hand aft so Will could see the molar. There was no filling, just a tooth, meaning this man was not the double that had taken Dalton's place. Will stepped back.

The president-elect released his lip. "Satisfied?"

"So far. I've confirmed who you are not."

"Maybe I can help establish who I am," Dalton said. "Remember the day you fell from the garage rafters?"

Will's mind flashed back to McConnell Air Force Base as he nodded at Dalton. Like a series of snapshots, Will recalled his mother's image, his father's departure. Will shoved the memory aside, trying to focus his mind on the present. A series of zigzag lines appeared in his field of vision. Will saw only a wiggling image of the president-elect. Blood started pounding in his brain. Another migraine coming. He heard Dalton's voice.

"Would you like to ask me some details about that day?"

Almost as fast as the onset of Will's migraine had begun, it faded. His vision cleared. Dalton was still in front of him, but in his mind, Will saw a much younger Dalton standing next to his mother, holding her in his arms, then looking up and seeing Will hiding in the rafters. "You were there!" Will uttered the words almost as a growl.

Dalton's eyebrows shot up. "You didn't know?" He let out a laugh of astonishment. "My God, I thought you always knew. I thought you might use that . . . against me if I didn't get you the assignment in Hawaii." All of a sudden, Dalton shifted uncomfortably, as though he had blundered.

Will took a step toward Dalton, anger surging inside him, as they stood face-to-face. "You and my mother . . . you son of a bitch!"

"Yes, for that I was." Dalton staggered back a step, gaining separation, although from his expression he looked a little stunned that someone would dare to refer to the next president of the United States in those terms.

"Choose violence," he said, "and I won't stop you. I learned goddamn well in prison how to take it."

Will halted, mentally taken off balance by the statement.

When nothing happened, Dalton's eyes began to water. He seemed to become detached, as though wrestling in some kind of private mental hell. "I'm sorry, but it happened. I met your mother before you were born, but I was married. Nancy and Jack lived next door. You came along. Then my wife died. Nancy helped me get through that. I found myself caring very much for her. That is the sad truth. You were too young to know the problems I created for your parents, but I was trapped in the middle of it and wound up involved beyond my intention." Dalton shook his head as if to clear his thoughts. "At this moment, you must feel intense resentment, but you have to put it aside for now so you can understand what else *has* happened, what else *is* happening, and why."

"Yes," Will seethed. "What *has* happened is you stole something that didn't belong to you, and what *is* happening is you're about to try it again."

"No, Will. Don't you think I've paid my dues to get where I am?" Dalton's eyes narrowed, a slight flash of anger showing through. "When I got back, I was full of rage. Abandoned for twenty years! How could my government allow me, and your father, to wither in Vietnamese and Ukrainian dungeons that long?"

Dalton shrugged as if to suggest that Will would find no easy answer to his question. "Well, they had their reason: protecting this country at my expense. But they did not forget us. They *did* rescue one of us. Me. Director Kraus was there when I landed in Turkey, and he offered three choices. I could tell my story to the world and get immensely rich from book rights, interviews, and the speaking circuit. Or I could choose to disappear." Dalton flicked his hand like a magician going *poof*. "A new identity, into the witness protection program with a nice lifelong income while allowing Anderov to continue in place. Or . . . ," Dalton's face took on the hint of a glow, "I could get even." He clenched his jaw, eyes darting around the room, then back on Will. "I could resume my own identity, and within the bounds of legality, Kraus would help me advance in politics. Before making my choice, though, he took me to meet Anderov. At first I wanted to strangle the life out of the man. Then Anderov showed me the scar on his leg where the Soviets had broken it to match my injury. Can you imagine someone agreeing to have that done to him and then spend three years posing as me in a POW camp? They didn't even tell the Vietnamese! That's when I began to understand the lengths to which some of us will go for our countries. I also learned to accept an imperfect world, but in that world my government hadn't abandoned me."

"Don't forget Stoner," Will added.

"Brad?" Dalton blinked, pausing a brief moment. "I can speak only for myself. I owe Kraus and his people, who by patience and perseverance made possible my being alive today, ready to become the president of the republic tomorrow."

"If I keep quiet," Will said.

The color drained from Dalton's face. He stammered, then cleared his throat. "At times, this government acts like the God of the Old Testament. On the surface, barbarously cruel. Only later, when we know the whole story, do its actions prove responsible. Keep in mind, if the government didn't care, you would not be alive now. And yes, your father and many good people died to ensure that the Cold War didn't turn hot. That was the responsible thing to do, and I suffered over twenty years on behalf of it."

Will shook his head. "If you're saying that without this escapade the collapse of the Soviet Union would have brought on a nuclear war, I'm not buying it. Those Kremlin leaders saw the inevitable. The Soviet Union collapsed because the system didn't work and went bankrupt."

"True, but do you think for a minute that Gorbachev, Yeltsin, and Putin got their power because they were nice men who suddenly saw the light and switched from a life of immorality to decency? Don't you realize Gorbachev took that momentous step—freeing the republics—in an attempt to maintain his control, a step he and his generals couldn't take without solid assurance that the United States would not seize upon the opportunity to attack?"

"I guess I'd have to ask him that question," Will said.

"Ask him about the orders for your father's and my deaths while you're at it." Dalton seemed to catch himself at the edge of losing control. He took a deep breath, his eyes casting about for an anchor, then finding one. "But Gorbachev no longer matters. What matters is what is taking place in the Ukraine. An impulsive move on our part, *your* part, could push the Ukrainian coup leader Podvalny in the direction the Soviet generals may have gone had they known their man Anderov was no longer in place. Right now, Podvalny, who has Islamic heritage in a hugely Christian country, sees America as his mortal enemy."

Will would have preferred to argue the matter of perceived threat from the Ukraine, but he and Gabbie had definitely seen a mobile missile on the move that last night outside Kharkov. He had seen Podvalny the day they arrived in the square, speaking from the podium next to Stayki, two skinheads in uniform, one of whom now had the power to go along with the rhetoric.

Will closed his eyes. Dalton had destroyed the memory of his mother. Dalton had flown the plane in which his father was shot down. The effort to protect Dalton's identity had nearly cost Will his life and may have cost Gabbie hers, but none of that was as important as what mattered if the statements about the Ukraine were true. He opened his eyes.

"I don't know. I just don't know what to believe anymore." Then, looking back at Dalton, he said, "I'll be thinking of my father and the dues *he* paid when you take that oath tomorrow."

It took a moment for Will's words to register. Dalton brightened. "All right then," he said, his manner again confident. He offered a card from his pocket to Will. "If you need to talk, I can be reached through this number."

The card was plain white, with nothing but a telephone number on it. "An access code is required. Punch in four-nine-four when instructed. That will get you through to either myself or Janet if we're available. Please do not discuss this subject with her or copy the number anywhere. All I ask is that if you change your mind, let *me* make the announcement. National security is at stake here. If I don't take the oath tomorrow, it may trigger a very unstable regime to act."

Will took the card.

"Fine," Dalton said. "I can't force you to remain silent until this crisis is over, but if you do, I promise you the time will come to properly bring the facts to light. If the American people want me to step down at that point, I will."

Dalton glanced at his watch. "Is there anything I can do for you? Anything at all."

"Find Dr. DeJean. Do you know who she is?"

"Yes, I've been briefed by General Kraus."

If Kraus did not have Gabbie, then Will guessed the CIA did have her. Would they lie to the next president? Probably, but Will decided to press-to-test. "Contact the CIA, the FBI, the Russians, for God's sake, and find out where she is."

"Consider it done. Hopefully, I can let you know at the affair downstairs." Dalton rose. "They told me you might be in attendance tonight. Is that right?"

"Yes."

"Good. Now I have to get going." Dalton led the way through the foyer, shook hands, then opened the door.

Janet appeared, looking anxious but relieved. She waited until Will exited, then she joined Dalton, both of them returning to the Presidential Suite.

Arline Haske escorted Will through the connecting room and out into the hallway. As the door closed behind him, Will looked at all the disarray and bustling people.

"Welcome to the sordid world of politics," Will said to no one in particular as Ganetta approached, offering him his cell phone back.

41

WHEN WILL RETURNED to Whitten's suite, Russ had on his tuxedo jacket and looked eager to party. Kraus summoned Anderov from the bedroom again.

Will checked Anderov's teeth, comparing them against the older X rays. The last molar had a filling that looked like the one in the X ray. After a moment, Will nodded.

"I trust you are satisfied," Kraus said

Will put the records back in the envelope. All the while, Kraus had his eyes glued on it as Will placed it inside his tuxedo pocket.

Then Kraus motioned Anderov toward the bedroom. He took the hint and disappeared. Turning to Will, Kraus asked, "We have an agreement?"

"For now," Will said.

"Good. You should also be aware that I have sequestered the crew from your flight out of Moscow. After the ceremony this evening, I'd like to have you join them for a full debriefing. There will also be some nondisclosure documents to sign. If you'd like, I'll have you picked up after the dinner and driven directly there."

Will felt uneasy. With all that had gone on since arriving stateside, Will had not thought about Boyd and his crew and the danger they might be facing. "Where is the crew?"

"At a secure location."

In no way did Will intend to become isolated tonight with the only remaining people besides Gabbie who had full knowledge of what had happened in the Ukraine. "I'd prefer to get there on my own," Will said, then thinking, *if and when I go there.* "Tell me where."

Kraus started to object, then checked himself. "All right, Fort Belvoir. You'll be escorted from the gate when you arrive."

"I'd like to talk to Colonel Boyd," Will said.

"I can't authorize that from here, unfortunately. You may contact them tomorrow." He produced a Palm Pilot, checked for a number, wrote it down on a card, and gave it to Will.

After an awkward silence, Whitten piped in. "Hey, party hardies, it's happy hour downstairs, and I'm already two drinks behind." He stood, invitations in hand, and caught his balance before taking a step toward the door.

Kraus moved ahead to open it, explaining that he would join them later. Whitten took Will by the arm and headed for the elevator. On the way down, he told Will about the seats he had reserved for the inauguration in the morning.

When Will and Russ Whitten walked into the Grand Ballroom, the festivities were already in full swing. They went through security and onto the reception line that Janet Mills and Henry Dalton had come down earlier to host.

As Will's turn came to shake the president-elect's hand, Dalton leaned toward Will's ear. "Nothing yet on the doctor, but they haven't all gotten back to me."

"Who hasn't?"

Dalton lowered his voice. "The CIA. I hope to have more as soon as I hear from them." Dalton turned to greet Whitten.

Will moved off, his mind full of doubts, emotions swirling as Whitten came from behind, placed his arm across Will's back, and ushered him toward the attendees, crowded around circular dinner tables. A six-piece military band was warming up to the side of the head table beneath red, white, and blue bunting that hung on all sides of the room. People flitted from table to table shaking hands. The lighting was dim, and it took a few seconds for Will to spot Dalton coming in from the reception line. He began holding court at the head table just in front of the stage, Janet Mills at his side. Former POWs clustered around the couple, engaging in animated conversation. Enough stars twinkled on the shoulders of the brass standing behind the head table to assemble a dazzling constellation.

The curtains were drawn onstage and a screen lowered. From a projector, a shaft of light beamed toward the stage. A cheer rose from the gathering. On the screen was projected a slide showing a young aviator, dressed in an olive-drab flight suit, his cap at a jaunty angle. The lieutenant's G suit was partly zippered so the leggings flared at the bottom, appearing almost like cowboy chaps. The smiling pilot was posed in front of a bomb-laden F-105 fighter.

One of the POWs to Will's right stood at his table and took a bow, to increased applause.

Russ Whitten shouted, "Yahoo, ol' Speed Jeans himself." Whitten weaved his way toward the man, dragging Will along. "That's his nickname because he wore his G suit into the bar after shooting down a MiG. Then he and I put down a lot of shooters together, if you know what I mean. Still do from time to time."

The projector cycled. The lieutenant in the speed jeans disappeared. In sequence, two more slides of pilots appeared to rousing applause. Then a roar exploded from the crowd.

The next slide showed Major Henry Dalton in the front seat of an F-105F. In the rear cockpit sat another officer squinting in sun glare. Even though the image was grainy, Will recognized the face of the man. His father.

Whitten sobered at the sight. "Ah, son. They shouldn't have—"

"I'm okay," Will said, but he was not. His father's presence pressed in from all sides. Emotions flooded over him like storm-tossed waves: anger, grief, frustration, longing, remorse. The crowd noise waned as though others suddenly realized there was a sad aspect to the photo. Will looked at his father's image, a rugged face with a mysterious half-smile, or was the cast of his mouth caused by the effort to squint? Will couldn't tell. There was so much he wanted to say to his father and so many things now he knew he could correct, but they had him boxed in. They had him thinking that if any good were to come from his father's death, it must come through his own silence, despite what he knew. The door to what happened to Jack Cadence would remain padlocked, barred, boarded over.

Will could not take his eyes off his father's image. "It's as though he's trying to tell me something."

"I feel it, too," Whitten said.

A father's smile or a grimace in the sunlight. Which was it? Did it even matter? Will wanted to shout for them to leave his father's image alone, but instead he stood unmoving like the picture on the screen, his eyes absorbing every moment of the view.

A *click,* and Will's father was gone. Another slide flashed into view, another cheer, and another, and another.

Jack Cadence was not coming back—ever. Will finally tore his eyes from the screen. He looked over the crowd. Near the far wall he saw General Stoner, talking with Colonel Bustamante. Stoner's gaze met Will's, held it, then shifted away.

"Stay cool," Whitten whispered. "We'll take care of that bastard when the time comes."

Waiters carrying huge silver trays crammed with dinner plates shuffled among the tables. Whitten maneuvered Will behind a place setting, then poured the wine. He handed Will a glass. "Toast fodder, and you don't want to be out of ammo."

The wine was set aside while Whitten introduced Speed Jeans—Gene—Boscal—and three other guests at the table.

A gavel rapped at the podium as the room brightened. Master of Ceremonies General Bradley Stoner strode to the podium, his deliberate movements emitting latent strength. He scanned the crowd as though reviewing his subjects, then took the microphone to introduce the chaplain who gave the invocation.

Stoner reminded Will of Podvalny, and he wondered if Stoner was ethnic Ukrainian. *Those two might even be related,* he thought, remembering Kraus's words that the link between Podvalny and Stoner's replacement had never been broken. Will shifted his attention to Dalton. The president-elect was staring, unsmiling, at Stoner, his attention riveted on the man.

"Ladies and gentlemen, please remain standing for the posting of the colors."

The band sounded ruffles and flourishes as the room darkened and double doors to the ballroom swung open. The color guard marched in. Then the "Star-Spangled Banner" began. A throaty chorus of voices joined in. The flag was positioned behind the head table as the anthem ended.

Stoner leaned over the microphone. "I'd like to propose a toast." He hefted a glass. "To the president of the United States."

"Here, here," the crowd echoed. "To the president."

Then Stoner turned to face Henry Dalton. He slowly raised his glass again. "To one of our own, the *next* president of the United States." Dalton barely cracked a grin.

"Here, here," resounded through the room.

Finally Stoner toasted the nation's fallen comrades. Then they took seats.

The dinner entrée was prime rib, and Will helped himself to the wine, deciding it would serve to numb his senses enough to tolerate Dalton's speech. As the meal wound down, Stoner interrupted the dinner music to take the microphone again. He announced a short intermission.

Dalton's reaction in the penthouse to the comment about Stoner had given Will the feeling that perhaps Dalton was unaware of Stoner's double. If Dalton was being kept in the dark on some aspects of Kraus's program and admitted such, it might cause Will to doubt Dalton's ability to control the presidency. Will might go public with the details of the switch. Dalton wants to lead the country, yet Will sensed puppeteer Kraus controls the strings to the presidency. Who and what else does Kraus control?

After the intermission, Stoner used the mike again to introduce Henry Dalton, who took the podium to standing applause.

Dalton began his presentation, the main topic being the need for continued military vigilance during these chaotic times. Will listened as Dalton seemed a little unsure of himself at times, stumbling over his words, as though he had other things on his mind, which, of course, he did. His closing words seemed to fit the tone of what Kraus had said about the Soviet leadership.

"The Communist state didn't collapse because its people were weak," Dalton said. "It fell apart because its *leaders* were weak, lacking in moral courage, corrupting its house from within."

A chorus of "Right-on"s erupted from the floor.

"We, in this room, survived our ordeals in prison because *our* leaders were strong."

A salvo of fists rose in the air to join a tumultuous cheer.

Dalton waited, drinking in the applause, then raised his hand for quiet. "Now, having prevailed, each of us has been given a second chance, a chance to serve our nation and our God, whether in the military, business, politics, or the many other human endeavors open to us. Our country didn't fail us, and we in turn must not fail it. We are average Americans who were placed in extraordinary circumstances, and because of that there are things that we can teach the world that no other group of average Americans can. We can teach them about *fear*. And about *pain*. And about how to endure both while succeeding. To each of the four hundred fifty of you who left Hanoi in 1973, I say thanks for your support. I would not be standing here tonight without it. Not all of us came back, and the pain of their loss is still with us, with the lives they left behind." Dalton's eyes sought someone in the crowd, stopping when they found Will. "With their children, their parents, their friends. To you, I say, only someone who has suffered a loss such as yours can truly understand your feelings. Some of us have, and all of us deeply care.

"Thank you, everyone, and I'll see you all tomorrow."

The crowd rose amid a thundering ovation as Henry Dalton, Janet Mills, and General Bradley Stoner departed.

42

AFTER HENRY DALTON'S OVATION waned, Will said his good-byes at the table. He glanced at the exit, anxious about Kraus wanting to quarantine him and wondering how to slip out unobserved. Suddenly, he felt a slap on his shoulder.

"Hey, pup," Russ Whitten said, as he staggered, then caught his balance. "We got a sortie laid on." Whitten swung an arm at the gathering. "We're gonna march to the memorial. Right now!"

Will scanned the sizable group.

"I'm with you guys," Will said. Though still uncertain about his security, he was eager for the safety in numbers.

"And hey," Whitten said, "in case we get separated . . . or I pass out, we meet for the inaugural tomorrow outside L'Enfant Plaza at nine-thirty. I'll bring the tickets."

Outside the hotel, at least a hundred ex-POWs were massed together, cavorting along as the group traversed L Street. Chilly air seemed to sober Whitten, his stride steadying. Will saw no sign of unusual activity other than normal traffic control by the police.

The revelers paid no mind to the cold air or the distance, finally crossing Constitution Avenue to walk along the grass beside the reflecting pool. A thin coating of ice had formed on the surface of the water. The Lincoln Memorial glowed in the distance, lit up ivory white in all its splendor. They followed the path to the entrance to the Vietnam Veterans Memorial. Will remembered when his odyssey began and what Henry Dalton had said in his Senate office about visiting the Wall. "Go. You'll cry. Everyone does."

Will stopped at the register of names, its pages lit day and night. He found his father's name and slab number, then walked the last twenty yards to the monument, a rift in the earth. Its long, polished black stones seemed to emerge then recede into the ground. Will ran his hand across carved names on the memorial's walls. There were so many, seemingly infinite in number, conveying to him overwhelming loss. When he found his father's name, and beside it the lie—the date of death chiseled in solid permanence—he felt again as though he'd been slugged in the stomach. In the dim light, he saw his reflection in the marble face coming from deep inside the monument, broken only by the names that ran through it. He looked away. Glancing upward into a coal-black sky, his mind drifted to another deceit.

Will thought of his mother and what Dalton must have meant to her. She was human, no matter how much in his mind he had placed her on a pedestal. Yet, if everything Dalton had said was the truth, he did not know if he could ever forgive the man . . . or the politician. Will now saw Dalton the statesman as merely a pawn, like Whitten and Bustamante. What troubled Will was how the pawns seemed to function like flunkies, half in the know, half in the dark, all doing what they thought was their patriotic duty. And once Dalton becomes president, what kind of power will Kraus, the king, have? Dalton owes the man everything. What do Whitten and Bustamante owe and to whom?

Will glanced up and down the path. The crowd had spread along the wall, but Whitten was nowhere in sight. In the murky light, everyone looked the same, all dressed in tuxedos. Anyone keeping track of Will would have to stay very close, and no one seemed to be sticking on his tail. *Were any of Kraus's or Stoner's people out there hoping to be led to Gabbie?* The sound of a police siren, far away, wafted through the air, then died.

Some of the ex-POWs began walking toward the Lincoln Memorial. Will started after them, glancing behind. No one pursued. As the group made their way up the monument steps, Will skirted around the side of the building, crossed the grass, and ran toward the Arlington Memorial Bridge, slowing only when his bad leg started to act up. Cars sped by, but none seemed to show any interest as Will brushed past a lone pedestrian who stared after him as Will limped past in formal dress. Will felt really out of place, took off his bow tie, and shoved it in his pocket. Once on the other side of the bridge, he spotted a Metro sign for the Arlington Cemetery Station.

No one came down the steps behind him as Will bought a ticket and mingled with a sparse crowd on the south platform. While he waited, he thought about Gabbie and how Dalton said he would get back to him once the CIA had responded. He remembered the card Dalton had given him with the special contact number on it. He found a pay phone, put a coin in the slot, and dialed, but heard a message at the other end stating his party was temporarily unavailable.

A train was pulling in, so Will hung up and ran to catch it, just making it aboard as the doors closed.

One other person had entered the car, a man about sixty who sat and began reading a paperback. The train headed toward Alexandria. Will looked out the window wondering what Kraus held over

Whitten. He had been through a lot, probably drank too much because of it, Will thought. Maybe it helps him forget. Maybe his connection has to do with what Gabbie saw in his folder. With Will, Whitten had always been vague about what his firm did, but Gabbie said he ran a high-tech outfit that made navigation equipment for the air force and navy. Both services use inertial and global positioning systems in their fighters. *Could Kraus have helped Whitten get contracts for those?* With Kraus's ability to ferret out intelligence, he might have inside information on contractor bids and the like.

Will shook his head. *Russ Whitten?* He's a good old boy, with a ton of guts. *Cheat the country he served?* No, and even if he did, that still didn't explain why Whitten was involved in the MIA scheme.

Will thought about other uses for standardized nav systems. Ballistic missiles came to mind. Air force land-based and navy sub-launched missiles have the same navigational needs.

The train pulled into National Airport Station. Will got off, caught a taxi back to the Alexandria motel, iced his knee for a few minutes, then crawled into bed. Thoughts of Gabbie's safety crowded his mind. He stared up at the ceiling, grappling with Dalton's and Kraus's explanations, wrestling with the memory of his parents, the treachery that seemed to sanction the belief that two wrongs make a right. He decided not to try Dalton's private number again in the event it gave away his location. No telling what might happen while he slept, and he did need rest. Despite the plausible things he had heard, Will felt little security in the darkness of the motel room.

Up before dawn, Will dressed in the casual clothes he had purchased the day before. He grabbed a quick bite, then used the cellular to call Whitten's room. No answer. He tried Dalton's private number and got the recording again, so he boarded a crowded Metro train to L'Enfant Plaza where he was to meet Whitten. When Whitten didn't appear, Will made his way to Independence Avenue across from the Capitol Building, hoping to run into Whitten there.

At precisely ten o'clock in the morning, he watched silently from across the mall, without Whitten, as Henry Dalton placed his left hand on the Bible, raised his right hand, and took the oath of office.

The band struck up "Hail to the Chief."

Well, it's done, Will thought, but something felt terribly wrong about it.

The inaugural parade began. Will looked northwest toward the Mayflower. He used the cell phone to call Whitten's room again. Still no one answered, so he walked to the hotel.

The clerk rang Whitten's room and got no response. When Will asked to look inside the room, the woman refused. Will persisted, so a security officer was sent to check the suite.

While they waited, Will called the Fort Belvoir number Kraus had given him to see if Tom Boyd and the crew were there. The billeting attendant put Will on hold. A moment later, Will heard Boyd's voice.

Will had one thing on his mind. "Is Gabbie with you, Tom?"

"No," Boyd said. "She's not with you? Where'd you lose her?"

Will wondered if Kraus had someone listening in on the line. "Long story, but not now, Tom."

"I haven't heard a peep from either of you till now, but hey, Will, how about getting your butt out here ASAP. I'm told we're out of here soon's you two show up and we sign away our retirement, or whatever this stack of papers in front of me winds up costing us."

"I'll be out soon, but I've got an errand to run."

"Try and make it sometime before the spring thaw. I've seen so much of Nelson, I'm starting to talk like a lieutenant. Another day of this and I'll probably be thinking like one."

Will hung up, then wished he had asked Boyd whether the crew was really staying in the quarters at Belvoir as Kraus had indicated. He redialed the number, but the line was busy.

Just then, the security officer returned. The man shook his head to indicate that no one was in Whitten's room.

Will decided either Whitten was in harm's way, or he was doing what most folks do when they have a heavy conscience.

"He's drinking with his buddy," Will said out loud.

"What's that?" the clerk said.

"Is there a Boscal staying here?"

She checked her register. "I have a G. Boscal."

"Ring him, please," Will said.

She dialed and handed the receiver to Will.

A man answered. "Yeah?"

"Gene? It's Will Cadence. I'm looking for Russ Whitten."

"Well, you found his ass. Now if I could just get you to carry that ass outta here, along with the red, white, and blue puke that's all over the bathroom, I'd be the happiest som-bitch in the valley."

Two minutes later Will knocked on Boscal's door. When it opened, Speed Jeans stood in his underwear, bloodshot eyes the only thing not deathly white on his entire exposed body. He stood aside to let Will in.

Whitten lay prone on the bed. An empty bottle of Jack Daniel's was on the floor beside the bed. Will rolled Whitten onto his back.

Whitten moaned. "It's all over."

"That's all the som-bitch has said since he got here. 'It's all over. It's all over!' 'Nuff to drive a man 'round the bend."

Will took off Whitten's tuxedo jacket and foul-smelling shirt. "When did he get here?"

"Shit if I know. Like to woke my ass up at oh-dark-thirty."

Will pulled Whitten to a sitting position. "Help me get him in the shower."

A half hour later, Whitten sat on the bed, shirtless, a towel wrapped around his waist. He still smelled heavily of booze, but at least he could hold his head up and the dry heaves that started in the shower had stopped. He cradled a cup of steaming coffee in two shaky hands. Boscal was still in the bathroom cleaning things up.

Will sat next to Whitten. "What's this really all about?"

Whitten looked up with eyes filled with sadness. "They made me do it, Will."

"*Who* made you do *what?*"

Whitten lowered his voice. "Kraus and the DIA got their hooks in me. Three years after we got back from prison, one of Kraus's goons, the Secret Service guy who now covers Dalton's ass, came by. He told me they had information that I'd given secret details about our missile detection gear to the Vietnamese, info that had gotten a lot of our guys shot down. They were going to court-martial me." Whitten stifled a sob. "Shit-oh-dear, the gooks nearly ripped my arms off and now our government was going to finish the job."

Tears streamed down Whitten's face. "Then I was taken to see Kraus. That bastard ranted and raved about me being a traitor. *Me!* Fuck, I did the best I could, but you can't imagine how it was. The gooks made me look at a guy they'd beaten so bad, one eye hung out. I couldn't even recognize who it was. Yeah, you better believe I came unglued, spilled my guts, told them Viets what they wanted to know."

Whitten wiped at his face.

Boscal brought a cup of coffee from the coffeemaker in the bathroom and helped Whitten take a sip. Then Boscal sank into a chair to listen.

"Kraus said there was one way to make good. Told me I could '*get even*' in the process."

The whole world seems intent on "getting even," Will thought.

"He offered to set me up running a company." Whitten inhaled and held his breath, acting as though he might start the dry heaves again.

Will waited until Whitten relaxed. "Your electronics firm?"

"Yeah, I was making a buck printing out circuit boards and such. Kraus got me contracts for building superaccurate navigation chips for ICBMs. He said he had something cooked up for later that he couldn't tell me about. Anyway, the profits went back to DIA through bank transfers. His whole program was funded that way. No congressional oversight. Kraus said he couldn't go to the Hill with a plan like he had in mind. Ever since the Phoenix Program and the coup in Chile blew the lid off the CIA's clandestine ops, you can't run a secret operation past Congress. It'd be front-page news in the *Washington Post* the next day. So, they needed someone they could trust to manage their program close hold. Okay, I thought. If we ever had to level them Commie bastards, I'd have a hand in doing it." He paused. "It's all over, now."

"Why do you keep saying 'It's all over'?"

Whitten took two quick breaths, then gave Boscal a sideways glance. "Couple years ago, Kraus moved the program forward. He sent me this engineer, a software guy, who reworked the nav interface, only he made a few changes that ain't in the specs."

Boscal leaned forward. "You mean you let some propeller-head dork up our missile systems!"

"Not ours," Whitten groaned. "Theirs."

Will grabbed Whitten's arm. "What do you mean, theirs?"

"Kraus had me let Ruskie agents steal chips with the latest software algorithms, but, you see, the engineer had also inserted a routine that has a way of preventing proper trajectory if they fire missiles at us."

Boscal's eyes got wide. "You screwed up the Commie boomers? No shit?"

"Yeah, they're using bogus software."

Will shook his head. "Haven't the Russians tested the system?"

"Sure, but you got three go-sensors: acceleration, heading, and pressure, and only if the test missile was sent on a heading over the Pole to North America would it fail. They don't test them that way for obvious reasons. Ground testing don't show the problem neither. When the Russians insert a simulated heading they can't put launch Gs on it. If they use a centrifuge for launch Gs, they can't hold the simulated heading. And you gotta have the pressure change at altitude for arming. A feedback loop tells if any sensor is bypassed and, if so, the routine will cut out. Only launching a missile at North America causes the bug to work. The nav guidance and arming circuits go tits-up just after first-stage burnout. Shoot it in any other direction, it works like gangbusters."

Will got off the bed and stood in front of Whitten. "You mean if the Russians launch at us, they'll be shooting blanks."

"If they modified all their missiles, they can't hurt us."

"And the Ukrainians got their new missiles from the Russians," Will said. "They'd be firing duds, too!"

"Yeah," Whitten said, "and it's gonna happen."

Will felt a shiver. "What the hell do you mean?"

Whitten put both hands on top of his head as if to keep his suspicions inside. Finally, he dropped his hands. "It's all over. I'm thinkin' maybe there's gonna be a launch."

Boscal jumped off the bed. "Do you mean to tell us that those bastards *are* going to shoot missiles at us?"

Whitten nodded.

"And if they do," Will said, "they'll be shooting blanks and we'll retaliate with missiles that work."

"The fuck you say," Boscal said. "There ain't gonna be no war now. Tell 'em, Russ, this is all b.s., right? That stuff on the TV is just an exercise, ain't it?"

Will turned. "What stuff are you talking about?"

"Ain't you been watching the news?" Boscal said. "Just afore you got here they announced that the president's appearances at the inaugural parties have been canceled."

Boscal turned on the TV. NBC's Brian Williams was just finishing a special bulletin confirming what Boscal had said, adding that a crisis had come up in a former Soviet republic, the Ukraine. A military mobilization was in progress at the Pentagon.

"I don't know for sure," Whitten said, "but before Kraus left, he thanked me and told me I was about to get even."

"Getting even," Will said. "Again that term. You get even for the torture you endured. Dalton gets even for decades of confinement. Kraus carries a vendetta against Ukrainians, and his sordid mind has twisted it into a delusion that in the process of getting even, he's saving the world by wiping out the potential source of the next major war."

"Horse shit," Boscal said. "Maybe we got those assholes' missiles messed up, but they got no reason to shoot at us."

"Oh, they might," Will said. "What if they received a warning we were about to wipe them out? They'd be forced to try beating us to the punch."

"No way," Boscal said.

"Years ago," Will said, "the Soviets planted moles to detect our nuclear intentions. Kraus found out about it and learned the cipher the spies were supposed to use to warn Russia of a nuclear attack. Now Russ says Kraus let Soviet agents steal software that makes their weapons harmless. If Kraus then passed word that the United States is going to strike, the Russians and Ukrainians might knee-jerk react. The Russians can call the president on the red phone to raise hell first, but the Ukrainians don't have that luxury. If their leader Podvalny gets word we're about to plaster them, he's going to launch missiles! By the time the dust settles, the whole Eurasian continent is laid waste."

"But," Whitten said, "if the Ukrainians think they have a spy in the White House, they would know he wouldn't clear our missiles to launch."

"That's right, assuming Marshal Podvalny knows about Dalton," Will said. "Remember what puppet-master Kraus said? 'The link between Podvalny and Stoner has never been broken.' Podvalny may have worked with Stoner at some other prison in the Ukraine, and that's the only double he knows about."

Will thought about Stayki, the guy he killed at the grave site. Stayki knew about Dalton. He worked for Podvalny. Will considered that a certainty. If Stayki was Kraus's inside contact, and he definitely had one to set up the escape from the compound, Stayki might have withheld the details about Dalton and Jack Cadence from Podvalny at DIA's order. The Soviets were paranoid about secrecy and damn little became common knowledge at any level but the top, in Moscow. Podvalny might never have visited that small gulag near Kharkov before it was demolished.

"Marshal Podvalny may only know about Stoner," Will said, "but that's enough. Stoner is now the number *two* guy in the U.S. strategic force. Stoner can't stop a preemptive launch, but he *can* get warning to the Ukrainians! Kraus, too, can send the code to Podvalny, making him think it came from Stoner. As fiendish as it sounds, I think that's it." Will had another thought as he took Whitten by the shoulders. "Does Dalton know about the bogus software?"

"He's never been involved in it that I know of," Whitten said.

"If Kraus is true to form, he's duped Dalton, too," Will said, "and Dalton's our chance to stop this."

Will pulled out the card Dalton had given him, went to the bedside phone, and dialed. This time a woman answered. Will gave the pass code and was put through.

Janet Mills came on the line. From the sound of her voice, she was not in the mood for chitchat.

"Janet, this is Will Cadence. I've got to speak to the president."

"He's not here," she said.

"You have seen the news, right? This means life or death for millions of people. I've got to talk to him."

"You can't. They've taken him to the hardened command post. Plans for tonight have been canceled."

"Janet, listen. There is likely to be a missile exchange between the Ukrainians and the U.S. It can be stopped, but only if I can speak with President Dalton."

Will waited, but no answer came. "Janet?"

Finally she spoke. "Last night, your visit. He seemed so upset. Does this have something to do with that?"

"Yes."

Another pause. "I'd like to help, but *I* can't get through to him right now. All I know is a helicopter is on the way to pick me up in fifteen minutes."

"To go where?"

"To join him."

Will covered the receiver. "How far is it to the White House?"

"About four blocks," Boscal said.

Will uncovered the receiver. "Alert gate security to let me inside. I'll explain the whole thing when I get to you, but you've got to get me on that helicopter!"

When Janet Mills hung up, she turned to her aide. "Get me Thornton Bishop at the CIA."

Will put the phone down and grabbed Whitten, pulling him to his feet. "Get your clothes on. You've got to help me stop them." Boscal went to the door while Whitten pulled on his trousers.

As the door opened, a man in yellow tinted glasses stood blocking the exit. He held a pistol with a silencer on it. Will recognized the man. He was the stranger who had helped him from his car wreck in Hawaii.

The man wriggled the gun. "Let's everyone have a seat."

In the corner of Will's eye, he saw Whitten come alert. Then he heard a roar as Whitten hurled his bulk forward.

The gun coughed. The first shot hit Whitten in the chest, but he kept moving forward. A second caught him in the shoulder.

Whitten's hands were choking his attacker's neck as the man pumped round after round into Whitten's abdomen.

Will leapt after the pair as they crumbled to the floor. He saw the gun coming out from under Whitten's torso and wrestled it from the man's grip. It slid across the carpet.

The man reached under his trouser leg for something. A needle.

A gun fired past Will's ear. The man's head snapped back. The hand with the needle went limp. Will rolled Whitten over and looked up to see Boscal holding their attacker's weapon. Blood covered Whitten's shirt. He still had a grip on the man's throat. Whitten's eyes were wide with anger as he let go.

"Stop the bastards, Will," he whispered. "Don't want to have to make up for this where I'm headed." His eyes slipped closed.

Will laid Whitten's head on the carpet.

Boscal knelt beside Will. "I'll take care of him. You've got to go."

Will jumped to his feet and raced out the door. In the elevator, he mashed the lobby button. On ground level, he ran through the promenade and out the front door.

A taxi had just driven up and a guest was about to get in. Will shouted that it was an emergency and pushed him aside. As he dove in the back door, the taxi driver turned. "Hey buddy, what's this shit you're pulling? I ain't taking you nowhere."

Will scrambled back onto the sidewalk and started running flat out toward Pennsylvania Avenue. He crossed K Street against the light. Ahead he could make out the green grass of Lafayette Square. He ignored fresh pain in his knee, could feel tendons twinge and hear cartilage popping as he raced along.

Will heard rotors overhead. A big Sikorski of the type the president used was descending toward the White House. Will put on a burst of speed across H Street. As he neared the curb, his knee gave out. Down he went. He grabbed on to a light pole for support and pulled himself upright. An explosion of pain shot up his leg. He started off again, half-running, dragging his damaged limb, down the center of Jackson, across Pennsylvania, and to the rear entrance gate.

A man in a dark business suit stood by the guards. "Are you Cadence?"

"Yes," Will shouted.

"Adams. Secret Service. Photo ID, please."

Will whipped out his wallet and showed his card.

"Follow me," the man ordered.

Will began limping after Adams. When Adams noticed Will falling behind, he came back, threw Will's arm over his shoulder, and together they hustled toward the aircraft.

Meanwhile a black sedan pulled into the White House driveway. CIA director Thornton Bishop got out. Gabbie was with him. Bishop waved for Will to keep going toward the helicopter. Moments later, they were seated inside as the Sikorski lifted from the ground.

"Are you okay?" Gabbie shouted as she hugged Will.

"I'm feeling better already. What about you?"

"They shot my tires out, but I'm fine."

"Why didn't you call?"

"Someone shoots at you," Gabbie said, "it takes quite a bit of convincing to believe in them. I thought they might track you down when you answered, and I'm still not sure I trust them."

"Me, neither. How'd the CIA find us in Maryland?"

"They were on to us when you used the credit card at the cell phone store. They got there twenty minutes after we left. Then when you called Musser's number on the cell, they used satellites to triangulate our position."

"Talk it out later," Bishop shouted. Over the engine noise, he confirmed that they were indeed going to the alternate command post in Maryland to confront the president. He took Will's arm. "Let's hear what you have."

Will felt he had nothing to lose by talking now even if the CIA was in on the scheme. He spent the next few minutes explaining about the doubles and what was at stake. Everyone listened. Mills shuddered as Bishop confirmed Will's part of the story with the information the CIA was still trying to verify from Gabbie. Bishop had been working for months trying to piece together the intrigue surrounding some of DIA's activities involving a photo provided by Pam Robbins.

"When Pam Robbins claimed her copy had been altered and wanted back the copy she sent to us," Bishop said, "we checked it first and found it had indeed been altered." Bishop then ordered his case officer to lie to Robbins, and to DIA for that matter, about the CIA having an original version in order to keep the initiation of their investigation secret. Bishop put the surveillance team in Hawaii to monitor JTF and DIA activity. That's when the subject of the second photo, the Polaroid, came to light. Agent Phil Garcia intercepted the message being passed to Kraus at DIA in Washington. Then Garcia was ordered to follow Gabbie, since she had involvement in both Robbins photos. Through that surveillance, they learned details about American POWs in the Ukraine, and from Will and Gabbie they pinpointed the safe house in Maryland. The CIA was right now trying to locate Boyd and the C-141 crew.

Will handed over the card with the phone number Kraus had provided. "Trace that number and you'll find them."

The presidential helicopter nosed over and descended to a landing in the Maryland countryside, inside a heavily garrisoned military compound.

The pain in Will's leg had begun to ease as he, Gabbie, Janet Mills, and Director Bishop left the chopper and followed a marine colonel past a sign that read RESTRICTED AREA—DEADLY FORCE AUTHORIZED. They went through an entrance to the underground command post where a marine guard had them pass through a metal detector.

Once inside, a set of blast doors slid shut behind them. They went down a long corridor to an elevator that carried them deep within the structure. As they came out, a brigadier general appeared.

"If you'll follow me," he said, "the president would like you to wait in his quarters."

"Absolutely not," Janet said. "Take me to President Dalton, now."

"I can't do that, ma'am. We're on alert, and the president is in conference."

She indicated Bishop. "This is the director of the CIA. You know who I am, and you don't want to be the one who crosses us!" Janet yelled. "Call your boss if you have to, but get me in contact with the president now!"

All across the Ukraine, mobile missile trailers began erecting their launchers. Like moray eels, their ICBMs poked ugly green snouts out of cold dark grottoes.

Inside the Ukrainian combat control center, Marshal Podvalny pointed and shouted orders. Sector controllers were frantically transmitting commands.

43

INSIDE THE COMMAND POST, deep within the bunker, the new president sat at the center of a curved counter. To his right sat DIA Director Jarret Kraus. On Dalton's other side sat Secretary of Defense Warren Tillotson. Next to Tillotson was the chairman of the Joint Chiefs of Staff, General Richard Ellis. One row below, in a small theater-like setting, sat the army, navy, air force and marine deputy chiefs. Their bosses were split between the Pentagon and the Airborne Command Post. Two consoles, the launch apparatus for sending nuclear bombers aloft and ICBMs toward their targets, rose in front of the president and JCS chairman Ellis. Each console possessed a key slot and a code display below which were alphanumeric keypads. The president and the chairman had already inserted stainless-steel keys in their slots a few minutes earlier when DEFCON 2 had been declared, one step from all-out nuclear retaliation. To the right rear of the president was the aide who carried a black briefcase inside which were the cookies, the nuclear release codes for that day. Separate codes for General Ellis were kept by his aide, standing to his left. Both the president and the chairman had to be in agreement before Armageddon could be unleashed. Then the codes would be entered and the keys rotated simultaneously. Neither key was close enough for one man to operate at the same time. Ten feet directly behind the president and by a locked door stood a lone marine sentry, armed with a 9mm automatic. Only one guard was permitted. Two might present a problem since they could overpower the commanders, take things into their own hands, and actuate the launch commands. Telephone consoles and a microphone were positioned in front of all the decision makers. They peered ahead, through a wall of glass behind which uniformed men worked at computer monitors beneath a large world map. There were ominous red dots appearing in the area of the Ukraine.

General Ellis put his phone down. "Our satellites have detected blast doors opening on twenty-six silos."

The president picked up his red phone and when the Russian president answered, Dalton wasted no time. "Mr. President, what the hell is going on over there? That idiot in the Ukraine looks as though he's preparing to launch missiles!" Dalton listened intently during a long pause. "What do you mean you can't reach Podvalny?!" Then he listened as the Russian president asked Dalton a question in Russian. Dalton of course understood and assumed the question was intended to determine whether he, Dalton, was in fact the Soviet double who was speaking. The Russians were ready to turn over their wild card if need be. Dalton answered briefly in Russian, keeping up the deception, while his words raised curious eyebrows throughout the room.

While the president was on the line with Moscow, Secretary of Defense Tillotson took an incoming call. When President Dalton lowered his receiver slightly, Tillotson leaned toward him. "Sir, Janet Mills is outside with Thornton Bishop and wishes to speak with you."

Dalton took on a look of intense irritation, but wanted a reason to avoid conversation with the Russian president until he had a chance to speak with Kraus privately. "Excuse me a moment, Mr. President," Dalton said, then turned his attention to Tillotson.

"She says she also has a Major Will Cadence with her who can explain what the Ukrainians are up to."

Dalton slid his palm over the red phone's mouthpiece.

The secretary shrugged. "I'm just relaying a message, sir."

Director Kraus had overheard. He homed in on Tillotson.

"This is a crisis, not a call-in show!"

The president scanned the map, then asked, "Can any of *you* explain what's happening?"

All eyes focused on the president, and no one spoke until Kraus raised a hand toward the map. "Do we have time for guesswork or do we take action, Mr. President?"

Dalton turned to the marine guard. "Let them in."

"No, I know all about the major's information and it's flat wrong." Kraus's jaw locked as he glared at Dalton.

Dalton looked at the marine who had not yet moved. "Open that door, Sergeant!" He turned back to Kraus. "Meanwhile, you try to fill me in, all the way, Jarret."

Phones began ringing.

General Ellis shouted, "Too late. The Ukrainians have seven missiles in the air!"

Dalton looked at the map. "Those idiots!"

A moment later, Janet, Gabbie, Will, and Bishop burst in as the LAUNCH-ALERT flashed above the map display.

Kraus pressed his microphone button. "Give the orders to counterattack!"

"No!" Will shouted. "Those missiles are no good. DIA has rigged their guidance systems to go haywire."

Dalton looked at Kraus. "What?"

General Ellis bored in on Kraus, too. "Jarret, is that true?"

Kraus swung his arm in an encompassing arc. "Are you all crazy? Our people will be annihilated if we don't act!"

The map showed a flood of missile trails headed toward the United States from the Ukraine.

Dalton removed his palm from the red phone, then placed his free hand over the Launch-Command circuit. "Get our alert bombers in the air, and stand by with the ICBMs!"

The air force deputy chief of staff picked up his phone and passed the scramble order, sending Air Combat Command B-1, B-2, and B-52 bomber crews running for their aircraft.

The president and JCS chief's aides stepped forward with the missile cookies at the ready.

Dalton put the red phone to his ear and spoke to the Russian leader in English. "I'm only putting our bombers in the air, Mr. President."

Then Dalton looked up at the map. Fourteen tracks were arcing their way toward the United States. Dalton covered the phone again. "Give us the launch codes." The aides handed them over.

"No!" Gabbie screamed. "Their missiles won't work. Wait!"

The president and the chairman set the new codes. Then the two men looked at each other. The bombers could be recalled, but launched missiles offered no change of mind.

Will staggered toward Dalton. "Kraus is a lunatic bent on vengeance for what the Ukrainians did to his father. He engineered this madness and manipulated all of us in the name of patriotism. A code has been sent to the Ukrainians making them think *we* are preparing to attack *them*."

Deputy Chief of Naval Operations Admiral Sweeney joined in. "There are no missiles coming from any subs yet and nothing is coming out of Russia. You have one minute until the first missiles achieve trajectory!"

Kraus saw Dalton hesitate. "Every minute gives them time to launch a dozen MIRV missiles. That's another hundred twenty chem/bio weapons airborne while we chitchat, for Christ's sake."

Dalton looked at the map as the warning system displayed projected impact points around major cities in America.

"Kraus," Dalton said, "I need answers and fast. Is Brad Stoner another plant?"

The other members of the staff stared at Dalton, wondering what the hell he was suddenly talking about.

"Talk to him, Ellis," Kraus ordered. "We must launch now or risk the entire nation. These Ukrainians have loaded those missiles with binary chemical weapons capable of killing entire cities."

General Ellis looked preoccupied, as though he had not heard Kraus. His brow furrowed. "Kraus, you didn't . . ."

Kraus gave a small nod and his tone softened. "It doesn't matter. Convince them."

General Ellis shut his eyes, then sighed. "I've heard all I can stand from you. I can't continue this."

"They must be wiped out!" Kraus pounded the table. "Can't you see? No matter what, those people will try to destroy us."

Dalton noticed the impact rings begin to flutter and shift positions. "Hold it."

Looking up, the group saw missile trails begin to fade, and one by one the impact circles vanished.

"They're not achieving trajectory!" General Ellis said. "Sixteen tracks have disappeared. The chemical cocktail aboard them won't mix."

"The weapons will all be duds," Will added.

They watched as missile trails abruptly stopped just below the Arctic Circle.

Kraus looked at the map, too. "You fools. I'm trying to save us all." He tugged at his left trouser and in one deft move pulled a pistol from an ankle holster. Kraus spun from his chair and pointed the gun at the marine guard. The guard went for his weapon. A popping sound, like a round misfiring, echoed inside the chamber. The marine slumped to the floor.

"No one move!" Kraus pointed his gun at Dalton, then leapt to the marine's side. He pulled the pistol from the marine's hand and put down his own weapon, then snapped the slide on the 9mm, chambering a round into the breech.

With the marine's pistol now pointed at the president, he picked up the gun he had used to shoot the guard and tossed it to Ellis. "Cover them!" Then Kraus turned to the gathering. "The rest of you, move against the wall!"

"This man isn't the president," Kraus yelled, as he waved his weapon at Dalton. "He's a spy. Didn't you hear him speak Russian into the red phone a minute ago?" The aides, in confusion, eased toward the side wall as Kraus slewed his gun in their direction.

The deputy chiefs stood their ground, but seemed unsure of who the bad guys were. Janet backed near the door. Will stood beside Gabbie and Bishop, all of whom stared at the president as though trying to determine if he indeed was the Soviet double.

Dalton remained at the console until Kraus leveled his gun at his head. "Move," Kraus shouted. The president dropped the red phone. It fell off the counter and swung like a pendulum from its cord. He eased past Ellis and stopped a few steps away.

Kraus moved to the president's console and turned his attention to General Ellis.

"Turn the key, Richard."

Ellis faced Dalton. "Yes, Stoner is a Russian mole. His mission, like Anderov's, your double, was to relay a warning code if he learned we planned to launch an unprovoked nuclear attack." He turned to Kraus. "You maniac, you sent Stoner's preemptive warning to the Ukrainians, didn't you?" General Ellis stood, red-faced, as the words hissed from his lips.

"It was time to fix the problem, Richard. Either now or later some idiot over there or in the Mideast or Asia would find the mechanism to annihilate us. This will put an end to the threat forever."

"And us, too."

"Nonsense. In the fifties, thirty to forty weapons were exploded each year around the world and all that happened was downwind a few sheep died and the leukemia rate went up. Turn the key, Richard."

Ellis swung his gun toward Kraus. "No." He squeezed the trigger. Nothing happened. He turned the weapon in his hand and stared at it.

"You never had the big picture *or* a grasp of details either," Kraus said. "That gun's plastic with one Kevlar bullet. How do you think I managed to get it in here?"

Kraus aimed his pistol at Ellis. "Do your duty."

Ellis put down his gun and placed his hand on the key. "I will." He pulled the key from the slot and tossed it into his mouth.

The roar of the 9mm was deafening. The key flew from Ellis's tongue. He clutched his chest and fell over his chair. The key trickled along the floor and came to rest at Will's foot.

Kraus's gun barrel swept toward Will. "Pick up the key."

Will made no move.

The weapon shifted to Gabbie. "Pick up the key, Cadence, or she dies."

Will bent down and grasped the key.

"Now, place it back in the slot."

"Don't do it, Will," Gabbie pleaded.

"One more word from you and I shoot!"

Silence. Then a low shrill sound was heard, an imperceptible but angry voice at the end of the red phone.

Secretary of Defense Tillotson spoke. "The map. Look." Kraus glanced upward. Red dots began pockmarking Russia, indicating the opening of ICBM blast doors.

"Now, Cadence," Kraus ordered, "before the Russians have a chance to launch!"

Will, eyes riveted on Kraus, limped slowly past General Ellis and stopped by the console.

"I'm not kidding," Kraus said.

Will held the key above the launch-command slot.

Kraus turned the president's key to the launch position. "Do it!"

Will remained motionless. He could hear the upset voice coming from the red phone. "Talk to me, now, Mr. President, or else I'm forced to act!"

Kraus heard it as well. "You've seen how those Ukrainians and Russians are, Cadence. Podvalny will stop at nothing. Neither will the Russians. Put an end to all of them. You have this one chance to get even for what they did to your father."

"And what do I do about what *you* did to my father?"

"Kraus," Dalton said.

Kraus glimpsed Dalton, standing off to the side.

"Shut up. We had to eliminate Jack Cadence. If I hadn't saved your ass, the Russians would have finished you off, too. Now they may succeed."

"Try this detail," Dalton said. He raised a hand toward Kraus's weapon, smiling. "The marine's gun has only one bullet. A precaution."

Kraus glanced down at his gun. "You're lying." The gun was still aimed squarely at Gabbie.

Dalton started toward Kraus.

"Stop!" Kraus screamed.

Dalton kept coming.

Kraus brought the weapon to bear on Dalton who bobbed to the left as the gun roared.

Dalton's arm flew backward. Down he went. On pure adrenaline, Will lunged past Dalton and reached for Kraus.

Instinctively, Kraus flicked the gun at Will and squeezed the trigger.

The pistol did not fire.

Will batted the gun aside and launched his right arm at Kraus's jaw, his fist landing hard on the mouth. Kraus tumbled over the console and landed in a heap. Gabbie sprung toward the gun, grabbed it, and held it on Kraus's motionless form. Then she noticed that the slide on the weapon was full aft. The gun was empty. By now the generals were all over Kraus, pinning him to the floor.

"Hold it!" Dalton gasped as he got to his feet, blood streaming down his shirtsleeve. He picked up the red phone. "Mr. President," he managed. "You see your map? We are not launching. I repeat, we are not launching." He leaned over the console and deleted the coded entry. "There will be no retaliation." Then he repeated his words in Russian.

Silence enveloped the room as Dalton awaited the Russian president's response.

"Good," Dalton said. "Now, for God's sake, send your people down there and get control of what's left of Podvalny's arsenal!"

A collective sigh filled the room as indications of blast doors closing swept across the map of Russia.

"Recall the bombers." President Dalton slumped down in his chair as the air force deputy chief issued cancellation orders.

Gabbie, Will, and Secretary of Defense Tillotson rushed to Dalton's aid.

Dalton turned to Tillotson. "See to the marine."

"I already have. He'll survive."

"And Ellis?"

"No."

"Goddamn it." Then he faced Will. "I had no idea Kraus was this ruthless."

Gabbie popped the clip from the 9mm. It fell to the floor, empty. She made sure no cartridge was in the breech. "You knew he had *two* rounds."

Dalton waved his hand as though it did not matter.

"And you made him shoot his last one at you."

Dalton looked down at his bloody sleeve, then at the crowd gathered around him. "Soon I may find myself wishing Kraus had been a better shot."

Gabbie ripped his shirtsleeve apart. "I won't, and I thank you for taking a bullet for me." She looked at Will. "You, too." Then she made a quick bandage out of Dalton's shirtsleeve and wrapped it tight over the wound while an aide called for the president's physician.

Dalton gazed up at Will. "I believe I have an announcement to make to the people in this room and the country."

"We need to get you to medical attention," Janet said.

"Not until I clear this up. I've been well taught on how to function under pain."

During the minutes before Dalton gave his speech, Will filled Gabbie in on the rest of the events that had transpired in the Mayflower. In his dramatic national radio address, the president bared his soul to the American public. An hour later, after learning that the C-141 crew had been safely rescued at Fort Belvoir and Stoner had been apprehended, Gabbie helped Will walk out of the command center.

Will took in a great breath of fresh air. "What'd you think of the president's resignation?"

"Oh, he came across straightforward in there. I liked the way he underplayed his own role in stopping a nuclear disaster, while not once mentioning his wound."

"When the whole story comes out, the country just might cut him some slack, but he's history. We'll have a new president in a few hours."

They made their way out of the tunnel into the light of day.

"From what we know about Operation Shadowmaker, they'll find out exactly how much Colonel Bustamante, Major Chase, and others connected to Kraus's scheme knew. They'll be dealt with accordingly, but this whole deception has me wondering about something else," Will said softly to Gabbie.

"And that is?"

"Wondering who my father might really be. Dalton had an affair with my mother."

She turned him to face her, took his left hand, and opened it. "Dupuytren's, the hand malady your father had, it's hereditary. Comes on slowly as one ages. You've got it."

He looked down at his hand. The tendons of his last two fingers were stretched, tiny outlines visible under the skin.

"That's the onset stage. I noticed it when I put my hand in yours the second night we made love." She traced the tendons with her index finger. "I've known for a long time who your father was."

Will pointed the way. They climbed a tiny knoll that covered the bunker. At the top, they could see rays of sunlight beaming under shimmering clouds to the west. Will looked at Gabbie. Her face shone in the soft light, happy now, with him. She was courageous, a woman the likes of which he might never be lucky enough to meet again. He hoped she had come to feel about him the way he felt about her. They might not attain happiness ever after, but if she wanted to, he was ready to give it a try. Will leaned heavily on his good leg. "Thanks for sticking by me."

"Sticking by *you*? I was in charge, remember."

"I remember. And I still owe you one."

"You owe Josef and Jim Dansky in the Ukraine a Mercedes, or at least two new bikes. I'm not sure you can afford what I'm due, but I'm ready to start collecting."

She hooked her arm in his and took the lead helping him down the hill.

He ambled along, haltingly in tow. "Do I ever get to be in charge?"

"Maybe, after you're all paid up."

When they got to the staff car that was waiting for them, Gabbie stopped. A look of foreboding crept across her face. She turned to Will. "What if Kraus lied and there are more than two doubles?"

About the Author

Ralph Wetterhahn served in Vietnam with the Air Force and Navy, completing 180 combat missions. *Shadowmakers* evolved from his true-life experiences searching for MiAs from southeast Asia to the gulags of Russia and Siberia. His previous nonfiction book, *The Last Battle: The* Mayaguez *Incident and the End of the Vietnam War*, received the 2002 Colby Award for "a first work that makes a significant contribution to the public's understanding of intelligence operations, military history or international affairs." His third book for Carroll & Graf will be the next installment in his series on missing-in-action from America's wars, an on-site investigation of the WWII bombing campaign fought over Japan's Kurile islands. Widely read in *Air & Space/Smithsonian, Popular Science,* and *Leatherneck,* Wetterhahn lives in Long Beach, California.